Praise for **THE PERFECT STRANGER**

A wild, delicious romp of a saga. Imagine Jonathan Swift, Terry Pratchett, Kurt Vonnegut – and Kafka - conspiring with Mistress Poesia herself.

Harris has invented a new and divinely erudite & comedic genre: Real Magicalism.

A devilishly good journey with a multiplex of literary lyrical splendors, crafted (& crafty!) linguistic play, and incisive social/political relevance.

You will laugh out loud!

—Judyth Hill, author of *Dazzling Wobble*

Liberally sprinkled with incredible, unique images, Harris's unconventional "Perfect Stranger" evokes the impression of Richard Brautigan cartwheeling down an Escherian Stairwell: Very creative, certainly strange, and possibly dangerous.

—Kenn Amdahl, author of *The Land of Debris and the Home of Alfredo*

As charming and unpredictable as Terry Pratchett's Discworld, while maintaining edgy, over-the-top Vonnegut-like satire. Filled with biting humor, clever wordplay, and dollops of generosity…a compelling read.

—Laurie Marr Wasmund, author of *Clean Cut and White Winter Trilogy*

With a poet's eye and ear for the most unsettling but telling detail, Gregory SETH Harris has brought forth a unique and complex novel—a tour de force—more often than not a farcical indictment of social mores, if not the human condition.

—Robert Milo Baldwin, author of *Love & the Ost Soldier*

The Perfect Stranger brings together sharp social satire, brilliant insights into human nature and delightfully adept writing to weave a fantastic tale. If Camus had a sense of humor, he would love this story of the stranger who enters a closed society and rattles its mental blocks.

—Judah Freed, author of Making Global Sense

ISBN 978-1-7355494-0-8

Publisher's Cataloging-in-Publication data

Names: Harris, Gregory Seth, author.
Title: The perfect stranger / by Gregory Seth Harris.
Description: First trade paperback original edition. | Denver [Colorado] :
BookCrafters, 2020.
Identifiers: ISBN 978-1-7355494-0-8
Subjects: LCSH: Satire—Fiction.
BISAC: FICTION / Satire. | FICTION / Absurdist.
Classification: LCC PS374.A28 | DDC 813.6 HARRIS–dc22

Publishing assistance by BookCrafters, Parker, Colorado.
www.bookcrafters.net

To Joan,
Here's to the sweat
blood, and tears and joys of
the writer's life. Keep on scribbling,
of nothing else it's good therapy
Love and respect
Greg

THE PERFECT
STRANGER

Gregory SETH Harris

To Stephanie Selene Anderson
*without whose support
this work may never have been written*

ACKNOWLEDGEMENTS

IT TAKES A VILLAGE to write a novel. Little did I suspect when the pages that follow were but a seedling of an idea tickling my youthful imagination, it would take a family of friends and acquaintances to bring what I then envisioned into full flower.

I start by thanking Anita Kushen & Associates, most especially Gabriel Gianes for championing an early, unfinished version of what is here published. Gabe's enthusiasm, coupled with his recognition of all I was attempting, buoyed me through many a moment I was tempted to abandon my quixotic quest to construct a novel like none before it. More importantly, Gabe steered me away from a subsequent draft wherein internal doubts resulted in my watering down some of the exuberant risks I'd taken in that original draft. For that I am eternally grateful.

Going back to this novel's origin, I owe a debt to Harriet Freiberger of the Steamboat Springs Writer's Conference and author Charlotte Hinger whose guidance prompted my opening pages. Having finally found a door to open my tale, I could then begin a circuitous journey—a journey which took more years than I care to admit; a journey of stopping, starting, repeatedly setting the manuscript aside to tend to that annoying necessity called earning a living.

A shout out to dear friends, Chuck Rhoades and Mary Lou Brubaker, who perused a completed first draft and provided their thoughtful suggestions. So too, a warm thank you to Sheri Keasler, Robert Milo Baldwin, Su Urban Wright and Dar Tomlinson who helped me navigate the opening chapters, taming my excesses while containing their bafflement as I insisted on ignoring all conventional wisdom as to what agents and editors (and by extension, readers) were clamoring for. Lana Hayward, Lise Larson Pyles, Laurie Marr Wasmund, Leslee Breene, Tom Reeves, Linda Tebedo, Diane Jones and Henry LeFevre also deserve credit, helping hone my fiction skills, leading to a modest handful of published short stories before I gained the confidence and wherewithal to finally tackle this novel.

I owe a tremendous debt to Barbara Test, as well as Mark and Stephanie Anderson whose support and generosity allowed me at times to escape the real world for extended periods. Sequestered in some hotel or cabin, I could thus indulge my imagination in its love for the absurd and its sordid affair with language. Thereto, I owe a debt to my dear friend, Shawn Edwards, who gifted me with Random House's **Word Menu** which became my Bible and constant companion, remaining so to this day.

I've little doubt I've absorbed many-a trick of the trade and whatever additional mastery I can boast to the myriad creative personalities who have populated my universe. While not directly contributing to the enclosed novel, Tupper Cullum, Woody Hildebrant, Jerry Smaldone, Judah Freed, Roseanna Frechette, Ted Vaca, Ira Liss, Edwin Forrest Ward, Stewart Warren and Ricki Harada all warrant my sincerest thanks and appreciation. No doubt, I've missed a few names. I hope I will be forgiven

As this novel went through its final gyrations, I turned to Rocky Mountain Fiction Writers Trish Hermanson, Joan Jacobson, Joseph Farris, Michele Stuvel, Chris Devlin, Eric Stallsworth, Jenna Martin, William Cowie, Chris Winiecki, Jason Evans, Julie King among others to help in its final tweaking.

Rounding out this illustrious family, I extend deepest thanks to Mari Anne Christie, Jennifer D. Munro, and Michael Annis for their skill, expertise and insight. . .doubly so to Sarah Martinez, who has been my lighthouse, guiding me through the final steps of this journey.

And no one deserves more thanks than my wife and beloved partner, Colette, for her patience and tolerance while watching me wrestle all the demons creative flesh is heir to. I can scarce express the depth of love and gratitude I owe to her still waters and undying faith. You are indeed the love of my life.

It does indeed take a village to write a novel. Thanks to those named above, and to the many, many others not here mentioned, I've been able to strive, thrive and prevail. My sincerest thanks to all.

—Gregory SETH Harris

KNOW THYSELF

~

HEAL THYSELF

Chapter 1

From the first he offended us. Without meaning to, i'm sure, but still. The very sight of him was repugnant—tho no one could quite say why; not a one of us could point his/her finger & say: that's it, there it is—that's why he annoys us so. Those inclined to speculate blamed it on his walk—it being disjointed somehow, as if the lower abdomen or the hips perhaps, were stiff, even paralyzed. This made his body jerk rather like a cocky chicken as he groped his way thru our narrowed streets. Still, his gait was no different from many of us—from most of us, in fact.

Maybe it was his hair, an unkempt tangle of knots shooting out in all directions as if his head were on fire. Or perhaps his dark, sullen stare—eyes blacker than ravens, feathers dulled by dust, seeming not to look @ anything exactly. Whenever he tramped thru the animal prison or paused to pet a statue, whenever he loitered in a public restroom where we watched him thru the mirrors—whenever his eyes brushed across anything, it was as if he looked but didn't see.

"He's too tall," our Aryan-Pygmies complained. "Why, you'd break your neck if'n you was to look him in the eye. He needs to be brought to his knees." The 7-Footers Club argued he was too short, that his lack of height was an affront to their (& thus to everyone's) integrity. A torture rack was recommended to stretch him to a more suitable length.

"If you ask me—" Sidney Whelps of S&M's Boyskin & Tanning Salon expounded to patrons @ Gus's Barbershop/Lingerie Boutique, "he's too skinny. The more fat, the more skin. And skin is good—skin is gold."

"Skinny's fine," Lou Swire, head of our Dept of Walls, countered. "I think it's singful, he goin' round talkin' to hisself. Specially when there is so much to be learnin' just liss'nin' to what all the fine folks 'round here have to say 'bout this, that, & the udder."

The rest of us agreed. We knew that should we ask, he'd have no opinion about the weather—that it could rain or snow or yodel for all he cared. Neither was he likely to support our cause—but then, neither would he side w/ our opponents. In fact, all factions were convinced he had no opinions worth even the breath it might take to udder them. He may as well not exist, a two-thirds majority concurred—only he did, thus requiring food, shelter, clothing; all of which, had he not existed, would have meant more for the rest of us.

Complaints flooded the district office from all sectors. Mrs Beverly Gloss wrote an impassioned limerick. Old Man Crawstilts refused to eat his supper—or take his medicine. Several members of Penis Envy Anonymous went on diets, a few even losing a pound or two.

Our office, however, had been aware of his presence the moment he crawled past our DO NOT ENTER sign. He was not the first—& no doubt not the last—to slip past the mines, the barbed wire, the watch dogs, our blatant lack of WELCOME signs. A few even dared stay beyond the two-day limit our Constitution graciously allots to show tolerance twd those we don't like; but when the stay stretches past a week, on into two weeks, into a month or longer—well, files have to be made, surveillance stepped up, officers have to work thru their coffee breaks. This makes everyone's day unpleasant. People get cranky. Lieutenants snap @ file clerks...who stick pins in dolls adorned as administrators...who cut wages until everyone from the janitors to the interrogation staff are screaming for Truth, Justice & better rates on their dental insurance. Pretty soon, it's chaos & everyone's annoyed. Something has to be done.

And so, a fortnite into the interloper's unwarranted intrusion, a new folder was added to the files of anyone who could afford to be anyone—a folder labeled 'S-'.

* * * * *

ON ONE PARTICULAR MORNING the weather was behaving very much like a woman bickering before her mirror over what to wear. Should i be moody? Maybe mysterious? she asked herself. Perhaps cloudy? Put on a chilly air. Maybe tease w/ brief bits of sunlight. No, she mused while sipping tea & contemplating another bonbon. Stripping away her gray kimono, deciding instead on cotton white, she slipped into sultry sunshine. She let her golden mane tumble down, sele cted a

2

chemise of soft baby blue w/ scattered white clouds. But then, unable to settle on an appropriate pair of shoes, she withdrew her radiant smile, turning her thoughts to darker brooding. Lightning flashed in her eyes; she thundered, spit on rooftops. Till thoughts of her lover, their last amorous encounter, dissolved her cloudy disposition. She softened her hue, slipped gingerly from behind her dark veil. Her tears were drunk thirstily by her brown-skinned sister, the Earth, whose grass skirt shimmered in a brisk, soothing breeze. The moist air exploded in pungent aromas. The Mistress of the Sky slipped on a blue blouse decorated w/ flocks of peaceful clouds, her yellow head radiating from the sky's throne.

Thus contented, she smiled down upon two men: the shabbier one seated on a marble step, head buried in his palms; the other sneaking up behind, clad in a well-pressed navy-blue button-down uniform, a wooden club quivering in his uncertain hand.

"Young man, how dare you cry on our library steps!" the man brandishing the club demanded. A yellow badge taped to his breast pocket, the uniformed man stood poised, tapping one of his well-polished shoes in perfect syncopation to the rapping of the billy club in his upturned palm.

S- (for so it was) looked from the scar atop the round bald head, to the man's belt—hooked in its last hole—& finally to the vacant green eyes peering from under two thick hedges of admonishing eyebrow.

"I didn't know these steps belonged to the library," he confessed, wiping a soiled cheek w/ the back of his hand.

"He didn't know these steps belonged to the library," the man echoed, repeating it again @ the top of his lungs. "HE DIDN'T KNOW THESE STEPS BELONGED TO THE LIBRARY!"

The Chief of Police—for so the yellow badge read—bent lower, nearly touching S-'s runny nose w/ the round, bulbous tip of his own. "And where do you think the good citizens of this town would put their library steps—if not in front of their library? You do see the library there, don't you?"

S- glanced over his shoulder @ a tall stoned structure held up by columns, some fluted, some flat, some covered w/ plastic ivy. A few columns were placed together, others apart, several inserted crookedly or horizontally such that it was necessary to either climb over or crawl under to reach what, for lack of a better word, might be called an entrance. Upon closer inspection, he saw towering arches haloing each doorway as well as stained glass windows placed as randomly as the columns. Just below the red-tile roof that seemed intent on puncturing the lower

3

stratosphere, was a fresco w/ carved & protruding figures of warriors & horses, wisemen & women. Or so S- supposed. The figures—intricate, sensuous, ornate tho they were—seemed haphazard such that a woman's belly might seem to be giving birth to a horse's snout or a wiseman's head might be joined to a warrior's buttock. S- could just make out a series of worn letters scrunched-together, letters that read: LIBARY&LITERARYINFIRMARY.

"You do see the libary there?" the Police Chief repeated, correcting his pronunciation.

"Y-y-yes," S- stammered, reaching to wipe away his one remaining tear. Before S- could complete the act, the Chief of Police snagged the offending droplet, expertly depositing it in a glass vial pulled seemingly out of nowhere. The law enforcement officer assured the startled S- that said tear would be subject to intense laboratory scrutiny, chemical analysis, carbon dating & other related torturous processes until it had given up the last of its conspiratorial secrets. S- could expect the bill later.

S- stared @ the pudgy-cheeked police officer, noting the spastic wrinkles wiggling across the Chief's broad forehead, a similar twitching btwn the officer's pressed lips.

"So, is it a crime to cry on libary steps?" he asked.

The Police Chief heaved a sigh, holstering his club as his beady green eyes began to twinkle. He slid down next to the inquisitive interloper. "Let me tell you something, my boy. Not only is it *not* a crime to cry on the libary steps..." (the C of P paused, looking both ways as if about to approach a dangerous intersection) "...but some people do it every day. Indeed..." (he paused again, draping one arm around S-'s slumped shoulder) "...some even bring a tin cup for others to throw coins in. Those passing by will ask—w/ a great deal of formality, mind you–'Dear sir, why are you crying on our libary steps?' And the crier, who is usually practiced in the art of elocution, will go down on one knee & expound a long list of excuses. Then, depending on the delivery & sometimes the skill of his elocution—not to mention the quality & timbre of the crier's well-orchestrated whimpering—the passerby will toss a few coins into his or her cup."

The Police Chief paused, releasing his arm, allowing S- time to respond. As the stranger merely stared @ his own tattered shoes, the C of P continued:

"I might add, this town is known for its criers. Why, many of our weeping willows have gone on to worldwide acclaim. Some of our most famous give college lectures. See, college kids are big on these crybabies. And of course, criers are always depressing others, thus converting more criers. Why, in a good year, we get as many as half the town crying on these steps. It's hilarious."

S- sniffled, looking wide-eyed @ a few passing pedestrians. "So you laugh while half your town is crying?"

The Police Chief arched a brow. "Actually, i find the whole affair rather curious," he chuckled, rising & dusting off his pants. "Not that i object to crying, mind you. But i fail to understand why anyone would cry on our libary steps. Now the court steps, the church steps, the steps of city hall—even i've done my fair share of crying on those. But the libary steps? C'mon, my boy! You see, whatever reason you might have for crying, there's a book in those there hallowed halls that proves conclusively crying is nothing but a waste of saltwater...good saltwater @ that."

S- gazed back @ the imposing structure, its stained glass sparkling w/ reflected sunlight. He glanced around, taking note of a soft breeze kicking up its heels as it slid sinuously thru a small grove of teenage birch trees. The aromas of lilac & lavender strolled elbow to elbow down the sidewalk. Several starlings glided on a small gust of wind before dive-bombing into the grove, chirping a few catcalls @ the passing aromas, who turned up their noses, pretending to ignore them.

"Here, i'll prove it to you," the C of P suggested. "Tell me why you're crying?"

S- averted his gaze, his lower lip beginning to tremble. He stifled a sniffle. When he opened his mouth, nothing came out. Finally, he shrugged.

"You don't know why you're crying?"

S- shook his head.

Again the Police Chief slid down next to the peculiar stranger. "Let me ask you this, then: what brings you to our fair town?"

S- felt the warm puffs of the Police Chief breathing down his neck. His lips quivered as he struggled to complete a coherent sentence. Several fragments jettisoned from his throat, but nothing the C of P could make sense of.

"I don't really know," he finally confessed.

"You don't know? HE DOESN'T KNOW!" the Police Chief shouted @ the top of his voice. Looking askance @ the cowering stranger, the officer softened his tone. "Then how did you get here?"

"I don't know."

"HE DOESN'T KNOW!"

"I was led...i think."

"Now that's something," the C of P conceded. "You were led. HE WAS LED! But by who? Or should that be 'whom'?"

S- shrugged.

"HE DOESN'T KNOW." The Police Chief sidled closer, again draping one arm around S-'s bony shoulder. "Now, let me get this straight: you were led here, but you don't know by who...whom?...who."

S- nodded.

"Curious." The Police Chief scratched his bald head. "So why are you following this person...this person whom, who you don't even know?"

Staring @ his shoes, S- shrugged. After a long silence, he offered: "Because i must?"

"Because you must. BECAUSE HE MUST. And why must you?"

Again S- shrugged. "I just must."

"HE JUST MUST. But why...because this person told you to?"

S- nodded reluctantly.

"Well, if he told you to...then it must be the law. AND I'M ALL FOR THE LAW. I DON'T CARE WHAT THE LAW IS. IF IT'S A LAW, I'M ALL FOR IT." The Police Chief studied S- from the corner of his eye, rubbing his chin, then scratching his scar. "So...tell me, what does this person look like?"

S- gazed directly into the Chief's questioning eyes. "I don't know."

"You don't know?" The Chief sighed. "Of course not. HE DOESN'T KNOW. Well...is he tall?"

"Sometimes."

"Interesting... Does he wear glasses?"

"I've never seen his face."

"I see... Does he eat his pizza w/ a fork? Or does he fold it in his hands?"

"With a fork, i think." S- pondered a moment, his eyes shifting as he strained to recall. "But i'm not really sure."

Again the Police Chief sighed. Placing both hands on his knees, he raised himself up. He walked slowly & deliberately around S-, whistling as he went, one eye pinned on the peculiar stranger. As an added precaution, he readied his handcuffs.

"So, you obey the law of someone you've never seen? Someone whose name you don't even know. Someone who you don't even know what he looks like. Are you sure it's a him?"

"No...sometimes he isn't." Thinking further, S- added, "Maybe that's why i'm having a hard time finding him."

"No doubt," the C of P agreed. "So this person...why would he—or she—choose to come here...to our micropolis?"

6

S- shrugged, glancing up @ the C of P whose rotund figure momentarily eclipsed the sun. "I don't know...that's why i'm looking for him."

"You're sure of that?"

"Yes...i think."

"Even tho you don't know what he looks like. Even tho you never met him. Even tho... Look, tell me this: how will you know it's him when you do find him?"

S- turned away, his jaws beginning to twitch as his eyes bounced about their sockets like squirrels trapped in a cage.

Sensing the stranger was on the verge of tears, the Police Chief continued. "If you don't know who he is or what he looks like, how do you know he's the one who told you to come here?"

"I always know when it's him."

"You do?"

"Yes."

"How?"

"I don't know how...i just...i just always do."

"HOW!"

S- startled to attention. He clutched himself, his body jerking in spasms as he rocked on the balls of his feet. Incoherent murmurings bubbled from his throat as he curled into a quivering ball.

Pulling out his club, the Police Chief readied his aim. S- continued to shudder as, under his breath, the Chief debated w/ himself: *the back of the head, maybe? One swift blow to the front skull?* Several passersby paused, staring @ the officer, their eyes egging him to strike...& to strike hard. The Police Chief balked, his resolve melting.

He cleared his throat & adopted a conciliatory tone. "Look, i have tremendous respect for the law. I doubt if anyone has greater respect for the law than i do. As i said, I DON'T CARE WHAT THE LAW IS; IF IT'S A LAW, I RESPECT IT, SO HELP ME, PUP...i would be the last person to encourage anyone to break the law." The Police Chief holstered his club. "But...how can you follow a law made by someone you don't know, someone you've never seen, someone you might not even recognize when the two of you do cross paths?"

S- continued to rock as he observed several pedestrians sauntering by: a woman dragging a toddler twice her size; a man folding a newspaper, tucking it under one arm, removing the paper, refolding it, tucking it under the other arm; two kids, one sneaking something out of the other's pocket, the other sneaking it back, slipping it

7

into another pocket, the first kid stealing it back again, all the while the two walking arm-in-arm as if the best of buddies. He craned his neck, studying the libary's carved figures: a woman's arms extended, her hands lopped off, appearing several yards over, loaded w/ fruit offered to a wounded warrior, his mouth gaping, his neck straining, his own arms chopped off as well. He then looked directly in the Police Chief's frowning eyes. "How can i know until i find him?"

"Good point. GOOD POINT," the Chief acknowledged, seating himself again next to S-, wrapping an arm around S-'s shoulder & pulling the trembling stranger tightly to him. "So, you think he's here? Now. In this town."

S- nodded.

"What if i assured you, that as Chief of Police, i keep close tabs on the comings & goings of everyone in this, our micropolis. When a stranger enters our midst, believe you me, i know about it. Prior to you, why no one has entered our town in..." (the Chief extracted a note pad & began flipping its pages) "...three years, seven months, twenty-one days, eight hours & twenty-five minutes—rounding up, of course. If this stranger had entered our town, believe you me, i would know about it." With an air of triumph, the Police Chief repocketed the pad.

"But i know he's here."

"Even tho you don't know what he looks like?"

"I know he's here."

"Even tho you don't know where he's staying?"

"I KNOW he's here."

"Of course you do." The Chief sighed as he patted S-'s knee. "So, where are you staying, young man?"

"Staying?"

"Home. Where is your home?"

S- shrugged.

"Didn't this stranger tell you to seek shelter?"

"No. I figured when i got here, he would tell me what to do next."

"And he has! He has, my boy. I was talking to him the other day & he told me that if i was to see you, i was to tell you to seek shelter. 'Seek shelter,' that's exactly what he said. In fact, i know just the place. It's got a roof, a couple of walls—four, i think—& most of a ceiling...&, w/ a judicious application of soap & water, you might even find a window or two.

"Don't just sit there, my boy. Let's get a move on. You see that yellow mistress up there?" The Chief cocked a thumb twd the twinkling sun. "She may not be smiling too much longer. This place is a fair distance. If we don't head out immediately, it might not be there by the time we are."

S- rose quickly, his eagerness to be led matched only by the Chief's eagerness to lead him. He dusted the dirt from his pants-seat as he observed the police officer do, then turned one last time to gaze @ the jumbled structure calling itself a literaryinfirmary. He recalled someone once saying how books contained all the reasons why it was pointless to cry. Still he hesitated, till the Police Chief tugged @ his elbow, assuring him he could return later—tomorrow if he so wished. Vaguely reassured, S- allowed himself to be pulled along.

* * * * *

THE YELLOW MISTRESS IN THE SKY was indeed on the brink of shifting moods. Rumor of her lover's philandering having reached her ear, her sunny disposition began to slip behind a thick partition of gray, ominous cloud. Tho she'd peek out every now & again to check on the newcomer, she eventually succumbed to her mounting grief, hiding her moist cheeks behind a black veil she wore the rest of the afternoon—finally crying her eyes out till well into the evening.

S- & the Police Chief trudged thru the winding streets, the Chief bidding hello to persons they encountered, often pretending to tip an invisible hat or inquire how a bed of geraniums might be doing. He frequently paused to pet a dog or throw a stick for the neighborhood kids to chase. As for the townspeople, they waved, echoed his hellos, smiling as if their jaws ached, staring spellbound as the two men strutted by. They took particular delight each time the Chief reached over & took S- by the elbow to steer him in another direction.

S- found himself delighted by the waving, the smiles, the nods, the occasional winks of townsfolk directed twd their Police Chief. He was amazed to see a friendliness he had somehow missed. Had they always been so amiable? How had he failed to notice? He listened attentively as the C of P offered tidbits on the various persons they passed: how the whiskers on Mr Cartwright had grown an annual rate of eight inches a year until his forty-fifth birthday, when the growth slowed to six & a quarter inches; how Mrs Wainwright heard voices in the walls & how the walls had told her to add an extension to the back of her home just in time for the birth of her triplets; how the Wellingsworth boys would leave home six months each year to live completely different lives w/ the Bellwethers, then return when the weather got colder—neither Mr & Mrs Wellingsworth or the Bellwethers suspecting a thing.

9

Finally, the Chief talked about the place to which he was leading S-: "It's an attic: a garret actually, a very fine garret, located just above a very fine house... located, in fact, just below the roof of that very fine house—in btwn the roof & the top floor, to be exact.

"The Smolets live there." The Chief regarded S- from the corner of his eye. "You ever hear of the Smolets?"

S- shook his head.

"A fine family, a noble family—one of the oldest & most respected families in town. Mr Smolet runs the town's largest bank & pizzeria. Noble tomato sauce flows thru that man's veins." The officer stopped, placing a hand on S-'s shoulder as if to indicate what he was about to say being worthy of undivided attention.

"You probably haven't heard of H. Herrington Smolet, have you? I thought not.

Well, H. Herrington saved this town from near inevitable disaster. He was a great uncle, twice removed, to the present head of the Smolet family, & a great great uncle he was. Single-handedly he established the Principles of TP Etiquette @ a time when divisions in TP Theory threatened to plunge this micropolis into civil war. Families had split apart over this issue. Why, the last person we ever executed had poisoned a second cousin after they got into an argument during a family barbecue—& all because some people believed when you put a roll of toilet paper in a dispenser, you set it so the end flaps over, while others insisted the end should flap down."

S- stared @ the Chief, who, swiping glistening beads of sweat from his forehead & picking @ a scab, continued walking, stopping only to pull out his billy club & tap it against his upturned palm as he explained further.

"H. Herrington (the H stands for Horatio) had the patience of a saint. One morning while nursing a hangover, he flipped a coin exactly 1,291 times. When he recorded his findings, he found that six hundred & forty-three times the coin landed on heads & the other six hundred & forty-eight times it landed on tails, clearly in favor of toilet paper being dispensed w/ the flap down. Of course for years the scientific community quibbled over these findings, but when others repeated the experiment, 53% of the time tails became the clear winner by @ least five, sometimes as many as nine points. Based on these findings, the town council was able to get four-eighths of the members awake to vote in favor of the flap down & under, so once again people in this fair town could enjoy their family barbecues without being @ each other's throats. And H. Herrington Smolet is the man we have to thank."

The C of P again stopped, this time aiming his club @ a manor whose gate the

10

two were approaching. The manor was set farther back, away from the street: so far back, in fact, the architects thought it advisable to erect a second gate, then a third. The house's foundation bore three stories on its formidable shoulders, w/ a front porch propped up by columns similar to those of the libary. One of the upstairs rooms opened onto a terrace, while another was crowned w/ a chocolate syrup cupola. Just looking @ it gave S- a toothache.

The Chief pointed to the uppermost floor. "That's your new home."

Out of the corner of his eye, S- noted a downstairs curtain shifting.

When the officer jabbed the doorbell w/ his billy club, the sudden blare of trumpets startled S-. The flourish of rapidly ascending notes, followed by a police siren & the high-pitched whistle of an air-raid siren, culminated in the resonating bang of a Chinese gong.

A man of equal lack of stature to the Police Chief appeared, his beach-ball belly magnified by three plateglass doors separating him from the outside world. His cheeks as red as stop signs, his shocking white hair parted to the right, his beady blue eyes consuming everything they feasted on, the man unlocked the innermost door. Fiddling w/ a set of combinations, he opened the next door. Finally, he broke the glass to a red metal box marked IN CASE OF EMERGENCY, from which he pulled a key to unlock the third door. Extending what S- took initially to be frankfurters but quickly realized were four fingers & a thumb, the man shook the Police Chief's equally beefy digits.

"Howdy do. Howdy do, Mr Smolet," the Chief chimed, clicking his heels & flashing a military salute.

"Howdy do," the banker echoed, eyeing the Police Chief cautiously thru a pair of thick, dark-framed glasses.

"I understand, Mr Smolet," the Chief continued, cradling his billy club & rubbing his scab, "I understand you might have a garret that you might be willing to let out, providing the price & the prospective renter might be of the proper mettle."

The town's most prosperous banker squinted @ the ragged figure standing behind the Police Chief. He removed his glasses & squinted some more. He pursed his lips, his jowls moving up & down, his triple-chin quivering as if he were chewing on something.

"Well, uhhm, gee…" The banker spoke slowly, in a hoarse monotone, his jaws still chewing as the corners of his mouth turned slightly upward. "…i just might, Chief. I just might @ that. C'mon in, lad…Chief, show him how to wipe his feet— &, ah, frisk him for fleas, will ya?"

After wiping his feet & passing flea inspection, S- was led into a spacious foyer where he was instructed to make himself @ home—tho not touch anything. S- stared @ the garish wallpaper, glancing occasionally @ the whirring ceiling fan & shifting his feet in the plush, artificial grass-like carpet. Meanwhile the banker & Police Chief returned to the front porch.

"Where'd you find him?" the banker asked, his frankfurters resting on the Police Chief's shoulders.

"He was crying on the libary steps."

"Hmmm. I see...one of those."

The Police Chief nodded.

"You find out anything?"

"Not much. Says he's looking for somebody; doesn't know who, tho."

"Doesn't know who, huh?"

"Doesn't even know what this somebody looks like."

The banker pursed his lips, rubbing the lowest of his three chins. "Interesting." His jaw jiggled as he chewed on the Chief's intelligence.

"He's loony," the Police Chief offered. "A loon in search of a perfect stranger."

"Maybe." The banker nodded, his eyes, along w/ his thoughts, clearly elsewhere.

"That's why i brought him here...to you. Btwn the two of us, i figure we can keep a close watch on him." The C of P looked both ways before leaning in closer. "In the end, we'll probably have to...you know. But you never can tell—he may come around. If anyone can shine a light into that blank stare of his, i figure it would be you, Mr Smolet." The Chief of Police smiled & winked.

The banker ceased chewing, his ice cold stare magnified by the thick lenses of his spectacles. "Good job, Chief," he pronounced, patting the Chief's belly, unbuckling the C of P's belt & pulling it one notch tighter. "Once again, you have proven yourself an invaluable member of this community."

Extracting a thick, elegantly packaged cigar from his breast pocket, the banker handed it to the Chief. The Police Chief's eyes widened, accompanied by a broadening smile as he accepted the offering. He ran the cigar under his nose, whiffing its sweet earthy aroma, crinkling the gold-tinted cellophane wrapping. He thanked the banker, pretending to kiss the ring of the clammy hand the banker extended him.

"Every time he leaves the house, you signal by flashing the curtains," the Chief instructed. "And i'll have a man on his skinny tail. You can depend on it."

"Thanks, Chief. I'll let you know what i can get out of him."

After shaking frankfurters, the Chief of Police sauntered away, sniffing the cigar, smiling & occasionally turning to wave the cigar @ the banker who smiled & waved in turn. Exiting the third gate & rounding an intersection, the Chief ducked down the closest alley, loosening his belt & discarding the cigar in the nearest trash can. Slamming the lid & wiping his hands, he whistled a skewed tune—the same tune he had struggled w/ while interrogating S- on the libary steps, a tune he would continue to struggle w/ all the way back to headquarters. Occasionally, as he strolled along, he would shake his head. "Crying on the libary steps," he chuckled. "THE FOOL WAS CRYING ON THE LIBARY STEPS!"

Chapter 2

LIKE MANY A COMMONWEALTH, ours had been settled by persons escaping persecution: persons hoping for a better life somewhere where they might be the persecutors instead of the persecuted. Founded circa 1643, or thereabouts, by one Reverend Taylor Brittlebaum (or Reverend & taylor Brittlebaum—the records are ambiguous), our town is best known for its lack of a name; our four-sighted founders believing this a foolproof method of rendering our borders difficult to locate. Stretch your maps the length of any dining room table & you might—if you're lucky—stumble upon the solitary unidentified dot that is our micropolis (the one w/ no roads leading in or out); but, more likely, you'll mistake us for a misprint or, better still, a speck of dried debris even your most aggressive thumbnail can't quite dislodge.

From what few untampered documents remain, our historians trace the original Brittlebaums to somewhere west of Iceland, north of Rome, south of Never-Neverland & east of Eden. These earlier Brittlebaums, according to said documents, had flourished on the outskirts of a great micropolitan trade-center—a center since having sunk into the great lake upon which it was once a thriving island.

Legend has it pride, vanity & too many obese in-laws had sunk the economic mecca. The Brittlebaums, as well as the island's other noble families, were said to have suffered from that all-too-common malady of believing themselves better than anyone else. As our economists attest, competition fuels perfection, thus many were the families perfecting the upward turn of their noses & the downward sway of their regard—including the Brittlebaums. Unfortunately, when among the older, more established families, the Brittlebaums were easily outshunned.

14

When uncivil war erupted, the unfortunate Brittlebaums found themselves crying 'Uncle'—a euphemism for verbiage our linguists allege to be unprintable. The once proud Brittlebaums were reduced to servitude &, as the poor, downtrodden & disenfranchised are wont to do, they turned to religion for solace. Decades of devouring humble pie & self-deprecation led eventually to one branch of Brittlebaums (headed by the aforementioned Taylor Brittlebaum) moving family, animals & loyal congregation elsewhere. Months of arduous travel—by boat, by wagon, by creaky caravan—finally resulted in Brittlebaum & company settling this territory, leveling its mountains, deforesting its hills, rerouting its rivers & generally bringing the landscape to its knees.

Meanwhile (so our anthropologists tell us), several Brittlebaums contracted a rare genetic disease traced back to the old country. The Reverend Brittlebaum; his older brother, Aaron; & their kid sister, Meg, simultaneously contracted an inability to see anyone different from themselves. Whatever the difference—perhaps a physical attribute (e.g. height; slender waist; silky, full-bodied hair), or the proud swagger in another's gait, or whether one called a couch a sofa or spelled theater 'theatre'—those born on the wrong side of said difference found their toes constantly stepped on, found themselves forever interrupted in conversation & pushed about as if they weren't even present. Should said persons fail to correct the offending difference, said persons eventually found themselves under a horse andor carriage owned/driven/rented or leased by a Brittlebaum, or descendant thereof. The situation proved not w/ out its tensions.

Complicating matters—or so our geneticists assert—the Brittlebaum myopia transferred randomly onto succeeding generations, perhaps skipping one generation to take up residence in the next. To make matters still worse, the descendants bypassed usually contracted that more universal of genetic diseases: the desire to be as different from Mumma & Pupa as humanly possible (while still gaining mention in any last will & testament, of course).

Thus were there years stretching into bloody decades when the original colony seemed destined to run each other over & out of existence. Inbreeding strengthened the Brittlebaum gene; outbreeding diluted it. Factions formed, dissolved, formed again. This might have gone on forever had not another clan, unnoticed by 'high' Brittlebaums, migrated into our fertile territory.

The Woodbees were an industrious race, able to turn whatever the land offered into useful, practical, wealth-generating material. Upon entering the province, Woodbee wealth centered mostly around the manufacture of honey & the transformation of trees into lumber. Thus 'low' Brittlebaums—those w/ clear enuff vision to discern the vagrants—dubbed the unwanted intruders 'Woodbees.'

Much has transpired since those first Woodbees infested our settlement, including a great deal of intermarrying. Even high Brittlebaums found certain advantages in accumulating the Woodbee propensity of turning labor—especially those of others—into wealth. For the privilege of marrying a Brittlebaum (& later just to sleep w/ one) a tax levy was exacted. Another levy exempted one from being mistaken for thin air—thus lessening one's chances of being run over by a Brittlebaum horse andor buggy. In effect, much/most of the Woodbee wealth eventually found its way into Brittlebaum coffers.

Woodbees, however, in addition to being an industrious race, proved consummate breeders—something Brittlebaum descendants had trouble mastering the mechanics of. Eventually, 'Woods' came to outnumber 'Brits'...& to insist on having equal say in the exacting of any taxes or levies, as well as in the selection of which minorities should receive the most shaft. For decades Brittlebaum offspring (the D'leBaums, the Rittl'baus, the D'baums, et al) held firm their positions of power, cautioning how the "undue burdens of privilege would prove overtaxing to those of lesser constitution." The Woodbees, however, accustomed to the undue burdens of being overtaxed, persisted & continue to persist in their pursuit of being so unduly burdened.

Altho descendants of Taylor, Aaron & Meg Brittlebaum continue to have final say, Woodbees have nevertheless been making substantial gains by buying, leasing, renting-to-own as many chairs on our City Council as they could fit their ever-widening posteriors into. Thus was the state of affairs when the dark-eyed S- entered town & stood gaping @ the decorative wallpaper adorning the Smolet Manor foyer.

* * * * *

WHILE THE POLICE CHIEF & the banker convened on the Smolet front porch, S-stood mesmerized by the lifelike wall pattern engulfing him on all sides: tree after golden-boughed tree, their muscular limbs brimming w/ heart-shaped leaves of legal tender. Gnomes & pointy-eared elves crouched in the tall bent grass gathering raw, uncut rubies. Others seated on sapphires the size of boulders stuffing lapis lazuli into burlap bags stamped: FOR DEPOSIT ONLY. Nearby, fellow gnomes cast fishing poles into a sparkling river of gold-finned trout & silver-scaled carp, their gills exuding diamonds that bubbled & bobbed to the surface.

S- felt the floor rumble beneath him. He turned @ the sound of approaching

16

footsteps. The returning banker halted inside the doorway, his blinking blue eyes peering thru S-, his sagging jowls chewing on something.

"What say you & me step into my cocoooon?" Smolet finally suggested, stretching the last word beyond its normal capacity. Seizing S- by the arm, the banker led the stranger to a dimly lit room that might have doubled as a junk yard.

The banker gingerly stepped around makeshift mountains of spreadsheets, file folders, bank ledgers, deposit slips & what proved to be an entire encyclopedia on economic exploitation: "from A to Z," their black & gold embossed covers boasted. A bulldog of a mahogany desk squatted in the far corner, backed by a pudgy-cheeked easy chair, both seeming to glower @ S- w/ guarded suspicion. A gutted bookshelf; a credenza, its doors wide open; & a souvenir case purged of its contents, stared back @ him as if pleading for rescue. Several portraits of persons w/ severe expressions sneered down from above a false fireplace. Smolet motioned for S- to sit in one of two chairs facing the mahogany desk.

"Excuse the mess," the banker entreated. "I rang for the housekeeper but...you know how wives are." Smolet smiled wanly as he grappled twd his easy chair.

S- sat as instructed, watching as the banker again began to chew on something. Smolet's jowls moved up & down as he glanced around the disheveled office. He removed his glasses to rub the bridge of his nose. About to speak, the banker abruptly dropped to his knees, the room quaking from the impact, a small avalanche erupting from one of the piles of debris. Yanking open a lower desk drawer, Smolet rummaged thru its contents, nearly climbing inside as pens, erasers, ink pads, rubber stamps & many a paper airplane flew up & about the room. Some plopped on the desk, others tumbled to the floor, a few crashed atop the other piles, setting off additional avalanches. Sweat beaded the banker's forehead. "It has to be here somewhere," he assured himself. "It just has to be."

S- observed several musty odors cringing in the room's far corners, clutching their throats & gasping for breath. He eyed the thick burgundy curtains lined w/ gold tassels & considered opening a window, wondering if additional light might aid the banker's search as well as provide the stale odors some much needed relief.

He heard an "Ah, hm," only then realizing the room had grown silent.

Smolet was seated @ his desk, leaning forward. His pale blue eyes, magnified by thick lenses, were lasered in on S-. The full patch of brilliant white hair curled atop the banker's head like a sleeping cat.

Smolet folded his hands. "So..." he asked slowly, chewing his words carefully, "What exactly do you DO?"

S- felt his neck hair bristle, a shiver snaking up his spine. Something about the question frightened him. His frantic eyes scanned the carpet, certain the last word must have fallen to the floor & shattered into pieces.

"You do DO something, don't you?" The banker stood, steadying his bowling ball of a figure w/ the desk's help. He waddled to the side of his desk, draping one leg over its corner. "Everyone must DO something."

The financial officer crossed his flabby arms, removing his glasses. He resumed his chewing. "It's the prime function of all civilized societies. Certainly, there was a time when more, shall we say, *primitive* societies were content to merely BE. But the DOers drove them out. Took over their land a long time ago.

"Around here, young man, we DO." The banker waddled back to his seat. "We DO," he repeated. "Everyone DOes. DO unto others before they have time to DO unto you—that's the successful man's motto." Leaning forward, Smolet studied his potential tenant from head to tattered shoe. "You do DO, don't you? Or do you UN-DO?"

S-'s eyes sought a hasty retreat. He noted again the muffled cries of the room's myriad odors. He looked to his own shadow, which abruptly ducked for cover when a wedge of light suddenly sliced thru the room.

"Excuse me, dear..."

A woman stood in the doorway, her bleached hair a raging ocean frozen in mid-crest. "I know you rang a while ago, but i was—" The woman gasped.

S- jerked his head, looking around to see what might have frightened her.

"What is *that* doing in my house?" she screamed. Her eyes flared as her alligator slippers snapped their sharp teeth.

"THIS IS NOT RIGHT," she shrieked in capital letters. "HOW DID HE...? WHO LEFT THE DOOR...? THE BASEMENT, SOMEONE LEFT THE BASEMENT WINDOW OPEN! CALL THE EXTERMINATOR! NO, THE FIRE DEPT. GET A PLUMBER. I WANT HIM OUT! DO YOU HEAR ME? GET HIM OUT!"

S- noted his shadow crouched atop the shadow of a chair. Looking down, he saw he too was crouched atop his chair, ready to spring forward or jump back, tho unsure which direction might serve him best.

Smolet, meanwhile, had catapulted to his feet & rushed to the woman. Stepping btwn S- & his raving wife, he massaged her shoulders & patted her head. "It's all right, my little jelly roll. Don't worry. It's all under control."

"This is not right.... I want a divorce."

The banker kissed his wife's powdered cheeks. "It's okay, my apple dumpling."

"I mean it this time. You keep that thing here one minute longer—" The woman gasped again, her eyes bulging as her mind entertained the unimaginable: "YOU'RE NOT PLANNING TO RENT THE ATTIC TO HIM, ARE YOU? I won't have it. Do you hear? You do & i'm leaving. I'm taking our favorite children & leaving. Do you hear me? I mean it."

The banker continued to implore his wife. "You have to trust me, my sugar-coated strawberry. I know what i'm doing," he whispered. Despite her agitation, the woman's voice dropped several decibels, her tone softening. Her slippers ceased snapping & merely hissed. When she again saw S-, she shivered. "I can't stand to even look @ it," she declared.

"I know," the banker cooed. "But it's all under control. I promise." Gently, tho firmly, Smolet steered his wife out of his office. He closed the door, bolted it & fell against it, sighing heavily as he ran a stubby hand thru his thick thatch of white hair, his forehead dribbling w/ perspiration.

He flashed S- a smile. "She gets a little excited. I'm sure she'll warm to you just as I have."

Foraging among the junk piles, he found a handkerchief & dabbed his forehead, then the back of his neck. S- returned to his seat as the banker's jaws again began chewing on something.

Digesting whatever it was, the financial officer plodded back to his chair, plopping down heavily. He lifted a framed photo from the corner of his desk, examined it & set it back in place. He rubbed his hands the way S- had often seen flies do. Removing his glasses & leaning forward, the banker looked directly @ his new tenant.

"I tell you what. You & me son, we're gonna be a team. How would you like that?"

S- sat motionless.

"This will be our little secret." The banker looked about, waddled over to the door & pressed one ear against it. He walked around his cocoon, running his hands under all surfaces, checking behind the drapes before plopping in the chair next to S-. Again he looked around, then leaned over & whispered. "As far as anyone knows, i'm hiring you as my new ass't janitor... But in truth, we're part-ners."

"Partners," S- repeated after some hesitation.

"Partners," Smolet smiled. "Your job will be easy. All you have to DO...is whatever i tell you. No questions asked. Just DO it. So...whatever i ask, you go like this..." The banker nodded his head several times. "Try it."

S- moved his head up & down.

"Good...good. I knew you could DO it. You're a natural." The banker patted S- on the wrist. "Now, straighten up this mess."

S- rose as the banker sat back & chewed. Each time S- picked up an item, the banker pointed to where the object should go. Soon the financial officer was smiling broadly, imagining himself a famous conductor standing before a world class orchestra.

"I understand you're looking for someone," the banker interjected when S- was almost done. "We have ways of finding missing persons. Why, our cemeteries are full of 'em. Perhaps i can be of assistance."

S- paused, eager to hear more. But the banker fell silent, again masticating on something. When the office was back in order, Smolet's eyes again peered thru S-. "I guess i need to find you a key," he said, fingering the chain around his neck, a flat key glistening from its base.

"Actually, on second thought, you might want to use this entrance." The banker jumped up & drew back the thick curtains. With concerted effort he yanked, cursed & grunted until the stubborn window finally acquiesced.

"Just so as not to disturb the missus, you understand. Just go around the side there. There's a giant mulberry tree w/ a short, stout trunk. You can't miss it. It looks just like a giant mulberry tree w/ a short, stout trunk. Take the branch jutting north-to-northwest. It'll lead directly to your room. Call me if you need anything.

"And, ah, welcome to the family...partner."

Chapter 3

NOT SINCE 330 BC when Ptolemy built the great library [sic] of Alexandria has more style & ostentation been expended on such a literary infirmary as ours. And no one was more proud of this fact than our head libarian, Neimann Gorge, who sat smiling smugly as he gazed about his lofty office—a grand rotunda of fluted pilasters & inlaid bookshelves crowned by a golden-domed, crystal-chandeliered ceiling. Erected during an epoch when knowledge was akin to gold, considered more essential than bread—when wisdom was proven more effective in quelling one's enemies than bullets or betrothing one's sister—Neimann's palatial surroundings featured the most advanced architectural affects lauded in that bygone era. Closing his eyes, he pictured the lower levels: the towering labyrinth of portals, galleries, study chambers, conference rooms—separated not by walls but by Roman columns arrayed w/ Greek-Corinthian capitals, connected by graceful archways. Higher up, reached by a circular, spiraling ambulatory were the chapels, alcoves & the twelve 'basilicas of learning,' each capped by high-vaulted ceilings, their walls stuffed beyond capacity w/ what Neimann affectionately dubbed his absolute bestest of friends: that is, his books.

His fingers laced & resting comfortably on his abdominous bookbelly, Neimann relished the accumulating echo of footsteps, page turning & endless whispering, the drone rising to hover in the upper chambers like invisible bats. Vaguely he recalled an ancient legend: was it something about a tower of bubble, or babble? But then, he reassured himself, dealing w/ troglodytes was the price an erudite cosmopolite such as himself paid for the privilege of being the town's highest salaried libarian.

Neimann glanced @ his attire. Tho not his habit to concern himself w/ outward appearance, something had possessed him to dress impeccably that morning. He had pulled his tweed vest & jacket out of storage, donned a powder blue silk shirt, navy blue cravat & matching slacks. He had stood before his morning mirror painstakingly parting his dark curly afro this way & that, attempting in vain to somehow subdue his long cucumber face, his floppy elephantine ears. But there seemed little he could do to alter the features fate had seen fit to grace him with.

He glanced @ his watch, the hands miniature figures of his venerable heroes: Socrates & Plato. Mz Pritt would be by any moment. He wrung his hands, admonished himself for nibbling his nails. He inventoried his office, finding solace in the reassuring presence of so many close friends. They crowded around in all shapes & sizes: tall, slim, short, thick; leather bound & paperback, vellum, lambskin, pigskin, the economical peasant-hide; some maroon, some maize, vermilion, beige, roan, russet, all colors really. Their bookmarks sticking out like panting tongues, some leaned like ladies of the evening; some sat, napped, frolicked; others stretched out on their bellies like babies in cribs, or w/ pages spread-eagle on the divan, across throw pillows or snuggled up to cushions. Those on the bookshelves stood like so many soldiers guarding his sanctuary; stern & resolute—determined to fend off the forces of darkness, prejudice, superstition & ignorance.

books

His thoughts returned to Mz Pritt, their impending conference. Neimann resolved to be firm: gentle, yet unyielding. He would voice his displeasure, but not @ the expense of her feelings, of course. Thus decided, he resumed his nail biting—that is till the all-too-familiar dulcet tones of Mz Pritt interrupted his snack.

"May i come in?" she chimed.

Neimann bolted upright. His feet, having slovenly found their way across the edge of his desk, slammed onto the carpet. His peaceful revelry squealed on its brakes. He felt a peculiar sensation suggestive of the hair on the nape of his neck standing @ attention. He might have been mistaken, but his face felt beet red.

"I beg your pardon, Mz Pritt. I seem to have been lost in my own intellection." Neimann reached for the nearest object, a thin volume of ancient witticisms which he held to his chest like a frightened child might clutch a teddy bear.

Mz Pritt entered, three inches taller than Neimann in her high heels. Her sleeveless red dress clung to her hips, the neckline revealing just enuff of her breasts to send Neimann imagining what it might look like a few inches lower.

"If you're busy i could come back," she offered, parting her lips in a smile Neimann found disconcerting.

"No, no. That's alright, Mz Pritt." He struggled to gain control of his Adam's apple, wondering who was playing w/ the thermostat. Didn't they realize heat rises & hovers in his office? Someone should teach these Neanderthals to be more considerate.

"How can i be of service of to you?" he heard himself ask.

"The bookends, Mr Gorge. You said i might stop by to look @ your bookends."

"Bookends? Oh, yes! Bookends—there." He pointed to an antique arabesque coffee table. Among the lounging periodicals & reference material were two hand-crafted, heart-shaped bookends embellished w/ tail-wagging puppies & kissing doves.

"Why, these are adorable!"

As Mz Pritt bent to scoop up the bookends, Neimann saw—or imagined he saw—the outline of her...well, her undergarment. How were the scholars & schoolboys of this learned institution to keep their thoughts on their studies when members of the staff went about attired like common...no, he wouldn't think it, much less say it.

Her stockings swishing, Mz Pritt sidled up to him & thanked him profusely. Why did she wear that perfume? he wondered. And insist on smiling that way? And what was wrong w/ her eyes? Her lashes were fluttering like hummingbird wings.

Fumbling w/ his book, then tossing it aside, Neimann moved away, explaining how the bookends were a gift from a silly schoolgirl who—or so he suspected—had a ridiculous crush on him.

"She has good taste," Mz Pritt responded, her dove gray eyes seeming to pierce thru the libarian.

Neimann slammed his knee into a chair. "Well, yes," he found himself agreeing, his Adam's apple once again in a state of rebellion. He forced a smile. "You know these schoolgirls. Too bad. She was a promising young Aristotle." He looked off in the distance, recalling thin tapered fingers twisting the end of dark cascading hair, a young mind poring over tomes of antiquated philosophy.

Neimann faced the window overlooking the southern precinct of town. Flat-topped, squat bldgs bullied their way into the foreground, their squared shoulders denying all challengers any right to dominate the skyline. Farther back, visible more in Neimann's imagination, were the mansions/manors/palaces of the privileged, their classical architecture modified by influences of early Brittlebaumesque—luscious lawns, expansive gardens, encircling moats. A shadow fell over him. The sun ducked under a lone cumulus cloud, returning Neimann to the present. He turned, staring blankly @ Mz Pritt.

"I wonder, Mz Pritt...i have just finished a mesmeric book. In your reading have you ever stumbled upon the works of Saska Swamin?"

Mz Pritt smiled. "I don't believe i have."

"Then allow me to acquaint the two of you." Neimann motioned Mz Pritt to the chair facing his desk. Reaching for an anorexic volume of natural lambskin, he propped himself on the corner of his desk, resolving to discuss the matter of Mz Pritt's attire another time—when they were better acquainted, he told himself.

"Saska Swamin," Neimann began. "Slender as she is, is a tasty morsel." He pressed her slim spine to his thin lips, looking inward a moment before proceeding. "A bit abstruse for conventional scholars, but Swamin, heavily influenced by the Myst Sticks, concluded that each of us—you, me, the janitorial staff, even those nasty Nabors living next door—we all possess w/in us all the wisdom of the ages."

Neimann tossed Swamin aside as if she were no more than a book. He paced the room, hands clasped behind his back. "Problem is: just as each of us have instances when we can't quite remember a word, a title, or the name of an acquaintance, each of us can't remember what we knew when we first enter this existence."

Mz Pritt crossed her legs, shook her head & brushed the hair from her eyes.

"Life," Neimann said, rapping his knuckles on the window ledge, "is thus a quest to remember, to recall if you will, what we all already know deep down inside."

He retrieved Saska Swamin & opened her fluttering pages @ random. "Ah! Here Swamin elucidates her position on what she calls 'Hombres d'Garbiage,' those who in their ruinous ignorance pull the rest of us down to *their* noxious state of perniciousness."

Neimann began reading: "'Hombres d'Garbiage reinforce our mistaken assumption that we are less than we truly are. Some even exalt in their baser nature, convincing others to do the same. Thus we hire ourselves out to stress factories, servants to their (& ultimately our own), less-than-perfect nature. In the evening, we return home to lead lives of quiet defecation. Only the enlightened, the occasional brave, the uncommonly foolish—or the lucky—break thru the chains of the status woe to move ever closer to that wisdom etched in every atom of each our own beings.'"

Neimann slammed the book shut & slid it back on its shelf. As Mz Pritt offered no response, he continued:

"Swamin further asserts that it is the bounden duty of those of us—we scholars, savants & lettered luminaries, even the lowly-but-learned shopkeeper, the compassionate butcher & the freakishly-gifted Dreg—it is the bounded duty of

24

those of us who unearth bits & pieces of our higher nature to enlighten the ignorant *other* as to anything we can happily recall.

"Lately i've been rereading one of my favorite thinkers." Neimann turned, retrieving a modest volume sprawled in the center of his desk. "Hiqmat al-Ishrag. This is his masterpiece: **The Breaking Wind of Reason,** a brilliant vivisecting of the encumbrances of human ratiocination."

Neimann noted the hem of Mz Pritt's dress resting slightly above her knee. He noted also the smoothness of said knees & a small patch of darkness btwn those knees, which led him to imagine—no, he would not allow his thoughts to go there.

He glanced @ his watch. The lanky Plato pointed just past 12 while the diminutive Socrates gazed up @ 11. "Oh dear, look @ the time. It always seems to fly when i'm in your company." He blushed upon realizing the unintended importation of his remark. "I'm needed in surgery before my one o'clock discussion group. You really ought to join us sometime, Mz Pritt."

"I'd love to, Mr Gorge. But your lectures seem to be scheduled when i'm on hospital duty. But thank you for these darling bookends." Mz Pritt rose. "Maybe i can return the favor sometime..." She extended her hand. "...Mr Gorge."

Neimann accepted the soft silky palm. "Neimann. Please. Call me Neimann."

"Okay, Neimann. And please call me Kate."

"Okay...Kate."

The invisible tentacles of Kate's perfume wreaked havoc on Neimann's sense of equilibrium. She turned & left, leaving the memory of her smile & the subtle swivel of her hips. Neimann stood smiling, staring @ nothing in particular. Then he recalled the reason he had summoned her. He cursed himself: he had avoided the moment—again.

Buried under the books on his desk was a slender pamphlet on libary etiquette. Again he skimmed the brief section subtitled "Dress Code," baffled as to why there was no specific suggestion on how to deal w/ provocative attire. And there was nothing forbidding the use of lipstick, rouge, perfume. Not even mascara.

* * * * *

OUR LEARNED LIBARIAN was humming a lilting ditty as he scurried down the spiraling ambulatory. Anyone spying behind a bookshelf or peeking thru the wall-hangings might have reported Neimann as being in high spirits. A more astute agent, however, would have discerned a nagging hint of serious consternation tugging on his guarded

25

smile. The great institution that was his libaby had of late received serious threats from those who advocated bulldozing it in favor of additional parking. Even the memory of the hem of Mz Pritt's dress creeping above her knee could not forestall the reemergence of Neimann's deepening concern.

Plans to expand libary services, to reach those most in need of relieving their impoverished lot via the Holy Grail of knowledge, were perpetually blocked by what Neimann called a scandously sciolistic City Council, its most common complaint being that all knowledge seemed to do was give people ideas—this in a paradisiacal epoch when all the right ideas had already been established, enshrined, homogenized, notarized & perfectly codified into city law. Thus the literary infirmary—despite centuries of lavish ostentation—had recently fallen onto hard times. The current municipal council considered Neimann's pride & joy a mere watering hole for dried-up old geezers who thought themselves smarter than their less-educated superiors. Tho its interior had hitherto been left untouched, the libary's exterior was in a miserable state of disrepair. The proposed facelift was held up in so many committees & modified by so many consultants that, finally, a group of promising high school architects was commissioned to complete the project in exchange for free movie passes.

Assuming a brave face, Neimann strolled the ambulatory, waving to myriad, sundry & divers truth-seekers. "Chew slowly," he cautioned a homeless couple devouring the glossy pages of a sodium-free, low-fat cookbook. He extended a silent "shush" to Rebecca Shale of our Pro-Life Movement. Hair in curlers, stockings rolled down to her shins, Mz Shale came every morning to debate **The Encyclopedia of Natural Philosophy**. "The nerve of some books," she ranted thru clenched teeth. Despite her badgering & proclivity to stick gum btwn its more intractable pages, the encyclopedia held firm, insisting plants, birds, animals, insects (& by implication, those nasty Nabors next door) were all *living* entities…& that thus, to be *truly* pro-life meant to defend *all* living things. "It's a commonist plot," Mz Shale rebutted, slapping each volume silly, threatening them w/ matches, terrorizing them by wielding pictures of heavy-duty, state-of-the-art paper shredders.

Neimann waved to the Siamese twins, Herman & Hermine, camped out among the books on theoretical science. For weeks the twins had been conducting endless experiments using Lincoln logs to prove conclusively that i before e, except after c, superseded all the contemporary nonsense about E equaling MC-squared. Neimann contemplated the potential implications of their controversial theory, adroitly sidestepping as a tumbling body plummeted from an upper chamber. The human projectile landed w/ a dull thud several floors below. Without breaking stride, the head libarian made a mental note to move the books on suicide to a lower level.

Pushing thru a set of double doors, Neimann stepped into the brightly lit INFIRMARY. He was greeted warmly by rows of bedridden patrons, arms andor legs wrapped in gauze, their bandaged bodies propped up by pillows. Reading lamps cast amber halos above each patient's head. Many balanced books on their laps, most shaking their heads in dismay. Libarians in starched uniforms dashed from patient to patient, taking temperatures, dispensing aspirin, antihistamine, valium & qualuudes in a frantic— Neimann would say 'Sisyphusian'—attempt to stave off infections precipitated by the cuts, scrapes & bruises the pursuit of knowledge is heir to.

Neimann negotiated the maze of hospital beds, arriving finally @ the opposite end where a swinging door emphatically insisted: KEEP OUT—STAFF ONLY. He snatched a surgical mask hanging from its peg. Nudging the door w/ his shoulder, he stepped into another brightly lit room. An array of medical machinery purred along one corner, panels spewing digital numbers, lights flashing, graphs firing lightning bolts across dim green flickering screens. A series of clicks, beeps, chugging & hiccups were emitted in a random tho soothingly rhythmic sequence. Sprawled on a narrow operating table lay a live mummy, connected to the blinking/hissing/humming machines by a network of clear tubes & interlacing blue, green & red wires. Four men in surgical gowns worked in silence, heads bent as each hunched either over the patient or the purring machines.

First to acknowledge Neimann was a scarecrow w/ a stethoscope, his five o'clock shadow pushing half past eleven. The man nodded before nudging the elder, slightly hunchbacked physician standing next to him. The older man, his face a fishnet of deep-set wrinkles, greeted Neimann w/ a smile, followed by a friendly wink.

"Dr Buncle," Neimann returned the greeting.

Jotting a few notes, dotting his t's & crossing his eyes, Dr Carl Buncle, DMS, set his medical chart aside. Pushing back his bifocals, he rubbed his prodigious pockmarked nose, then gestured twd the wiry-headed scarecrow whose reddish-yellow thatch of hair jutted out in all directions. "I believe you know Dr Oswald, our literary heart specialist."

Dr Oswald extended a hand in mock greeting. His surgical tools arranged in descending alphabetical order, he proudly displayed his accomplishment to an all approving Neimann, himself a devotee of reverse alphabetization.

The libarian further acknowledged Drs Scurvy DVM & Cataract DDT, @ that moment comparing labels on their surgical gowns. Each referenced various mentors, medical advisors & esteemed mental patients on the importance of the comfort, fit, status & utility of surgical attire.

"One, after all," Dr Cataract asserted in a deep resonating voice, "one cannot affect the proper surgical cut should the shoulder of one's arm be restricted by too tight a seam."

"Or the hem of one's sleeve flop listlessly about, thus obstructing one's view of the offending artery," the younger Dr Scurvy added, stroking the goatee of his otherwise hairless head.

Nodding his approval, Neimann turned his attention to the gurgling moans of the patient strapped to the surgical table. Said patient had begun to squirm to an alarming degree. When Dr Oswald suggested the gauze around said patient's mouth might be obstructing the poor chap's breathing, Dr Buncle came to the patient's aid. Neimann's eyes widened as he recognized the scruffy beard, the mole on the left cheek & the jaundiced countenance.

"Well, well, well. If it isn't Erle Greaves," Neimann tsk'd tsk'd, shaking his head. "I warned you it would come to this."

"Water, water," the patient groaned.

"Yes, water," Neimann repeated. "The very substance of life. The true nectar of the gods. But the gods can't help you now. I warned you seminary school would be a despoliation to your unmitigable inquisitional endeavors." Neimann wagged a finger.

The patient struggled, lifting slightly before his head fell back, the heavy clunk sending the surgical tools on the adjoining table rattling. Fear momentarily seized Dr Oswald's face.

"You went too fast," the libarian continued. "Too much truth...too rapidly consumed...can be almost as detrimental...as blind *ig-nor-ance*." Neimann enunciated the last word clearly. All four physicians nodded in agreement.

"Well, gentlemen," the senior surgeon suggested, "shall we scrub in?"

As the four men headed for the sink, Neimann leaned over the semi-delirious student. "So tell me, Erle...where does it hurt?"

The patient groaned, clutching the edges of the table as spittle spewed from his mouth, running down his cheek. Neimann knitted a brow as Erle emitted a low gurgling sound. The libarian leaned closer, placing his ear as close as he dared for fear of becoming infected. "What was that? Speak slowly."

The seminary student swallowed saliva, choking, coughing, struggling for breath before murmuring, "Mer-re-ac."

"Merreac? Merreac?" Neimann's eyes brightened. "Ah, Meriac! Yes, that forerunner of our own demicratic system. 'All men six feet tall are created equal,' they claimed, the proof of which being self-evident in that each person being of six feet in height had exactly seventy-two inches.

"This is rather serious," Neimann informed the surgeons, that moment returning to the operating table. Dr Cataract twitched his nose as if detecting an offensive odor. Dr Scurvy gazed @ the libarian thru youthful, questioning eyes.

"Meriac built a great empire on that principle," Neimann elaborated, "drafted a constitution, got their God to notarize it—all the while enslaving anyone having merely two feet. And they overran any civilization w/ the gall to feel ten feet tall, slicing those who refused to capitulate into two relatively equals halves, making two fives—then, calculating two plus five equals seven (that is, one more than six), they declared this a blatant sign of hubris, if not downright witchcraft. Anyone caught thus, was burned @ their steaks...& all reasoned out w/ perfect mathematical precision." Neimann glanced @ the patient.

"Someone, my dear Erle, should have directed you to al-Ishrag's **Breaking Wind of Reason**."

The libarian bent low, his lips nearly brushing Erle's ears. "You see, my dear Erle, reason is merely a tool human beans use to justify whatever it is they desire. Everything begins w/ DE-ZI-ERR. We want something; we convince ourselves it's our right—our *divine* right—to have it. If necessary, we juggle words, alter definitions, reinterpret sacred texts—texts we ourselves write & edit, then attribute to our Gods...&, if anyone dare dispute our alleged logic, we bayonet them into agreement."

Neimann stepped back to allow Drs Buncle & Oswald room. The four literary surgeons circled the table, each respectively clutching a scalpel, a pair of forceps, a can of soda, or a pick ax.

"And that's not the worst of it, my friend. Should our infallible reason still fail us, we fall back on anti-reason, on the irrational: faith, passion, God, PUP, majority rule, or that most universal of all lines of reasoning: *i'm-bigger-than-you-so-you-better-do-as-i-say*—something i'm sure they never bother to elucidate @ Seminary U."

Neimann signaled the four masked men to begin, looking on as four sets of surgical eyes exchanged questioning glances.

"Where should we operate?" each seemed to ask.

"Obviously he needs to have his head examined," Dr Cataract suggested, his forehead already sweating profusely. "Shouldn't we start there?"

29

"With all due respect," Dr Oswald proffered, "I suggest we cut away the heart. His heart is obviously the culprit." Referring to the most recent issue of his favorite medical comic, Dr Oswald proceeded to explain how the heart, thru a complex network of electrical impulses regulated by neurological synaptic connections, was attached to the mouth.

"The heart drives him on, but should he taste whatever it is his heart so desperately desires, he soon tires of it. Then his heart tells him to find something else. As long as the heart is in control, he will never be satisfied. Ergo, removing the heart is the most equitable corrective."

"Yes, but what about the feet?" Dr Scurvy interjected. "Everything begins w/ the feet. Because we have feet, we have mobility. What is mobility? Freedom! Freedom to go anywhere, even places we don't belong. Remove the feet, you restrict mobility. Perhaps he'll stay away from the places that fed him the forbidden fruit which has him so sick to his scrutinizing stomach."

"Then why not remove the stomach?" Dr Buncle challenged. "Or the ass, for that matter? The patient is obviously an ass. He places his trust in his mind. Using his mind, he convinces his mind that the mind is not to be trusted. Where's the sense in that? He's an ass, i tell you—i say remove the ass."

"Or the fists." Dr Cataract offered, being the only attending physician w/ a psychiatric degree from the University of Froid. "After all, babies form fists long before they extend handshakes. The clenched fist is the first act of rebellion. Amputate the First Cause & you truncate all that follows."

Neimann bit his lower lip, exchanging a pensive glance w/ the bloodshot eyes of Dr Buncle. "I think it's clear, gentlemen," the head physician concluded. "The only way to be sure we extricate the insidious cancer is to amputate the whole person."

"Agreed."

"I agree."

"Me, too."

Reaching for his medical clipboard, the elder surgeon slashed a big X thru the patient's chart. Extracting a fresh sheet, he doodled a chicken, endowing it w/ well-proportioned ample breasts, followed by a rooster equally well-endowed tho w/ opposing genitalia. After giving the rooster the round bald head of Dr Scurvy, the moustache of Dr Cataract & the long, floppy ears of Neimann, he set the medical chart aside.

"Gentlemen, shall we get started?"

All heads concurred.

Neimann too donned his surgical mask. Stepping back, he looked on admiringly as four huddled shoulders hunched over the prone figure of a once promising religious scholar. He watched the wizened face of Dr Buncle furrow, knit-one & purl-two his salt & pepper brows. The mottled complexion of Dr Cataract seemed to change color the deeper his scalpel dug. The youthful face of Dr Scurvy looked on w/ wide-eyed wonder, his hands deftly commanding a sponge w/ which he soaked up every spilled drop of blood, sweat, or root beer. The tiny dilated eyes of the literary heart specialist also looked on w/ pleasure as the others called out in reverse alphabetical order, "suture, suction, needle, forceps, clamp, chain saw..."

When Neimann checked in w/ Socrates & Plato, he exclaimed w/ surprised disappointment that he had to go. "I'd love to watch you finish, but my lecture commences in a few short minutes."

Not certain whether the surgeons were paying attention or purposely ignoring him, Neimann silently backed out of the room, his elbows pushing open the door. Removing the mask, returning it to its peg, he retreated thru the INFIRMARY, musing upon the bedridden, half-drugged patrons smiling back in stupored satisfaction, completely unaware they could—most likely would—be next.

Chapter 4

EARLIER THAT SAME MORNING, while Neimann had been fidgeting before his unforgiving mirror, the town's newest resident awoke in his new apartment, surrounded by unfamiliar walls & an oppressively low ceiling. A narrow sliver of sunlight spilled onto the floor, providing just enuff illumination for S- to observe his shadow @ the far end of the room, already up & active. Crouched before a narrow window, a metal pail @ its feet, the shadow dipped a cloth in the pail, lifted the dripping rag, wrung it out & applied it to the grimy, bug-stained glass. His shadow rubbed vigorously, the window squeaking in protest. As the stubborn layer of dirt dissolved, more sunlight somersaulted into the apartment, bouncing off the walls until its yellow radiance permeated every corner of the stark room.

S- sat up, allowing his eyes to adjust.

Tossing the rag aside, the shadow waved S- over. Together the two peered out the window @ the yawning, sleepy-headed town still in its pajamas. A spindly church spire towered in the distance, its pointy head piercing a herd of pink-tinged low-flying clouds. Several flat-headed warehouses, their chimneys raised, bared their bulging bellies, their half-shut eyes blinking into the full force of the rising dawn. Congregations of oaks, maples, elms & their evergreen cousins began their calisthenics, shaking their leaves, waving their limbs, a boisterous drill sergeant of a breeze insisting they keep moving.

S- & shadow noted the houses in the foreground as grander than those in the distance, their siding dotted w/ colorful gumdrops, their porch columns decorated in striped candy canes. Sugar-coating sparkled on the eaves; whipped cream lined & chocolate syrup crisscrossed the gingerbread roofs. S- pointed out the lush, giggling lawns; his shadow, the sedate, shimmering ponds & the peaceful, priest-like sycamores. Sculpted fountains bubbled w/ irrepressible laughter, rims brimming w/ effervescent orange, grape, or lime soda. As S- sized up the myriad-colored flowerbeds, his shadow admired the trimmed hedges partly obscuring the many moats, while morning glories devoured the barbed-wire fences. Immaculately groomed robins & tuxedo'd blue jays alighted onto elaborate gardens, no doubt in search of the choicest of gourmet earthworms.

S- turned to survey his bedroom. He noted the narrow bed, its soiled mattress, a splintered cedar chest & the room's only chair upon which lay folded sheets, blankets & a depressed-looking pillow. He followed his shadow into the adjoining room—a 'LIVING ROOM' according to a conveniently displayed label. Man & shadow stood elbow to elbow, inventorying a ragtag assortment of furniture: a young, nearly lifeless, gut-spewing futon; an elderly tho still alive-&-kicking wooden rocking chair; a middle-aged, multiple-bandaged, one-armed loveseat; & an innocent looking three-legged footstool staring up @ its three elders w/ a bemused look of humbled reverence. The floor was a motley assortment of frayed carpet & throw rugs. In a lone corner, a badly tarnished brass lamp stood sentry. Outside the room's lone window, a muscular multi-boughed mulberry winked in the moist air, its early-budded leaves shaking ever so slightly. S- & shadow waved back.

Together they explored a third room. Curtained off, the step-down compartment proved little more than a narrow walkway. A clothesline had been strung from one end to its opposite corner. Crude, makeshift shelves were held in place by chipped & crumbling cinder blocks while a frayed towel had been tacked over the small square window. Below said window, a child-size amputee of a desk leaned on bowed legs. A bored broom & listless dust mop stood in the far corner while dozens of coins lay strewn about the floor as if abandoned or left for dead.

Abruptly his shadow froze, clutching S- by the elbow. S- too had heard it: a light tapping emanating from the living room. Retracing their steps, the two quickly identified the culprit as one of the throw rugs. Cautiously lifting it, they discovered a trapdoor. A silent debate ensued, S- wishing to ignore the rapping, his shadow insisting they investigate. Thru frantic hand gestures they reached a compromise, agreeing to both raise the door @ the same time…only slowly.

"Oh dear!" a startled figure called out, falling backward, barely saving itself from tumbling down the steep narrow steps. S- stared in amazement into the wide frightened eyes of Mrs Smolet. Regaining her composure, the lady of the house smoothed her yellow apron & retouched a few cracks on her heavily powdered cheeks. A dark horizontal crack formed btwn her lips. Despite her precarious stance, she curtsied. "Top of the morning to ya."

Her pinched nose twitched nervously as her bunny rabbit slippers rubbed their ears together & wiggled their cotton ball tails. "On behalf of my vendorable husband, myself & our three adorable children," she called up, "I wish to extend our hardiest salutations."

S- & shadow stared @ the woman, then @ each other. S- noted the quiver in the woman's voice; his shadow noted a similar quiver in her hands.

"I trust your existence here will be pleasant & fruitful, as i'm sure it will be for us. Our family would be honored if you would condense to join us for breakfast." Again Mrs Smolet curtsied.

S- & shadow continued to stare, suspecting a trick should they venture farther. The banker's wife stomped up the ladder, coaxing, cajoling, finally tugging. "Here," she instructed, "let me show you how to use the stairs. You put one foot here. Now the other down there...good! Now take the first foot & repeat...very good. Now the other.... Yes, that's it. You *are* trainable!" she exclaimed.

His success spurred the lady of the house to mounting optimism. The icicles lining her smile soon melted. After S- had descended to the bottom step, she embraced him, igniting sparks of static electricity as her pompadour brushed against his uncombed tangle of knots.

S- offered no resistance as the lady of the house steered him to a room labeled GUEST LAVATORY. She shoved him inside, firmly closing the door behind him. S- stood stunned, his heart palpitating as he & his shadow looked around. They examined the THRONE & experimented w/ a FAUCET that boasted HOT & COLD. S- sniffed the SOAP cradled in the SOAP DISH, his shadow fascinated by the WASH CLOTH & the GUEST TOWEL. S- ran his hand across the cool flat surface of the MIRROR, which doubled as a MEDICINE CABINET. When he pressed against it, its door popped open. Waiting for his heart to calm, he picked up a COMB, then its companion, a BRUSH, his imagination further piqued by something labeled RAZOR. When his shadow pointed to a HAMPER on which rested a pile of clothes marked PROPER ATTIRE, the two engaged in a silent debate, a debate that soon grew heated. Despite S-'s protest, the shadow pulled @ S-'s rags, attempting to replace them w/ the proper attire. A new debate ensued over the mechanics of what were labeled SHOELACES. The debate might have continued indefinitely had they not overheard the lady of the house conversing w/ someone.

"Good morning," she chimed cheerfully on the other side of the door, her tone laced w/ sugary inflection. "And how are you this lovely morning? Gitchy-gitchy-goo. Oh, don't you look thirsty... And you, too. Wake up, you little sleepy-head!... What's that, Phil? Well, no, not really... Charlie's been a bit preoccupied of late. He's got a lot on his mind, you know..."

S- cautiously cracked open the bathroom door, his shadow poking its head thru. At the end of the hall, haloed in a soft glow of sunlight, Mrs Smolet bent over a thriving jungle of houseplants. With one hand she tenderly examined a few fronds, in the other she held a watering can.

"Watch your language, Mr Potty Mouth," she admonished a rubber plant. "What Mr Smolet & i do in the privacy of—" The banker's wife stopped, abruptly wheeling around as S-'s shadow ducked back into the bathroom.

"We'll discuss this later," the lady of the house whispered. Setting down the watering can, she marched twd the bathroom, half-ordering, half-coaxing S- to come out. When he timidly emerged, she sighed, taking note of the misbuttoned shirt, the pant zipper @ half-mast, the shoes misstrung & untied.

"I see i need to fill you in about the rules," she announced, slipping btwn S- & the door lest her houseguest consider a hasty retreat. "Rules are the keystone to unireversal happiness," she asserted, taking his hand & pulling him twd the sunlight. "I can't elephantsize enuff: life would be a vendorable paradise if people would simply submit to all rules & social statues." She reached in her apron pouch, pulling out a dog-eared manual.

"These are Saturday's rules..." She allowed S- to touch the smooth, laminated cover. "...related to the upstairs interior of the house. You can never be too well-rehearsed on the rules. Personally, i recommend you prescribe to the RuleBook-of-the-Month Club...for your own good."

S- nodded, his usually blank stare showing signs of interest. Mrs Smolet allowed him to hold the book, delighted as he turned the manual over in his hands, thumbed its pages & whiffed its faint scent of talcum powder. She smiled benignly, adjusting his zipper, feeling his biceps & rebuttoning his shirt. As she glanced into his dark, deep-set eyes, the noses of her slippers twitched. Pressing her cheek to his, igniting more static electricity, she took his hand, offering to introduce him to "the only true friends any mother could hope to have."

Urged by her insistence, S- bid hello to Mz Aloe Vera. He shook a green paw of Mr Phil O'Dendron & waved to Mrs Coleus, hanging high & flanked by her extended family of recently potted clippings. He greeted Fern said to be from Boston & Violet who had traveled all the way from Africa. When his offered hand was brusquely snubbed by a dapper, somewhat pretentious rubber plant, Mrs Smolet bade S- to pay no attention. "Mr Uppity is having a bad day," she informed him. "Ignore him. If you ask me, someone's asking for a serious clipping."

Before S- could react, Mrs Smolet dropped to her knees, bending over his shoelaces. As her hands moved deftly, she glanced up @ him, her lips curved into a smile. The tail of her slippers twitched in delight. When she stood, she fondled the manual still clutched in his hand.

"You know, young people today fail to depreciate the painstaking effort w/ which we older & wiser formulate these rules. Laws are not obituary, you know. Kids today come out of their mother's wounds thinking they're PUP's answer to free will, thinking they already know everything there is to know. In factuality, all they really know is how to stain their diapers & cry about it afterwards.

"I'll need this back." Delicately prying the manual from S-'s grasp, the lady of the house continued. "I'll bring you your own rule book." Winking, she waltzed her fingers up his chest, sending a shudder down his spine. S- stared as she raised herself on tiptoe, rubbing her pointed nose against his chin, closing her eyes & puckering her lips.

"Mind your own business!" she suddenly snapped, turning to glower @ the Boston fern. "Keep it up, mister, & i'll be giving someone a root canal!"

Returning her gaze to S-, her expression softened. "Maybe we shouldn't be seen going downstairs together," she whispered, toying w/ his zipper. "Why don't i go down first. You wait a few minutes, then follow." Twitching her nose, her slippers twitching in turn, she kissed S-'s chin before turning to depart.

As she descended the stairs, the lady of the house stopped momentarily, looking back over her shoulder. "You & me," she smiled, "I can tell we'll get along famously...provided you follow the rules." Wagging her finger & winking, she turned & disappeared, the memory of her beehive hairdo dominating S-'s confused thoughts. He stood a moment, the lingering whiffs of talcum powder tickling his nostrils as he overheard the faint murmurings of Violet & Mrs Coleus. Grumbling in the background, the Boston fern shook a disapproving frond while the rubber plant issued its dire warning.

* * * * *

SEVERAL WRONG TURNS LATER, precipitated by a contentious argument w/ his

36

shadow, S- finally located the room labeled DINING AREA. He entered to find the entire Smolet family seated around a long, elegant table. Mr Smolet sat in a silk bathrobe, sporting a false beard that handily doubled as a bib. Pausing from buttering his toast, the banker waved S- in, assuring him there was nothing to be afraid of.

"Come in, my boy. Come in. We won't bite."

S- entered warily, aware the room had gone silent the moment he stuck his head in. He passed behind the head of the household, seated next to the lady of house. Mrs Smolet bowed her head, averting her eyes as her cheeks grew crimson, competing w/ the rouge she had seen fit to touch them up with. At the end of the table was a chair labeled GUEST. S- made for the chair, conscious of a leering set of harsh blue eyes watching him thru narrowed eyelids. Said eyes belonged to a husky, half-boy half-man whose lips scowled & whose teeth were bared right down to their molars. Next to the boy-man sat a mere wisp of a girl, her marble cheeks unblemished, her eyes locked in on her pancakes. The girl's jet black hair had been twisted, teased & otherwise cudgeled into an arrow piercing thru one side of her skull & out the other. At the head of the table, opposite S-, was an even tinier pipsqueak of a girl, this one in pigtails. Squirming as if sitting in itching powder, she brandished a spoon, more interested in how far she could toss her oatmeal than in how much of it she could consume.

"Don't sit down yet," the lady of the house cautioned, blushing as she diverted her gaze. "We believe in demicracy here, don't we, kids?" Despite the lack of response, Mrs Smolet continued. "Nothing can be done w/ out the full consent, or a majority vote, from our ildustrious family...that is, unless Mr Smolet invokes his veto."

Mr Smolet set down his butter knife, picking up a napkin & dabbing his robe & false beard, both mildly splattered w/ oatmeal. "Let me introduce you to our—as my wife so aptly put it—industrious family. You know, of course, Mrs Smolet: the food that nourishes my loins, the gravy on my dumplings, my leg of lamb, my breast of chicken. Round here we call her Mrs Sticky Buns." The banker smacked his lips & kissed the air.

Mrs Sticky Buns waved off her husband's comment. "He's such a sweet talker," she rejoined, patting her rouge & pulling back a few stray hairs.

"And here is the Adam of my apple." Mr Smolet pointed to the boy-man seated across from him. "My son, Bill, tho around these parts we call him Buck."

Buck cocked his head just enuff for S- to reconfirm the glower of the icy blue stare. The boy's platinum hair had been scooped high into a double-decker ice

37

cream cone. S- glanced @ the boy's plate, piled high w/ waffles, pancakes, oatmeal, scrambled eggs, sausage, ham & bacon—a veritable mountain doused w/ butter, syrup & blueberry preserves. A formidable platoon of plastic soldiers guarded said plate, armed & prepared to fend off any incursion. Armored tanks surrounded his placemat's perimeter. An airstrip ladened w/ jetfighters & stealth bombers secured the territory encompassed by the rest of the table.

"This is our oldest daughter, Penny," Mr Smolet continued, indicating the taller of the two girls. Penny glanced up, tho not @ S-. In one tiny porcelain hand, she clutched her fork tightly as she stared @ her father, who swiftly directed his glance elsewhere.

"And this is my little Pearl." The banker pinched the cheek of his younger daughter, light-haired like her brother, hazel-eyed like her sister, oatmeal-splattered like her father. Wielding her catapult of a spoon, Pearl aimed globs of oatmeal @ random objects, mostly in the vicinity of her father's head.

"Pearl, stop that," the banker chided. "We have a guest."

Still standing behind his chair, S- noted additional troops scattered around the table: some kneeling behind the salt & pepper shakers, a few crouched atop the butter tray. One stood waist deep inside the sugar bowl. As Buck chewed his breakfast, he redeployed several troops, testing their bayonets, re-aiming their rifles in S-'s direction.

His older sister, meanwhile, poked & prodded her blackberry pancakes, their innards bleeding strawberry syrup. A colorfully coordinated array of buzzers & bells aligned the perimeter of Penny's placemat. Centermost was a miniature gong w/ a tiny mallet attached by a string.

"Pearl, behave," the banker chided again, oatmeal whizzing past his head, landing on the LINEN CABINET.

Mrs Sticky Buns tapped her husband on the wrist. "Now, Charlie," she chimed, "You should be proud. Last week, she could barely shoot that far."

"I know we're supposed to encourage these kids to be themselves," the man of the house sighed, cleaning his glasses & inspecting his beard, "but can't they be themselves some other time?"

S-'s eyes met the banker's. Mr Smolet winked & flashed S- a devilish grin. His short stubby fingers began a casual, somewhat surreptitious stroll twd young Pearl's bowl. The banker affected a whistle, his eyes pretending to spot something fascinating on the ceiling. When the girl looked up, the banker's fingers leapt into her bowl, scooped up a gob of oatmeal & plopped it in his mouth.

Pearl squealed as her father pinched her cheek. Mrs Sticky Buns looked on fondly. The elder sister scowled, refusing to look up while Buck again displayed his molars. When the boy-man shifted in his chair, several coins fell from his pockets & rolled across the floor.

"So, Buck," the beaming father began, "what do you say? Should we let my new ass't janitor here sit @ our table, guard our leftovers, maybe even contemplate our women?" The banker's eyebrows rose in succession, each trying to top the other.

Several more coins tumbled from Buck's pockets as he redeployed more troops in S-'s direction.

"What say you, son?"

The boy scowled, again baring his teeth as he stared down each person @ the table in turn. "Only if you apologize to Edmund," he finally insisted, his voice cracking slightly, his lips on the verge of quivering.

"Who?"

"You know who. You wouldn't even look @ him," the man-child hissed. "Didn't even say hello."

"Now, Buck," Mrs Sticky Buns cautioned.

"What is he talking about?" the banker inquired, looking around the table, avoiding all eye contact. "Penny, do you know what your brother's mumbling about?"

Penny shrugged, the tip of her arrow quivering.

The banker turned to his youngest. "Pearl, do *you* know what your brother is talking about?"

"He's talking about his friend Edmud."

"Edmund!" her brother corrected.

"Edmud? Edmud?" Smolet queried.

"Edmund!"

"Edmund who?"

"Edmund Radcliffe," Buck fumed.

"Who?...You mean that two-faced boy, the one who talks out of both sides of his mouth?" The banker snatched off his glasses, staring @ his son in wide-eyed disbelief. "You better watch yourself, young man." He wagged a threatening frankfurter. "You better not be seen in the same room w/ that...that... If i ever catch you bringing him or any of his kind in this house—"

"He already has," Pearl volunteered.

"Is that true? Is...that...true? Answer me!" The banker slammed his fist on the

39

table. Silverware rattled. Plates & dishes leapt like frogs. Several of Buck's soldiers collapsed or prostrated themselves. "How dare you sneak that sorry excuse of a Woodbee in under my nose!"

"I didn't sneak anyone!" Buck screamed. As the boy jumped to his feet, his chair scraped like machine gun fire. "He came thru the front door!"

"Sit down," the banker ordered, "& don't you ever raise your voice to me!" Father & son locked eyes as silence fell like a bomb. Pearl froze. Mrs Smolet & Penny pretended to be engrossed in their breakfast.

The banker repeated his demand: "Sit down, i say, before i come over there & knock you down. How dare you bring that, that, THING thru our front door? What if someone saw?" The banker returned his glasses to his face, his magnified eyes flashing incredulous disbelief.

Reluctantly, Buck slid back into his seat. "I introduced you to him," the boy whined, protruding his lower lip into a pout, "but you pretended like you didn't even see him."

"Nonsense," the banker huffed, removing his glasses & waving them for everyone to see. "Do you have any idea how much these cost? Do you? Do you think i would have paid good money if they didn't work?" His cheeks flushed. He returned the glasses to his face, squinting as he looked around the table, daring anyone to challenge him.

"This is how my children talk to me," he complained, addressing S-. "I feed them, put a roof over their heads, provide the best education Oneness can buy....& this is how they repay me: bringing imaginary friends over just so they can torment their dear Pupa! Imagine bringing the enemy into your very own home."

"He's not our enemy," Buck mumbled.

Again the father slammed his fist, sending Buck's left flank into spasms of sheer terror. "I've had just about enuff of you! Are you thru w/ breakfast?" The banker glared @ his son. "Which reminds me: where were you yesterday, young man?"

Buck's eyes bolted to attention, his back suddenly stiffening, a few coins tumbling from his pockets.

"According to your professors, somebody skipped out on World Domination three days in a row."

Mrs Smolet touched her husband lightly on the arm. "Careful of your blood pressure, Charlie."

"Now Mrs Sticky Buns, i have a legitimate gripe. Who pays for his uniforms? Who fronts the laundry bill? Getting all those blood stains out isn't cheap. And now i hear my own son could be flunking War! How do you fail World Domination? You simply annihilate everyone you can't force over to your side. How difficult is that? But you can't annihilate anyone if you don't show up."

"Remember what the doctor said," his Sticky Buns persisted.

"How do you expect to graduate w/ honors if you keep cutting War?"

Penny looked up from her plate, glancing first @ her father, then @ her brother, who sat rigid & silent, his hairdo in slow meltdown. "Pupa, could you please pass the pepper?" she asked.

Smolet reached for the shaker, absentmindedly passing it to his eldest daughter. "From here on, young man, i'm personally walking you to the bus stop & making sure you get on that armored tank. Do i make myself clear? ....In the meantime, i'm revoking your voting privileges."

"Pupa!"

"Don't Pupa me!"

Buck bolted up & stomped out of the room. S- shivered as he heard an invisible door slam. As if on cue, more of Buck's soldiers assumed positions of surrender.

The banker turned to his oldest daughter, watching momentarily as she sprinkled pepper over her strawberry syrup. "Now, Penny, my little pumpernickel. What do you say? Should we let this peculiar foreigner join our breakfast table?" Smolet cocked a thumb twd S-. "I'll have you know i've rented him the attic for *your* edification. Think how high you can get someone like him to jump. And who better than this year's most highly prized debutante to teach him a lesson or two in abject rejection & humiliation?"

The banker's eldest daughter slammed the shaker to the table. Aiming a defiant stare @ her father, she grabbed the nearest bell & shook it vigorously.

A maypole of a man clad in a plaid three-piece suit & matching Swiss hat burst thru a side door. Wielding an attaché case, the man tread thru the room in squeaky new wing-tipped shoes. Gingerly placing the case on a corner of the breakfast table, he snapped open the locks, raised the lid & bent over to savor a whiff of its genuine leather lining. A glob of oatmeal, in perfect trajectory, splattered among the legal-sized documents contained therewithin.

"Good shot," both mother & father rejoined. The lady of the house encouraged her youngest to try it again, this time w/ scrambled eggs.

"Mr Smolet," the undeterred maypole began, his nose raised, his upper lip stiff, his pointed chin swaying back & forth to his own internal music. "As Mz Penny's school-appointed lawyer, it is my duty to inform you that this personage..." He

41

paused, looking about until finding S-, who still stood behind the GUEST chair. "Oh, there you are...that this personage is an uninvited intrusion to my client's psychological, emotional & social stability. His presence cannot be tolerated...@ least not w/ out the prerequisite series of tortuous litigious proceedings necessary to put my client's mind & social well-being @ ease. My card, sir."

Btwn bites of toast, Mr Smolet reached for the card.

As the lawyer departed, Penny pressed a buzzer. This time a woman appeared, pushing a dumbwaiter while talking ninety-five miles an hour as she negotiated around the dining table. When she came to a screeching halt near the eldest daughter, she applied fresh powder on the said daughter's cheeks, reapplying lipstick & using tweezers to remove bits of oatmeal & scrambled egg from the girl's blouse. When the woman vanished, Penny lightly tapped the gong. A man w/ a camera appeared, first measuring the intensity of light around the girl, then pacing the room snapping pictures, one shot from every possible angle, the final shot to include both her & S——both instructed not to smile. Just as quickly, the photographer was gone.

"Here, my gravy-over-dumplings." The banker handed his wife the lawyer's card. "Put these w/ the others, will you?

"As for you, young lady," he addressed his eldest daughter. "I seem to remember your voting privileges being tied up in litigation @ the moment. I wouldn't want to prejudice the judges by vacillating on their suspension @ this crucial moment in the delicate legal proceedings."

The banker leaned back, his lip curling on each end as he brushed his false beard to remove toast crumbs.

"Well, well, well. As Pearl is too young to vote unless ably guided by the wisdom of her parents, & as my Sticky Buns is wise enuff to know i'm always right in these matters, it would seem the vote is unanimous: the newcomer stays. Sit down, my boy, pull up a chair.

"Ah, ah, ah," his wife admonished as S- plopped himself down. "Remember to keep your elbows *off* the table. Them's the rules."

Chapter 5

GREAT CITIES ARE OFTENTIMES LINKED to the contributions they bestow on the advancement of civilization: Sparta, for instance, for being the seat of austerity, self-sacrifice & rugged discipline; Florence, the artistic flourish that began the Italian Renaissance; Paris for refined manners & championing the Rights of Man; London, the cradle of the stiff upper lip; Hershey, PA for its perfection of milk chocolate.

Had our unnamed micropolis made a bigger name for itself, we no doubt would be renowned for our cartels, our coteries, our cadres—congregating, confabulating, constituting, conspiring & clubbing being among our favorite pastimes. One sociological study even suggested the preponderance of the Brittlebaum gene coursing thru the general populace had resulted in most of our clubs & cadres being highly selective & exclusionary.

When, for instance, a group of Aryan midgets noted they all seemed lacking in height, they formed the Aryan-Pygmies—excluding anyone over four feet or of swarthy complexion. When two pairs of surgeons, sued for incompetence, turned to cutting hair for a living, only to discover each was prone to chew his/her nails, they formed the Nail-biting Barbershop Malpractice Quartet. Proudly our municipality boasts clubs for the hook-nosed & the gap-toothed; clubs for the tattooed, the untattooed, the mistattooed; for the left-handed, the under-handed & the ambidextrous. We've secret societies for those who get up on the wrong side of the bed, for those who don't put their pants on one leg @ a time & for those who never have bad hair days. There are even a plethora of one-person cartels exclusively for those excluded from all other coteries.

One of our more secretive cadres dub themselves LUGWORTS, tho actually our office had files on these scoundrels months before they thought to unofficially incorporate. The only person seemingly unaware of their existence was their very founder & leader, the inimitable & nimble-minded Neimann Gorge.

For months now, every Saturday afternoon the unsuspecting libarian would call to order what he called his BOOKWORMS ILLEGITIMA—an exclusive book club for those born out of wedlock (& other misc bastards). They assembled in the libary basement where battered, bruised & belittled books lined the perimeter of the room: stacked on tables, piled on radiators, crammed into corners to collect dust & cobwebs. It was here that books abused, confused or misused by overzealous browsers were brought for rebinding, rehabilitation & days of R&R on their road to recovery.

And so it seemed fitting that here also a motley crew of disenchanted youth, equally battered & bruised, gathered around a few randomly arranged tables for the clandestine purpose of studying the esoteric scribblings of authors our local authorities referred to as "sons-of-bitches." For what our agents reported to be an "excruciatingly interminable hour," Neimann Gorge would aim his nose twd the ceiling fan & extemporize on obscure writings condemned by our municipality as unfit for man, beast or toilet paper—never mind papyrus.

On this particular afternoon, Neimann entered the basement cubicle only to immediately be assaulted by a shrill chorus of hoots, howls & whistles. He blushed while he waited for the raucous commotion to die down.

"Nice duds, Bub," this from a thirty-two-year-old teenager, bulky in build, his dark hair & sideburns glistening w/ Nibian oil.

"Afternoon, Hector."

Hector cracked a few knuckles, shifting in his seat & readjusting his leg-iron.

Neimann greeted the bleached blonde shackled to him. "Afternoon, Ruth."

Chewing on a thick wad of pink gum, the big-boned Ruth fondled a cat-o'-nine tails, color-coordinated to her leather outfit. Neimann then smiled @ a human rag doll sporting a pencil moustache & tugging @ her lifeless bangs.

"Heidi. Good to see you. We missed you last week."

The rag doll glanced up, nodding a noncommittal hello while mumbling something no one could quite understand.

Neimann then smiled @ the freckled, crew cut, prepubescent named Rheum, toying w/ two pencils, pretending they were warships engaged in a fierce sea battle. Neimann turned to address the boy's older twin, a pasty-complexioned, button-nosed youth named Sedgewick.

"Well, Sedgewick," Neimann queried. "I trust we've arrived all in one piece today?"

A look of concern, bordering on panic, flashed across the boy's face. He began feeling about his person. He checked under his beanie cap, felt about his nose & lips, along his chest & down to his legs & feet. Systematically traveling up & down his arms, he discovered his left pinky missing. Searching his pockets, then his backpack, he located the missing extremity & reattached it.

Neimann meanwhile heaved his briefcase onto the lectern centered in front of the claustrophobic room. Feeling all eyes on him, the head libarian opened his briefcase & extracted his neatly typed notes. Spreading the pages across the lectern & wringing its gooseneck lamp into compliance, he beamed, harmonizing w/ the glow of amber light shining on the bold capital letters of his title page:

FREEDOM & THE WEASEL

by

Fontius T Pilot

Relieving an itch behind one ear, Neimann cleared his throat, mildly perturbed when all heads turned. A doorknob jiggled. The door attached to it creaked open. A mop-topped scrawny toothpick of a male poked his rusty head inside.

"Edmund," Neimann acknowledged the newcomer. "Still maintaining your tradition of tardiness, I see. Careful: nothing numbs the budding intellect like heedless habits."

The copper-headed juvenile, his long thin face a circus of freckles, slithered in, bidding everyone "Hello" from one side of his mouth, apologizing for being late from the other side. He slid lizardlike into the nearest empty chair.

"I was just about to begin," Neimann informed him.

Again clearing his throat & again scratching an ear, Neimann rapped a gavel, calling the meeting to order. Racing thru roll call, he called on Sedgewick as club secretary to read last week's minutes. As there was little in the way of old business & the thought of new business being repugnant to Heidi (who believed only in the Here & Now), said minutes were quickly dispensed with. Neimann then arrived @ the reason he assumed they all gathered so faithfully each Saturday in the basement of banned & battered books: for his weekly book report á-la-sermon.

Tho he'd deny it, Neimann lived for these recitations. There was something about having these young restless eyes glued to him, their pierced ears pinned to the rolling cadences of his deliberately convoluted, yet classically-structured syntax; each thought andor argument piggybacked syllogistically onto the next until the weight andor force of his compellingly pristine analytical acumen collapsed like a cresting wave onto their intellectual shores, oftentimes doubling back on itself to charge the beach again & again w/ even greater vigor. There was something about all this that caused Neimann to think—if only momentarily—that perhaps, yes, there was a PUP.

The Bookworm Preeminent was soon oblivious to the mayhem around him: Rheum rat-a-tat-tatting as his pencils competed for dominance on the high seas; Sedgewick yanking off a hand, setting it flopping fish-like on the table, prodding it w/ his other fingers; Ruth popping her gum, rattling Hector's chain & cracking her whip every time his lazy eye wandered too near the vicinity of Heidi's dirt-encrusted knees. For her part, the human rag doll surreptitiously slipped open a number of worn paperbacks, lifting a few lines here & there, crossing out the authors' names & substituting her own. Thus preoccupied, she was last to notice Edmund writhing in his chair, waving his skinny arms like a schoolboy frantically soliciting permission to use the bathroom.

Glancing up, the libarian paused. "Yes, Edmund. You have a question?"

"So this Nap-pol-leon guy," the boy asked from the left side of his mouth. "He actually said it is never necessary to *suppress* the truth...only to delay it till it no longer mattered?"

"*That doesn't make sense,*" Edmund's right jaw countered. "*This from the man who supposedly brought freedom & demicracy to the whole of—what did you call that continent again? The one—*"

"That's the point, idiot," Edmund's left jaw cut in. "These weasels lead whole populations to struggle, fight & die for privileges the weasels have no intention of granting the masses who sacrifice their lives."

"Like that other country you mentioned," Sedgewick chimed in, "the one that had slaves even tho—"

"Ever notice," Hector interrupted, "how these weasels claim to preserve demicracy, yet refuse to listen to views they don't want to hear?" Hector cracked a knuckle.

Descending back to earth (or @ least the libary), Neimann smiled paternally. "Exactly, Hector. The strategy is to refuse to even talk w/ someone until they agree to agree w/ you...& until they do, you insist *they're* the ones being unreasonable."

"Pret-tee clever," Edmund concluded.

46

"*It's deceitful.*"

"It is not," Edmund countered himself. "It's brilliant."

Hector cracked a few more knuckles. "So what you're saying, Bub, is these weasels are able to convince even those they oppress...to prolong their own oppression on the vague promise that if they fight & die to free others, they'll eventually be free themselves."

"Or get to Heaven trying," Edmund snickered. "It's brilliant!"

"*Yeah, but they can't keep the charade up for long!*" his right jaw countered.

Edmund's left nostril snorted. "As long as you keep waving the twin banners of PUP & country, most people will follow their weasels anywhere: even weasels they *know* to be deceitful."

"Which points back to what that other guy said," Sedgewick tossed in. "The one who said the history of all societies is the history of class struggle."

"Yeah, Bub: those w/ class...& those w/ no class," Hector chuckled.

Neimann's smile widened. He was about to toss in his own two & a half cents when Heidi stood, pushing back her chair. Primping her curls, she mumbled something no one could quite hear. As she continued, her voice modulated, her tone growing in intensity as she drove her point home. Everyone nodded, their eyes looking neither @ her nor each other.

"Here, here," Ruth shouted when the girl was done. "You know what they say: give the consumer a fish & she eats for a day. Teach the consumer to manufacture fish & she can never get enuff until all the real fish are gone & substitute, artificially-flavored fish becomes the norm." Ruth popped her gum in triumph.

"The demand ever-rising—" Hector added. "And the market keeps growing—"

"Till the place of the manufacturer is taken over by giant mechanical caterpillars," Sedgewick jumped in, "tools of the Woodbee weasel & the buck-toothed billionaire Brittlebaum..."

"...wreaking further havoc, Bub, on a system already about to erupt & collapse in on itself."

"HERE, HERE!" Ruth shouted again, cracking her whip for punctuation.

"Ka-pow! Kaboom!" Rheum added.

"Whoa, whoa," Neimann cautioned. "Slow down. You continue thinking like that & you'll have this libary shut down quicker than a Rhodes Scholar can find a table of contents. Ideas like that, you want to publish *after* you're dead. Otherwise you'll find yourself dead a lot sooner. But actually, I address that very issue—tho a bit more obtusely. Here, let me see...."

47

Rifling thru his pages, the libarian came to a section subtitled *The Weasel Eats His Lunch.*

"Here it is. Listen to this: 'In early epochs, we find a complicated arrangement of society into various orders: a gradation of social ranks, as it were. Our epoch, however, the age of the Brittlebaum, possesses one distinctive feature: the erosion of social ranks so as to simplify class antagonisms. Society as a whole has more or less split into two camps: one hostile, the other docile; one robust, the other robotic; one caviar, the other chopped liver; in other words, the consumer...& the consumed.'"

In no time Neimann was again transported. Even a persistent fly entranced by the jelly stain on the libarian's cravat failed to derail the bibliophile's concentration. The hour rolled on as Neimann exhorted, Heidi plagiarized, Rheum rat-a-tat-tatted & the others resorted to spitball fights & paper airplanes to bolster their attention spans.

When done, Neimann concluded his lecture by gathering his papers, imagining not six but six-thousand pairs of hands clapping in rapturous applause. Tapping the gavel three times, he called for a motion to adjourn.

"I...here...so...mooove," Hector grunted.

Ruth yanked his chain. "Behave yourself."

"Do i hear a second?"

"I second, three & fourth it," the bleached blonde scowled.

"Meeting adjourned."

Neimann smacked the gavel, returning his papers to his briefcase. His audience silent, he imagined them awestruck by the implications of what he had so persuasively laid @ their precocious feet. They would linger in the basement the rest of the afternoon, no doubt debating the finer points of all he had just bestowed upon them. Each sat motionless as they watched him exit. Only @ the faint sound of the elevator door swishing shut did they stir.

* * * * *

AS IF ON CUE, the Bookworms Illegitima transformed into the aforementioned Lugworts. They rose from their seats, gathering around one table (except Rheum, who, remaining seated, continued his battle on the high seas). Sedgewick poked his head out the door, looking both ways before slamming it shut.

Heidi was first to speak. "His fly was open the whole time."

"It's a fashion statement," Ruth giggled, cracking her whip as if to call a new meeting to order.

48

All eyes turned to Heidi, who smoothed her moustache & scratched her knee. "Everything is proceeding as scheduled," she announced. "How is the dictionary going?" She looked @ Hector.

"All done, Bub. They arrived back from the printer's yesterday."

"Good work. Sedge?"

Sedgewick reattached an ear beginning to peel off. "I've managed to strike a deal w/ the Klepto-Schizophrenics," he announced. "They've agreed to steal all the town's dictionaries. The hitch is, just before they change their minds & return them, we have to switch *those* dictionaries for our new ones."

"Excellent. We are about to strike a blow that will bring the weasels of the world to their knees."

"Ka-Pow!" Rheum inserted.

The left corner of Edmund's mouth scoffed, his right nostril snorting.

"What?" Heidi challenged.

"It won't work."

"Sure it will," Ruth quipped, snapping her whip w/ an air of authority. "Remember what we learned from **The Breaking Wind of Reason**?"

"*Look, we're not saying rewriting the entire dictionary isn't a clever tactic,*" Edmund's right jaw came to his left's defense, "*changing verbs to nouns, articles to adverbs, calling a Woodbee a Brittlebaum & a Brittlebaum a weasel...*"

"...but even if you manage to switch all the dictionaries in town," his left took over, "it could take years before it has any real effect."

"Look, Bub." Hector lurched fwd. "We've been thru all this."

"Revolutions start slow," Sedgewick reminded everyone. "As long as the masses are complacent, there can be no real change. The easiest way to convince people how miserable they are is to change the definition of happiness." Receiving a cold stare from his rusty-headed co-conspirator, Sedgewick threw up his hands. "You got a better idea?"

"*I always have a better idea.*"

"Yeah, right. We always have a better idea," Edmund's left defended his right.

Heidi sighed. "Then let's hear it."

Edmund smiled from both sides of his mouth.

"Well?"

The redheaded drainpipe of a man-child pressed a finger to his lips, using his eyes to direct the others. Sedgewick rose quietly & stood on a chair, feeling about the ceiling fan. Hector & Ruth, muting their chains, checked the window ledge, then

49

inspected the lectern while Heidi & Edmund systematically lifted & shook those books easily w/in earshot. As they again seated themselves, Sedgewick dove for a loose eyeball before it rolled under the table. Edmund leaned fwd, whispering from the right corner of his mouth: "*Do the initials B. S. mean anything to you?*"

Several heads shook, their eyes staring questioningly @ one another.

"Buck Smolet," Edmund clarified, rapping his knuckles on the table in triumph.

"KaBOOM!" Rheum shouted, raising his arms in victory as one battleship succumbed to a sneak attack from the other.

"OH, GEEZ!"

"Get real, Bub!"

"You got to be kidding."

"*No, really,*" Edmund pressed on, rising to his feet, leaning over the table. "*He should be here any minute.*"

Ruth sneered. "What good can a stuck-up rich kid be to us?"

"Yeah?" Sedgewick seconded. "What can ol' stuck-up Buck do for us?"

Edmund's left came to his right's defense. "Plenty. This entire micropolis is run on the One, right?"

"Oneness is an illusion," Sedgewick scoffed. "'A false god picking its own navel'...to quote Heidi."

Heidi blushed.

"Precisely. And who better to shatter that illusion than the son & heir of the greatest stockpiler of the One himself?"

The others looked @ one another. Hector conferred w/ Ruth. Heidi consulted Sedgewick. Rheum ka-powed! ka-boomed! & rat-a-tat-tatted!, his favorite pencil transformed into a fighter jet blowing its defenseless, sea-bound opponent to smithereens.

Heidi shook her head & pulled on her dull curls. "You're forgetting something, Edmund. That son-of-a-banker doesn't believe in anything except his own enlightened selfish interests. He'll never buy into overthrowing his own throne."

"Buck's as unreliable as a whore's love," Ruth tossed in, quoting from one of Heidi's lesser known works. (Heidi again blushed.)

Edmund glanced around the room, undeterred. "*Yes...but i've something Buck wants: a sister.*"

"Bub, the dude has two sisters."

"Right, but those he already has. *He doesn't give a hoot about those*, but my sister...*my sister*...Buck has his eye on her. *In fact, he can't wait to get his hands up her dress*...only Jasmine refuses to wear a dress...*or any clothes for that matter*... especially so some rich, gussied-up stud can try to undress her. *Jasmine couldn't care less about Buck*...& as everyone knows: the thing Buck can't have...is the very thing he wants most."

"Banker's privilege," Sedgewick quipped.

Ruth popped her gum & flicked her whip. Hector cracked several knuckles in slow succession. The others sat in silence, their heads shaking as they weighed the matter. When the doorknob jiggled, Ruth cracked her whip & shushed everyone.

"Speak of the—"

Her sentence hung incomplete. She ceased chewing, her jaw dropping as the handsome head of Buck Smolet poked its way inside. His clean face & dimples seemed to light up the room. His platinum hair hung like a lion's mane, his blue eyes two piercing beacons. Heidi's face flushed as Hector ceased his knuckle-cracking & Sedgewick abruptly snatched away his brother's pencils.

"Come in. Come on in," Edmund chimed, standing & waving Buck over. Smiling from the left side of his mouth, he draped one arm around Buck's broad shoulders.

Buck slid from Edmund's grasp to straddle the nearest chair, his arms dangling over the chair's back as his dimples continued to illuminate his chiseled face. "Sorry, i'm late. Almost didn't make it. But i've got a surprise for you." He puffed his chest out as he surveyed the motley assemblage of scruffy, wide-eyed faces.

The door opened wider as S- stepped thru the threshold.

Several jaws dropped in unison. Sedgewick's head about fell off. The only one not displaying surprise was Edmund. His freckles glowing like measles, the man-child leaned back on his heels, grinning from both corners of his mouth.

"So where's Jasmine?" Buck asked.

The room fell silent as Edmund's grin stretched even wider.

Chapter 6

HOW THIS COULD HAVE HAPPENED became the burning question down @ headquarters. Rumors spread faster than an unattended fire in a warehouse of incriminating documents. The supervisor on duty immediately dropped his tiddlywinks to meet the problem head-on. "How did the Smolet boy come to befriend this, this, this...interloper?" he demanded to know from those gathered around the wine cooler. "And why had Buck led what he knew to be a ticking time bomb to those repugnant Lugworts? That's like inviting a conflagration to ride shotgun on an oil tanker."

For days our entire dept was in disarray. Special agents had to cancel their naps to analyze all available data. Dozens of extra donuts were ordered in & every last packet of artificial coffee creamer was consumed during our quest to uncover the facts. We jotted notes, ripped said notes from our monogrammed notepads, crumpled those notes into fist-sized wads & practiced shooting baskets off the rim of our wastebaskets. Countless theories were conjectured, verified, debunked, revisited, revitalized, further discredited, then postulated again. Finally, someone had the good sense to leak one particularly plausible scenario to the tabloids, rendering it as good as fact—thus relieving all parties from further speculation. The truth, however, went more like this:

Earlier that day, after S- rose from the Smolet breakfast table, he returned to his garret. (This much our dept had gotten correct.) No sooner had he climbed thru his trapdoor when he sensed something amiss. He paused, listening to the creaks & groans of the wooden rafters. This told him little. His shadow meanwhile tiptoed about the furniture, soon alighting on something nestled on the footstool. The shadow waved him over. Exchanging glances, S- & shadow picked up a glossy manual, examining its cool laminated cover. **Rules of the Road**, Vol. MMCXXXIV, it read. S- fanned the pages, his shadow looking for other signs of disturbance. The crisp, virgin paper crinkled like dry leaves, puffs of talcum powder rising like smoke signals. As S- stifled a sneeze, his shadow seized him by the arm, its dark fingernails causing S- to wince.

Hear that? it whispered.

S- perked his ears, looking around the still apartment.

The shadow pointed. *It's from in there.*

S- crept slowly twd the curtained compartment, his shadow trailing in his footsteps. They heard what appeared to be whimpering. The muffled cries would pause a few seconds, resume, then pause again. The two drew closer, slowly pulling the curtain back. Staring out the window, his back turned to S-, was the banker's son, rubbing his eyes on the towel curtain, his shoulders heaving slightly. The boy's hairdo had entirely melted & dripped onto his hunched shoulders.

Via hand signals, S- & shadow debated. S- suggested they w/draw, his shadow insisting they continue fwd. A squeaky floorboard inserted a third opinion, prompting Buck to whirl around & hurl his watering blue glare in S-'s direction.

"What are you doing here?" the man-child snapped. "Who sent you? Are you spying on me?"

S- cowered, shaking his head as he fell into his shadow, who struggled to bolster S-'s trembling frame.

"Speak up, you drooling idiot! How long were you standing there?"

The veins on his forehead pulsing, the man-child sprouted fists, his cheeks turning into tomatoes. He charged, S- stumbling backward, tripping over his shadow; only the doorjamb saving him from falling over. Buck stormed by, the floor palpitating as he stomped into the living room. "No one invited you!" he barked over his shoulder.

His shadow dusting itself off, S- regained his composure.

Buck plunked onto the battered loveseat.

He lives here, the shadow whispered. S- too noted the casual way the boy's slouching posture conformed to the loveseat's contours.

"I know what you're up to!" Buck glared, aiming a loaded finger @ S-. "Don't think you have anyone fooled. You start out as ass't janitor, then worm your way up to groundskeeper, maybe even bank guard, right? Next you're thinking this qualifies you to own your own business: fixing lawnmowers or squirrel-mulchers, selling designer mops or reuseable toothpicks.... Pretty soon you're thinking you're good enuff to marry my sister. You stay away from my sister—both of them."

Buck snatched the manual resting on the stool, coughing while violently fanning its pages. Wiping his eyes, he scanned the title. "Mum's been here," he snorted, tossing the manual back on the stool. He fell back on the loveseat, clasping his hands behind his head. "She probably neglected to mention there are different rules, depending on which slippers she's wearing."

The man-child stared @ a spot in the rafters. S- located the same spot & stared @ it as well.

"Take it from me, you'll be so busy learning the rules, you won't have time to break any." Buck turned his head to face S-. His brilliant blue eyes narrowed, then softened. As he regarded the interloper, his arched brows relaxed; his gaze, no longer hostile, showed instead signs of curiosity.

Nudged by his shadow, S- slid onto the futon as Buck resumed staring @ the rafters. The boy crossed his legs, his tense jaw beginning to chew on something. "Now your rules," he continued, "your rules—@ least for today—probably say: keep your mouth shut, agree w/ what you're told, stay away from Dregs & don't make waves."

Buck reached for the manual, skimming the opening pages. "Yep, just like i thought. Same as Edmund's, tho yours say you can covet another man's wife. That's interesting." Buck paused a moment, rubbing his chin as he chewed on a new thought. After a long pause, he tossed the book aside, glancing @ S-.

"Edmund's this real good buddy of mine. People don't like him tho...'cause he refuses to follow the rules.... But you can't really blame him. I mean, why follow rules that are stacked up against you? That's like ensuring you'll always be miserable. At least if you refuse to cooperate—lug the wort, as they say—you have a fighting chance. And, as everyone knows: it's fighting makes the world go 'round."

S- nodded as Buck rose to pace the room. The broad-shouldered man-child ran his fingers up the floor lamp & across its tasseled shade. He tapped on the back of the rocking chair, setting it in motion. Every time the rocker threatened to stop, he gave it an extra shove, as if giving an added push to a child on a swing. The rocking chair squealed w/ delight, prompting S-'s shadow to hop on for the ride.

"As to me," Buck continued, "I was born w/ the rules rigged in my favor. According to *THE* Book—the granddaddy of all rule books—the Gods, the forefathers, the Notary Publics, the very stars illuminating the sky," Buck pointed to the rafters, "all had me in mind when they created the status sphere. 'Let there be

RIGHT!' PUP declared—& there i was. Only you know what? It's less boring when you ignore the rules.... Sometimes it's more fun to break them...just to get the ol' heart pumping again."

Buck scooped up **Rules of the Road**, balancing it on his palm like a pizza. He steadied it on one finger & twirled it before tossing it in S-'s lap. He then plunged back down onto the loveseat.

"Mum keeps moving my bedroom. Every time i come home, my bed, my clothes, the dresser, my soldiers are all moved to another room. I usually come up here till everyone's asleep. She always leaves a light on tho. I'll give her that much."

S- stared @ the rule book, then @ the slouching man-child on the loveseat w/ his brilliant platinum hair dangling loose, the chin defiant.

These human beans like to use other people's ears to hear themselves think, his shadow whispered. S- nodded, offering Buck full use of the apartment anytime the boy so wished.

"Thanks." Buck cocked his head to study S-. "This room doesn't get much sunlight.... Neither does that one." He indicated the room he had just come from. "Which is why i like it." As he sat up, he flashed a smile, a set of dimples lighting up his cheeks. "Hey, you want to come to a meeting w/ me? It's over @ the libary."

S-'s eyes also lit up. He recalled the marble steps...the rotund, cherry-cheeked Police Chief...& something about books proving why crying was a waste of good tears. He nodded, his shadow adding that nothing would please them more. S- repeated the comment out loud.

"Great!" Buck slapped his thigh & rose. "You can meet Edmund.... He's got these friends he wants me to meet. Why, i'm not sure. They're...ah, bookworms...& me & books—" He shook his head. "I mean, give me a hand grenade any day.... Actually, to tell the truth, I'm only going 'cause he promised his sister might be there."

Within minutes S- was following Buck down the trapdoor & thru the Smolet Manor. They passed a frowning Penny on the second floor. The girl was consulting her attorney, who jotted notes, shaking & nodding his head (sometimes simultaneously) as his client gestured. She waved both hands, once or twice pointing @ S-. S- followed Buck to the first floor, sidestepping Mrs Sticky Buns, on her knees scrubbing the lower steps.

"Gotta get this done before the housecleaner arrives," she complained, scouring vigorously. "Don't want the hired help to think we live like pigs."

They passed Buck's father, mumbling to himself while searching the hallway closet, too preoccupied to acknowledge them.

"I think you'll like Edmund..." Buck said as the two stepped onto the front porch, "even tho he'll probably treat you like you're stupid. Just don't take it personally. He does that to me too."

"Last one over the moat is an enemy informant," the boy declared, charging ahead of S-.

* * * * *

By the time S- & Buck reached the street, the weather was a cantankerous old man complaining ceaselessly about his gout, his lumbago, his in-laws, his trick knee (from an old war wound) & his rheumatoid author rightus. The blustery sky coughed, wheezed, spit & grumbled about every little thing. Cowering clouds scooted by, racing to escape his finicky wrath. The crotchety old man mussed hairdos, knocked off hats, kicked dust into faces. He rustled treetops, harrassed discarded wrappers, tore @ loose newspaper, ran unleashed poodles out of town. The more buxom a pedestrian, the more likely the old lecher would shove his chilly fingers down her blouse or lift her skirt to check the lace-trimming of her underwear.

Buck found an empty can his feet took delight in kicking, the old man's erratic breathing adding push to shove. The hapless can clanked & clanged in protest, attempting several times to roll out of range or seek a gutter. Buck's foot, however, always found it & kicked it farther down the road. The sidewalk soon spawned sauntering pedestrians, crisscrossing each other, strolling in pairs & trios, jostling packages, cursing stray dogs, talking more to themselves than each other. Many ducked inside doorways as S- approached. Others dove for cover should a horse-drawn carriage & buggy charge by. S- struggled to keep up as Buck marched to his own internal rhythm, broken only when the boy diverted from his path to kick the can or wave to someone.

"Yo, Clyde!" he greeted a burly man in a pink tutu & spotted leotards. Chewing a cigar, the man stood outside a butcher shop, waving to passersby & fluffing out his tutu & examining it for lint.

"Kill any innocent lambs lately?" Buck shouted from across the street.

Clyde waved & nodded noncommittally.

"Ol' Clyde's a legend," Buck explained, his dimples flashing, his eyes sparkling w/ pride. "His late granddaddy discovered the secret to savory, mouth-watering, tender meat. Guess what it is?"

S- could only shrug.

56

"C'mon, guess."

S- thought a moment, his shadow doubling their effort. Both gave up & shrugged.

"He tortures his animals," the man-child conceded, grinning @ the concept. "See, he starts when they're young. Doesn't give them room enuff to stand or even sit. And never allows 'em a good nite's sleep. The more miserable their existence, the tastier they sizzle." Buck moved on. "It's kinda like what they teach us in World Domination: the more miserable the Pee-Ons, the tastier our caviar."

When the two entered what a prominent billboard heralded as the BUSINESS DISTRICT, S-'s eyes widened. Scantily clad storefronts became the norm. Arrayed in silk bloomers & lacy black see-thru brassieres, the stores sold everything from bug spray to puppy pulverizers to kids' diaphragms. Sale signs were scrawled in scarlet lipstick, outlined in mascara & accented further w/ tricolor eye shadow. The larger dept stores donned fishnet stockings on pillars painted in flesh tones, their smooth thighs petering down to supple ankles & teetering on high heels w/ exposed toenails. Door entrances curved like busty bodices. Corsets announced OPEN FOR BUSINESS. Doormen beckoned the casual browser, promising their superfriendly salespersons would not only not bite ("unless you enjoy that kind of thing") but, should you prove credit-worthy, there might be no end to the services said salesperson would render—complete satisfaction being guaranteed.

Falling farther & farther behind Buck, S- finally paused, intrigued by an erotic display of nuts, bolts, double-screws & wrenches. Continuing on, he rounded a corner, nearly colliding into Buck, who had stopped @ a storefront, its window cluttered w/ black & white & color photos.

"You like photography?" Buck asked.

S- glanced @ a life-size photo of a toddler in black garter & pampers, peering upside down thru spread legs.

"Ever know in your heart something is real—even when everyone around you tells you it's not?" Buck looked @ S-, his usually confident brows tentative. "Sometimes i think, if i could learn to take pictures, I could capture what is *really* real. Then, if my dad or some puffed-out-chest of a colonel tried to tell me different, i could hold it up & say, 'oh, no it's not—here, see.'" Buck looked again @ the display. "Edmund's dad runs a photography shop. Don't tell anyone, but i was planning to turn that little room in the attic into a darkroom."

You still can.

S- echoed his shadow. "You still can."

Without responding, Buck walked on.

Again S- struggled to keep up. He glanced @ the bowlegged old man in the sky. Nearly out of breath, his pale cheeks spent, the old man was being helped over the horizon by a patient niece, her hair a golden fleece, her dress decked in turquoise. She smiled over her shoulder, once or twice winking @ S-. Her eyes twinkled as she paused to teasingly lift Buck's mane & blow hot air on the nape of the boy's neck. Buck immediately slowed his pace, abandoned his military march & lost interest in the can. He fell into a more leisurely saunter.

Leaving the business district, the two entered the MUNICIPAL PARK & NATURE OBSERVATORY. No sooner had S-'s shoe felt the plush softness of the green grass than his shadow threw off its shoes to frolic like a puppy gone ape. The mature elms & flowering apple blossoms grinned from ear to ear. Poplars, gathered in groves, were discussing the sudden change in weather while towering cypress stared bemused up the sky's wide billowing dress. Starlings & finches warbled & whistled; crows were outright laughing.

Still a few paces behind Buck, S- passed a congregation of elderly maples mumbling something he couldn't quite make out. A giant oak joined the conversation, the maples nodding solemnly @ the oak's discerning comments. S-'s shadow paused, enamored by an even more massive oak, its venerable face ancient, knotted, gnarled & weather-beaten. S- also paused. The oak's multiple boughs stretched & twisted in all directions, its leaves beginning to sprout fresh green wings. Sensing two pairs of curious eyes gazing @ it, the oak raised an eyelid, blinked its giant eye & smiled down on them. It jerked its head, signaling that Buck was getting away. S- thanked the oak & hurried on, his shadow lingering a moment before following.

Lost in his own thoughts, Buck barely registered S-'s approach. S-, breathing heavily, had run to catch up. Together the two stepped off the curb, leaving Nature's Observatory & returning to the town's paved streets. A few blocks later, S- recognized the friezes & the scrunched-up letters announcing: LIBARY&LITERARYINFIRMARY. He stopped, puzzled as to why the walk had not taken nearly as long as his walk w/ the Police Chief.

"C'mon," Buck coaxed. "It won't bite."

Negotiating the pillars, even going down on their hands & knees, the two eventually stepped thru the imposing double doors, the bright lights & opulent architectural design dazzling in its splendor. S- stood transfixed, his brain barely able to comprehend the magnificent aura some might mistake for the very halo of Heaven—or @ least Heaven's port of entry. The clamor of footsteps, subdued whispering & everywhere the turning of crinkling pages filled his ears to near confusion. Old men w/ long faces & tall women thin as giraffes conversed in soft whispers. Younger women tugged @ their curls as they pored over parchment & paper. Younger men & older boys bit their lower lips, rubbed their peach fuzz, occasionally glancing up to study a swaying hip or the curve of an exposed calf. Too overwhelmed to gauge where he was going, S- collided into a tall willow tree of a woman, dressed in red, her perfume grabbing him by his defenseless nostrils & refusing to let go.

"Young man," she scolded. "If you don't watch where you're going, who's to say where you'll end up."

S- stumbled fwd, the room beginning to lose its balance. Heat rushed to his face, coursing from his brain to his fingertips as his stomach began to churn.

"Pardon me. I believe you dropped this," someone uttered. He felt a book thrust into his chest as the room began to spin. He clutched the book, his other hand reaching to find a wall. The spinning slowed, tho only slightly. His heart pounding, he feared the wall might collapse or the floor beneath him open to swallow him whole.

He's getting away, his shadow screamed, its voice faint & distance. *After him. Quick!*

S- wobbled fwd, colliding into several moving bodies before collapsing inside what proved to be an elevator. Of its own volition, the elevator door closed; it jolted into motion & deposited him in the basement. Only when the door opened did the spinning subside. He stumbled out, clasping a well-worn paperback. **Photography for Idiot Savants**, the title read.

Tumbling fwd, S- caught a glimpse of Buck waving him over before disappearing inside a doorway. Using the wall to anchor himself, he staggered fwd, coming to a door labeled CONFERENCE ROOM. When he entered, numerous eyes did double-takes. Several jaws dropped open. Someone cracked a whip. Another's thin face else cracked a smile, grinning from ear to twitching ear.

Chapter 7

As SOLE PROPRIETOR of our town's largest bank & pizzeria, Charles Dinero Smolet could trace his bloodline all the way back to Meg Brittlebaum's butler. True, over the centuries, the Smolet jean pool had taken many a detour, wandering thru the poorly harvested cornfields of penniless ploughboys, down dimly lit back alleys, past the empty banks of Casanova vagabonds & second-rate concert pianists & finally thru one notoriously silver-tongued traveling trapeze artist. Turn-of-the-century Smolets were in fact on the brink of extinction—worn down by poverty, petty thievery & a propensity to marry for love...that is until the first in a line of Smolet geniuses strolled into town in a secondhand baby carriage.

The first of these geniuses, Smolet 'the Great'—in addition to having extorted a world-renowned secret tomato sauce recipe—had devised a new mathematical system known only to the Smolets: a system based on the revolutionary notion that one & one did not equal two, but rather a bigger One—a One, in fact, twice as big as either previous one. In such a system, two & two could not possibly equal four, as there was no such thing as four—or two for that matter. If they were together, they were One; if they were separated, they were one & one.

Of course, everyone initially laughed @ Smolet's great-grandfather, then a young unkempt bachelor living in the same garret S- now found himself occupying. Economists refused to believe one & one could possibly equal One; some things, they argued, could not be mixed, oil & water, for instance; fire & ice, peace & prosperity. It was the beautiful Annabelle McDougal who first saw the wisdom in what the young iconoclast was advocating.

According to legend, @ the behest of burgeoning maternal instincts, Annabelle began visiting Smolet in his poorly lit garret w/ the self-appointed mission of guiding him to the strait & narrowed. Despite Annabelle's persistent pleas, however, Smolet held fast to his lunacy. It was Annabelle who changed her mind—after seeing the farther sun & a wholly ghost emerge into a giant One. She reported being swept off her feet, giving her soul up to it completely. In glowing narration she detailed how her body seemed aflame as she fell under its influence; how happiness shot thru her cerebral cortex, her hippocampus enjoying an extended holiday as all grew singular. She felt the sensation rise into her breasts until she feared she would explode from sheer ecstasy. Every One came together. Everything *was* One.

Initially Annabelle divulged none of this to her fellow townspeople. She repeated the story instead to her Sunday school classes. Gradually, as the children grew older & their impressionable minds grew rigid, the attitude of the entire town changed. A few ads strategically placed on park benches, in fortune cookies, on chain-gang apparel...& our citizens swung over to Smolet's point of view, the sitting council voting his theories into fact.[1]

As one might imagine, this revolutionary system made adding, multiplying, subtracting, even long division remarkably easy. Everything @ Smolet's First Pedestal Bank & Pizzeria was greatly simplified—except the sauce, of course. All accountants & tellers needed to know (in addition to how to chop vegetables, grate cheese & preheat the oven) was that one & one equaled One. There were fewer mistakes. There was little difficulty in hiring competent personnel or finding qualified replacements should any more uppity employees organize a strike.

And patrons came to prefer the system. They always knew how much they had in their account. There was little need to pore over monthly statements, quarterly reports, yearly interest payments, or spend hours balancing checkbooks. The sum total was always One. Thus they could concern themselves w/ more pressing matters: whether to have their pepperoni w/ green pepper or mushrooms, whether to add extra cheese, or try one of the daily roadkill specials. They could leave financial concerns in the hands of the experts—which is to say, in the plump capable frankfurters of our town's most prominent financier: Mr Charles D Smolet himself.

While Buck & S- were rubbing elbows w/ the Lugworts, our illustrious banker, snug in his cocoon, leaned back in his easy chair staring up @ the portrait of his great-grandparents. Smolet the Great, a whiskered tyrant in his old age, hair parted

---

[1] To this day, the Smolets grace our temple pews every other alternate Sunday. The church, for its part—in sermon & in song—pontificates the virtues of Oneness, reminding those in attendance how the word "one" appears 473 times in the Holy Text (soon to appear 509 times in the forthcoming revised edition).

down the middle, smiled arrogantly thru turned-up lips, his black eyes scowling. A thin, pale woman w/ a fierce hooked nose & beady eyes stood behind him, one hand clenching his shoulder like an eagle claw.

The banker then glanced @ the photo of his wife perched in its frame on the corner of his desk. With forced smile & thick platinum ringlets, Mrs Smolet stared back @ him thru gray bewildered eyes. Eleanore Smolet, neé Eleanore T D'baum (aka Mrs Sticky Buns), claimed direct descendency twice-removed from the original Brittlebaums. The banker grimaced @ his wife's long face & wide creased forehead, characteristics of many a Brittlebaum descendant.

The banker then peered @ the similar furrows of Sur Harry D'leBaum, his uncle-in-law, head patriarch of the only remaining family able to claim direct Brittlebaum descendency once-removed. The razor-nosed aristocrat sat brooding in one of the armchairs. Freshly taylored in a dark business suit, the coat no doubt padded to obscure his severely sloped shoulders, Sur Harry suffered a self-imposed speech impediment: he refused to accent the same syllables as those accented by what he called the "comMON herd." Mere minutes after Buck & S- had departed for the libary, the cane-swishing aristocrat had rung Smolet's doorbell.

The two men exchanged furtive glances, Smolet painfully aware that w/out the padded coats, the stuffed shirts & platform shoes, Sur Harry was less than half the man he purported to be. A dark suede derby hat rested in the aristocrat's lap, a hat the aristocrat patted as if burping a baby. In his other hand, Sur Harry clasped a black cane, using it periodically to keep @ bay a barrage of flies only he could see.

After mulling over some private thoughts, Sur Harry finally broke the uneasy silence. "This is not like the old days, CD...when a WoodBEE didn't know ENuff to look both ways BEfore crosSING the street. There's hardLY aNY point in hitCHING up a horse & bugGY aNYmore."

The banker nodded in sympathy. "Believe me, Uncle Harry. I'm as concerned as you are."

"AfTER S-elecTION one of our first acts should be REmoving all 'cauTION' signs.... WouldN'T hurt to take down a 'Yield' sign or two eiTHER." Sur Harry lurched forward to swat a fly, then sat back, burping his derby.

The banker chewed on his uncle-in-law's words, rocking gently in his chair.

"Now i hear these fools are advOcating we eliMINate war: that we acTUally make friends w/ our eNEmies," the old man spat. "They even have the gall to quote the GOOD BOOK: someTHING ABout turnING the otHER cheek." Sur Harry tugged on his earlobe. The furrows on his forehead rippled in waves.

"What they fail to menTION is when the Good PUP said "cheek," he meant *butt* cheek. Sometimes i get so anGRY i could kick a LugWORT."

Sur Harry rose, frantically swishing his cane as if flies were attacking from all directions. After knocking several to the floor, then pulverizing them into the carpet, he sat down, returning the derby to his lap. "I know what the GOOD BOOK says, CD. No one has skimmed the CliffsNotes more than I have. If you read btwn the lines, it clearLY states the best way to PREserve the One is to PREserve the Two: those who the One faVORS & those who those-faVORED-by-the-One, *don't* faVOR. 'A peoPLE w/out 'n eNEmy doth make eNEmies of themselves.' ZacheRIot, ChapTER 11, Verse some*THING*-or-ot*HER*, footnote 3. *That's* what the GOOD BOOK says." The old man scoffed, pretending to spit. "What's the point in beING supeRIor, if there's no one to look down on? Tell me that."

Sur Harry jumped when his nephew-in-law abruptly bolted from his seat. The aristocrat stared disconcertedly as the banker frantically pulled down a set of business journals, rifling thru the vast volumes of the **Encyclopedia of Banking & Finesse**, then fanning the glossy pages of the *Periodic Economic Forecast*, backtracking to scour the *Swimsuit* issue twice.

Sur Harry eyeballed his nephew impatiently, several times mock-pretending to smack the banker on the back of his head. Finally the aristocrat rose, setting his hat on the mantle before pacing the length of the fireplace. Staving off a mild onslaught of flies, he periodically stuck out his tongue @ the gild-framed portrait of Mr & Mrs Smolet the Great, muttering "Smolet The Fake" under his breath. As our town's chief financial officer continued to rummage, Sur Harry sidled to the souvenir case, crammed almost past capacity w/ plaques, blue ribbons, medallions & trophies, most engraved w/ the name William or Buck Smolet. Sur Harry stuck a finger down his throat, pretending to gag before pivoting on one heel to whack an invisible fly foolishly resting on the banker's desk.

Smolet startled, pausing in his search to glance @ his uncle, his astonished blue eyes sizing up the puny aristocrat.

"I trust you've REceived the file on this new felLOW, this...this...this—"

"S-."

Sur Harry nodded, smacking the side of the desk.

Abandoning the encyclopedias, the town's most powerful financier waddled back to his chair.

"They say this one is worse than the last," Sur Harry continued, stabbing the carpet w/ his cane.

"Hardly worse than R-," the banker suggested.

"Worse. Much worse. I eVEN heard the two are broTHERS—& eVEN tho the misSUS & me starTED that ruMOR, it doesN'T make it aNY less true. You know what will hapPEN if the Woods get their claws in him. Btwn these starRY-eyed rubBLE-rouSERS & those CONfounded town crybaBIES, our BElovED microPOLis is going downhill faSTER than a virGIN in one of my canDY stores."

The banker chewed in silence. His uncle jabbed the carpet like a trash collector stabbing loose wrappers.

"Don't worry about this guy," the banker offered, leaning back & lacing his fingers before strapping them around his bulging stomach. "I've got this one under my thumb."

"Don't make me laugh, CharLIE. EveRY time one of these do-do birds show up, it's a pitch batTLE to the veRY end."

"Maybe not this time; I've rented him my attic."

"You've what?"

"Even hired him @ the bank. He'll be under constant surveillance. Someone watching his every move."

Smolet planted his feet firmly, bracing himself lest his uncle's cane become a baseball bat & his own head a softball. With his desk securely btwn them, the banker calculated his skull to be just beyond the aristocrat's swing—unless, of course, his uncle rounded the desk.

Sur Harry stared bug-eyed @ his nephew, twice raising his cane, both times lowering it as if concluding this was only a dream; surely his nephew-in-law couldn't be that stupid—could he?

Mustering what little nerve he still possessed, the banker leaned fwd, folding his hands, resting them on his desk. "No one ever thought to befriend one of these... these...whatever he is. Just think, if we can pull him over to our side, we might win by a landslide...not even need to rig the tally."

Still, Sur Harry's dark BB-sized eyes bore into the banker. Undeterred, Smolet rose, moving to stand below the portrait of his grandfather, Smolet the Grating. He gazed up fondly @ his deceased Grampupa, known for his kindness to animals, politicians & poppy plants—known also for his time-proven tactic of annoying people until they finally gave up & acquiesced to even his most blatantly unreasonable demands. Smolet then looked to the portrait of his father, Smolet the Semi-Great. An 'adequate' financier by most historical accounts, his father's true genius lay in the way the man hand-tossed pizza crust, a technique successfully passed on to the son now staring up @ him. As a youngster, CD had cringed before his bumbling sire, regarding the pigeon-toed stutterer as an incompetent imbecile. Now, for the first time, the banker weighed their similarities: both enjoyed perfect vision yet wore thick-lensed glasses; both had been applauded for their vigor & physical prowess, yet as adults ate voraciously—no doubt for the same reason: to dissuade, discourage or @ least diminish any damage caused by an onrushing Brittlebaum carriage.

The banker heard his uncle sigh. He turned to face the overbearing pipsqueak.

"You know, CharLIE. There a ruMOR goING 'round 'bout this son of yours, a ruMOR me & the MISsus didN'T eVEN start."

"Who? Buck? What...about...Buck?"

"Whaaat abooout Buck?" Sur Harry mimicked. Wheeling around, the aristocrat stomped twd the souvenir case, yanking its door open & grabbing the larger of its many trophies.

KILLBALL
FIRST PLACE
Bill "Buck" Smolet

the engraving read. Sur Harry wielded the trophy like a barbell. "That WoodBEE girl, the one who runs ARound in the nude...the one camPAIGNing for this GrimSPOON felLOW. I hear your preCIOUS Buck has been sniffING 'round her like a houndDOG @ an oPEN garBAGE pail."

"Oh, ballshoot!" the banker retorted, steeling his back & curling his frankfurters into fists. "Buck's a secret agent," he blurted before he could stop himself. Removing his glasses, Smolet stared down his uncle in defiance. "It's for his final project... for his World Domination class. It's all hush-hush...even his professors don't know about it. That Buck is such a sneak," the banker added, faking a smile. "He takes after your side of the family. Take my word, he's using that Radcliffe kid to infiltrate that subversive bookclub."

"The LugWORTS?"

Smolet nodded. "Rather ingenious, wouldn't you say? Even our best agents haven't been able to do that."

Sur Harry glared @ the banker, reluctantly returning the trophy to its case. "I hear that RADcliffe boy's been in this house."

The banker returned the glasses to his face, avoiding his uncle's gaze. "I haven't seen anyone," he mumbled.

65

"I did you a big faVOR, CD; letTING you marRY INto good, top quaLIty BrittLEbaum stock. You're not goING to let that boy of yours ruIN your faMILy's chanCES of recoVERing your DIluted gene pool, are you?"

"He's a boy!" the banker chuckled, lumbering back to his desk.

"A boy w/ a man-size you-know-what. A boy ABout to graDUate GlaDIator U— PROvided you can get his misguiDED testoSTERone back on the warpath! I've seen the boy's REport card, CD. We all have. He's been writTEN up twice for quesTIONing who our real eNEMies are. Once he asked if we eVEN neeDED eNEMies! I'm telLING you, CharLIE, we run out of eNEMies & we are done for. ANYone who would eliMINate our need for eNEMies...*is* our eNEMy."

As Sur Harry brought his cane to bear on a mounting swarm of invisible flies, Smolet bolted to his feet. The financial tycoon dashed around his desk twd the coat closet. Yanking the door open, he disappeared inside. Coats & jackets, umbrellas & raincoats, loafers & wingtips were soon flying like kamikaze birds. Hats & boots whizzed passed the aristocrat's head; coat hangers rattled @ his flat feet. A can of insect/vagrant repellant barely missed Sur Harry's skull; a rubber galosh bounced off his shoulder pad. Before the second galosh could land, the aristocrat had retrieved his derby & slipped out the door.

When the closet was sufficiently gutted, the banker sank in an exhausted heap. His chin shook fiercely as he chewed on something he couldn't quite devour. "It's got to be somewhere," he reassured himself. "It's just got to be."

* * * * *

"COME IN, *COME IN*, sit down," Edmund greeted the wary S-, a wry smile curling both corners of the skinny boy's mouth. As S- complied, Sedgewick rose, offering his chair & finding another. Detaching an ear, the boy placed it on the table, centering it so as to hear the more clearly all about to transpire.

S- sat hesitantly, clutching **Photography for Idiot Savants** to his chest as he glanced around the table. Now & again he looked to Buck for reassurance.

Edmund gave Buck a friendly pat on the shoulder. "We were just talking about you," he grinned.

"Where's Jasmine?" Buck asked again, glancing around the table.

Several eyes exchanged looks. A body or two shifted in the seats to the rattle of leg irons, but no one volunteered a reply.

"Hi, i'm Heidi," the rag doll of a girl addressed S-, playing w/ her dun-colored curls.

"And i'm Sedgewick."

"Ruth."

"Rheum."

"You can call me Hector, Bub."

"And this is Edmund." Buck reached to return the friendly pat his rusty-headed friend had extended him.

"Sorry, Buck," his friend replied. "Jasmine was called away. She's campaigning for Filkin Grimspoon, you know. He's pledged to dress the clothesless—& you know how she feels about the clothesless. Said she might stop by later, tho." Edmund winked to the others, several lips slipping into vague smiles.

"So what's your feelings about the clothesless epidemic, Bub?" Hector leaned in twd Buck, his dark greasy hair glistening in the flickering overhead lighting.

"Me?" Buck shrugged, leaning back. "I think it's a shame...a sin maybe. I mean, if everyone's naked, how will you recognize the enemy? Or who to look down on? And how would *they* know who to look up to?"

Heidi's voice quivered, her tiny hands shaking as she mumbled something no one could discern. Everyone save S- & Buck nodded in agreement.

"Personally, I think nakedness shouldn't be mandatory...*but a choice*," Edmund suggested.

"So how would you end the plight of clotheslessness?" Ruth addressed Buck, her cat-o'-nine poised, her jaws grinding her gum until it popped like random gunfire.

"Well, gee," Buck fumbled, scratching his head, brushing back his mane of wild hair. "I haven't really thought much about it. You could always kill off anyone opposed to equal access to adequate attire."

Rhuem jumped up, kapowing & rat-a-tat-tatting, using everyone in the room as targets. Shushing his brother, Sedgewick slammed an angry palm to the table, his ear leaping in the air, flipping over like a pancake. "Is that your solution to everything?"

"Well, no," Buck faltered. "It's not the *only* solution. I mean, we do live in a demicracy & in most demicracies we try to give lip service to all solutions—@ least those we can half-tolerate. But you have to admit: might may not *always* make right, but it does eliminate anyone who'd dare tell you different."

S- noted a flurry of furtive glances. Silence loomed, broken only by the faint clanging of leg irons. Ruth toyed w/ her whip & popped her gum. The girl Heidi tugged @ her lifeless bangs, glancing down @ several books she seemed to be editing. Edmund's eyes were pinned on S-, except whenever S- glanced his way, @ which time the man-child would roll his eyes like a pair of dice; no matter where they landed, they always came up snake eyes. Finally the one called Hector cracked a few knuckles & changed the subject.

"So, Bub, who you supporting come S-election?" Running a hand thru his hair, the overage teenager dabbed each sideburn w/ the greasy excess.

Before Buck could answer, Edmund cut him off. "*Jasmine's got her heart set on this Grimspoon guy.*"

"Yeah," his other cheek joined in, "he's promising a shirt on every hanger."

"*A skirt in every hamper.*"

"Shoes in every closet."

"*A hat on every coatrack.*"

"And a raincoat set aside for rainy days."

Hector & Ruth rattled their chains. "In your dreams, Bub."

"*What? You don't think he can do it?*"

"Grimspoon can't win," Ruth contended, cracking her whip to strengthen her argument. "Not in a million uncounted votes."

"Why not?" Edmund challenged, winking @ the others. "*We all know what wins S-elections....* Yeah, it's not who you are, right, Sedgewick?"

"*...or the weight of your convictions.*"

"No," Sedgewick jumped in. "It's how much the One is on your side."

"Et-et-et-et-et-et-et-et!" Rheum jumped up, leveling the room w/ an imaginary spray of machine-gun fire.

"My sister can get pretty passionate when she puts her heart into something," Edmund continued, rolling another pair of snake eyes. "*You wanna tickle her fancy...* tickle her pink..." He turned, looking directly @ Buck. "*You help her candidate & she'll love you to death.*"

Hector cracked a volley of knuckles & nodded. The others each rolled a pair of snake eyes, except Ruth, who popped her gum & put away her whip. From the corner of his eye, S- noticed Rheum sneak some pencils his older twin seemed to be hoarding.

"So how's the old man doing?" Edmund inserted, leaning back, balancing precariously on the back legs of his chair. "Still having trouble seeing what's right in front of him?"

Buck huffed in disgust. "He has no trouble seeing this one." He pointed to S-, S- cowering as the others glanced his way.

"Must be tuff..." Heidi broke in, her voice cracking, her cheeks glowing crimson. "It must be tuff living w/ someone so blind to common cents."

"Not to mention the shivering of the clothesless," this from Sedgewick.

"*With such poor eyesight, it's a wonder he can read the combination to his bank vault*—but, come to think of it, he probably has that memorized."

"Are you kidding?" Buck scoffed. "The only thing worse than his eyesight is his memory. He's forever looking for things he can't find."

"Yeah, Bub." Hector looked to Edmund, both rolling their snake eyes in unison. "He *must* have the combination written down somewhere."

"He has to," Buck conceded. "PUP help us all if he ever forgets how to open the vault."

Several Lugworts bit their lips as Edmund seemed to count his fingers. "Wouldn't it be funny…" he finally ventured, only to stop mid-sentence. He raised an eyebrow & looked around the table.

"What, Bub?"

"Oh...*nothing.*"

"Go 'head, say it," Sedgewick urged, repositioning his ear more in Edmund's direction.

"It was just a passing thought...not even worth…"

"C'mon, say it." Ruth unfurled her whip & readied her wrist.

"Yeah, let's hear it," they all chimed in.

"Okay." Edmund sat up straight, leaning fwd & glancing around the table. "I was just thinking how funny it would be if say, *someone got hold of the combination, broke into the vault & handed all the One over to Filkin Grimspoon.*"

"That would be funny, Bub."

"A regular riot," Sedgewick chuckled.

Rheum tossed in an imaginary hand grenade: "KaBOOM!"

"*Only,*" Edmund cautioned, wagging a finger, "*who would have access to where the combination is kept?*"

Almost in unison, the Lugworts rubbed their chins, their snake eyes looking every & anywhere save @ Buck or S-. Heidi smoothed her moustache. Hector rattled his chain & re-greased his sideburns. Ruth removed her gum & stuck the pink wad under the table.

"I hate to bust your bubble," Buck finally interjected, "but ripping off the One would be like signing your own death warrant. Don't think for a minute they'll have any trouble tracking you down. Every cadet @ Gladiator U would earn extra credit to search & destroy every last one of you."

"That's true," Heidi rejoined, clearing her throat, scratching a knee. "As soon as you purchased your candidate, they'd nail you to a tree."

"Okay, then," Edmund speculated, "what if, instead of stealing the One...*all you stole was the combination?*" Edmund looked around the table, his gaze landing finally on Buck.

Hector leapt to his feet, nearly dragging Ruth w/ him. "That's it, Bub. It's brilliant!" He looked to the others, surprised by their blank, questioning stares. "Don't you see? That way no one gets the One. The Brits, the Woodbees, would be forced to rely solely on their own empty rhetoric. They'll stumble over their own shadows. Then everyone will see them for the weasels they truly are. It's genius, Bub." Hector slapped Edmund on the back.

"Grimspoon *might*...just *have*...a *chance*," Edmund spoke slowly, his eyes aimed @ Buck. "Jasmine would be so happy...*sooo happy*," both sides of his jaw concluded simultaneously.

"It would serve my old man right," Buck added, chewing on the idea.

"All we need," Sedgewick offered, "is someone w/ access to your father's First Pedestal & Pizzeria."

"You mean like a doughboy? Or a bank teller?" Hector asked.

"Perhaps one of the employee's kids?" Ruth conjectured, rolling her dice & rewinding her whip.

Her fellow Lugworts observed a moment of silence. From the corners of their eyes, they watched as Buck sat up straight, his sparkling irises working overtime, his dimples pulsating as several thoughts took form inside his handsome, square-jawed head.

"I can do you one better," he finally offered. "Pupa has hired a new ass't janitor—someone who will have keys to every office...& easy access to every trash can & ashtray, every bathroom stall & heating duct—someone he considers so naive & malleable, he'll probably try to mold him into the son i can never be."

"Whiiissh! Kapow! Et-et-et-et...rat-a-tat-tat," Rheum inserted, his pencils going @ it in one last pitched battle.

"Who, Bub?"

"Yeah, who?" Sedgewick asked.

"Who?" Heidi & Ruth repeated in unison.

Buck cocked his thumb twd S-.

"Kapow! Kaboom! Whoooosh! Glug, glug, glug, glug!"

As all eyes bore into him, S- squirmed as far back in his chair as its stiff back would allow. He pulled **Photography for Idiot Savants** to his chest as if the book might stop a bullet. He looked to Buck for reassurance but the man-child's gaze had turned inward, his thoughts clearly elsewhere.

70

Edmund stood, his chair scraping the floor as he reached over the table & gingerly plied the book from S-'s grasp. He placed it flat on the table & leaned farther in as he spoke gently. Using short, simple declarative sentences, he outlined the new plan & S-'s crucial role in it—both sides of his mouth working in perfect unison.

Chapter 8

As the elevator ascended, S- stood behind Buck & Edmund, his shadow opting to use the stairs. S- turned **Photography for Idiot Savants** over in his hands, recalling how the book had come into his possession. Inspecting the glossy cover, he noted the book's solid heft, its dog-eared pages, the highlighting a previous reader had indulged in. According to the liner notes, the book was a 'how to' manual featuring 133 pages of easy instructions, 47 color diagrams & simple-to-follow details for constructing a fully operational darkroom. As an added bonus, it promised time-proven techniques on shooting & framing award-winning photographs & family portraits.

S- thumbed the rough-edged pages, barely listening as Edmund informed Buck of a thin-curtained window thru which someone standing on tiptoe might get an unobstructed glimpse of an unclad Jasmine powdering her private areas. Both sides of the redhead's mouth worked in unison to secure Buck's undivided attention. The banker's son eagerly probed his freckle-faced friend for additional details. The two men-children stepped from the elevator, marching in sync, heads practically glued together as they made twd the EXIT door. Slowed by the sudden onslaught of bright lights, clacking typewriters, low murmuring & voices everywhere urging, *shhhh, shhhh, be quiet,* S- quickly fell behind his oblivious companions.

"Young man," a female voice screeched, its piercing intonation seeming to come out of nowhere. Two manicured claws dug into S-'s shoulder. "You leave w/out checking that out & i'll have you arrested."

S- froze, feebly acquiescing to his captor's determined clutches. He stood helpless, watching the exit doors close behind Buck & Edmund. He turned to recognize the same willow of a woman he had encountered earlier. Mz Pritt raised a thin, perfectly penciled eyebrow as her steely gray eyes bored into his guilt-ridden countenance.

"You can't just abscond w/ books." The towering brunette's gaze softened as she wagged a playfully admonishing finger. "Not w/out the proper credentials. We need blood tests, D&A samples, a note from your second grade language arts teacher. At the very least, we need a voter registration card." Mz Pritt cocked her authoritative eyebrow. "Follow me," she ordered.

Glancing around, hoping a Lugwort or two might come to his rescue, S- followed the libarian's lavender scent, disconcerted by the confident clicking of her high heels & the arousing swish of her red dress. As he marched in step, he marveled @ the proficiency of the libary staff racing to & fro. Some ran to the aid of student-scholars tumbling from balconies andor stubbing their toes on little known facts. Others swarmed over those groaning from upset cognizance or complaining of brain hemorrhaging, the beleaguered staff shaking thermometers or dispensing first, second &—when necessary—third aid.

Mz Pritt halted @ a desk brimming w/ fresh carnations. The pink, yellow & lime green petals matched perfectly the office supplies & color-coordinated reference books. She lightly tapped one of two heart-shaped bookends as if it held some secret power, then rounded her desk & sat. S- shifted from foot to foot while she began a cheerful hum, bustling about her tiny kingdom. Uncovering her typewriter, she extracted a crisp application form, seemingly out of thin air. She snapped it cleanly into the typewriter carriage, pulling in her chair until her posture was perfectly straight & rigid.

"Name?" she asked, looking @ the typewriter. When the typewriter failed to answer she turned to S-, repeating the question.

"Don't tell me," she waved him off, typing 'S-' in the space provided. "Now think carefully, this next question is considerably harder. Address?"

Her fingers brought the typewriter to life as S- described which blocks to walk down & which blocks to turn off of to get to the Smolet Manor. Confusing Buck's route w/ the more circuitous route favored by the Police Chief, S- had to start over several times. Mz Pritt, however, remained undeterred, not minding each fresh start—this, after all, she assured him, was her *raisin d'être*.

"And how are things going this afternoon, Kate?"

S- glanced over his shoulder as a man his own height & of similar build approached. An awkward grin stretched across the man's elongated face. As the man conversed w/ Mz Pritt, his hands drew wild concentric circles, occasionally swan-diving into a pocket only to pop out immediately to scratch an ear or rub the tip of his ski-slope nose. On one occasion, the two quivering hands grabbed the edge of the desk, whereupon the quiver ascended into the man's throat. S- looked to the name tag, then to the flushed face of Mr Neimann Gorge, Head Libarian.

His voice now half an octave above normal, Neimann sensed he was being watched. He turned, his eyes alighting on S-. His words trailed off mid-sentence. The shaking ceased.

"Aren't you...? By, Gorge, you are! I must say, this is a veritable honor." Grabbing S-'s unoffered hand, the libarian sandwiched it btwn his own, shaking S-'s limp hand till both their bodies began to vibrate. "I'm Neimann Gorge, head curator of this well-lit museum of erudition." The head libarian spread his arms so as to indicate all that surrounded him.

"I see you wish to withdraw one of our remarkable progeny." Neimann poked a finger btwn S-'s crossed arms, sneaking a peek @ the book clasped there. "Ah, yes: Förseņbớrger's **Photography for Idiot Savants**...curious choice, i must say." He pursed his lips as he tugged an earlobe. He looked to Mz Pritt, who smiled back thru twinkling, dove-gray eyes. He turned again to S-.

"Perhaps i can interest you in more apropos perspicacity." Extracting the book & setting it on Mz Pritt's desk, Neimann seized S- by the elbow, attempting to lead him away. S- deftly slipped from the libarian's grasp, snatching the book up & clasping it defiantly to his chest. Clearly outmaneuvered, the libarian smiled, acquiescing w/ a shrug. Glancing @ Mz Pritt, he assured her he would handle "this one."

The head libarian made light banter as he directed S- twd the ambulatory, his comments frequently interrupted by bawling andor screaming clientele. "So tell me what you think of our humble micropolis so far?" he asked, dodging a patient rushed by on a stretcher, sidestepping another getting mouth-to-mouth & a third being slapped back to her senses. In a jumble of sentence fragments, S- recounted a few vague impressions of his stay thus far. He prattled nonsensically, reassured by the libarian's seeming complete lack of interest. He stood aghast, however, when the libarian stopped in mid-stride, Neimann's eyes suddenly wide & brimming w/ interest.

"So you've met my precocious bibliophiles!" the libarian gushed w/ pride. "That Hector is really something, isn't he?"

S- raised a confused eyebrow as the libarian walked on, opting to answer his own question. "A late bloomer, i grant you—but the secret to his success," the libarian looked around in all directions before continuing in a whisper, "is that ball & chain, Ruth. She's a real mother, isn't she?" The libarian chuckled, his voice returning to normal. "See, when he's studious, steadfastly adhering to his studies, she offers herself up to him—but...the moment he sets his books down to seize her: whoosh! Twenty lashes. And that's just w/ her tongue. Heaven help him if she ever uses that whip." Again the libarian looked around, craning his neck so as to see around corners. He continued in a whisper. "Tail btwn his legs, he returns to his books, vainly hoping that should he finish just one more chapter, ingest one more epic, write one more luminous dissertation, he can actually have her. Thanks to her ruthlessness, he's the very paragon of self-sacrifice & discipline. And, as I am sure you know, self-sacrifice is the key to eternal success." The libarian winked.

Reaching the top landing, Neimann led S- into the rotunda that was his office, urging his guest to take a seat. Not wishing to disturb the many books sleeping every & anywhere anyone might sit, S- perched himself on the edge of the divan.

"Now Heidi: there's an interesting study of neurosis morphing into genius," the libarian continued, reclining in his desk chair, his feet finding their way to the desk's edge. "I tell you, i get rather a thrill watching her slither among our more obscure tracts & dust-riddled documents...always checking over her shoulder, afraid someone might be watching—which, of course, they are. She pilfers a half-baked idea here, another piping-hot tidbit there, kneading it all into a pungent, sometimes putrid, dough that nevertheless rises savory & golden brown...chocked full of insight, foresight & what, in hindsight we'll be embracing as profoundly original."

The libarian lowered his feet & sat fwd, looking S- in the eye. "Today our authorities can hardly stomach her; tomorrow, after they grind her into the ground, they'll laud her as being way ahead of her time."

S-'s shadow wandered to the window, gazing down @ the brick forest of tired-looking warehouses. A curlicue of a breeze circled a crumbling chimney & whistled thru the holes in a rusted drainpipe. In the window's peripheral vision, forlorn-looking factories stared back, worn down by sheer boredom andor obvious neglect. A few arrogant skyscrapers snubbed their noses @ their lowly neighbors, the more seasoned storefronts bending on sore knees, hunching their weary shoulders & staring back thru blank, unwashed windowpanes.

The shadow turned as Neimann rose & approached, nearly stepping on its toe as he rummaged for something among the bookshelves. "There is a book you absolutely must read," the libarian declared, turning to look @ S-. "You see, we must sculpt your quintessence from the ground up so as to better gird you for the onerous, dare we say, mortiferous journey ahead. It is, after all, paramount you survive in one relatively whole piece...@ least until... Well, let's not get ahead of ourselves.

"Ah, here it is!" The libarian stretched on tiptoe to pull down a thin, lanky, oversized book. He blew its dust, turning the dark mahogany cover over & over. "Note the large print: so as not to strain your weak vision, all the better for you to see what truly matters. And see here: it contains more pictures than text. You'd be surprised how often words impede our accurate apperception of entelechy. Believe it or not, i found this in the children's section." Neimann held the book @ arm's length. "Imagine such sagaciousness written for those prone to diaper rash. But then, who among us is as wise as an untainted child, eh?" Neimann winked & pressed the book to his lips before trudging over & handing it to S-. S- stared down @ its bold, brash title: **Antz from A to Z.**

"We must start you from the ground & work our way up," Neimann encouraged, pushing the book more firmly onto S-'s lap. "And what, i ask, is closer to the ground than the ant? You see, my boy, you have your queen ant—the absolute monarch of the ant kingdom. She has all the power." Neimann paced his desk, his voice gaining confidence as he spoke. "Whatever she says, goes; her will is your command. Then you have your worker ants...& your soldier ants...they work andor die for their queen—no matter how arbitrary or selfish her puny whims. And you have millions upon millions of ten*ants* who also suffer her every sneeze. And lieuten*ants* to rein in any devi*ants* should the undisciplined masses get *ants*y or, heaven forbid, turn recre*ant*. But...when the queen & her immediate kin (i.e. the domin*ants*) become *ant*iquated, well that's when thousands, then millions of *ant*agonists turn anti—*ant*i anything the queen or her next of kin have to say." Neimann ceased pacing to stare @ S-.

"You see, it takes all kinds to ruin a world. But these ants & their human counterparts all have one thing in common: they are puny...hardly worth the effort required to take note of them—until they invade your picnic table."

Neimann swiveled around, searching for another book, this one buried in the clutter on his desk. "Aristostaphones' **Moths**," he announced. "A paranoid schizophrenic, Aristostaphones, but even in schizophrenia there are moments of stark illumination...& this book is one of them." Neimann draped one leg over his desk corner & sat on the edge. "Aristostaphones saw clearly how human beans— men, women & everyone inbwtn—are driven by an insatiable thirst for the very thing that will destroy them."

Neimann tossed the bulky peasant-hide edition into S-'s lap. "Can you guess what that is?" he asked.

S- shook his head, turning the book over, admiring the flaming illustration of a moth, its wings consumed by fire.

76

"Freedom," Neimann said, rapping his knuckles on the desktop. "Freedom. You see my friend, freedom is a drug: an addictive drug. When first we taste its fruit, there is this rush, this high, this exhilaration, this sense of being in possession of infinite possibilities—& that intoxicating delusion that this is indeed a benevolent universe." Neimann raised an eyebrow as his ski-sloped nose lifted, nearly pointed to the ceiling. He spread his arms as if to embrace the entire world.

"But, w/out even perceiving it, that sensation dissipates, replaced by a vague yet all-too-real anxiety. And we think: 'If only i had more freedom, this anxiety would go away.' So we scratch & claw for more freedom, willingly ripping out the hearts of anyone who insists on *their* freedom over our own.

"We blink & find ourselves @ war. Not only w/ those around us, but mostly w/ ourselves. So we think: if only i had *more* freedom; didn't i have more once? Who took it? Where did it go? There it is: they took it?" Neimann pointed, his finger aimed @ an invisible other. "Get rid of them," he ranted, "& i, we, those of us who really matter, will finally be free!"

Neimann turned to S-, his hands balled into fists. "Result: we become paranoid schizophrenics marching @ a mad dash for that illusive drug, freedom—when in truth, my boy, it is harmony & balance that truly lead to human happiness...for it is *happiness*, not freedom, we are truly clamoring for.

"Here, take these books. Relish them as long as you need. Devour them till your stomach is full. When you're done, regurgitate everything you've learned. Then bring them back."

S- rose slowly, his shadow inquiring about the blood sample, the D&A test, the note from his second grade language arts teacher. When S- reiterated his shadow's question the head libarian waved him off. "Not to worry. I understand there's a sample of your teardrop on record. They'll be no escaping us now.

"When you finish those books, i've got an excellent introductory opus on rodents & bipedal weasels. You learn how to negotiate around those slippery creatures & you just might live past your thirty-third birthday." The libarian wagged an encouraging finger.

After shaking S-'s hand till both their bodies quivered, the libarian led S- as far as the ambulatory, pointing the way to the lower floors. S- ambled the winding walkway cautiously, fearful of being accosted by another well-manicured claw. Dodging many an avid reader suffering from upset cerebellum & the ever-alert nurse-libarians rushing to their aid, he located a NO EXIT sign. Its door refusing to cooperate, he waited until someone entered from the other side.

When he stepped into the piercing sunshine, a butterfly fluttered inches from his eyes. A robin sporting a red tuxedo chirped overhead, several blue jays echoing its comments. A flock of yellow-tailed sparrows circled his head, wheeling skyward to form an arrow his shadow eagerly followed. S- broke into a run to keep up.

* * * * *

THE WINGED WELCOMING COMMITTEE made a beeline for the MUNICIPAL PARK & NATURE OBSERVATORY, flitting around trees & over bldgs, swooping under awnings & low-lying eaves. No sooner had S-'s feet touched the green earth when his shadow somersaulted, running in & out of crocus beds, diving headfirst among dahlias & chrysanthemums. S- circled the wide rim of a tranquil lake, its blue & diamonded sunlit shimmer reflecting everything surrounding it in reverse. As ducks quacked, rabbits zigzagged & chipmunks foraged, wild roses tossed their incense high onto a conveyor belt of cool breezes. Remembering the wizened old oak tree, S- waved his shadow over, the two simultaneously locating the massive trunk, its boughs & branches towering over its friendly neighbors. The two approached, the oak raising an eyelid & flashing its broad smile. Shifting slightly, the ancient oak gestured for the two to sit. It shifted a few exposed roots to create a crude resting place for S- to balance his books. Setting **Antz from A to Z** & **Moths** aside, S- turned to the introduction in his photography manual.

His back pressed against the oak peering over his shoulder, S- studied the black & white photos, turning the pages slowly, mostly for the tree's benefit. A few of the photos captured children playing sadly; others were of men smiling thru granite cheeks. Several spotlighted beautiful women disguising ugly thoughts, usually behind made-up faces. He paused, staring long & hard @ a photo of angry bldgs longing to blow off steam. One photo revealed a bridge bored out of its beams, contemplating suicide, calculating carefully just the right moment to take a group of approaching picnickers w/ it. The photos, according to the author, were award-winners—exemplary examples of capturing what words could hardly hope to express.

The oak rattled its branches. S- noted the surrounding foliage waving frantically as if to gain his attention. Craning his neck, he saw a rotund figure waddling twd him, shaking its head & tapping a billy club in a fat upturned hand.

"NOW HE'S GONE & DONE IT," a booming baritone barked.

S- closed the book as he glimpsed the yellow badge dangling from a puffed out chest. The Police Chief stood over him, his nose bright red in sharp contrast w/ his dark blue uniform.

"YOUNG MAN, HOW DARE YOU...How dare you...How dare, ACHOO!" The Police Chief holstered his club to pull a handkerchief from his back pocket. He buried his nose in the hankie, the force of his next sneeze sending **Antz from A to Z** & **Moths** tumbling to the ground.

"Pardon me," the C of P sniffled, his voice a cross btwn a whining schoolboy & an angry duck. Wiping his nose & sniffling again, the Police Chief stared down @ S-. "Don't you realize people will assume you're stupid, seeing you read in public like that?" He blew his nose & repocketed the hankie. "You'd have to be. After all, if you already knew everything, there'd be no need to read, would there?" The officer placed his hands on his hips.

"FORTUNATELY FOR YOU," he abruptly shouted, "EXPOSING ONE'S IGNORANCE IS ONLY A MINOR OFFENSE." Rubbing his nose, the C of P lowered his voice to a near whisper. "It is clearly written (albeit in invisible ink, mind you) that a gentleman must take great pains to appear smarter than he actually is. Around these parts, my boy, it is wiser to *pretend* to be wise rather than spend years acquiring the knowledge no one around here acknowledges anyway. Otherwise, you may as well slit your own throat now & spare my office the trouble."

The C of P circled the oak, fingering its rough skin. After circling once & circling back, he stood over S-, his legs apart, his arms akimbo. "You do realize how much trouble you're in? DO YOU EVEN REALIZE HOW MUCH TROUBLE YOU'RE IN?"

S- noted a mockingbird alight on a branch nearby. Its wings akimbo, the bird flitted up & down, mimicking the Police Chief—even tossing in a pretend sneeze.

"ACHOO!" the Police Chief seconded. Retrieving his hankie, he blew his nose, then crossed his arms, the kerchief dangling from one hand. He narrowed his watering, bloodshot eyes to study S- from head to foot. Raising the hankie, he blew w/ such force the mockingbird bolted. S- watched the bird fly away, too frightened to look back. Folding the kerchief, the C of P stuffed it in a breast pocket, continuing to sniffle, talking in a nasally whine.

"It hasn't been a day..." he began, "...HASN'T BEEN A DAY. NOT TWENTY-FOUR HOURS. But let us review the facts." The officer pulled out a pad, flipping it open & rifling thru its pages. "DAY ONE: SUBJECT IS INTRODUCED BY NONE OTHER THAN YOURS TRULY (meaning me), TO ONE OF OUR TOWN'S MOST RESPECTABLE CITIZENS (meaning Mr Charles D, as in Deniro, Smolet).

"DAY TWO." (He flipped to the next page.) "NOT EVEN BEFORE OUR FAIR SUN COULD SET..." As the officer continued, S- became distracted by several sycamores pretending to snore, their snores growing louder the longer the C of P droned on.

"ARE YOU LISTENING?" the officer suddenly shouted, his runny nose inches from S-'s startled face. Again finding his place in the note pad, the C of P continued: "...subject falls into cahoots w/ persons repugnant, recalcitrant, repulsive, reprehensible & ready to rip apart all this fair province reveres as righteous & proper." The C of P snapped his pad shut w/ an air of triumph. "Don't think we haven't...DON'T THINK WE HAVEN'T BEEN WATCHING YOU."

Looking around, his face reddening, the officer changed his tone. "Forget that last line," he advised. "Pretend you didn't hear that."

Stepping back, the C of P eyed S- thru narrowed eyelids. His nose twitching, he grabbed his kerchief, his stern glare beginning to lose heart. He slid down next to S-, his voice lowering to a whisper. "Now don't get me wrong, some of those Lugworts are good kids. Just caught on the wrong side of their best intentions, if you ask me... tho Rheum & Heidi would make excellent divans. So would that Sedgewick kid if the lad could just keep himself together. But that copperheaded nose-wipe of a snake, Edmund...bad news."

The C of P blew his nose, sending several swallows scattering. "Too bad," he added. "Edmund's father & me go way back. In the old days, we used to loiter where guys like us weren't welcome. Used to pretend to smoke fancy cigars, steal baby carriages & harass the homosapiens. Alas," he sighed, "times change. These days Perman runs a respectable business, pays his bills—which pays my bills—cheats on his taxes only up to the legalized limit. How on PUP's brown earth he could have sired such a son?" The C of P shook his head, repocketing the pad, then running the kerchief under his dribbling nose.

"But you can't tell ol' Perman that. No, sir. NO SIR. Ol' Perman considers that two-faced rapscallion of his as honest as the Pope himself.

"'But he talks out of both sides of his mouth,' I try to tell him.

"'So does the Pope,' Perman answers.

"And he's got me there...so i throw my arms up...wipe my hands of the whole mess.

"BUT YOU," the C of P suddenly shouted, aiming a loaded finger, "YOU'RE A MESS I'D BE HAPPY TO CLEAN UP."

S- stared down the barrel of the Chief's twitching finger. When S- cowered, the

C of P's tone again softened. "What's that you're reading?" he asked, reaching for **Photography for Idiot Savants**. "So, @ least you admit you're an idiot. They say that's the first step." Raising his head, his nose beginning to itch, the C of P groped for his kerchief.

"Of course," he continued, the hankie poised to catch a sneeze that never came, "there is always the ONE...the only ONE who can truly save you. Your fate—as well as the fate of us all—is really in *his* golden digits, *he* whose silvery beard flows on into the banks of forever." The C of P pointed to the sky—or rather the oak's massive, intertwining branches obscuring said sky.

"Who's that, you wonder?" he asked S-. "I can tell from that quizzical frown on your clueless face." The Chief leaned closer, looking both ways before whispering, "I wasn't going to say anything @ first...but I ran into that fellow you've been looking for, this stranger of yours."

S- cocked a brow & the C of P nodded in response. "Over @ Pete's Cafe Olé & Bail Bond. We split a bagel. Seems he's partial to chives in his cream cheese. Anyway, he told me where he's been trying to lead you all this time."

S- cocked the other brow & the C of P nodded in the affirmative.

"He wants for you to discover the ONE—the ONE & Only, the true source of all wisdom & well-being. Told me he'd been hoping you'd discover it on your own. He's been leading you to PUP, my boy." Stifling an urge to sneeze, the C of P pressed the kerchief to his nose.

"Come to think of it...tomorrow is Smolet Sunday. The entire Smolet family will be @ the synachurch-temple, lapping up all the wisdom HE-from-which-all-things-come & to-which-all-things-we-own-eventually-go, has to offer.

"If you want, i'll let PUP know to expect you. I'll let this friend of yours know you'll be there, too."

Several crows cawed overhead. The towering oak began a soft whistle, its eye rolling as it pretended to scan the heavens. S- gave the C of P a noncommittal nod.

"Good." The police officer patted S-'s knee. "Then it's settled. If any ONE can enlighten you on the virtues of the One & the infinite wisdom that comes from knowing one's place—if any One can set you free, never mind the cost—PUP's the ONE."

Tugging S-'s arm, lifting him till they both were standing, the Chief of Police gathered the books, dusting S- off & insisting on escorting S- home. Leading S- along a different tho equally circuitous route as the day before, the officer looked all ways before crossing each intersection. Btwn sneezes, he would bark commands, then urge S- in a whiny whisper to ignore that last remark. Whenever he wished to impart more friendly advice, the officer would pull out his kerchief & speak thru the folds in the cloth.

When the two arrived @ the Smolet Estate, the C of P offered S- a hand mounting the mulberry. S- negotiated the boughs & jutting branches, the C of P standing below, scribbling notes, stifling sneezes & occasionally waving up @ him. After blowing his nose, the Chief slipped the note under a stone marked w/ a red X. From beneath a neighboring stone he pulled a crushed cigar, whiffing it despite his clogged nostrils. Kissing the crinkling wrapper & whiffing it again, he placed the cigar proudly in his breast pocket. Before turning, he clicked his heels & saluted a narrow gap in an otherwise drawn curtain. When the gap closed, he about-faced, whistling as he negotiated the moat & closed in succession each of the three iron gates. Somewhere in the distance a dog barked. Closer to Smolet Manor, several alligator snapped their jaws.

Chapter 9

"YOU KNOW, you really shouldn't pick your nose."

S- jolted to attention, the tiny pinprick of a voice seeming to descend from the rafters. **Rules of the Road** tumbled from his lap as he clutched the arms of the rocking chair. A cloud of talcum powder rose from the manual as it dive-bombed onto the cluster of books circling his feet like so many army tents.

Glancing over his shoulder, S- beheld the shiny, heart-shaped face of Pearl Smolet, her head peeking thru the trapdoor, green specks flickering in her otherwise hazel eyes. Climbing in, she stopped a few feet from the rocker. "No one likes you, you know." Her voice was matter-of-fact. Surveying his apartment, she shrugged, then looked @ him again. "But that's okay. Nobody likes anyone, really."

S- shifted in his seat, intrigued by the creature less than half his size—half the size of anyone he had met thus far. Tho he couldn't say why, he sensed this creature—maybe even others her size—was fundamentally different from those who towered over her. He motioned for the girl to sit.

Never taking her eyes off him, Pearl plopped onto the futon. "You're not to be trusted, you know."

We're not? his shadow asked.

"Why not?" S- inquired.

The girl shrugged. "That's what everyone says. We read about you in our history book."

What did it say?

"What did it say?"

"Not much, really. The picture was taken @ nite. We couldn't really see you. And the things you did were so bad, they blacked them out so it wouldn't laminate us kids."

"I wonder what i've done?"

"Whatever it is, the best thing for you to do is to get out of town."

S- nodded. Instead of rising, however, he rocked in his chair, furrowing his brow.

"If you're contemplating suicide, i'll help," the girl volunteered, her eyes brightening.

"I'd like to go," S- offered after a while, "but i'm looking for someone. I can't leave till i find him."

"Is he fat & wears these loud Hawaiian shirts & a hat like hunters wear in the jungle?"

"Maybe."

"Does his round face come down to a pointy chin & his hair stick out under his hat like helicopter propellers?"

S- stopped rocking. "Sometimes."

"Do his floppy shoes point in opposite directions?"

Heat rushed to S-'s face, his heart beginning to pound. "You've seen him," he exclaimed.

"He was here earlier asking for you. He left you something."

"What?" S- leaned fwd, his hands outstretched.

"Nothing," Pearl grinned, kicking her legs w/ delight & giggling.

S- fell back in his chair, rocking slowly as his eyelashes fluttered uncontrollably.

"That's what Pupa said," the girl added. "If you was to ask what it was, me & Mummy were to say it was nothing. But it isn't nothing, cause i snuck it out & took a peek...& it's definitely not nothing. What's the matter w/ you?"

S-'s cheeks burned crimson. "I don't know," he stuttered. "It's like there's this alarm in my head."

"You should come to school. We have alarm bells going off all the time...mostly they're false alarms, tho, so nobody pays attention."

S- studied Pearl as she rose to inspect the room, one arm clasped behind her back, clutching the other @ the elbow. The girl pulled loose furniture threads, picked up or kicked aside his books, flicked the lamp on, then off...then on...then off. S- watched, admiring her pigtails: taut like tied rope, limp & dainty as they dangled down her back. The girl refused to stay still, fidgeting & squirming, pivoting perpetually as she roamed the room. When she ran out of corners to inspect, she whipped around & lowered her brow. "Are you in love w/ my sister?" she asked.

S- rolled his eyes as he searched for an answer. "I don't think so."

"You will be."

Pearl sat again, pointing to **Rules of the Road**. "It's in the rule book. You fall in love w/ Penny. Mummy faints in udder disgust. Pupa calls the extermenite but before they can get here, Buck hangs you from that mulberry tree—that one there." She pointed out the window. "You better not screw it up—or else they'll really be mad."

As she spoke, her flickering eyes cast a spell over him. Thoroughly enchanted, S- found himself wishing he had a camera. "What about you?" he asked. "What does the rule book say about you?"

"Me?" Pearl huffed, pulling a pigtail. "I'm a spoiled brat. I never do what i'm supposed to. Just like my brother. Only Buck gets to inherent the weight of the world on his shoulders...& all the privies thereof. I don't inherent nothing. So my job is to ruin things for those who do."

The two sat a long moment, Pearl yanking her pigtails, S- waiting for the alarm in his head to subside.

"Hey, you want to see something?" Pearl jumped to her feet.

"What?"

"What that man left you."

"But you said—"

"Yeah, but no self-respecting spoiled brat is going to do what her parents say. Like i said, my job is to ruin things." Pearl leaned in, cupping her hands around his ear. "I snuck it out," she whispered. "It's in my room. Wanna see?"

S- nodded, the girl gesturing to follow her down the trapdoor. Tiptoeing & signaling him to stay quiet, she led him to a room he took to be a junkyard. Mountains of stuffed animals lay mangled & bruised, battered till their innards oozed onto the floor. No surface seemed immune from doll parts of all shapes & sizes: some missing arms, some w/ torn legs or gouged eyes; some w/ fingers crudely taped, clasped or pinned into place. Abandoned toys & doll accessories lay everywhere, the only sense of order being a shelf above the narrow bed. Neatly aligned was a row of stuffed kittens, their eyes life-like, their innocent wonder peering out in all directions.

They look so life-like.

"They look so life-like," S- repeated.

"They were," Pearl responded, "once. Good thing you're potty trained," she added, wagging a finger. "Mummy said I had to potty train those. But this way I don't have to. Problem solved." Dropping to her knees, reaching under her bed, Pearl pulled out one, then a second, then a third even larger box.

"This stuff is what he left you." She opened the first box. She lifted several plastic bottles. DEVELOPER, STOPPER & FIXER were written in bold letters on otherwise identical labels. 'Keep out of reach of favorite children' was added below in parentheses. From the second box she removed several smaller boxes. In one, stamped FRAGILE, she lifted the lid to find a dozen tinted light bulbs. From another she hoisted a camera. When she raised it to look thru the lens, she found a note taped to its bottom.

"Look @ this." She handed the camera to S-.

Scribbled in flamboyant handwriting was the message:

Sometimes i eat my pizza with a fork.

Sometimes i use my hands.

Dropping the camera, S- clung to the bed, his stomach churning as the room began to tilt. Pearl's face grew distorted, her lips moving to no sound. As her words gradually became audible, the room righted itself & everything returning to near normal. S- released his grip, his face burning, his dry throat tasting like cotton. He reread the note several times.

"What is all this stuff?" Pearl asked, diving further into the box. She held up a TIMER & a THERMOMETER. S- found scissors & tongs, plastics trays & material to build a follow-the-numbers towel rack—items he recognized from **Photography for Idiot Savants**. From the largest box, Pearl unwrapped something labeled ENLARGER. S- stared @ its black surface, its silver knobs & white markings. When he finally stood, he had to clutch the bed post, his legs still wobbly, his head threatening again to spin out of control.

"I know how we can sneak this stuff up to your room," Pearl suggested, smiling like the act would be the height of her day. "You repack the boxes. First i need to scout out where everyone is. Then i'll show you a secret passive."

Still reeling slightly, S- repacked the boxes, his unsteady hands not entirely up to the task. His shadow stepped in to assume command. When together they closed the last lid, Pearl reappeared, whispering about some coast being clear. Leading S- on tiptoe, she steered him into another bedroom, this one more spacious & efficiently arranged. Its walls, woodwork & furnishing were bedecked w/ unicorns, most in pink & purple pastels. A veritable art gallery of paintings lined the colorful walls. Dominating one wall, portraits of horses, puppies wearing pants, & grazing lambs were artfully rendered from dried breakfast food. The fermented blackish green-blue mold added a surrealistic texture S- found both intriguing & disconcerting.

The adjacent wall featured portraits of young men or older boys captured in moldy waffles, fritters, crumpets, granola & poached eggs, their eyes sunny-side up. The largest, centermost picture was titled "Heel, boy!" wherein a devilishly gleeful dark-haired beauty rode a bare-chested man crouched on all fours. The beauty's sparkling spurs drew blackish-red ketchup stains from the wincing man's love handles.

Despite Pearl's urging him to hurry, S- felt compelled to stare. His shadow also lingered. Their eyes moved simultaneously to the mural on a third wall: a semi-abstract-expressionistic rendering of a woman, part goddess, part superhero. Scantily clad, voluptuously curvaceous, the busty maiden wielded a hula hoop, a flock of men-children called in from tending sheep or playing marbles, no doubt to compete in jumping thru.

While S- stood immobile, Pearl headed for the walk-in closet, pulling wide its sliding doors. Disappearing behind the color-coordinated wardrobe, stumbling over shoes, sandals & slippers, she made her way to the far end where she pulled down a hidden panel.

"This is the door you're supposed to use to conduct your sorted affair w/ my sister," she whispered. Leading S- up a narrow, winding staircase, they eventually arrived @ another moveable panel, this one opening into his garret. "Don't tell anyone i showed you this. You're not supposed to find this until Pupa promotes you from ass't janitor to ass't to the ass't ass't vice president. That's when you become uppity & so blinded by self-importment, the Bored of Directors—that's my Uncle Harry—warns you to keep your place...or else. Then in a fit of outrage, you begin to covert the boss's—that's Pupa—you begin to covert the boss's daughter—that's Penny."

Setting the boxes down, S- scratched his head, heaving a heavy sigh. "How am i to remember all that?"

"Oh, don't worry," Pearl counseled. "It'll be in your rule book. They'll include that section when you're ready for it. In the meantime, just don't screw up. Otherwise they'll like you even less than they don't like you now."

* * * * *

"RISE & SHINE!" The muffled words crackled from the loudspeaker positioned

87

over S-'s bed. "How is my little sugar dumpling this morning?" the announcer continued. "Did i hear you whisper my name in your prayers last nite? What i wouldn't give to have tucked you in. Oh, well, mustn't think such thoughts, 'specially on Smolet Sunday."

According to **Rules of the Road** (Sunday supplement), S- was to report to the Smolet living room @ O-900 hours for a quick inspection before the family headed to the synachurch-temple & mosque. Arriving w/ seconds to spare, S- stumbled in, his shoes untied, his shirt misbuttoned.

He found Mr Smolet busily lifting cushions, pulling sofas & chairs from against the wall, peeking behind & under everything his paunchy physique could maneuver. Detecting S-'s presence, the banker bolted to attention, nonchalantly replacing the cushion in his grasp. He plopped down in a plush, self-reclining easy chair, stroking his false beard as he eyeballed S-.

"So, my boy. Yesterday you were a stranger to this fair community. Today you could become one of its most cherished citizens." The banker winked, then rubbed an eye w/out removing his glasses. "Here, slip this in your pocket." Smolet handed S- a folded stack of bank notes, urging him to put them in his back pocket before anyone saw.

"Sit down," the banker gestured. "Take a load off your feet. If you kneel down on all fours, crouch down a little lower, you'll make an excellent divan."

Following his partner's instructions, S- dropped on all fours, positioning himself in front of the banker's chair. The banker propped his feet across S-'s back, lacing his satisfied frankfurters behind his thick head of white hair. Soon after, Mrs Sticky Buns fluttered in, dressed in a flowing salmon-colored gown, wafts of musk-rose rising from her person like steam billowing up from a manhole.

"Where are the children, Charlie? They know we're running late." The mistress of the manor immediately detected subtle alterations in the arranged furniture. Cushions stuffed haphazardly were promptly righted; chairs positioned cockeyed were corrected; the sofa two inches from the wall was repositioned to the required one & three-eighths inches specified in the rule book, its seat pillows re-fluffed to the proper density as all the while Mrs Sticky Buns prattled on about a peach cobbler...or a cobbler named Peach...or who used to be a peach till he failed to promptly repair the shoes she'd hoped to wear that morning (neither Smolet or S- could decipher which).

Her husband, meanwhile—while responding w/ an occasional "Yes, my little tender loin"—examined the size, shape, contour & texture of the unlit cigar he held

@ arm's length. Below him, S- groaned, the weight of the banker's feet seeming to increase w/ each passing moment.

"Pupa, why do i have to go to church!" Buck barged in. The man-child stomped his feet in defiance. Bare-chested, clad only in military-issue pajama pants, Buck's fierce mane of hair hung down to his squared shoulders. He refused to give ground to his sister, attempting to force a clean shirt onto his resistant torso.

"If i have to go, you go, too," Penny insisted. Still in her nitegown, the middle daughter's hair had been twisted & shaped into an ice pick clamped tightly into both sides of her head.

"Why do we have to go, anyway? We haven't gone in—"

Smolet waved frantically to his children, pressing a thick finger to his lips. He pointed twd his feet, suggesting one never knew when a ten*ant* might be listening.

Mumbling in protest, threatening to take the matter up w/ his superior officer, Buck submitted as Penny pulled the shirt over his muscular frame, her motions quick & efficient. She hung a tie around his neck, wrapping, twisting & tightening it in three angry jolts. "I sure hope you inherit the world soon," she snapped. "Maybe then you'll learn to tie your own dam noose."

"There's my little pudding pie."

Mrs Smolet clasped her hands as a sleepy-eyed Pearl staggered into the room. "Aren't you just the most adorable…"

Pearl rubbed her eyes, her dress inside out, her panties donned like a hat, cocked to one side on the girl's uncombed head.

Mrs Sticky Buns turned to her husband. "Will you look @ that, dear? Our little Pearl is learning to dress herself." The proud mother pinched her daughter's cheek, showering her precious little angel w/ praise as she reorganized the girl's attire to meet Sunday rule-book specifications. The two older siblings grimaced as they looked on. Their little sister meanwhile fidgeted & rebelled, howling in shrill fits of protest.

"There, don't you look like a phospherous young lady?" Mrs Smolet concluded, having won their tussling match. "Now go get today's rule book." The whimpering Pearl slumped away. Penny quickly followed, stating she needed to find Buck's pants.

Resigned to his fate, Buck adjusted his tie, moving to the head of his father's newest divan. "You're coming, aren't you?" he asked S-.

"That's right. I almost forgot," his father said, lifting his legs & planting his feet on the floor. "Get up, my boy. Can't be seen in church w/ dirty knees—@ least not on your first day."

As S- stood, Buck brushed the dust from S-'s back & pants legs. The boy then knelt to tie S-'s shoes, standing again to re-button the shirt.

"I was telling our new friend here, how going to synachurch will turn him into one of the most cherished citizens in town," Smolet confided to his son.

"Yeah, right," Buck grinned, winking @ S-. "Anybody who's anybody worships @ the altar of PUP. Why, PUP can make you the richest man in town...next to Pupa, of course. Then, next day, turn you poor as a peach pit, just 'cause HE feels like it."

"Not just because HE feels like it," Smolet Sr corrected. "Because of how you make *HIM* feel." The banker pointed to S-. "You have the power to make HIM love you...or to fill HIS heart w/ wrath. HIS divine whims are @ the mercy of your unwashed, poorly manicured fingertips. Remember that. And don't forget to tip HIM generously." The banker winked @ S- & patted him on the back pocket. "That way HE knows how much you *really* love HIM."

"Let's go," Mrs Smolet urged. "Buck, where are your shoes? Make sure you choose a pair that doesn't clash w/ those pajamas. Charlie, will you stop cavorting that cigar. Remember what the GOOD BOOK says: 'On the seventh day, PUP quit smoking.' Penny, what are you doing wearing Buck's pants?"

Penny had reappeared in a pair of men's dungarees, the leg cuffs rolled above her ankles. Her matching mechanic's shirt had apparently belonged to someone named AL. Perched precariously atop her ice-pick hairdo was a baseball cap declaring, 'Let he who is without sin buy the first round.'

The lady of the manor gasped, her hands covering her mouth. "And what do you think you're doing, young lady?"

"I'm going as Buck."

"You can't. It's not in the rule book."

"Then amend the rule book. Pupa does it all the time."

Mrs Smolet whirled around to her husband. "Charlie, would you talk some cents into your Penny." Dashing past her eldest daughter, Mrs Sticky Buns whisked up the returning Pearl lest her youngest be "morally continuated by her sister's blasphony."

"Penny, listen to your mother," Smolet huffed, rising to his feet. Tiptoeing to the doorway, verifying his missus was gone, the man of the manor pulled out his cigar & savored its aroma. "Why would you want to go as a boy, anyway?"

"So PUP will stop staring @ my legs."

"Nonsense. HE's not staring. HE's just making sure your skirt is the proper length & your knees are clean."

"If i wear pants, maybe HE'll stop drooling long enuff to listen to my prayers."

"Have you ever heard of such a thing?" the banker chuckled to S-. "Kids today. What makes you think he doesn't listen to your prayers?"

"Everyone knows HE *loves* boys while HE only *pretends* to like girls. You're always quoting HIM yourself: "99 & ½ pennies doth not a buck make.""

"Ludicrous chapter 13, verse 24, corollary ^," Smolet informed S-. "Words to live by."

S- looked on as father & daughter began a verbal wrestling match, their bodies rigid, their tongues doing the tumbling. When one tossed out an argument, the other hurled it on its back, slamming it to the floor, trying his/her best to pin it to the mat. His dimples having a field day, Buck gleefully refereed, tossing in dialectic landmines whenever his father resorted to the age-old argument, "Because I'm your father & I say so." Flustered even more when his daughter refused to be bought off, the banker finally yielded, throwing up his arms, removing his false beard & acquiescing to the cross-armed Penny's foot-tapping insistence.

Sorry the match was over, Buck tossed in one final landmine. "What will Mummy say?"

Smolet took a long lingering look @ his cigar. "Nothing," he concluded. "I'll just write an addendum in her rule book. After all, it's Smolet Sunday. PUP reminds us that the man of the house is the undisputed kingpin head."

"You got that right," Buck winked @ S-.

The banker kissed his cigar, then scraped a match behind S-'s ear. The match hissed, sputtering into flame. Smolet pretended to light the cigar. Puffing like a dragon, rolling the cigar from one side of his mouth to the other, he cast his eye on the corner china cabinet, its cutlery & flatware. Its gold-rimmed wine glasses glistened in the slanting beams of the morning sun.

"Tell your mother to get in here," he instructed, not addressing anyone in particular. "And tell her to bring her rule book, some Write-Out & a pen."

Both Penny & Buck exited.

S- remained, watching his boss, landlord & partner feel above, behind & beneath the glass cabinet. Eventually the banker lifted the delicate latch, checking under & behind each silver spoon, elegant platter & brandy sniffer, shaking his disappointed head as he rummaged for something he failed to find.

* * * * *

THE CATHEDRAL KNOWN AS the TEMPLE of PERPETUAL PUPPINESS—& its adjoining coin laundromat—had not gone unnoticed by S-. The day he arrived, S- nearly collided into its neo-gothic, art-deco brickwork. He recalled gazing @ its arched windows, its flying buttresses & pinnacled turrets. At that time, it was the tallest structure in town, its skyscraping spire easily dwarfing its residential & business neighbors. Yet over the few weeks S- had prowled the streets, its pinnacles & belfries seemed to have shrunk below the monumental office bldgs & newer skyscrapers that now lorded over it. The synachurch temple & mosque sat tucked away in a mini-shopping mall boasting a dry cleaners, a beef jerky emporium, a daycare/adult arcade center, a haberdashery for nudists, a surreal estate agency & a We-break-it *and* Fix-it repair shop. Even as S- & the Smolet family approached, the cathedral seemed to shrink back as if in fear he or they might scuff its holier-than-thou polished & waxed tile floors.

"I want you children to be on your best beehivor," Mrs Smolet warned, tugging @ her white gloves, pulling them off, putting them back on. "We have a guest here & i want you to show him the pauper way to behoove in church."

However unassuming the outside of the temple, its inside proved the opposite. A somber, reverent mood radiated from every wooden beam, every stained-glass window, every statue lining the high-ceilinged walls. The glass windows depicted scenes of winged creatures wearing birthday hats, blowing out candles & bearing the burnt bodies of vanquished enemies as proof to humble, genuflecting believers that their PUP was indeed merciful. The statues & statuettes were of robed or armored figures w/ eyes that moved as they peered down on the murmuring masses entering the synagong halls. So numerous was the entering crowd of worshippers, several deacons in coattails & high hats were rearranging collapsible, stackable plastic pews & doing a slovenly job of it. All about, parishioners stubbed their toes or rammed their knees into the unforgiving hard plastic. A volley of curses & strident invoking of PUP's name echoed off the vaulted ceilings. Ever vigilant, Mrs Sticky Buns kept covering Pearl's ears lest her youngest be subjected to the coarse, corrupting language.

"Yes, it is a serious problem," Mr Smolet conceded to S-. "One the synagong has wrestled w/ for centuries. But if you notice, every few feet the church fathers have placed a confessional booth. That way, when you stub your toe & voice your displeasure by coining a four-letter word or using PUP's name in vain, you can immediately step inside a booth & confess—"

"And since on average it takes six hours & twenty-three minutes for PUP's arch-accountant angels to record a sin," his Mrs added, "these minor transmissions can be analed immediately & never enter the books."

"Good morning, Mr Smolet...Mrs Smolet...kids...& a particular good morning to our special guest." A man w/ thinning brown hair matted down w/ holy grease approached; his slender grin stretched seemingly beyond the sides of his face. Before shaking each hand, the man ran his palm thru his hair, allowing said hand to slip easily in & out of every palm it shook. He had barely grasped S-'s five digits when his own was gone. "I'm Reverend Hickey," he smiled, "but, please, call me Hal."

Even as the Reverend spoke, he turned from S-, throwing the longer of his two lengthy arms around Smolet. The two men whispered like a pair of bees exchanging rumors of stolen honey as they led the procession of Smolets (& their special guest) to the Smolet family pew. "Ester," he called to a purple-haired woman of swarthy, prunish complexion. "Could you get a holy cloth & dust off these seats?

"Please forgive us," he apologized. "We received but short notice you & the Mrs would be gracing our pews. I trust you all have been in the best of spiritual health & enjoying eternal fiscal bliss?"

Mrs Smolet answered promptly, launching into a report on the stellar behoovoir of those under her care, along w/ an assessment of each child's attitudinal tendencies, which all in all added up to each being sure to gain admittance into the right-hand pocket of the ONE & only blessed PUP. While she spoke, the Reverend maneuvered inbtwn the Mr & Mrs, his back turned to the former, his greased palm turned upward. The head of the Smolet family removed a cigar from his breast pocket, wrapped a bank note around it, followed by another & another, before slipping it into the Reverend's lightning-fast grasp.

His grin extending even farther past his pointed ears, the Reverend bowed to Mrs Smolet. "Well, enjoy the sermon," he bade the entire family. "May you all be as the One would have you." He motioned for the family to sit.

"Since it is Smolet Sunday," he turned, addressing the banker, "we offer our town's chief financier & owner of the Smolet First Pedestal the chair of eternal honor." The town's chief financier followed the Reverend. Polite applause rang out from the pews as the two mounted the altar before disappearing, neither to be seen again till the end of the service.

S- looked about, observing a sea of faces, some pale, some painted, some polite, some prim, some polished, some plastered. The front-most aisles were overflowing— overstuffed it seemed to him—w/ the Temple's more obese parishioners. S- surveyed the crowd, noting the more rotund the worshipper, the closer they seemed allowed to sit near the altar. Those merely plump were seated farther back, while the lean, sleek & downright scrawny were confined to the rear or restricted to the balcony. White gloves seemed to be the fashion rave. All the chunkier, better-dressed mothers wore them, often removing one or both to whack a pudgy, unruly child across the head.

The Smolet pew was an elegant, ornate, enclosed box located on the second tier, allowing S- to gaze down on the bulkier members of the congregation. S- noted a similar box opposite them where a razor-thin face also surveyed the crowd. At times the man, a derby hat cocked on his tiny head, seemed to leer @ S——or perhaps the entire Smolet family. Seated next to the tiny man was a shriveled grasshopper, disguised as an elderly woman wrapped in a woolen shawl. While the man swung a cane wildly in the air, the woman took delight in spitting on those below, most of whom had the foresight to bring umbrellas.

As the milling congregation was settling in, S- grew aware of numerous mothers pointing his way as they whispered to their children. So too w/ various men, who whispered among themselves, nodding or shaking their heads. When the low murmuring permeating the crowd subsided, the overhead lights dimmed. Subdued slivers of sunlight streamed thru the stained-glass windows, casting the church's musty interior in an eerie semi-darkness—until a bright spotlight homed in on a deep purple, sumptuous throne lowered thru the ceiling. Collapsed on the throne— either sleeping or dead—lay a marionette, its strings barely visible in the glaring spotlight.

The chords of an organ began, accompanied by the shifting of people in their chairs, the crinkling of starched dresses, the rubbing of panty hose, the scraping of peasant-leather shoes & an occasional soft whack of gloves atop some fidgeting young skull. Several parishioners developed coughs. Too busy observing the congregation, S- missed the moment the marionette sprung suddenly to life.

Raising its head as the pupils of its button eyes rolled, then lifting its arms, the marionette sat up. All coughing ceased as the organ sustained a low, drawn-out, mournful chord. The marionette reached for the nearby chalice & took a drink, the red liquid trickling down its cleft chin & onto the vest of its dark, pinstriped, three-piece suit.

Who among you has not been tempted to change the divine order of things I have bestowed on you? the marionette began, its hoarse voice crackling thru the loudspeakers. As it spoke, the marionette flailed its arms, bobbing its head, its pupils rolling inside its sewn-on eyes. Occasionally it jerked one leg, then the other as it pranced about the pulpit.

What greater compliment could I have bestowed upon you, than that I should have created you in MY image...w/ no strings attached? The puppet looked first to

94

the right, then to the left of the congregation, all speechless w/ awe. *And to guide you on your divine journey. I am the ONE, the one purpose, the one cause, the one & only true bank account. There is only one PUP...& the One is His Prophet. Repeat that.*

In unison, the entire congregation repeated: "There is only one PUP...& the One is His Prophet."

I gave you the One that you might all join together in fiscal brotherhood—eternal & interest-bearing. That the poor might ascend to the fruits of my money-bearing truth... that they too one day might be rich in eternal, monetary bliss...that the rich might taunt, humiliate, exploit & thus shame them to greater heists...that the poor in spirit, the poor in accessories, the poor in midriff bulge might receive tangible proof in the abundance of Oneness—that they may witness the ever-expanding girth of those of you who take up more than your fair share of these holy pews, knowing that they too might expand in girth should they surrender to the greater One...to inhabit this infinitely consumable universe...that they too might eat, drink & make merry... till their belt buckles burst."

S- felt his heart pound, fearing for his life as the marionette looked his way before reaching for a nearby censer. Lifting the lid, it extracted two pinches of snuff, which it snorted into either nostril of its round red nose. It then jumped in great leaps, balancing by one foot on the arm of the throne, then somersaulting to the next arm, walking up & down it as children walk along a train rail. Maintaining its balance, it perched cross-legged on the high back of the throne as it reached in its vest to check its pocket-watch. Finally it leaped to the edge of the pulpit, its arms swishing, its body swaggering, like a pirate breaking into song after fending off a swarm of relentless attackers.

The greater good is in the larger belt size, the puppet pronounced, protruding its own belly in demonstration. *Leather belt, cowhide, snakeskin, silk, cotton, synthetic or made of genuine boyskin—it doesn't matter. It's the girth that matters. Check your libaries, your zoos, your prisons, your institutions of hirer learning: are not a disproportionate number of your criminals, your sinners, your Dregs, your freethinkers, your unDoers—those dishwashers of discontent—thin? Skinny is as skinny does, as my GOOD BOOK says. Where the skinny gather, there will you find the rumbling bellies of blasphemy...those hungry to consume what you, not they, have gathered. Where there is fat, there will you find overabundance, there will you find the contentness of cows, the contemplation of sheep. There will you find those ready & willing to suckle the wisdom-teats of PUP, ready to suck on my wishbone*

& its promise of perpetual Oneness—where everyone is rich & those who are not @ least wannabe.

Not a sound, save the booming, crackling voice of the puppet could be heard as S- glanced around. Those in the foremost pews chewed on the puppet's words like cows chewing its cud. The organ fell silent. No one coughed. No child fidgeted. While the eyes of the women & children were riveted to the marionette, who again checked his watch & snorted more snuff, the men's eyes continually alternated btwn watching their PUP & scrutinizing S-. S-'s neck hair bristled when the marionette leapt high in the air, nearly losing its balance as it landed in front of the pulpit, its scratchy voice even more vehement, its large, rolling eyes often aimed directly @ S-.

There are those among you, even some of you in this, my holy house of worship... some of you who have been cavorting w/ the slender of belt. You have listened to their thin whiny voices, sympathized w/ their lack of stylish attire...sat impassively as they plotted to take from our very mouths what is not theirs & distribute it among themselves & their PUP-forsaken kind. But I say unto you, whether you be four-hundred pounds—a well-fed, muscle-endowed, headstrong son-of-a-banker—or a newly arrived citizen to this community, you are no better than they...for there is only one One & the PUP be His profit! Repeat after me: there is only one One & the PUP be His profit!

"There is only one One & the PUP be His profit!" the congregated repeated in ragged unison.

Nay, you are no better then they—unless...unless, of course, you don a turncoat & rise above them. Ascend to the One. Smote their disreputable intentions; refuse to be suckled by their lack, nay, by your own lack; join the greater-giving family of eternal high-interest-bearing Oneness. Working, praying, paying taxes, tithing what is left cluttering your purse to the great, the one & only One, currently housed @ the Smolet First Pedestal Bank & Pizzeria. Only then can your belt size, my belt size, every One's belt size, increase w/ each face-stuffing year on into infinity.

The marionette jumped from the altar onto the front aisle & pranced one-legged, its other leg tangled in its strings.

Will you do it? Will you join w/ your fellow congregation & contribute to the eternal One?

As if on cue, the entire congregation shouted, "YES! YES! YES!"

Repeat after me: There is only one PUP...

"There is only one PUP!"

...& the One is His Prophet.

"And the One is His Prophet."

There is only one One...

"There is only one One."

And PUP be His Profit.

"And PUP be His Profit."

The strains of the organ rose among the chorus of voices. The congregation jumped to its feet, clapping in time to the music. The puppet leapt back on stage, flying about the altar piece, which housed a candy-striped tabernacle behind a statuette of three pilgrims bribing a winged, well-fed messenger. Finally the marionette collapsed on its throne, knocking over the chalice as the spotlight went out & the throne ascended to the ceiling. From all corners of the room, handwoven plastic baskets appeared. Temple deacons approached each person as the singing congregation tossed in coins, bank notes, jewelry & an occasional firstborn (these promptly tossed back). When the basket came to S-, he sensed all eyes were upon him. Nudged by his shadow, he reached in his back pocket & unloaded the bills given him. Immediately a cheer went up. For the next half-hour, while the congregation sang in four-part disharmony, S- was patted repeatedly on the back.

When the service ended & the crowd began to press twd the exit doors, S- caught a glimpse of the Police Chief milling among the crowd. Dozens of roly-poly citizens pushed their way up to shake the officer's hand andor pat him on the back. Others came to shake S-'s hand. Women gyrated in awkward positions to kiss his cheek & tried in vain to coax their frightened offspring to say hello to the "nice stranger." He received several invitations to stop over for fried okra & chicken gizzards in exchange for taking out some garbage.

S- found himself swept along by the crowd pressing in from all sides. No sooner did he spot sunlight & begin to push twd it when he was suddenly jerked backward. He heard screams as a callous hand seized him by the throat, releasing him only to pummel his chest, then drag him into a nearby confessional. The man punching him was a patchwork of body parts, carelessly stitched together, his punches more like soft ribbing than solid blows.

"Get out of here," the man hissed thru sallow teeth, his eyes delirious & bloodshot. "You know not what you do!"

A swarm of parishioners crowded into the booth. The Police Chief tackled the assailant, others grabbing an arm or a leg. The man kicked, ranted & raved as they pinned him to the floor. "You know not what you do," he spit @ S-. "You bring the bread of destruction. The wine you serve is fire!"

"Easy, Erle. Easy. Settle down." The Police Chief, sitting on the man, spoke calmly. A wizened-faced older gentleman arrived, toting a black bag. Opening the bag, he extracted a syringe, filling it w/ a clear amber serum. "Hold 'em still," he instructed as he poked the needle into the squirming man's arm. The man struggled, but to no avail. As the needle was extracted, he lost all will. Seconds later, he lay unconscious.

"Don't mind him," the Police Chief counseled S-, his wry grin less than reassuring. "He's a patient from the literary infirmary. Escaped apparently." The C of P arched a brow twd the man w/ the needle. "Carl, I trust you can handle things from here."

The elder gentleman nodded. Grabbing S- by the shoulder, the C of P led him out of the booth to the tepid applause of those looking on.

S- was again surrounded by numerous beefy & buxom parishioners expressing sympathy & reiterating their offers for all the okra & chicken gizzards he could eat. His cheeks burning, his heart continuing to pound, he was only slightly relieved when Mr Smolet waddled twds him. Barely able to speak, the banker explained in a hoarse whisper that he had somehow worn out his vocal cords. During the family's march home, Mrs Smolet could not refrain from praising S-, her hands barely able to restrain from hugging him, pinching his cheek, squeezing his hand andor copping a feel each time they fell behind the others. Only when Pearl sidled up & took his hand did S-'s racing mind begin to calm down. He walked on in silence, the words: YOU KNOW NOT WHAT YOU DO ringing in his ears, his shadow occasionally adding:

Maybe he's right...maybe we don't.

Chapter 10

"I CAN'T BELIEVE IT!" Buck ranted, slamming the FIXER & DEVELOPER onto their assigned shelf. The man-child—his hair scooped, frosted & sprinkled into a tasteful vanilla sundae—wore a ratty T-shirt proclaiming, "I'D RATHER BE KILLED BY FRIENDLY FIRE.' Done assisting in the darkroom, he stomped into the living room, the floorboards quaking as he kicked every loose coin stupid enuff to be in his way. S- trailed @ a distance, weighed down by a vague sense of guilt—this despite his shadow's insistence he had done nothing wrong.

"You're a traitor," Buck railed. "I can't believe it! I introduce you to my friend... who invites you in on an honest-to-PUP real secret conspiracy...& you immediately turncoat...all in exchange for all the okra & fried chicken you can eat!"

S- struggled to make his tongue move. Yet every time his lips parted, his thoughts collided, spasmed, then capsized. An incoherent jumble of intransitive verbs, imperfect participles & dangling modifiers tumbled forth in an order even he knew made no sense. "No amount of chicken gizzards..." he stammered, faltering & starting over. "I only meant..." he began again, his throat constricting, his mouth feeling like sandpaper. "I would never...@ least not...i mean..."

"Then why! Why?" Buck kicked the futon, dropping listlessly onto the loveseat, disheveling the hairdo his oldest sister had spent all afternoon perfecting—the girl proud of the added sprinkles & tinge of chocolate syrup. Buck closed his eyes, bitterly savoring the raunchy taste of unadulterated betrayal.

Twilight having descended, the garret was shrouded in shadow, the last vestiges of daylight squeezed out of the faded sunset. Buck rose to switch on the lamp. He pulled its chain, flinching when the bulb exploded, a brief flare petering out as it hissed like a dying snake exhaling its last breath. Buck yanked the chain again. He cursed, resorting finally to kicking the stand & cursing some more.

"Your dam light blew out," he snarled, collapsing in the rocking chair, his arms crossed, his nostrils flaring. "You have any extra bulbs?" Buck folded his legs beneath him, setting the rocker in motion.

S- about-faced. Returning to the darkroom, he located the box of tinted bulbs. As an afterthought he seized the camera, his shadow nodding in agreement, grabbing a roll of film as well. As if extending a peace offering, S- handed camera & film to Buck, the boy sneering as he snatched the gift, adding a few muffled curses.

Spurred by Buck's furious rocking, the floorboards groaned in protest, S- ignoring their painful pleas, wondering instead if he would ever get back on Buck's good side. Stepping out of fist range, he turned his attention to the floor lamp. He exchanged bulbs & pulled the chain, disappointed by the faint red glow.

"Take off the shade," Buck suggested.

S- removed the lampshade, stepping back & frowning. He turned, observing Buck open the camera & jam in the film roll. "Where did you get all that cash?" the boy inquired, snapping the camera shut. "The cash to buy off PUP."

As S- explained, the floorboards ceased complaining. Buck planted his feet firmly, his eyes turning inward as he chewed on something. His face grew brighter. S- realized his own eyes were beginning to adjust. Everything in the room became strikingly visible. He could clearly distinguish the furniture, their shadows looming large, their edges sharp & distinct. He observed the walls gently breathe in & out. The creaks & moans coming from the rafters now synchronized w/ the crickets outside.

He flinched, almost jumping back when Buck's shadow rose despite the man-child remaining seated. While Buck tinkered w/ the camera, his shadow traipsed along the rafters & disappeared into the darkroom, reappearing to take an interest in S-'s shadow, who, like S-, had been watching it in rapt fascination. It smiled, playfully protruding its belly as if pretending to be pregnant. It clamped two fingers together to suggest a cigar, which it proceeded to puff on fiercely. Falling to its knees, it mockingly feigned a desperate search for something—lifting the futon's shadow, peeking under it, shrugging its shoulders before lifting the loveseat's shadow & so on.

"What so fascinating?" Buck asked, straining to see what S- might be staring @. The shadow froze, tho only for a second. It clicked its heels, giving a mock salute. Buck seemed not to notice. It stuck its tongue @ the boy. Buck returned to fiddling w/ the camera. Soon the shadow grew emboldened, tossing mock hand grenades, pulling down its pants & wagging its bare butt every time Buck glanced in its vicinity.

"Here you go." Buck handed S- the camera.

Feeling the camera's heft, looking thru its lens, S- aimed @ Buck's shadow. The shadow primped its hair & struck several poses. S- snapped photos as rapidly as the shadow changed positions.

"What the hail are you photographing?" Buck grumbled. "The rafters? There's not enuff light in here. Wait till we get outside."

S- aimed the camera @ Buck, adjusting the aperture & continuing to snap pictures.

"Look, if you're trying to get on my good side, you can forget it." Buck knit his brow, unaware his shadow had pranced behind him, making deer antlers, then devil horns behind the boy's head, adding a goatee on Buck's chin.

"You need to decide whose side you're on," Buck advised, again setting the rocker in motion. "Remember what that girl Heidi said: 'You can't have your caviar & eat it, too.' Pupa is only using you, you know."

S- lowered the camera & perched on the edge of the loveseat. "Why? What could he want from me?"

Buck eyed S- a second, then drew a deep breath. "Look, the first thing they teach us @ Gladiator U is to know your enemy: know what they think, how they think. Know what they eat, how they hold their fork, what side of the bed they sleep on, if they hug their pillow or punch it while they dream. Pupa hired you as a symbol: proof that even someone as…even someone like you will bow down to the One.

"You're the great unknown. No one knows what you will do. No one knows what to do w/ you. All they know is you can't be ignored. Even the blindest Brit can't help but see you."

Buck fell silent, the floorboards beginning to groan. After a long pause, he continued, "Who knows? Maybe Pupa will have *you* bribe the S-election officials. Hail, they might even run you as a dummy candidate. But mark my words, by the time all the bribes are tallied, you'll have your toes stepped over so many times, the doctors will prescribe amputation to stave off the oncoming gangrene. Better take some pictures of your toes now so you can remember what they look like."

Slightly alarmed, S- removed his shoes, snapping photos of his pedal extremities from as many angles as he could contort his body into. He handed Buck the camera for additional shots from other angles, including an aerial shot capturing the tip of S-'s nose pointing btwn two fanned-out feet. Buck was zooming in on individual toes when S- observed the boy's shadow lost in thought. No sooner did the shadow snap out of it when Buck announced he had a great idea.

"What if you become a double agent? Better still, you can be a triple double agent...one who pretends to be a Brit spying on a Lugwort while pretending to be a Lugwort pretending to spy on a Brit pretend-spying on a Lugwort. No one's been *that* devious!" Buck grew animated, mussing his hair till it dribbled down both sides of his face. "The trick is—i learned this in Espionage 101—never decide whose side you're really on. See, if you *don't* know, how is anyone gonna pin you down? With that deadpan expression of yours, I bet you could pull it off."

S- looked to his shadow. Pursing its lips, narrowing its eyes, the shadow shrugged.

"This will work," Buck insisted. "You play along w/ whatever Pupa says. 'Yes, sir' him to death. Nod your head, bow on your knees, kiss his ring. Every time his clothes get even a hint of lint...be there to brush it off. When his pants creases get stuck in the furniture, help him pull them out. Do everything you can to gain his complete confidence. And do the same for the Lugworts. Nod when Heidi mumbles. Agree w/ both sides of Edmund's kisser. I don't care whose side you're on, really. Just don't mess up my campaign to surmount Jasmine."

Buck's shadow again grew lost in thought. "It's funny," the man-child mused, "all the years i've been whoopsidoodling Brittle girls—vanquishing their virtue, as we call it @ Gladiator U—& it hasn't taught me a thing about how to deal w/ a real girl. There's something about Woodbees...especially their girls. You know what i mean?" Buck pursed his lips.

"Of course you don't. I don't know what i mean myself. Brittle girls, they crumble when you hold them. I mean, toss a fake grenade & they freak out, get all indignant. Touch them in the wrong place, they get all sticky & start oozing all over you. You end up using a lot of soap. But a Woodbee lacks that certain something Brittle girls are trying so hard to fake. You have to be more than cunning to whoopsidoodle a Woodbee girl."

Buck paused, searching S-'s face for a reaction. The man-child's shadow stood beside him, stroking its chin. It leaned in to whisper in Buck's ear. "I'm thinking maybe of taking some pictures of Jasmine," Buck announced. "With a little luck i figure i might get one that captures how she makes me feel. Maybe she'll be so swept off her feet, she'll drop her guard, maybe even surrender w/ out a fight."

Buck's shadow grew somber, its head bowed as if in prayer. "I can't tell you how much i want to be the one to pull her pants on," he continued. "Or be the first to wrap

102

a skirt around those soft thighs...& be there to zip her in. PUP, how I long to fasten her brassiere...then slide those milky arms into a silk blouse, button her in, leaving the top couple buttons undone just enuff to reveal that sweet hint of her..."

Buck blushed, lifting the camera to hide his reddened cheeks. He snapped several pictures of nothing in particular. Heaving a sigh, he announced it was getting late: time to search out where his mother had moved his bedroom.

"You have a big day tomorrow," he reminded S-. "Your first day @ work. Don't forget to keep your eyes open & your ears peeled. When you find that combination, i want to personally hand it to Edmund, right in front of Jasmine."

The man-child rose, ambling to the trapdoor. When he turned, he clicked his heels & flashed a military salute. His shadow repeated the gesture, adding a thumbing of its nose. S- grabbed the camera, disappointed to find the film was out of frames.

* * * * *

"WAD THE SAMUEL HILL i need an assist*ant* fur?" Stubbs Farrago frowned, leaning on his mop & challenging the banker w/ a suspicious stare. The bank janitor & the bank president each stood their ground, said ground being the basement of the Smolet First Pedestal Bank & Pizzeria. A few yards away, S- stared @ his new shoes, hands clasped behind his back.

"Now, now," Mr Smolet urged, placing a friendly set of frankfurters on the janitor's stiff shoulder, chewing on a thought before forcing a wan smile. "In the seventeen years you've been w/ us, you've never had an assist*ant*. Think of all the wisdom, the skill, the experience, the know-how you've accumulated. Don't you think it's time you passed some of that precocious wisdom on to a younger generation of up & coming maintenance injuneers?"

"Hail, Mr Smolet. Meaning no disneglect but he ain't even one a us." Stubbs extended the arm that held the mop in the general direction of S-. S- stood motionless as the banker discussed the pros & the janitor countered w/ the cons of creating the coveted position of ass't janitor.

"True, he's not one of us *now*," the financial officer conceded, "but who's to say what he could do. You teach him the skills of wielding a mop—the up & down stroke, the back & forth maneuver, the circular sweep, the figure eight—& i'll attend to his moral edification. Btwn you & me, we'll forge him into something any bank—federally insured or no—would be honored to have attending to its floors & polishing its doorknobs. What do you say, Stubbs?"

The banker pulled on the key dangling around his neck. S- watched the two men: the skinny one in a gray uniform jangling a thick set of keys, the banker in his five-&-a-half piece suit fingering the single key. Both stood near a door painted w/ the ominous warning:

PRIVATE
FOR NO ONE ONLY
KEEP OUT
THIS MEANS YOU!

"It ain't right, Mr Smolet. I remember how i had to beg fur weeks t' get this here job. Back then i was competing w/ my second cousin & if it wasn't fur me accidental-like chopping off a few a his fingers w/ that machete i happen t' be carrying—in case i ran into a watermelon or sumpin'—you might a hired him instead. Now this fella jest comes in off de street, no references, no 'xperience & you hire him on da spot."

"Listen," the banker whispered, pulling his employee to one side, "I know it seems strange, me wanting to hire one of *them*." Both men locked eyes, then glanced over @ S- before locking eyes again. "But i have a good reason. This here is a S-election year, right? Doesn't it seem strange one of these guys suddenly appears in *our* town?" Receiving no answer, the banker repeated the question: "Doesn't it?"

Smolet reached in his coat pocket, producing a full set of keys more formidable then the measly set the janitor held. The two men jangled their keys in unison.

Stubbs finally nodded, tho barely.

"What i'm thinking," his superior continued, "is there is a conspiracy afoot, perhaps precipitated by a more radical faction of Dregs—the ones that give the rest of your kind a bad name. Where there is one of these guys," the banker indicated S-, "there's got to be more. You follow?"

Again Stubbs nodded.

"Now suppose we hire one...sorta like a test dummy. And suppose he can't cut the mustard...like everything he does is wrong & we make his life shear hail. Do you think he'll be running back to his buddies & saying, 'C'mon, i know where we can get jobs & maybe even impregnate a few poor men's daughters'? You get my drift?"

"Loud & clear," Stubbs responded, grabbing his mop handle by both hands. "You can count on me, Mr Smolet. I'll teach this guy everything he needs t' know t' be a miserable failure."

"I know you're the man to do it," the banker smiled, resting a hand on the janitor's shoulder. "Only be subtle. Think of it like fishing: you don't pounce on the fish right away. You pretend to be going along w/ its plan to steal your worm...& just when it thinks it's going to get away scot-free...WHAM, you reel it in." The banker pulled a cigar from his breast pocket, broke it in half & handed the smaller half to the janitor. "As my great Grampupa used to say, 'It ain't torture if it's fast & painless.'"

"I gets your drift," Stubbs confirmed, momentarily resting his chin on the two hands clutching the mop, the half a cigar pressed btwn his lips. "Come here, son," he called to S-.

S- approached cautiously, looking from banker to janitor to banker, his look more a plea for mercy than an expression of confidence.

"So, youse wants to learn my job, does ya?" the janitor asked. S- nodded unenthusiastically.

"Well, you done chosen yourself a fruitful career," Stubbs boasted. "Anywhere you goes, there are floors to be swept; halls to mop; linoleum to be scrubbed, scoured & waxed; shelves to be dusted; trash cans t' be emptied. You master these skills & dere ain't nowhere youse can't go...provided you gots de right set a keys." The janitor jangled his keys proudly.

"Come here now...let's first introduce you to your new coworkers: bleach, pneumonia & scouring detergent. I'm sure you & the fellows will get along famously."

As if he had just inherited a full-grown son, Farrago led S- thru the basement, introducing him to each door, extending special caution regarding the door marked:

PRIVATE
FOR NO ONE ONLY

"No ways you wanna go in dere," he cautioned. "I ain't never been in dere myself. The only one gots a key is Mr Seedy Smolet hisself."

Seedy Smolet, meanwhile, had waddled twd his office, pausing when coming to the door marked FURNACE ROOM. He stopped, looking both ways, lingering until Stubbs & S- moved out of view. Gently turning its knob, he tiptoed in. Reemerging a short time later, he dusted off his pants w/ his equally dusty fingers, a look of disappointment clouding his otherwise dejected countenance.

* * * * *

UPON ENTERING HIS OFFICE, Smolet abruptly halted, taken aback by the glaring eyes of three impeccably dressed men.

"Hope you don't mind, CD. We took the liberty to let ourselves in."

The banker squinted, removing his glasses to allow his eyes time to refocus. Tho better lit than his home office, his bank office was a near duplicate of the cocoon he enjoyed @ home. Waddling cautiously around his desk, he carefully avoided eye contact, certain the three sets of eyes lasered in on him were there to devour him alive. The banker reached in a desk drawer, pulling out a false beard & donning it like a bullet-proof vest.

"Rubin," he addressed the bug-eyed elder seated closest, wearing a porkpie hat. "Carl," he nodded to the silver-haired Dr Buncle, also seated, @ that moment wiping his bifocals. "Good to see you, Ira," he acknowledged the hairy-armed, broad-chested man standing near the fireplace. The latter scowled as his fierce eyes scoured the office.

"How's the barber business?" Smolet asked, easing himself slowly into his chair.

The barrel-chested man merely snorted, his tattoos seeming to echo the sentiment, his biceps emitting a silent "hmmph." Smolet turned his gaze to Dr Buncle, whose wizened face bore @ least a hint of civility, if not patience.

"Carl, it was nice to see you @ synachurch yesterday." The banker smiled, returning the glasses to his face.

"Likewise," the doctor muttered.

"It's been awhile since i've been there myself...being busy & all guarding the One that guards us all—as i'm sure you can imagine." Smolet reached for a fresh box of cigars, tearing off its wrapper, lifting the lid & offering cigars all around. The doctor shook his head. Old man Rubin wheezed. The barber crossed his arms & snorted.

"I've been busy myself," Dr Buncle commented. "We performed a delicate operation a few days ago, CD. The patient was suffering from post-traumatic thinking-outside-the-box syndrome—which is becoming increasingly common these days. Had to do a whole-person vasectomy. Only when we went to stitch him back together, we were told our One had run low. Not only did we have to reuse old thread, we had to release him way too early."

"Most unfortunate," the banker sympathized, crackling the cellophane of the cigar he clutched @ both ends.

"Allow me, Carl," the elderly Rubin cut in, shifting in his chair, his lidless eyes homed in on the banker. "Chuck, we've known each other a long time. I knew you when you were crawling around in designer diapers. It was your father—PUP bless

106

his bank roll—who first backed all my bologna, even when my detractors said i was full of it. I owe my entire empire & all fifty-seven varieties to your pupa. You & me go back a long way, Chuck." The old man paused, removing his hat & gazing unblinkingly into Smolet's blinking baby blues.

The banker leaned back, chewing as he listened, twirling his cigar in one hand, tugging his beard w/ the other.

"For months now, i've been trying to withdraw my One from this here financial institute. And i think you know why. So has Carl here. And Mr Fuse, too." A quick snort came from near the fireplace. "And @ least half a dozen other friends & business acquaintances i could name."

"Now, Rubin," Smolet interrupted, sitting fwd & laying aside his cigar to place his palms flat on the desk. "I have never denied you or any of our patrons the One they have coming to them—regardless of whether any of you buy an extra large pizza or not. That's our policy here."

"On paper, yes," the bologna baron countered. "But what about in hard cold cash?"

Smolet snatched up his cigar, his Adam's apple playing elevator in his throat, his cheeks draining some of their color.

The barber pulled a slip of paper from his pocket & waved it. "How do we know these here promissory notes are even worth anything? Come S-election, how do we know we won't be told they're as worthless as that last time?"

"That's absurd," the banker huffed. "Whoever told you that is still reading from the *old* history book. If those securities were worthless, do you think we would have taken the trouble to print them on such high-quality paper? Hold it up to the light, Ira. Go on! See those watermarks? Notice the hidden insignia of someone's sweet little grandma holding out a chocolate double-fudge cookie.

"And look here. I even signed them with this gold pen." The banker yanked a cigar-sized, gold-plated pen from an elegant rosewood pen & pencil set. "In silver ink, no less. What more assurance do you need? The Smolet First Pedestal Bank & Pizzeria would never advance monies w/ out the requisite One to back it up."

"How do we know that, Charlie?" Dr Buncle pressed, glaring over his bifocals as he locked eyes w/ the banker.

"Look @ our books, Carl. Everything is in perfect order." Opening his lower desk drawer, the banker produced a green ledger, plopping the cumbersome book on the desk & turning its thick, stiff pages. He gestured for each of his guests to step fwd & look.

"How can we tell?" the bologna baron grumbled, rubbing where there should have been a chin. "We look @ your books, all it says is one, & one...& one."

"It's coded," the banker assured them, "in case one of the cleaning staff starts snooping around. See, the ONEs in capital letters are bigger than the ones in lower case. And the Ones w/ a capital O are worth more than the oNes w/ a capital N & so on. Plus the ONes w/ two capital letters are bigger than the onEs w/ only one capital &—"

The doctor cut the banker off. "Our sources tell us you Brittles are proposing rounding up Dregs for the Turkey Shoot."

"It's bad enuff," the barber jumped in, "you Brits okey-dokey'd your right to legally mistake a Dreg for a Canaan."

"Now, Ira," the banker objected, "I am not a Brit. I may have married Sur D'leBaum's fourth favorite niece, but i assure you, i'm as much a Woodbee as any of you. But you've all got to face reality: we're almost out of Canaans. They're not reproducing like they used to—out of pure spite, if you ask me."

"That's the point, Charlie."

Dr Buncle removed his spectacles, aiming them @ the banker. "We're almost out of Canaans. Now they want to use Dregs...& maybe, perhaps, a few 'unsavory' Woodbees—or so it would seem."

"Be reasonable, Carl. Rubin. We have to shoot somebody."

"Do we?"

"Now, Carl. I'll not have such liberule views expressed in the presence of my wife & children's photos." Smolet glanced down @ the smiling Mrs Sticky Buns, then to the family portrait of Buck, Penny & Pearl, taken when all three refused to say 'cheese.'

An uneasy silence hovered in the room. The unflinching stares of Dr Carl Buncle, DMS; Rubin Samwish, Esq; & current alto tenor for the Nail-biting Barbershop Malpractice Quartet, Ira Fuse, challenged the equally unflinching baby blues of the president & CEO of the Smolet First Pedestal & Pizzeria.

Finally, Rubin Samwish shattered the uneasy silence by coughing up a fur ball, wrapping it in his kerchief. "We intend to advance our own platform," the old man wheezed, "whereby we shoot cans instead."

The banker smacked his cigar against the desk, his eyes incredulous. "It won't work," he blurted.

The old man ignored the objection. "Maybe fruit & vegetable cans to begin with...moving eventually to soup cans or perhaps baked beans...& after that—"

"CANS CAN'T RUN!" the banker shouted, whacking the cigar until it broke in pieces. "Cans can't duck. They can't hide. Not of their own free will! And S-election is all about free will!"

"Someone can throw them," Ira insisted, uncrossing his arms, clenching his hands into fists.

"I'm sure some clever entrepreneur can come up w/ an invention that can toss cans in some helter-skelter fashion," Dr Buncle calmly injected. "Think about this, CD. You said so yourself: you're more Woodbee than Brit. Your own great-great grandchildren—especially the not-so-great ones—could one day be hauled off &—"

"Won't happen," the banker snapped, wielding the bent cigar like a limp sword. "The ONE protects the one who protects the One!"

"Which is why we want *our* One protecting the one that matters most: one's self." Rubin puckered his dry lips & rubbed the few antenna-like hairs poking up atop his otherwise bald scalp. "We've been hoodwinked for the last time, CD. Sources tell us... You tell him, Carl."

"Rumor has it the Brittles are pushing to revamp the voting system. Plus they intend to raise the non-tax."

"Including shipping & handling," Ira added, spitting in the fireplace.

"Not only that," Rubin chirped in, "they're proposing some new so-called minimal Sir-tax."

"Now, Rubin," Smolet countered, "let me explain: a Sirtax is not a real tax. That's why it has a 'Sir' in front of it, w/ a capital 'S' no less. As for the non-tax, someone has to pay for the privilege of not being taxed. Think about this. We can't afford to have our wealthy reduced to wondering where their next five-course meal is coming from. That would be a public relations nightmare!"

"You've been selling us short, CD," this from the bologna baron. "Don't lie to us, Charlie. And don't forget where you came from."

"We want to see our One," Dr Buncle insisted.

"With our own eyes," Ira weighed in.

Crumbling what remained of his cigar, the banker leaned back, his chair groaning under the added pressure. He glanced quickly @ the portrait of Smolet the Great scowling down on the three puny visitors. Loosening a coat button, Smolet threw his arms up, clasping his hands behind his head. "I'd be only too happy to open the vault for you," he conceded. "I assure you there is plenty of One to go around. Why, the vault's industrial-size hinges are ready to burst @ their seams from all the pressure. Their very rivets are strained to capacity, there is so much One. Why, a wealthy man's mistress would need two lifetimes to reduce him to the poorhouse.

"That's a joke," the banker informed his unamused audience.

The bologna magnate looked @ the doctor, who looked back @ the barber. "We believe you," Rubin concluded, puckering his lips. "So, let's see it."

"*Un-for*-tunate-ly," the banker added, staring into the condescending glare of Smolet the Grating, "we can't open the vault on Mondays. Every Monday is a Sabbath in the banking business—not for the staff, mind you, but for the One. You know how the One needs its rest to grow strong & remain vibrant. Sorry." The banker threw up his fat fingers. "But you can come back any other day & i'll be happy to open the vault for you."

"I told you," Ira huffed. "Let's go."

The bologna baron rose slowly, his legs wobbling. Dr Buncle came to the old man's assistance. "We'll be back again tomorrow, Chuck. First thing."

"Oh, but not this week," the banker cautioned. "The vault is closed every Monday & every day this week. Sorry." Again he threw his hands up. "It's a security measure. We've received reports terminal mites, arachnids & other assorted bugs may have infiltrated the bldg. We're doing a thorough sweep of all spider webs, ant colonies, hornets' nests.... You know the routine. But security assures me it should only take a week—provided all goes well."

"Let's get out of here." Ira stormed twd the door, slapping the cap he yanked from his back pocket onto his wavy head of hair. "I told you this would happen. He's a turncoat."

"Fine, Charlie," both older men hissed, Rubin putting on his hat.

"If that's the way you want to play...but we will be back next Tuesday. And we'll be encouraging all our friends to be here, too." The bologna baron inched unsteadily twd the door, Dr Buncle guiding him by the elbow as the two followed the barber's thudding footsteps. After the old man crossed the threshold, the doctor turned back.

"How long do you think you can keep this up, Charlie? Don't think we don't know what you're up to. When the smoke finally clears, you won't be on the winning side...not this time. Good day, CD."

The doctor closed the door gently, Smolet hearing it slam. The banker stroked first his beard, then the key dangling under it. As he fingered its flat cool surface, he absentmindedly chewed on something—something his stomach could not quite digest.

* * * * *

110

"So, HOW WAS IT?" Buck glanced over his shoulder @ S- leaning against the darkroom doorjamb. S- shrugged, his legs about to buckle under, his head longing for a soft pillow. He watched indifferently as Buck held a roll of negatives up to the muted red light.

"These are some interesting pictures you took. I don't remember you taking any of these. When did i do all these goofy poses?"

Stifling a yawn, S- again shrugged.

"Here, look." Buck rose, pulling S-'s arm, refusing to let go until S- acquiesced.

His eyelids drooping, S- scanned the negatives. To his mild surprise, the world on film was reversed. What in life had been light was now dark, while what was dark had become clear. He saw a bleached-out Buck, pretending to be pregnant, a broad, dimpled smile illuminating a translucent face. He saw another Buck, posing like a proud father smoking a cigar, & a third Buck crouched on all fours like an approaching tiger preparing to pounce.

"When did you take these?" Buck asked.

When S- saw the photo of Buck holding two curved fingers up, the other hand forming a beard, he realized the real Buck—the one of flesh & blood—was missing... as if the real Buck was see-thru & only his shadow existed.

"You look beat," Buck observed. "Rough first day, huh?"

S- handed Buck the negatives, dragging himself to the living room. The man-child followed, listening as S- recounted in tired phrases the high & low points of his day. He spoke of a clock that seemed to run backward & a staunch supervisor w/ an endless repertoire of rules, policies & optional procedures—most of which seemed mandatory. Buck barely listened as he continued studying the negatives.

"Whatever you do," he warned, "don't become a Scarburrow."

Removing his shoes so his shadow could rub his feet, S- gazed up quizzically.

"You know: someone who burrows holes in their own flesh so as to remember what it's like to feel. Even worse, you could become a Menial: all of life's joy drained out of you till you find it a chore just to be nice to people.

"You know what?" Buck added, his eyes brightening, his dimples beginning to glow. "These don't really look like me @ all. We've got to get some of these developed. You're good."

S- glanced out the window, mildly amused @ the evening breeze playing the mulberry's higher branches like a tambourine. A few stars popped out to listen. Fireflies lugging lanterns searched the darkening sky for whatever it was fireflies search for. S- heard the cries of several twigs snapping, unaware a pair of size 12½ shoes were steadily creeping twd the mulberry tree. Inside said shoes were the clumsy feet of Edmund Radcliffe. Once under the tree's canopy, Edmund pulled out a crowbar, then stealthily slid around the house.

Dressed from head to foot in black, the rusty-headed would-be cat burglar scouted out all directions, finally slinking below the windowsill to Mr Smolet's cocoon. Applying the crowbar, grunting from one corner of his mouth, cursing from the other, he managed to snap the latch, diving to the ground lest the sound of cracking metal alert anyone inside. Hearing only crickets, he slipped the crowbar inside his jacket & proceeded to raise the window.

Three floors above, Buck coaxed S- into returning to the darkroom. Neither suspected Edmund @ that moment coiled in a heap inside the banker's office. The Lugwort waited for his eyes to adjust, his nose twitching @ the cacophony of stale odors permeating the stuffy office. He stood slowly, his eyes making out the fireplace & mantle, the desk & bookshelves lining the walls. He bristled on hearing a doorknob jiggle, freezing when a swath of yellow light dissected the darkness, slicing it in half, catching the tip of his formidable loafers. A silhouette stood in the doorway, a human beach ball seeming to stare directly @ him. The man-child ducked into the shadows as the beach ball whipped off its glasses & felt about like a blind man, stumbling into furniture as it found its way around the desk. His hands shaking, his heart pounding, Edmund swiftly slithered thru the opened doorway, gently closing it as he exited. He stood a moment, his entire body quaking, the harsh light in the hallway glaring down on him.

Prancing proudly (even jauntily) down the hall, the triumphant cat burglar crawled up the stairs one step @ a time—despite the watchful eye of Pearl standing @ the top landing. Clutching a doll, its limp arm precariously clasped to its body, the girl stared him down. Edmund pressed a finger to his lips, his eyes pleading for the child to not give his position away. As he neared the landing, Pearl dashed away. The coast now clear, Edmund fearlessly climbed the stairs into the garret, his crowbar raised in hopeful anticipation of encountering an accommodating numbskull.

S-'s shadow heard the squeaking first. Buck's shadow turned to investigate. Likewise S- & Buck poked their heads thru the curtain, catching Edmund slinking ever closer. Caught in mid-sneak, the redhead abandoned his crouch, snapping his fingers & sheathing his crowbar, insisting he almost had them.

"Sorry," Buck welcomed his friend, "we didn't hear the doorbell."

"*That's because i broke in.*" Edmund removed his gloves, unzipping his jacket & plopping onto the loveseat. While the scrawny intruder slouched in his seat, his shadow rose, sniffing the air, inspecting the room, searching for spy holes, eavesdroppers & potential bugs—as well as taking note of any & all loose coins.

S- & Buck also sat, Buck's shadow regarding Edmund's shadow w/ annoyed suspicion. S-'s shadow observed them both.

Edmund set aside his crowbar & played w/ his gloves. "I came to tell you... *Hector & me were talking.* We decided we should all meet this Thursday nite. *At my place*, above my old man's shop."

He glanced around the room, removing his ski cap & mussing his unruly moptop. His shadow ducked inside the darkroom, sniffing the chemicals, feeling around the shelves, taking note of the loose change scattered about the floor. Moments later it reemerged, cupping its hands as it whispered in Edmund's ear. Edmund's freckles brightened. His nose began to twitch.

"What's that smell?" he asked.

Buck answered, "The chemicals, probably." His shadow protruded its chest & gestured twd the darkroom. "We're just about to develop some pictures."

Buck's shadow leading, Buck rose, waving for Edmund to join them. He pulled back the curtain; S- & Edmund followed him in.

"*What's all this? You turning into my old man?*" Edmund mocked. As he spoke, his shadow shoved Buck's shadow into a corner, Buck's shadow jabbing back. Edmund rolled his shifting eyes. "*What is it w/ you petty boars-wha-zee & your pseudo-art?*"

"Give the guy a break," Edmund's left jaw countered his right.

"*You know this stuff will rot your brain, don't you? Sure, it starts out as a pleasant diversion, a boars-wha-zee attempt to ignore real suffering while the world degenerates...*"

"Go easy on him. He's your friend."

"*...but before you know it, you end up its slave, consumed by its self-indulgent demands. Believe me. I saw what it did to my old man. And neither of you are immune.*"

"Well, maybe he is." Edmund pointed to S-.

While Edmund spoke, his shadow & Buck's fell into fisticuffs. Buck's threw the stronger punches but Edmund's proved more adept @ slipping btwn the wall's cracks, leaving Buck's shadow swinging @ bare wood.

"Yeah, but this guy is a natural," Buck rebuffed, indicating S-. "He can catch on film what the rest of us don't even see—even what's right in front of our faces. Imagine us sending the newspapers snapshots of Commissioner Dicker's fat fingers deep inside the municipal cookie jar...or members of City Council taking the oath of office w/ their fingers crossed behind their backs. Imagine if the voters got to see that."

Edmund again rolled his eyes as his shadow mounted a sneak attack, pouncing on Buck's shadow from behind. When Buck's shadow hurled it to the ground, it kicked Buck's shadow in the groin.

"His heart's in the right place," Edmund's left jaw offered.

His right jaw huffed. "*But his reasoning is a donkey's ass.*"

Edmund pivoted, retreated to the living room & plunked onto the loveseat. As one hand toyed w/ his crowbar, gloves & cap, the other felt btwn the cushions, his shadow guiding it to the more lucrative coins.

"*You think like a mosquito,*" Edmund cautioned when Buck & S- reemerged. "Like Sedgewick & Heidi," his other side agreed. "*Or worse, like that pesky Mr Gorge.* To bring about real change, we need something more dramatic—something explosive. We need to really shake things up."

As Buck & Edmund's shadows continued to challenge each other, S-'s shadow slipped back into the darkroom, retrieving the camera.

"The real problem, Buck, *is men like your father*—meaning no disrespect—*& your weasel of an uncle.* Men like these have always hoodwinked the masses, cleverly removing the 'm' & turning the masses into asses—jackasses, if you want to know the truth. *You feed a jackass a little hay, let 'em get drunk, have their little bray* & the asses will delude themselves into believing they're actually happy...*or @ least content.*

"And every time a few of the stupid asses start to get wise, *the Powers-that-DO create some diversion*: find a scapegoat...*or better yet...*resurrect the Boogieman. *Soon enuff, the trembling asses are killing each other off...*believing it's their patriot duty to massacre each other while the Powers-that-DO keep score, sending out for donuts & coffee."

Buck listened in silence while his shadow tried to call a truce w/ its dark rival.

Noticing S- snapping pictures of a bare wall, Edmund cocked an irritated eyebrow, addressing S- for the first time. "How you coming w/ the bank combination?"

"It was his first day," Buck interjected. "I doubt if they've even given him his own keys yet."

"*We're depending on you.*" Edmund reminded S-. The redhead reached for his gloves & slapped them in his palm. "If we don't get to the One first, all hopes of affecting the S-election will be lost."

"Wait a minute," Buck objected. "I thought all we wanted was the combination so no one could open the vault. Who said anything about taking the One?"

"*If all goes as planned, we won't need to.* But as you-know-who once said, 'a smart soldier always has a back-up plan.' *That's what we want to discuss on Thursday*— our back-up plan. *And you both need to be there.*"

Edmund stood, retrieving his crowbar & ski cap. He donned the cap, slipped the crowbar in his jacket & zipped it up. Grabbing his gloves, he walked to the window & sized up the mulberry. Tho the window stood open, he nevertheless pulled out his crowbar & pried the window higher. Crawling thru, he clung onto the nearest bough & shimmied his way down. His shadow, meanwhile, lingered, mock-boxing w/ S-'s & Buck's shadows. When the two shadows converged on it, it hissed like a cornered cat, dove out the window & scurried down the rustling branches to join its human counterpart.

Chapter 11

As FILKIN GRIMSPOON jounced about his limo-carriage, he bit his lower lip. A legal pad lay cradled in his lap. According to conventional wisdom, his campaign's ultimate success would lay in his ability to appeal to the lowest common denominator. His pencil having scratched three pages' worth of complex algorithmic equations, no matter how he calculated, he kept arriving @ the same conclusion: the lowest common denominator of any number was always one. He couldn't argue w/ the facts. He moistened his lips as he noted further: the only difference bwtn one & One...was how big he made the 'O.'

Next to the aspiring lawyer-turned-politician, his young niece also jounced about the carriage, her face buried in a book. Having suffered multiple paper cuts from her avid reading, her slender fingers were covered in bandages. She read in rapt attention, @ times reading aloud bits of trivia she felt worth sharing. Directly across from Grimspoon sat Bubba J Gumm, his champagne manager; next to Bubba sat the cross-eyed cosmetologist, Geri Riggs.

"These little home 'pow-wows' are critical to our S-election hopes," Gumm was explaining to the nodding Mz Riggs.

As much as Grimspoon hated these pow-wows, he knew Bubba was right. And since hiring Mz Riggs, his campaign had done a 180. Born w/ a needle in her mouth & several thru her nose, the long-legged strawberry blonde possessed an uncanny ability to intuit every voter's fantasy. Grimspoon marveled @ how in mere nanoseconds she could transform him into an object of voter worship. At one rally he was a bronzed beach bum, his blond, freedom-loving hair blowing in an artificially salted breeze. At another he was a silver-haired MD expertly signing off

116

on medical charts while stoically staving off well-cleavaged tho morally challenged nurse-practioners. And then a transvestite w/ a bewitching tiny mole above his upper lip & a heart of such good-natured innocence, it tugged relentlessly @ the purse strings of the mainly male audience. Mz Riggs had it w/in her cosmetic & haberdashery powers to work wonders.

"Listen to this, Uncle Filkin," his niece interrupted his musing, Grimspoon's eyes rollercoasting the smooth contours of Mz Rigg's crossed calves. "'Since the beginning of time there have been three basic needs of humankind: food...shelter...& clothing. For centuries food was w/held from the masses by the powerful and gluttonous—'"

"The wide of girth," Grimspoon interjected.

"'—but eventually,'" the girl continued, "'during the epoch of men & women like G-, J- & L-, a moratorium was declared against starvation. That no one be allowed to starve to death become a moral imperative—thus welfare was created.'"

"You mean taxes were increased," Gumm quipped.

The girl shrugged. "'But when the welfare system began to drain the One, the wide of girth took away people's shelter instead, & homelessness became an epidemic.'"

"That's very interesting, Mouse."

"Ah, ah, ah," Gumm scolded. "Tonite, she's Belinda."

"Sorry...my pet name for her," the politician explained to Mz Riggs. "When she was yay high, she used to sit in some corner, quiet as a mouse, chewing on her braids & staring @ her shadow." Grimspoon smiled @ his niece, who returned to her text.

"'So for centuries the disenfranchised suffered from homelessness, till the era of M-, P- & Q-. Now homelessness is a thing of—'"

"We're here," Gumm broke in, pointing to the corner townhouse of a residential complex. "Remember," he cautioned, "this is Woodbee territory. We use the cheap champagne. Not only can't they taste the difference, but the lingering aftertaste will remind them of you long after we're gone."

Grimspoon peered out @ what he recognized as a typical Woodbee abode. Falling short of the elegance & grandeur of the manors, mansions & palaces inhabited by your average D'leBaum, Rittl'baus, Smolet, or Dimpleson, Woodbee apartments, townhomes & residential suites nonetheless possessed their own modest charm. With their bent for all things practical & utilitarian, the industrious Woodbee had devised & perfected abodes lauded for their self-sustaining, self-waxing, self-serving, self-involved & self-seeking features. The particular house before him touted several ostentatious extensions—rendering it self-righteous as well.

"A man's home is his hassle," Gumm quipped, quoting Chin Pow Kung, ancient sage & composer of the world's most quoted fortune cookies.

"Homes have a way of eating their owners out of house & home," Grimspoon countered, also quoting the ancient sage.

Still, these self-regulating units did manage to take out their own garbage, Grimspoon reminded himself. And most were self-protecting as well: maintaining surveillance around the clock, their antennae ever on the alert lest a burglar, solicitor or Jehovah's Witness ascend the high porches to ring the booby-trapped doorbells.

"Come in, Mr Grimspoon," a smiling, silver-haired man greeted the politician. "I'm Dr Buncle, but please call me Carl. Come in, all of you. We're in the central feeding room." The doctor held a large pair of tongs, which he used to point the way.

As they entered the unit's centermost room, the doctor lifted the lid from a decorative plastic tub. He reached w/ his tongs to extract a cut of raw meat, which he promptly tossed twd a feeding duct. The meat immediately disappeared, swallowed by the house's interior w/ a long slurp, followed by a satisfied belch.

As the town's leading opposition candidate entered, he smiled & waved to the myriad curious, suspicious andor skeptical faces gathered therein. Mz Riggs sprung immediately into action. Within minutes the tall, gangly politician was sporting half a moustache & half a beard; the other half of his face was clean-shaven. This, Riggs later explained, was to show solidarity w/ the clean-shaven among the guests w/ out alienating those of a bohemian bent. The checkered sports coat & tie were to appeal to anyone into checkers or chess, while one foot in argyle sock, the other sockless would strategically win over the professional class but show sympathy for the clothesless. As several in the room seemed to have raised children & apparently barely survived the experience, Riggs finished by pinning a SAY *YES* TO YOUTH IN ASIA button to her boss's lapel. Several heads bobbed up & down in silent solidarity.

While Mz Riggs busied herself w/ her boss's attire, Mssr Gumm proved equally industrious. Champagne glasses were swiftly dispersed, each fluted tumbler filled immediately & never thereafter allowed to reach half empty (or half full, as Grimspoon was instructed to say).

"Thank you, Geri." The politician acknowledged his ass't before introducing his champagne manager, who, w/ the flair of a magician, produced complimentary beer nuts & salted cashews, which he passed around by the bagful.

"And this is my niece, Belinda," Grimspoon added. "Ordinarily she's be home doing her homework but her parents asked me to watch her while they settle a domestic dispute by trying to kill each other.

"Let me start by thanking you all for being here & for graciously granting me this opportunity to address some of the more pressing issues no doubt weighing on your pocketbooks." Feeling his face flush, the politician swallowed several times, his Adam's apple going into spasms. As a stalling tactic, he raised his glass in salute, looking about the room, his glance pausing each time he encountered a familiar face.

Ira Fuse stood in back, his dark eyes scowling, his tattooed arms crossed, his nostrils flaring. As Bubba had forewarned the politician, Fuse, along w/ the rest of his barbershop quartet, had been pushing for a hefty tax on reckless baldness. "You tax 'em for losing their hair," they argued in harmony, "& they'll do everything in their power to save andor restore it."

Seated near Fuse was Calman Norr, the town's most antiquated coroner. Next to Cal was his lifelong friend, Poppy K Cox, the town's most antique antique dealer. Commanding three chairs btwn them were the Shale twins: Eunice, who headed the Dept of Grievances (Petty Division), & Blanche, founder of the Institute of I-Know-You-Are But-What-Am-I?, said institute in a current uproar over Blanche's refusal to retire. Within the sea of faces, Grimspoon spotted Police Chief Willoughby. Half in uniform, the other half sporting Hawaiian shorts, the Chief of Police dabbed his forehead w/ a kerchief, his nervous eyes ever on the alert, darting like a traffic cop looking all ways simultaneously.

"Before we go further," the Chief interjected, clearing his throat, "BEFORE WE GO ANY FURTHER, let us state FOR THE RECORD that this meeting, THIS MEETING, is of level 3 classification—PROTECTED BY STATUTE vi paragraph 19 & statute viii paragraph 12, of the right-to-assemble-for-the-purpose-of-disassembling clause—THUS REQUIRING any spies, ANY SPIES, DOUBLE AGENTS OR TURNCOATS FOR HIRE to present, I REPEAT, TO PRESENT SAID LICENSES, that we may be able to determine what may or may not be said during this FRANK & OPEN discussion."

As no one present spoke (our surveillance team being exempt from said statutes by virtue of their not having paid attention), Dr Buncle opened his tub to remove a choice cut of seasoned kid's feet, tossing the cutlet down the feeding duct, which promptly swallowed it, slurped, hiccupped & burped. Twice.

The Police Chief continued. "Very well, VERY WELL, THEN. LET IT BE STATED THAT AS NO LICENSED SPIES HAVE ELECTED TO IDENTIFY

THEMSELVES, we may proceed with the utmost confidence. LET IT ALSO BE UNDERSTOOD that henceforth, for the duration of this meeting, I shall speak @ a normal volume, refraining...REFRAINING FROM LOUDLY ARTICULATING ANY VALUABLE INFORMATION TO INCRIMINATE THOSE WITH WHOM I PRETEND TO ENGAGE IN FRIENDLY CONVERSATION." The police chief nodded twd Grimspoon, signaling his permission for the politician to proceed.

"Thank you, Chief Willoughby." Grimspoon shifted in his seat, one eye trained on the notebook Bubba had slid in his lap, flipping to the INTRODUCTORY REMARKS. "First," the politican read, "I would like to explain my decision to come out in full support of the clothesless."

Several chairs shifted as numerous sighs were heaved. "What do any of us care about the clothesless?" Fuse snorted, his hands balled into fists. "If you want to know the truth, it's the nakedly bald we should be worrying about."

"I t-too, b-beg to differ," Eunice Shale joined in. "I'm t-tired of my hard-earned One going to support those who c-can't keep their p-pants on. I say t-tax the clothesless."

"B-believe me, I f-feel your f-frustration, Eunice," the politician mimicked.

Bubba rolled his eyes & shook his head, sighing as he flipped the notebook to another page.

As Grimspoon read the pr-prepared text, he raised his arms, allowing Mz Riggs to slip on an oversized undershirt & replace his checkered tie w/ a solid black one. "B-but d-d-don't you see? This b-bias against those unable to dr-dress themselves is part of the Brittle plot to k-keep us @ odds w/ each other."

Again Bubba rolled his eyes, shaking his head.

"I ain't got no problem wid bald people...or the clothesless," Cal Norr declared. "Baldness is jest PUP's way of sayin' when the hair goes, the body ain't too fur behin'. But tell me, young fella...what's dis I here 'bout youse aposing da rights a dead people? Da dead need protection, too...spes'ly gainst dere so-called loved ones, who would rather scrimp on a cheap flea-bidden coffin, radder den purchase for dere dearly departed a coffin scrumptious enuff for da dead to be proud to be berried in..."

"What eggactly is your po'sition on Nibian oil?" the antique dealer cut in. "Ev'rybody knows nuthin' polishes & pretects genuine artificial wood like pure adulterated Nibian oil. But now all this artificial, im'tation Nibian oil is floodin' the market."

"Youse can't ignore da rights of dead people," the coroner persisted, "jest cause they can't exactly says what dey wants. It's our duty t' speak for the deceased & to defend their right to be berried in coffins of the highest quality...whether their cheap ash relatives can afford it, or not."

"Some of this so-called im'tation oil is act'lly squeezed from the processed pulp of Canaan mulattoes," Cox continued. "Which is false advertising: unregulated false advertising @ that!"

As each citizen defended his/her enlightened self-interest, a low but persistent grumble percolated from the feeding ducts. Gumm & Riggs meanwhile came frantically to their employer's aid. Riggs rapidly switched wig after wig after wig, each hairpiece growing fuller in thickness in hopes of placating the barber. She applied opaque white makeup to Grimspoon's increasingly flushing cheeks, displaying great skill in making said cheeks appear sunken & sickly. As a finishing touch, she replaced his bold black tie w/ one sporting a bearded skull & tattooed crossbones.

Bubba, meanwhile, employed both hands, flipping pages back & forth, deftly dog-earing every subject currently under discussion, his glib employer skillfully modifying, clarifying, @ times extemporizing on his varying unwavering positions. The politician called both for respect twd Nibians as being nearly almost fully human, while acknowledging that the only good Nibian was one crushed & pulverized so as to extract the maximum quantity of their natural oils. He insisted both on respect & reverence twd the deceased while acknowledging that should said deceased rise up & assert their wishes, he would be among the first to certainly listen. He further petitioned for empathy & compassion twd those suffering chronic hair loss while simultaneously acknowledging that each hair dislodged did perhaps diminish one's stature on the scale of full humanhood & thus, by logic, might diminish one's human privileges.

Seeming to have placated coroner, barber & antique dealer, each of whom grew less inclined to interrupt, the politician turned back to his defining issue.

"On our way over here," he asserted, "my niece reminded me of our long struggle for equality. How for centuries our forefathers fought & sacrificed to conquer starvation. And they did. Eventually. And how for centuries the disenfranchised then suffered from homelessness. Now homelessness is a thing of the past. All that is left is the clothesless & the underclothed."

"Humph!" Blanche Shale challenged, looking around as if hoping to rally support. "It's bad enuff the less fortunate go around baring their souls...do they now have to bare their butts as well?"

121

"But don't you see, Blanche?" Grimspoon pushed the notebook aside & resisted the starched white shirt Riggs struggled to slip his arms thru. "We eliminate clotheslessness & all the basic needs of all humankind will be met...guaranteed forevermore. We won't need to quibble about such things again."

"What's wr-wrong w/ quibbling?" Eunice blurted, her cheeks puffed, spittle flying. "We stop qu-quibbling & half my st-staff are out of a j-job!"

"It's the wide of girth we want to put out of a job," Grimspoon countered.

Noticing Eunice & Blanche exchange glances, then glower @ the politician, Bubba covered his eyes. "Who wants more champagne?" he shouted, pressing the notebook back in Grimspoon's lap, then tossing out bags of beer nuts like fireworks.

"But to do that," Dr Buncle proposed, "we need to turn to the One...& to do that, we need to tax someone."

"Someone that is not us," another voice chimed in, numerous heads nodding in agreement.

"I still say we tax all bald egos," Fuse insisted, pounding the palm of one hand w/ his fist. "No offense, Chief, but people are always losing hair. We might never have to tax anyone else again."

"But they'll all just s-start w-wearing hats," Eunice offered.

"Then we'll tax hats...maybe head scarves & wigs, too."

"What if we pooled our One?" the politician suggested. "Each of us in this room, we gather our One—w/draw it from the greedy fingers of those who have historically used it to keep us @ each other's throats. What if Woodbees, bald & hair-endowed, living & dead, proponents of pure Nibian oil & those inclined twd artificial substitutes...what if we all joined w/ Nibians, w/ Canaans, w/ Dregs— "

"N-not w/ Nibians."

"Yes, Nibians," Grimspoon insisted.

"Cert'ly not wid dem Canaans."

"Yes, w/ them Canaans...& even those nasty Nabors living next door."

Despite being swept along by his own rhetoric, the politician paused, his natural inclination to push on curtailed by Gumm, who had flipped to a notebook page headed:

PREGNANT PAUSE
Take deep breath...
follow w/ woe-is-me sigh

Quickly scanning the subsequent text, Grimspoon followed its instructions to a T. At the first hint of fidgeting & muffled coughs, he started from the top, repeating everything he now knew would resonate, making sure he used words of three syllables or less, speaking slowly & smiling till his jaws ached. Riggs, meanwhile, frequently softened his dry lips w/ lip gloss—pink, she insisted, calculating a few men in the room most likely swung the other way.

* * * * *

SEVERAL DAYS SWIFTLY ELAPSED. Days in which Grimspoon champagne flowed increasingly down the gullets of more & more converts. Days in which S- mopped many a floor, squeegied many a window, emptied many a wastebasket. Days in which Smolet rummaged thru those same baskets, scoured those same floors, checked behind the very drapes S- dusted & along the sills of the windows S- washed. For the bank's new ass't janitor, each day dragged listlessly into the next. Stubbs Farrago seemed never far from sight, his crooked finger forever poised to point out some missed speck of dust or wag back & forth in condescending disapproval.

On Thursday morning a loud banging catapulted S- out of a bone-weary slumber. The day was fully dressed, the sky wearing a bright blue skirt, the sun poking her shining face inside S-'s window, tsk'ing him for letting such a beatific morning pass him by. Larks, chickadees & bullfinches clung to tree branches, serenading the dragonflies & wasps returning from vacation. Roses & lilac bushes opened their shutters to air out their petals, sending both bumblebee & yellow-jackets into fits of drunken ecstasy. A groggy S- slipped from beneath his ruffled sheets, his shadow struggling to hold him upright as it attempted to rub the sleep from S-'s eyes. The banging from below persisted.

S- dressed himself, using **Rules of the Road** as a guide, his shadow running a comb thru his uncooperative curls. Both struggled w/ the shoelaces, S- finally throwing his arms up in despair. His shadow, too, soon gave up. Prompted by a sudden eerie silence below, S- gingerly lifted the trapdoor, insisting his shadow climb down first.

At the far end of the hall, Mrs Sticky Buns was consulting Violet & Mz Vera in a low whisper. She paused abruptly, turning & smiling @ her houseguest. Strapped to her hands were pan covers she wielded like cymbals. A flat straw hat rested uneasily atop her pompadour, with a blue, orange & purple band wrapped around the hat's base. A sash of similar colors was strapped across her bosom, her blouse, skirt & slippers coordinated to clash. On her feet two buck-toothed slippers wiggled their chipmunk noses, their puffed-out chests draped w/ identical sashes & sporting tiny buttons similar to the one pinned to Mrs Smolet's sash. 'My ONE is bigger than your ONe,' the iridescent buttons read.

S- blinked several times before cautiously descending the steps.

"Well, good morning, my little sugar cookie. Did i wake you from dreaming of me?" The lady of the house sashayed up to him, her smile dripping w/ syrupy sweetness. Hearing first one, then another door open, she immediately backed away.

Buck appeared barefoot in military briefs, pulling on his camouflage pajamas. An IF YOU CAN'T BUY 'EM, BOMB 'EM T-shirt covered his broad chest. "What the hail is all that racket?" he complained.

Across the hall, Penny stood in her doorway, her hair coiffured into an ocean liner split in two against her iceberg of a skull. Donning knickers several sizes too large, the girl bent to tie her army boots, her floral tank top an intricate array of gasping flowers, their stems strangled by a merciless onslaught of poison ivy vines.

"It's the first ofvicious day of S-election season," their mother cheerfully announced. She slammed the pan covers together. CRASH! BAM! BANG! "That seasoning we all get to choose whoever your father thinks should reprehense us @ the bullot box!" CRASH! BANG! The lady of the house herded her protesting offspring down the stairs. "Your father & sister are waiting down below," she called after them. Pivoting, she winked @ S-, lowering her eyelids & puckering her lips, adroitly blocking his every attempt to slip past.

"How come you leave your trapdoor locked @ nite?" She smiled, lowering her voice. "You afraid the sugar fairy might come & scoot you off to Never-Neverland? What if someone had killed everyone in the house except for me," she pouted, "& i came up for someone to console me?"

S- stood speechless. Mrs Smolet furrowed her forehead, her long pinched nose twitching, her crow's-feet twinkling like warning lights. Her pouting lips broke into a broad smile as wafts of perfume rose from btwn her breasts to slither up his nostrils. Flanked by his shadow, S- squeezed around the lady of the house, hurrying to join the others in the dining room.

The entire room was decked in the same colors as Mrs Smolet's sash. Orange, blue & purple balloons, ribbons & festooning streamers hung from the chandelier, the lamps, the hanging plants. The tablecloth was a tricolored flag, the usual china replaced by ceramic replicas of Mrs Sticky Buns' button: "My ONe is bigger than your One" arced around the top rim; "No, my ONE is bigger than your oNE" arced around the bottom.

"Our fair city's colors," Mr Smolet explained, using his beard to wipe orange toast crumbs from his lips. "Sit, my boy. Sit.

"This is a very, very special day for you, is it not?" The banker removed the unlit cigar from his mouth & leaned over the table. "S-election season is the most august time of year. When else does the fate of our entire micropolis rest solely in the mind & fingers of yours truly; i mean you, my boy." The banker aimed his cigar @ S-.

"Here, we believe in debate, in listening w/out objection to the misguided opinions of others. Then, just @ the point when we & our opponents can barely stand each other, we cast our respective bullots. And, in case of a tie...in case their pros & our cons are evenly divided, who gets to cast the deciding bullot in favor of truth, justice & a more comprehensive everlasting One?" Smolet cocked a questioning eyebrow & smiled broadly.

"You, my boy. Think of the power, the responsibility, the burden...a burden i would be only too happy to relieve you of...but that wouldn't be demicratic, would it? So today, you & i take a stroll to the City & Counting Bldg, where we verify, clarify, certify & rarify every bone in your judicious body...till we turn you into a lean, clean voting machine." The banker dabbed both sides of his grin w/ his beard, returning the cigar to his thick lips.

"Now I know what you're thinking. You have to report to work. Your magnanimous supervisor, Stubbs, will no doubt be waiting to demonstrate the finer points of mixing ammonia w/ warm water. You, dedicated employee that you are, want to get in early so as to brush up on the mop-pushing techniques you've been practicing all week.

"But this is far more auspicious." The banker brandished his soggy cigar. "So important that i will lead you personally up & down, back & forth, over & around the hallowed halls of our Municipal Complex. And when you leave that bldg & hurry twd work, you will hold in the palm of your tiny little trigger finger, the fate of all that you see around you."

S- looked @ all that he saw around him. Guarded by a formidable deployment of plastic warriors, Buck was wolfing down a stack of blue pancakes. Penny poked listlessly @ an abstract arrangement of purple hashbrowns & orange eggs Benedict. Pearl, her pigtails sporting orange ribbons, was firing globs of blue oatmeal @ anything that didn't move—& everything that did.

"So what do you say to that, my boy?" Smolet blinked @ S-.

Several coins tumbled from Buck's pajamas. The man-child winked @ S-, his dimples twinkling in impish delight. Aware his father was eyeballing him under disapproving eyebrows, Buck sought to create a diversion. "Mummy, could you pass that purple stuff?" he asked.

The lady of the house complied, promptly passing the dyed bacon while humming cheerfully & reaching to squeeze S-'s outstretched hand. In cascading squeals of approval, she stated how proud of him she was, adding that the right to cast a bullot was a rite of plastage, that he was becoming a man & more like a son to her. She too winked, her hand releasing his fingers to reach under the table & caress his knee.

His face flushed, S- looked around the room. Penny sat silently, stabbing the life out of her breakfast. Across from him, Pearl made faces, giggling every time she aimed her threatening spoon in his direction. Mr Smolet chewed on the cigar clamped btwn his lips. S- glanced repeatedly @ Buck, the man-child seeming to do everything in his power to avoid eye contact w/ his father.

"Your Uncle Harry has been asking about you," the banker finally ventured, removing both his beard & glasses, setting them aside.

Buck glanced up, his dimples caught off guard. "Who, me?"

Mr Smolet fumbled thru his pockets. He produced a wad of fresh banknotes. "He wants you to come & see him sometime today."

The banker removed the band around the crisp legal tender. He counted silently, his mouth moving, his cigar bobbing up & down. "Now that S-election is approaching," he interrupted his counting, "seems only fitting i increase you kids' allowances."

Buck & Penny sprung to attention, their respective forks coming to a halt. Their eyes focused on their father's counting fingers, their imaginations counting along.

"Of course, I expect each of you to put this One to good use." Their father paused, detecting a grimace or two, or a hint thereof.

"Yes, sir," Buck assured him, removing a few soldiers to provide the expectant One safe passage.

"Okay by me," his sister responded. "Whatever you say, Pupa."

"Buck." The father turned to his son. "What time should i tell Uncle Harry to expect you?"

"Ah, um." Buck looked around the room. He sat back, coins tumbling as he set his fork down. "Not tonite," he offered squeamishly, glancing @ S-.

"There's no time like the present," the banker countered, fanning the bills, raising them to his nose, fanning them again.

"I'm helping a friend w/ *his* homework," Buck explained.

126

"You can help your uncle w/ his homework." The banker whiffed the bills again. "This S-election could be our tuffest yet. What could be more important than contributing your all to the sound defeat of those who would send you, your family & ultimately all our hopes for world supremacy to the Turkey Shoot?" The banker's brows wriggled like worms: first one, then the other, then both together.

"You've been bellyaching for months about no longer having a worthy enemy, one we can ruthlessly slaughter w/out the slightest regard twd their humanity. No one is more dedicated to ensuring we never run out of enemies than your Uncle Harry. The man has spent his life identifying people worthy of our utmost contempt. Let's say tonite...about sixish?"

"But i really need to help this friend," Buck protested. "He's having trouble w/ his search & destroy technique. Total annihilation doesn't come natural to some people &—"

"Now, Buck." The banker put on his glasses, magnifying his baby blues to twice their normal size. "I commend your dedication, but you've said so yourself: mass mutilation day in & day out can get tedious. A brief ceasefire will give you time to rebuild your resolve, gather new strength, restock your arsenal. A break will do you good. It's only one nite. Remember, son: all of history's great empires have had to endure painstaking periods of peaceful coexistence. But what better time to amass new, even more devious methods of attack?" Pausing long enuff to allow his fatherly wisdom to sink in, the banker added, "Let's make it 6:30."

His dimples drooping, Buck reluctantly acquiesced.

"Good. In fact, we'll go together." Smolet slid several bills past Buck's broken line of defense. Buck hesitated, waiting for his father's attention to turn to Penny before begrudgingly snatching up the bills.

"As for you, young lady," the banker addressed his eldest daughter, "you have your graduation fest coming up."

Penny sulked, her ocean-liner hairdo unable to sink any lower. The girl stared @ her uneaten breakfast, her right hand clutching a fork, her left thumb poised over her favorite buzzer.

"You may think we're trying to sell you off to the highest bidder," the banker suggested, "& certainly the higher the bid, the more this speaks of the bidder's willingness to give his all for you—but actually it's your happiness that concerns your mother & me most.

"No, wait. Hear me out!" the banker urged as Penny's thumb began a threatening descent. He turned to his wife for added support. "Isn't that right, Sticky Buns?"

"Abstinutely," his wife cheerfully confirmed, momentarily pausing from massaging S-'s knee.

The banker reached for his false beard to wipe his forehead. "Remember when you were younger? All those Dregs, Woodbees & whatnots—giving up their lunch money to jump thru your hoop? Don't you think it's time to bring those hoops out of retirement? Time to begin polishing your gyrating hip technique? Boys love it when you do that. Graduation will be here before you know it. There's many a Brittle boy willing to put his very soul into hock—maybe even take out a high interest loan—just for the chance to jump inside your hoop.

"Once you're married, w/ a good lawyer, you can get even more out of him—more than that school-appointed lawyer is getting out of me now."

Smolet resumed counting the banknotes, repeatedly starting over as Penny turned her breakfast into a bull's-eye, her fork a four-pronged arrow gouging @ its center.

Mrs Smolet removed her hand from S-'s knee to come to her husband's aid. "And as you know, dear, you could net far greater One if you—"

The banker panicked, clutching his wife's arm, interrupting her mid-sentence as Penny's tiny fist rose. The girl's hand descended in slow motion, her defiant eyes challenging both parents in a duel of wills.

The banker swiftly slapped all but one bill on the table, sliding them smoothly past the rim of Penny's placemat. His daughter's fist fell away from the buzzer. The final banknote the banker slid twd his youngest, who promptly piled half her oatmeal on it.

As Smolet reattached his beard, his eyes suddenly widened. He jumped up w/out a word, racing from the room as fast as his jiggling body could carry him.

Mrs Smolet flashed a weak smile, returning her hand to S-'s knee as she addressed her children. "Now, kids, to prepare ourselves for the upcrumbling campaign, we have new rule books for everyone." The lady of the house clasped her hands in delight. She triumphantly pressed one of Penny's buzzers, a dumb waiter appearing, pushing a cart on which four crisp, hot-off-the-presses, shiny new manuals glistened.

"Buck." She reached for the uppermost book & passed it to her son. "You must under no circumcision be seen w/ anyone of the female perspiration clad in nothing. It isn't decent. Under no circumcision, young man—be it in pubic or in private.

"Young lady," she addressed Penny, "there is many a wolf in Woodbee clothing, of sound bidding age, mind you, who would love nothing more than to sink their hard, hairy teeth into your soft pink..." Mrs Smolet paused, looking over @ her youngest. As Pearl was currently engrossed in aiming oatmeal @ S-, the lady of the house continued, "...who would love to sink their hairy teeth into your precious petals. An extra eighth-inch of mascara, a few generous dollops of perfume, a strategic fluttering of eyelashes in the direction of some weak-kneed Brittle stud-muffin might just prevent such a tragedy from occurring, young lady. This manual will give you lots of helpful hints."

As Penny declined the manual, Mrs Smolet slid it beside the untouched banknotes. "At least take it. If nothing else, use it to balance a wobbly dresser or that lopsided vanity of yours.

"And as to you, our honored guest," Mrs Smolet slipped the third volume twd S-, a syrupy smile oozing from her lips, "seeing as you are new & unstudded as to the regular rules, perhaps you would benefit from some private tudoring. We can start when you get home tonite." She ran a polished fingernail along S-'s unshaven chin, the hand then reaching under the table to gently reassure his knee. Almost as an afterthought, she handed Pearl the fourth manual, cautioning her youngest not to get oatmeal on it—which her youngest promptly did.

Chapter 12

As OUR CHIEF FINANCIAL OFFICER waddled down the front porch steps, S- fell in two paces behind, a camera slung around his neck. After negotiating the moat & three iron gates, the two were soon weaving around bystanders & among pedestrians, the banker waving to anyone & everyone—especially those not looking his way. S- took to snapping pictures. He took several shots of someone gardening & a few more of someone mugging the gardener. He captured an action shot of a prostitute sitting on a john & several of a woman tossing away a child who kept crawling back. His lens followed the lazy loops of circling starlings, then adjusted its aperture to take in a grove of shiftless adolescent alders, their burgeoning leaves spread open like green butterflies poised to take flight. Should a house hiccup or a storefront yawn, he was lightning quick in capturing that as well.

"Put that thing away," the banker chided, pulling a fresh cigar from his coat jacket & placing the wrapper in a panhandler's upturned palm. "You'll scare the pigeons."

S- capped the lens, only later realizing he hadn't seen a pigeon since he'd entered town. As he tagged behind, he observed the banker occasionally slip down an alley to rifle thru a dumpster, once or twice dropping to his knees to disembowel a trashcan. On several occasions his employer would find an unwrapped, perfectly intact cigar.

"I'm finding more & more of these," Smolet mused. "Curiously enuff, they're always my brand."

"There it is." The banker stopped abruptly, pointing a stubby frankfurter @ what appeared to S- to be a concrete bulldog, its sagging cheeks, muscular haunches &

puffed-out chest dominating the suddenly obscured horizon. "See that bldg there? That's where we hang our criminals for misbehaving. The bldg connected to it: that's where we try them for having misbehaved. And the bldg behind that is where we house our Bored of Education—that's where we get 'em to misbehave in the first place." The banker beamed proudly, turning to face S-. "You see, my boy: government is an intricately interwoven jigsaw puzzle—w/ a few pieces missing just to keep things interesting.

"Now, see that clock up there?" The banker pointed skyward, S- tilting his head till his neck cramped. "I get a shiver every time i see it."

S- stared @ a dome-shaped obelisk pointing like a middle finger @ the sun. A clock w/ faded numbers & mangled hands dominated its flat, stoic surface.

S- gestured to his camera, the banker giving an approving nod. S- snapped several pictures.

"That clock is a timeless reminder of how men—civilized men, mind you—have bent time to our own purpose. See, there was a time, long before you or i were even conceived, when most calendars had but a measly twelve months. Hard to believe, isn't it?" Smolet chewed a moment. S- continued to snap photos. "It was a third cousin of my great granddaddy's mistress who first observed how when we're bored—I mean, *really* bored—time seems to stretch on forever. Our psychologists call it the 'Bored Dumb Effect.' You'd be surprised how much time you can extract from a Menial by giving them really boring tasks. A clock may have only twelve hours, but those twelve hours can stretch on for a near eternity...& @ minimum wage, think of the savings. Quite a triumph in both time & financial management."

The banker sighed, walking on. "The only hitch is that the workers complain. A lot. An awful lot. But...give 'em a couple of holidays...name a few after their martyrs & what can they say? They'll endure just about anything—even think we're doing them a favor.

"Here we are." Smolet gestured w/ his chin twd a tall flight of concrete steps. At the top, a gray-faced, steel-eyed monolith almost dared S- & the banker to approach. MUNICIPAL CITY & COUNTING BLDG was chiseled above its entrance. The two mounted the stairs, S- perplexed as the steps grew steeper & higher apart the farther they climbed. Following the banker's lead, he began to crawl & claw his way up, both men on their hands & knees by the time they reached the solid oak doors. The doors' hinges squealed as the two struggled to open them wide enuff to pass thru.

S-'s ears were immediately assaulted by the clickety-clack of hurrying footsteps,

131

the incessant clicking of ballpoint pens, the squeaking of rubber soles on the shiny polished floors & myriad persons mumbling as if someone was actually listening to them. Many shuffled down the halls, seeming to ricochet off the stone pillars like unwitting pinballs, all the while toting briefcases, clutching notebooks, or rummaging thru handbags & satchels.

S- followed the banker past the double doors of the Dept of the Inferior, a long line of applicants gathered in front, extending around a corner & down the hall. Further on, Smolet shook hands w/ a magistrate he addressed as Juris, tho he introduced the one-eyed dwarf to S- as Mr Prudence. Likewise S- was introduced to the Vice Chair of Character Assassins, who took copious notes as he probed S- w/ a barrage of personal questions. S- answered as best he could, all the while staring @ a sign prominently displayed in the office window:

HELP WANTED
Experts Needed
NO EXPERIENCE NECESSARY

Leading S- up a stairwell, Smolet passed the Ministry of Proper Gander, next door to the Honorable Rigor Mortis, who held lifelong tenure w/ the Dept of Ideas Etched in Stone. Backtracking, they passed the Joint Committee on Snap Judgments, then the Office for the Administering of Mixed Metaphors. Finally the banker ushered S- thru a set of doors labeled VOTARY REGISTRATION. The padded doors opened into a waiting room, its walls plastered w/ laminated posters: life-sized sketches of human beans each stamped: *NOT WANTED.* S- scanned the various names: Wetdweller, Cockortwo, Nibian, Butterbutt, Dixsticks, Canaan, Blueboot, Erstwilder, Wignut, Handpanler. Along each poster's margins were a list of telltale characteristics: droopy eyelids, pear-shaped nostrils, knuckles bristling w/ chest hair, low test scores, pink cuticles, left-footedness, two pinkies, an innate inability to genuflect or cower before one's superiors....

Smolet lumbered over to the reception desk, where a three-eyed receptionist multitasked; she handed the financial officer a clipboard, a child-proof pencil & an application form.

"Sit," the banker ordered S-.

Smolet filled in the application as S- stared @ an even larger poster tacked on the door marked EXAMINATION ROOM. A life-sized diagram of an 'Average Voter' had been sketched w/ stick-figure accuracy. The diagram charted a voter's entire circulatory system, prominently highlighting the tiny moral center surrounded by horseshoe-shaped libidinal lymph-nodes & several winding corridors of self-interest. Also prominent were the bribery center (a pretzel-shaped organ said to register human ideals) & the jugular rectum, which, according to an *, was where most informed voters got their information. S- squinted to read the fine print relating to the effects of varying bribes on the pulmonary purse when the door swung open.

A man in a white surgical gown appeared, his polka dotted bowtie slightly askew, his moustache picture perfect. As the man sniffed the air, his rabbit-shaped nose twitching, his narrowing eyes zeroed in on S-. "I'm Dr Cataract," he announced in a deep, resonant voice S- found reassuring. "I'm filling in for Dr Coff. Jack is out sick today."

His nose still twitching, the doctor's lazy eye alighted on the banker doodling in the margins of S-'s application. "I'll be right w/ you," he told S-, lunging @ Smolet, yanking the clipboard from the banker's grasp.

"I suppose you intend to vote for him, too," the doctor scolded.

Smolet's startled blue eyes beat a hasty retreat as his cheeks flushed red. "I'll just wait here," he timidly reassured S-.

Leading S- into a small drab room, the doctor cleared his throat, ordering S- to undress, then sit on a narrow cot. While S- obeyed, the doctor plopped onto a rolling metal stool, eyeing his patient thru lowered eyelids, continually smoothing his moustache & clearing his throat. "All your clothes," the doctor insisted, noting S- had stopped @ his underwear. "We must be sure you contain no blemishes, no offensive moles, blackheads, or unsightly splotches that might impede your ability to make an informed choice." The doctor smiled, his own mottled complexion glowing.

While S- stripped further, shivering under the direct blast of a purring air conditioner, the doctor gathered a growing arsenal of pointed instruments, testing each tip before arranging them on a tray already stacked w/ saws, vices & an electric hand drill.

"Open wide," he instructed, rolling closer & pointing w/ his cleft chin @ S-'s mouth.

S- opened his mouth.

"Wider."

S- opened wider.

"Say ah."

"Ah...aghhhh!" S- screeched.

133

The doctor grimaced, tossing a spiked tongue depressor back on the tray. "Funny thing about pain," he huffed. "It's no laughing matter, is it?" He cocked a threatening eyebrow before picking up a scalpel. "Turn your head & hold still."

S- turned his head, instinctively pulling away just as the scalpel nicked his earlobe. *Ow!* his shadow screamed.

Dr Cataract rolled his stool back, eyeing S- from a distance, smoothing his moustache as his lazy eye drifted in its socket. He opened a metal drawer, rattling its contents as he extracted a pair of rubber gloves. Tossing the scalpel aside, he stretched the gloves, snapping them on violently as he stared cross-eyed @ S-.

"Make yourself comfortable," he instructed. "This won't hurt a bit." From an icebox, he pulled a metal tray piled high w/ forceps, a stethoscope, a plessor, various pliers & a small array of blunt, phallic-shaped devices.

"Are you comfortable?" he asked a moment later.

S- blinked.

Dr Cataract scooted fwd, displaying the stethoscope as if to demonstrate it wasn't pointed. Ice crystals coated its rubber surface. Without bothering to hook one end in his ears, the physician thrust it against S-'s chest, S- jolting, sucking in air as cold shivers ran the length of his body. When S-'s teeth began to chatter, Dr Cataract reached for a roll of duct tape. He tore a strip large enuff to cover S-'s mouth. "It's important you not make a sound. Otherwise this examination will be null & void." Twirling on his stool, the physician grabbed one of the phallic instruments, running its ice-flaked surface up & down S-'s bare back. When S- groaned, the doctor cast a disapproving stare; S- guiltily quieted down, struggling to endure the chilling discomfort.

"So, I understand you've come to town in search of someone," the physician queried, raising an eyebrow. "Is that so?"

"Yes-s-s." S- shivered, his reply muffled by the tape.

"Is that so?" the doctor repeated sharply, running another icy cold instrument along S-'s back.

S- flinched, nodding while groaning, his teeth still chattering.

"Take deep breaths," the doctor instructed. "Breathe in...breathe out." He rolled another instrument up & down S-'s stomach, S- clutching the sides of the cot.

"And have you found this person?"

S- shook his head.

"You're not lying to me, are you?" Dr Cataract eyed his patient suspiciously. He placed a cold pair of pliers against S-'s thigh. "If you're lying, I'll know. We have

134

ways of extracting the truth." He clicked the pliers. "Admit it: you've already found him, haven't you?"

S- shook his head insistently, his shadow coming to his defense, screaming in the doctor's ear. Cataract reached for more tape.

"We know why you're here," the doctor snarled, baring his molars, his once reassuring baritone taking on a harsh edge. "This innocent act isn't fooling anyone."

While S- cringed, his shadow pummeled the physician's shoulder & chest, tugged @ his arms & grabbed frantically to divert the pliers, which seemed bent on homing in on S-'s shriveling private parts. "Don't think you can waltz into our micropolis w/ that dull-witted expression of yours & destroy everything we've worked for. Now cough," the physician ordered, his voice curt & tinged w/ annoyance. "Cough, I said!" He reached for a larger set of pliers.

S- coughed, the doctor swiftly prying S-'s legs open & scooting close enuff to prevent S- from closing them. As Cataract fumbled for a handsaw, S- emitted an involuntary cry; his shadow raced to the door, banging on its window, relieved when the door flew open. Smolet slid his chalky-white head thru the opening, his baby blues twinkling w/ amused curiosity. "All done?" he asked.

"Not quite." Cataract smiled feebly, smoothing his moustache & adjusting his bowtie. Releasing S-, he yanked the duct tape off, S-'s head snapping back from the force. "Apparently our patient has very sensitive political reflexes. Just give us another minute." The doctor smiled, shoo'ing the banker from the room.

Rolling his stool back to the far wall, Cataract stared long & hard @ his shivering patient. He tested the point of his largest scalpel, jerking as a small droplet of blood beaded on his finger. "You enjoy living w/ the esteemed Charles Dinero Smolet, don't you?" The doctor raised a brow, sucking the blood from his finger. "And you'd do anything the good banker asked, wouldn't you?"

S- sat tight lipped.

"C'mon, you can tell me. You've heard of doctor/patient confidentiality, haven't you? I won't breathe a word to another living soul. I promise."

S- continued to stare.

"I need to test your reflexes," the doctor then announced. "Go over to that icebox & place both hands palms down on the surface." Cataract picked up the plessor, studied it, then replaced it w/ a ball-peen hammer. Tears streamed down S-'s cheeks as the doctor pursed his lips & raised the hammer. S- closed his eyes, bracing himself, relieved by the sound of the hammer being tossed aside. "Nothing wrong w/ your reflexes," the doctor concluded.

"One last test. I need to examine your tear ducts." Pulling a lever, converting the cot into a chair, he instructed S- to sit back down. "We'll need to strap your head in so you don't move. Just a minute while I get this in place."

S- felt a leather strap encircle his head, another tighten around his chin. Widening S-'s eyelid w/ his cold fingers, the doctor reached w/ his other hand for something S- could not see. His shadow however, sounded an alarm, jumping btwn the two men, kicking & pounding, roping its arms around the doctor's neck, yanking as hard as it could. When he heard the whir of an electric drill, S- assumed the worst. He closed his free eye, bracing himself as tears began to blur his vision. When the whir ceased, followed by a heavy kerplunk as the doctor tossed the drill aside, his shadow heaved a sigh of relief.

Cataract brusquely rolled away & gathered his instruments. "I guess you really *are* as stupid as you look," he muttered, shaking his head.

"Look." He turned to frown @ S-. "We have no quarrel w/ you. But that man out there..." He pointed @ the door. "Oh, forget it," he concluded, dismissively waving his hand. He shook his head again, dumping the tray of instruments in a drawer & slamming it shut.

"When you find this friend of yours—*if* you find him—you tell him we will not be trifled w/ or trampled upon. Not by the fat-of-face, not by the wily-of-wallet. If this stranger tells you to fall in line w/ Smolet & his cadre of conniving catamites, we won't hesitate to nail you to a tree. You got that? If you're smart, you'll report to us before you do anything he tells you." Cataract tore off his gloves with two loud snaps. He tapped S- gently on the knee. "All done," he smiled, smoothing his moustache, which promptly slid from his face, fluttering onto the floor. Retrieving the application, the physician dashed off a few check marks, doodled a noose around the stuffed pig the banker had drawn & signed the document w/ an elaborate flair. "You can get dressed now."

As S- put on his clothes, the doctor went to a medicine cabinet. "Here," he said, pulling out a vial of pills. "These are to make you feel docile. They'll help you stomach people you can't stand. That way you can keep a straight face even when certain people make you want to puke.

"These here...are to fortify your liver. So even tho you're docile, you don't turn into a liver-belly.

"And these...these are the latest in pharmaceutical immuno-innovation. They don't have anything to do w/ voting, really...but one capsule a day will help regulate all your common ailments: your colds, the flu, constipation, migraines, suicidal thoughts. All will be regularly scheduled...which means you can set up your doctor appointments months in advance. No waiting."

Handing S- one of each vial, the doctor closed the cabinet, patting S- on the shoulder & wishing him good luck, adding: "You'll certainly need it." Handing S- the application, he scooped up his moustache & disappeared thru a side door.

A smug & delighted Smolet greeted S- in the waiting room. Leaning over the receptionist's desk, the banker continued his recounting tales of S-'s heretofore unheralded heroism. "A champion of the common folk," the banker was telling the shifty-eyed receptionist, "w/ their all-too-common cents. Why, i've seen this lad save a small child of humble persuasion—the kind of child most parents of that economic scale wouldn't hesitate to throw over some bridge when the authorities aren't looking. I've seen this lad save a German shepherd boy from being run over by a carriage run amok, w/ no thought for his own safety."

The skeptical receptionist seized S-'s application, one eye canvassing the banker, another surveying S-'s shoes, another giving S- its third degree. She stamped the application in several places, then exchanged it for a notarized certificate Smolet immediately snatched up, offering half a used cigar in exchange.

Congratulating S-, wishing him happy bulloting, the receptionist eyed the others in the room, another eye watching the doorknob turn & someone enter, the third observing a mosquito set up camp on a suspiciously Wignutish nose. After the banker turned, she dexterously lifted the cigar half w/ a pair of tweezers & dropped it in a trashcan.

S- & Smolet left the City & Counting Bldg unaware of two pairs of eyes peering @ them thru the slats of second-story Venetian blinds. Dr Cataract reattached his moustache & smoothed it into place. Police Chief Willoughby picked @ the scab on his sunburnt scalp.

"Think you got thru to him?" Willoughby asked, watching the two round a corner & disappear from vision.

The physician shrugged, clearing his throat. "I don't know. One thing's for certain: he doesn't know his left from our right. We'll probably have to go to plan C."

"You mean D."

"Yeah, right. Plan D."

* * * * *

137

LATER THAT DAY, S- & shadow slumped over the luncheon counter in the Smolet First Pedestal cafeteria. Despite being late for work, w/ only half a day still remaining, both man & shadow felt spent.

"Quit dragging your feet!" they could still hear Stubbs Farrago demand. "Git your ash in gear." Clearly peeved over S- having gotten the morning off, Stubbs had elected to show his assist*ant* no mercy. "No, not that way! This way!" the janitor hounded all morning, grabbing the sponge & showing S- the proper way to scrub a toilet. "Is youse a new kind a' stupid?"

The janitor's braying, head-shaking & contorted facial expressions remained etched in S-'s mind. "I'd thought i'd seen all d' kinds a' stupid there was, but youse something new. Youse a genius @ being stupid. You musta been t' college, gotten one a' dem dere stupid degrees."

Yet, should Smolet waddle by, the Head of Maintenance Engineering would abruptly change his tune, slapping S- affectionately on the back. "That's it! Youse got it!" he would cheer. "D' boy's a natc'ral!"

"'Cuse me. I wuz toll ta giff yu this." A timid, almost imperceptible voice interrupted S-'s reverie. S- & shadow glanced up @ a familiar stranger standing on the other side of the counter.

"Sumone sed yu dropt it," the young man added.

S- gazed into a pair of vaguely familiar eyes. The face was similar to Stubbs's, tho less angular, the cheeks smoother, rounder, in less need of a shave. Gone were the pockmarks & worry wrinkles. The hands, neither cracked nor weather-beaten, held a slip of paper, gesturing for S- to take it. S- reached for the note, an alarm going off in his head. Heat rushed to his face as the walls throbbed & tilted, the room seeming on the verge of spinning out of control. S- clutched the countertop. A churning issued from his stomach as he opened the note.

Widen your lens, the scribbled note read.

"Who—? You're not—?" S- stammered as his shadow scrutinized the young face.

"I'm Weed," the man-child said, a slight wheeze in his breathing. "I wurk in the pisza dapartmint. I think yu wurk fore my o'man." The boy leaned over the counter, his apron crusted w/ dried flour & pizza sauce. "I wont to sey, im glad to cee yu wurking heer. I here wot peeple ar seying...i meen, thay sey that about awl us reelly...bot im glad Mr Smalet iz giffin yu a chanz."

While his shadow examined the note, S- questioned the man-child. Who had given him the note? What did the man look like? Did he say anything else? The boy

138

mostly shrugged. The man, he said, was tall tho small of stature...& kept turning his head, his baseball cap obscuring his face, his coat collar turned up. S- again studied the note, recognizing the flamboyant penmanship & the customary smiley faces on either side of the meticulous lettering. He mouthed its message:

Widen your lens.

Reaching for his camera, he gestured to Weed, who happily acquiesced to having his picture taken. The boy smoothed his hair back, proudly displaying his sullied apron. S- stood up & stepped back several feet. Not able to widen the lens any further, he nevertheless snapped several shots from varying angles.

"Awl my life tha people haff tolked abot me," Weed confided, looking everywhere except twd S-. "Sed i wood neveh mount ta much. But Mr Smalet, he gife me a chanz, on acount a my pa assin hem to. I starded out az a ordenary dohboy." Weed turned, looking directly into the camera. "Sence than ive bean imployie a da moth fore tymes. And peeple can till whan i make the crust or sumbody elze duz. Sum peeple onlee make a depozit whan thay cee me wurking behin da counta." Weed turned again, looking twd three similarly clad, crusty-aproned coworkers tossing pizza dough, monitoring the oven & taking cash deposits. "Lit me git yu a complamintary slise."

Before S- could decline the man-child was gone, consulting his coworkers before pulling two steaming hot slices of pepper jack/artichoke pizza from the oven.

"Dese ar da lass a da batch i maid," Weed boasted, juggling the hot paper plates as he slid one slice over to S-. S-'s shadow blew vigorously on the pizza, gesturing for S- to take a small nibble. His taste buds were soon dancing, his teeth demanding a bigger bite as his tongue savored a myriad of complimentary flavors. The gooey cheese stretched on forever no matter how far away S- held the slice, his shadow twisting it around its dark fingers.

Weed passed out napkins & utensils. "So tell me," he asked, his olive-green eyes shining, "yu purfer eeting pisza w/ a fork? Or do you fold it wid yore hans?"

The room again wobbled, S-'s shadow barely able to keep S- from falling over.

139

Chapter 13

SEATED ON AN OVERSTUFFED CHESTERFIELD, its plump upholstery nearly swallowing him whole, Buck squirmed. Beads of sweat formed a phalanx along his hairline, belying the calm demeanor he had resolved to affect. His military collar, starched & buttoned tight, made of his Adam's apple a virtual prisoner. The man-child tugged @ said collar as he surveyed his great-uncle's spacious living quarters, sizing up the high arched ceiling, the glitter & sparkle of the chandeliers, the plush furnishing w/ names like bergère, récamier & méridienne.

He glanced down @ his uniform, recalling Gladiator U's sacred covenant, specifically the precept that polishing bullets, mowing the battle grass & keeping one's uniform pressed & wrinkle-free instilled the discipline necessary for every cadet to meet all of life's adversaries. He had little doubt he was being watched. Neither did he doubt his not-so-great uncle was a doddering old fool, someone he—a seasoned, about-to-graduate, senior cadet—could easily outmaneuver in any battle of wits. Nevertheless, he resolved to downplay his dimples.

Slouched on the nearby bergère, his father chewed incessantly on something, his bloated belly protruding complaisantly over his peasant-hide belt. An ornate floor lamp cast an amber halo above the banker's snowy white hair. Smolet's eyelids were beginning to droop, that is until the sudden caterwaul of a cat in an adjoining room roused Buck's father into sitting up straight.

The furry flash of a limping tabby rocketed by, Sur Harry soon following in its wake. Clad in satin kimono & platform slippers, the aristocrat negotiated the dense forest of expensive furniture, balancing a wobbling silver tray, its contents jiggling w/ increased agitation the closer he drew near. Not one to pick up his feet, Sur Harry resorted to cursing, kicking or stomping on anything not animate enuff to move out his way. His lips pursed, his eyes scowling, the aristocrat nonetheless managed to smile @ his guests as he set the tray on an antique coffee table.

"CranDY?" He gestured toward a fluted decanter surrounded by similarly fluted crystal glasses. W/out awaiting an answer he poured, filling the three glasses w/ the reddish-brown liqueur. "Is our young man old eNUFF for cranDY?" he cheerfully inquired, handing the banker the first glass.

"'Course he is," Smolet responded, handing Buck the drink, then accepting the hastily passed second. Sur Harry lifted the third glass, holding it to the light as if to check for bugs or potentially subversive microbes. "Jeers," he declared as the three men clicked glasses.

Pretending to sip, Buck eyed his great uncle. Taking but a tiny sip, the aristocrat smacked his lips, his sunken BB-sized eyes again surveying the liqueur, perhaps for microbes disguised as floating bubbles. Buck grimaced as his father downed half his glass in one greedy gulp. Divvying the difference, the cadet sipped generously, smacking his lips w/ exaggerated relish, his uncle's lips curling in approval.

Sur Harry plopped down next to Buck on the plump plum-colored chesterfield. Brushing lint from his lapel, the aristocrat inquired if Buck knew the significance of that particular day. Buck eyed his father & uncle cautiously, half-stating, half-questioning if said significance was the beginning of bullot season.

Sur Harry smiled broadly, his eyes gleaming. "Right you are, young man. But there's someTHING more signiFIcant ABout this occaSION."

Buck's brows began to spar, one blue eye gazing curiously @ his father, the other cautiously @ his uncle. He studied the listless bubbles in his glass, finding no hint there either.

"Buck," his uncle announced, one arm draped along the back of the chesterfield, "this is the day you enTER manHOOD. No lonGER a mere boy flounDERing unDER the PROtective wing of your graCIOUSly wealTHY fatHER—this is the seaSON you step from unDER his oVERhangING roof INto the full force of your own well-tesTED OSteRONE."

Sur Harry tipped his glass, sipped his crandy & smacked his lips. He topped all three glasses w/ more crandy, cautioning Smolet not to nod off. "Now...to symBOlize that EVent," he continued, "from here on we will call you 'Bill.' No lonGER a mere 'Buck'; toDAY you BEcome a full, leGALly tenDERED Bill. Here's to you, Bill!"

"Here, here!" Bill's father chirped, father & uncle downing their crandy. Bill's uncle gestured for the man-no-longer-a-child to do the same. Feeling outflanked, Bill/Buck complied, straining not to grimace as the syrupy liqueur seared his throat. Setting his glass down, Buck felt the room begin to wobble. He gripped the arm of the chesterfield, his other hand clasping the sofa cushion.

"That's right, drink up," Sur Harry encouraged, patting Buck on the epaulette. "There's plenTY more where that came from!"

Outmaneuvered, Buck accepted another refill, vaguely aware of Sur Harry fiddling w/ the bulky ring the aristocrat wore, a ring Buck had never seen before.

"So i hear you've BEcome quite the sharpshooTER," his uncle remarked.

Buck gushed, gulped, smacked his lips & looked around w/ a vague sense of helplessness.

"Shoot, he can hit a bull's eye @ 1,000 pesos," his father chimed in. "Hail, he's hands-tied-behind-his-back one of the best killball players in the history of the sport." The banker readily accepted the refill Sur Harry extended.

"I see a bright fuTURE for someONE w/ your taLENT." Sur Harry squeezed Buck's military cuff, raising his half-empty glass in salute. Buck sipped cautiously. As the room reeled slightly, his father & great-uncle began a verbal tennis match. A vigorous volley of glowing tributes, lavish superlatives & unbridled hyperbole ensued. His cheeks flushed, his chest protruding w/ each compliment, Buck felt his muscles relax. He too began to volley, bragging unabashedly, answering each of his uncle's somewhat probing questions. He admitted freely how rape & pillaging had once left him baffled. It wasn't till his sophomore year, he slurred, that he finally caught on how most enemies lack any genuine feelings: that an enemy's screams were merely a cowardly ploy to gain a soldier's empathy & thus render said soldier momentarily vulnerable. Thereafter he always aced the pillaging part of any exam & as to rape he usually got @ least a B+ except when he got distracted by peering into the victim's tear-streaked face.

"I've even been doing some extracurricular reading on my own," Buck boasted, unbuttoning his collar & loosening his military cravat. "A friend turned me on to this pamphlet on the 'Anatomy of Evil.' Did you know we are actually the evil ones?" Buck looked to his father who had nodded off. He turned to his great uncle, whose brows had become straight lines, the dark eyes as serious as bullets.

"It's a stroke of Brittlebaum genius," Buck reassured his uncle's frowning jowls, "tho demicratic despots have known it for centuries. See, we push weaker civilizations around—refuse to treat them justly even as we assert we're being fair & impartial. When their resentment boils over & they lash out, brutally attacking a few of us...then we've got 'em. We call them 'evil,' brand 'em savages & condemn their wanton lack of respect for human life. Brilliant, huh?" Netting no response, Buck decided to plow further on.

"See, by labeling *them* evil, we grant ourselves the right to dish out all the evil we want. We get to kill far more of them than they could ever hope to kill of us. And even tho their peashooters are no match for our rocket launchers, they remain the evil ones. We even get to massacre their women & children & chalk it up to collateral damage—all the while declaring ourselves paragons of all that is good, just & civilized!"

In his exuberance, Buck failed to notice the change in his uncle's complexion. Sensing something suddenly amiss, the man-child ceased talking, his father's snores the only sound piercing an otherwise eerie silence.

"Not that i'm complaining," Buck offered, downing his crandy, half its contents missing his lips to dribble onto his cravat & crotch. He launched into an enthusiastic appraisal of the role of war in fanning the flames of unbridled patriotism; how it also spurred the manufacture & sale of all the nifty weapons he & his fellow cadets got to play with; how it further sparked the fierce fashion competition that leads to new uniforms being commissioned every few years...which in turn kept the garment, the fabric & other related industries afloat, which in turn....

As he blathered on, Buck desperately wiped his crotch area, attempting in vain to remove the expanding wet spot. Sensing futility & fearing his uncle's disapproval, he flashed a healthy dose of dimple. His tongue virtually paralyzed, he extended his glass, hoping his uncle might forgive & forget his bold indiscretion—or, barring that, @ least refill his glass w/ a little more crandy.

* * * * *

S- MEANWHILE STAGGERED HOME after a draining day @ the First Smolet Bank & Pedestal. Despite the mulberry graciously lowering a bough & his shadow's offer to assist, S- felt too exhausted to climb the tree's branches. He instead mounted the manor porch & passed sheepishly thru its three front doors. Immediately the hairs of his neck stood @ attention, his shadow also on sudden alert. The lights, which usually blared from every room, flickered quiet & subdued. The downstairs appeared deserted. The faint heartbeat of the grandfather clock & the distant hum of a well-fed refrigerator were all he heard.

As he ascended the stairs, he overheard whispering. The newly potted Iris, along

143

w/ several hanging spider plants, gazed on him w/ disapproving smirks. One flower pot over, Lily winked to him slyly. On the second floor, Phil O'Dendron, Aloe Vera & Mrs Coleus engaged in a heated debate abruptly terminated when they sensed his presence. The sudden silence proved deafening, its uneasiness broken only when a door opened & Mrs Smolet emerged from the master bedroom. A knot took root in the pit of S-'s stomach.

The lady of the house wore a tight, peach-colored sleeveless dress, its busty contours bedecked w/ sugar-frosted pastel pastries. A pearl necklace paraded around her long perfumed neck, its glimmer matching her two rows of perfectly polished teeth. Her platinum hair was no longer a roiling ocean but a cascading waterfall gliding down the sleek sides of a long shining face, thin rivulets & wisps of stray hair subduing the corrugated furrows of her forehead.

She half-slinked, half-swaggered twd S-, her feet bare, her toenails bright red, her toes tickled pink @ having shunned their slippers. Her breath's stale odor assaulted S-'s nostrils as she walked unsteadily up to him, tucking both his arms into the vise grip of her soft yet firm embrace.

The lady of the house pulled him downstairs, explaining that the girls had decided to eat supper in their rooms. And, as for the boys, she giggled, they were @ her Uncle Harry's, doing whatever men do when womenfolk aren't aground.

"I've found some interesting comets in your rule book," she slurred, steering him to the FAMILY DEN, pushing him onto the davenport. "I'd like to go over them w/ you," she purred, her pink powdered cheeks already beginning to smudge.

* * * * *

MEANWHILE, ON THE SOUTHERNMOST EDGE of the business district, Edmund Radcliffe fidgeted in a tattered armchair, picking @ its stuffing. His sparse apartment leaned like a drunken sailor on leave, its walls crookedly constructed above his father's switch, bait & tackle shop—which, for reasons known only to Perman Radcliffe, also sold photography equipment. A half empty bottle of root dangled from Edmund's limp hand: a bottle he had passed to Hector who had passed it to Ruth who had passed it back to Edmund. Both his companions sat on the sagging sofa, Ruth seated Nibian-style, her skirt wide enuff to impede Edmund's thought process. The chain shackled around her ankle curled like a sleeping snake, Hector on the other end of said serpent. While Hector rubbed his greasy sideburns, Ruth diligently inspected her cat-o'-nine tails for signs of wear & tear.

"He said he couldn't get away," Edmund sulked, his eyes sullen, one side of his mouth stubbornly refusing to join the conversation. "Said his old man insisted he visit his uncle." Edmund took a pull from the bottle & passed it again.

"Think we can still trust him, Bub?" Hector took a swig, passing the bottle to Ruth. "Even if he plays along for awhile, the Bub's bound to realize his privilege lies in maintaining the status woe."

"Hector's right." Ruth wiped her lips, adjusting her legs to further disrupt Edmund's concentration. "It's been that way thruout history. He's sure to turncoat eventually." Ruth handed the bottle to Edmund.

The three conspirators observed a moment of silence.

"Yeah, you're right," Edmund finally sighed. "Remember what Heidi once wrote: 'the stronger the man, the weaker his testicles.'"

"Yeah, Bub, & 'the younger the man, the louder his whore moans.'"

Ruth snapped her whip, stifling Hector's snorting giggle.

"How's your sister doing?" she asked Edmund. "She still got him by the killballs? Maybe she can get him to tow the line."

Edmund shrugged. "Not likely. The high & mighty Buck Smolet only stands there...staring @ her naked truth. I actually caught him once hiding in the bushes, taking pictures of her."

The three observed another moment of silence.

"What worries me, Bub, is this S-. Even if he finds the combination, what's to guarantee he'll give it to us? These mamsy-pansy, head-in-the-cloud types make me nervous. They're less predictable than madmen. At least you know the insane will do something crazy. With this guy, you can't even be sure of that."

"Will *he* be here?" Ruth cracked her whip, startling a fly in mid-flight.

Edmund shrugged. "Can't say."

The trio again observed a moment of silence, all three on sudden alert @ the turning of a doorknob. The door leading down into Edmund's father's shop opened, a female head poking its way inside.

"Jeez, Jasmine," Edmund bellowed. "Can't you knock?"

"Sorry." Slinking further inside, her pumpkin-shaped head aglow w/ acne, her chestnut hair tied into a spunky ponytail, Edmund's sister entered barefoot & naked, her well-toned body tanned & curvaceous. "Pappy needs you," she informed her brother before silently acknowledging his guests. "Sorry," she offered again, turning on her heels & exiting.

Edmund smirked. "Tell him i'll be right down!" Raking a few fingers thru his

145

hair, the man-child lifted his lanky frame, swallowing the remaining root. "Wonder what the old buzzard wants," he quipped as he exited.

Hector shifted on the sofa & cracked a pair of knuckles. Gazing askance @ Ruth, who methodically stroked her whip, he attempted to waltz a few crude fingers down a tear in her stocking. One hiss from her cat-o'-nine, however, & he reconsidered the maneuver, opting instead to crack a few more knuckles.

Down below, Edmund greeted his father w/ a feigned smile. "What's shakin', Paps?"

A stout man of medium-height & burly side whiskers turned from thanking a customer to peer @ his son thru narrow, wire-rimmed spectacles. "Sorry to disturb you, son. There's a young lady here. Says she's here to see you. 'Parently she doesn't know to go round back."

Edmund noticed Heidi standing just inside the front door. The letters: PERMAN'S SWITCH, BAIT, TACKLE THEN SNAP A PICTURE SHOP were etched backward in the window just above her head. Dressed as was her wont in contemporary rag doll, her shoes mismatched, the girl waved before bending to scratch a grime-encrusted knee.

"Isn't she a—"

"Don't say it," Edmund censured his father. "Besides, she's only half. She's a friend & a fellow bookworm—the only one among us actually published."

"*Besides,*" the other corner of Edmund's mouth joined in, "*in a truly egalitarian society, we incorporate the views of everyone—even the you-know-what.*"

The critical brows of Mr Radcliffe relaxed, replaced by a proud smile as he rubbed his whiskers. "You're right, son. Of course." He sized up the human ragamuffin, about to formally welcome her when his eyes were drawn to something behind her. "Well, i'll be," he remarked, his gaze fixed over the girl's shoulder. "Is that...? Why, it is!" The front door swung open as the rotund figure of the Police Chief entered.

"Why, Willoughby! What brings you here?" The store owner wiped his hands on his apron before graciously shaking the Police Chief's pudgy digits. "It's been ages."

"Perman." Chief Willoughby smiled back, glancing briefly @ Edmund & casting a quick wink @ Heidi.

"So good to see you," Perman continued, one hand caressing his friend's uniformed shoulder. "How have you been? Let's go in back. I can't remember the last time we just sat & chatted." Leading the C of P to the backroom, the store

146

owner called to his daughter, "Jas, honey, would you mind manning the counter? My daughter will help you find whatever you are looking for," he informed a customer milling about the fishing nets.

His father & the Police Chief securely out of earshot, Edmund wheeled around to Heidi, hissing thru clenched teeth, "Why didn't you go round back like i told you?"

"Hey, us Canaans have been going thru backdoors for generations," she hurled back, her thin dark moustache twitching in defiance, her tiny hands half curled into fists. "That tradition ends w/ me."

"*Well, look what you've brought.* He was probably following you."

"Let him follow," Heidi snapped. She trudged up the staircase. Edmund stared disgustedly @ the back of her dress, several of its buttons missing. He followed @ an angry plod, closing the door behind him w/ a gentle slam. He glanced contentiously @ Sedgewick, who had not only arrived thru the backdoor, but currently slouched in the man-child's favorite chair.

"Sorry i'm late," the one-armed Sedgewick spouted, removing his beanie cap & placing it on one knee. "I left a few thoughts @ home. Had to run back to get them. Where's Buck & that S- guy?"

One side of his mouth detailing the facts, the other providing editorial comment, Edmund updated the new arrivals. Kicking an invisible dog, he suggested they had best come up w/ a plan G.

Upon digesting the latest development & chewing on the subsequent implications, Heidi spoke @ length. Since no one could hear her & only Sedgewick cared to listen, no one bothered to comment when she was done.

"There goes our revolution," Edmund conceded.

"*Not necessarily,*" his other jaw contended.

"You wanna bet!"

"*Why would i bet you? As if you'd ever pay up.*"

"We're not really ready, anyway," Sedgewick offered, whipping out a paperback, its author's name blackened out, HEIDI KILBORN scribbled crudely in white lettering on top. He thumbed thru several pages before finding the appropriate dog-ear & reading out loud, "'Uprisings for, by & of the people are feasible only when general discontent has reached a boiling point, the populace no longer willing to tolerate decades of blatant systemic abuse.'"

"Exactly," Edmund asserted.

"*Horse twinkies,*" he countered himself.

Sedgewick closed the book. "The citizens of this micropolis are far too complacent. Many don't even realize how miserable they actually are."

"That's what i've been saying."

"Oh, shut up!"

"He's got a point, Bub. Remember Mr Gorge saying something about revolutions being started by those who think, but made real by those who feel."

"Precisely," Sedgewick enthused.

"And what has all this got to do w/ anything?"

"We've been trying to get people to think," Hector continued. "We'd get far better results getting them to *feel*. I've been working on a treatise which ties in perfectly w/ this discussion."

Ruth slid onto the floor, slipping btwn Hector's legs as he reached to unbutton the top of her blouse. Delving therein, he extracted several sheets of folded paper.

"He's been working on this all week," Ruth explained, her tongue moistening her lips while she set her whip aside.

"This is based on an observation Heidi once wrote," Hector began. "How the best way to get the herd to do what you want is by manufacturing what I've come to call a BIG FAT FIB."

"Not a skinny little fib," Ruth interjected. "Like all taxpayers go to heaven, or PUP only does it w/ virgins...but a fat fib."

"Listen to this." Hector arranged the pages. "'In general, the art of all truly great leaders, demicratic or dictatorial, consists in not dividing the attention of the mass asses whose support they need...but, rather, in concentrating their attention into a single fabulous fib. The more unifying the application of the fib—that is, the greater the magnetic lure of its falsehood—the mightier the thrust in disarming any impeding, inconvenient truth.'"

Hector gazed up @ the three pairs of blinking eyes riveted on him, aware all ears were focused on his every word. Ruth fingered his shackle, her other hand stroking his calf.

"'It belongs to the genius of a great leader,'" he continued, glancing in Edmund's direction. "'It belongs to the genius of a great leader to make even those enemies far removed from each other...seem to belong to a single category...the reason being, weak & uncertain characters (i.e. the greater of the mass asses) seeing themselves in a struggle against too many enemies...will typically allow objectivity & common cents to cloud their bias...this throwing open doubt...raising the question whether *all* others are really wrong & only themselves in the right.'"

148

Again Hector paused, savoring the feel of Ruth's fingers creeping up his leg, her chin stroking his thigh. Feeling something harden, he continued, "'This results in a paralysis of one's power. Hence different adversaries must always be clumped into one...the eyes of the herd focused on only one enemy. This strengthens their faith in your fib...enhancing their bitterness twd anyone foolish enuff to contradict their folly.'"

Hector rifled thru the papers until he came to the final page: "'Now the magnitude of a fib must always contain a certain factor of credibility...'" He looked around to be sure his audience was still following. "'...since most asses are not @ bottom consciously or purposely evil...but—guided by their fears, doubts & selfish interests—are easily corruptible. Thus they are more easily prone to fall victim to a BIG *FAT* FIB rather than a thin, malnourished one.'"

Hector folded the pages in triumph, his eyes drawn to the cleavage heaving inside Ruth's blouse. When he reached therein as if in search of additional pages, Ruth closed her eyes, her whip lying listlessly @ her side.

* * * * *

AT ABOUT THAT SAME PRECISE MOMENT, S- found himself scrunched in the corner of a davenport in the dim-lit ambiance of the Smolet FAMILY DEN. The room's every Fern, passion flower & creeping Charlie had been turned such that none could witness what was transpiring. To S-'s right: the arm of said davenport. To his left: the arms, legs, bosom, cheekbones & sundry misc moistened body parts of Mrs Sticky Buns. The lady of the house seemed incapable of sitting up straight as she perpetually leaned into S- as if she might topple over were he not conveniently positioned to hold her up.

A crisp new rule book, along w/ several companion-reference books, lay spread across the cluttered coffee table. On said table, two tall goblets of imported vine & a half empty carafe of similar liquid stood sentry over numerous porcelain nudes gazing up @ the human couple from indelicate positions. S-'s goblet stood untouched while the other was heavily smudged w/ powdered fingerprints, its rim smeared w/ lip gloss.

"Read this one," Mrs Smolet encouraged, grabbing her goblet & leaning into S-, her cheek pressed into his shoulder blade. S- read, Mrs Smolet mouthing along as if to aid his comprehension. Distracted by wisps of platinum hair tickling his neck & Eau d'demimonde wreaking havoc on his olfactory glands, S- found himself unable to comprehend anything. The only thing he knew for certain was the knot in his stomach kept winding tighter.

"Mummy, Penny won't play w/ me."

S- looked up w/ relief...as he had each of the many times Pearl, in pajamas & pigtails, had appeared.

"PUP dammit," the lady of the house exclaimed, plunking her goblet down & ushering the girl to the stairwell. "Mz Penny Smolet, you play w/ your sister!" she shouted up to the second floor. "How often do i ask either of you for a little priest of quiet. It's the least you can do after all my sacrivices!"

The lady of the house soon returned, flashing a broad smile beneath her stern eyes. Stumbling as she negotiated around the coffee table, she laughed as she fell against S-, forcing him farther into the edge of the davenport.

"I remember this one." Removing the hair from her eyes, Mrs Smolet pointed to one rule in particular. "It was in the book i had when Charlie courted me." The lady of the house read to herself, her lips moving in silence. When she finished, she bit her lower lip & sighed.

"He broke this one," she said, indicating the section subtitled "First dates, petting & other know-nos." She reached for a tissue. Smudging her mascara, she wiped away a tear. S- accepted the bunched-up tissue, stuffing it in his shadow's pocket.

"Thank you," she sniffled.

"Mummy, Penny's cheating." Pearl appeared again, a doll dangling in one hand.

"Dam that girl." Mrs Smolet pounced up & stormed from the room.

Deserted, savoring the feeling of a brief reprieve, S- fanned thru the rule book. He reviewed the TABLE OF CONTENTS, reading each chapter heading, contemplating titles like "Clandestine Kissing & its Aftermath," "When No Means Yes" & "Cunnilingus w/out Sin." The chapter heading "What To Do When the Husband Comes Home" gave him particular pause. He flipped to the chapter's opening page, pondering its subtitle, "The best defense is no defense @ all." A footnote referred him to an appendage & a section headed "After You're Caught & Killed." According to the instructions, he was to stay dead while the distraught wife & guilty husband hid all evidence, sending the kids away for the weekend & adding a fresh layer of cement to the basement floor.

As S- referred back to the TABLE OF CONTENTS, he heard the front doors open, followed by the cheerfully tipsy voice of his partner, landlord & employer.

"You won't regret it, son," the banker was insisting boisterously. "I guarantee it. I too had some wild oaks to sow. But i thank PUP the day i swallowed my pride, put aside my high minded ideals & married your mother."

Chapter 14

"I KNOW WHAT you were trying to do the other nite."

S- gazed up as Pearl plunked down in the rocking chair, setting the rocker in motion. A shockwave surged thru him, a pounding erupting in his chest. His cheeks burned despite his shadow whispering assurances that he had done nothing wrong. Yet if that were true, why had no one come to visit? Where was Buck, who usually joined him in the darkroom every evening? It seemed as if the man-child was deliberately avoiding him. The day before, Buck actually hissed when S- suggested they finish developing Buck's photos of Jasmine. The boy instead insisted he no longer cared a hoot about any dammed pictures, adding he was now a man & everyone had better start calling him Bill.

Also avoiding S-—perhaps even repulsed by his very presence—was Mrs Sticky Buns. As if etched in his photographic memory, S- clearly recalled her frightened, wide-eyed expression when she sashayed back into the family den, her dress half-undone. She froze mid-disrobing, the sight of her snoring husband sprawled across the davenport sending her scurrying from the room. Since then the lady of the house spent her evenings @ the Temple of Perpetual Puppiness, monopolizing the confession booths, clutching PUP's terry-cloth palm, waiting for Him to speak—which she was certain He would once He got over His anger @ her 'sinful transmissions.' The lady of the house even declined attending family meals, insisting there would be plenty to eat when she got to Puppiland.

S- winced @ the creaking of floorboards as Pearl rocked rambunctiously, her eyes rarely deviating from ogling him. The girl's shadow stood, smoothing its dress before traipsing about the garret, taking a vague interest in the stack of prints he had only that morning developed.

"You were trying to give Mummy a baby, weren't you?" Pearl's hazel eyes studied S-, her brows mildly admonishing. "You should read your rule book. It's my sister you're supposed to do that to.

"Anyhow," she continued, her shadow putting down the prints to stare out the window, "i don't blame you. Penny doesn't like you anyway. You need to give her flowers or something. Tell her how pretty she is—even if you think she's ugly. Girls like it when boys lie.

"Are you listening?" she asked a moment later.

S- nodded tho in truth he had been watching Pearl's shadow play peek-a-boo w/ the mulberry. The tree would shift its broad leaves to cover its eye, then spring them apart to reveal a face first smiling, then frowning, then sticking out its tongue.

"I'm trying to help you," Pearl persisted, still rocking. "Besides, when Mummy & Pupa cast Penny out for having your baby, i get to have her room."

S- glanced down @ **Antz from A to Z** & **Moths**, both books gazing up @ him forlornly. Having read each twice, he sensed their growing restlessness. He imagined them feeling abandoned & unloved. "I need to get to the libary," he announced. "Only i'm not really sure i remember the way."

"Boys," Pearl sighed, shaking her head before jumping to her feet. She placed her hands to her hips. "My sister is right. You *are* completely worthless. C'mon. Let's go." She extended her hand, clasping his & giving him a gentle tug. Her shadow quickly dashed over, finding his shadow's hand. S- grabbing the books, the foursome made their way down the trapdoor, the rocker continuing to rock long after the quartet had left & were stepping off the front porch.

As they strolled the downtown streets, an increasing multitude of pedestrian traffic surrounded them: an ocean of faces & bodies, the more rotund among them seeming to take great relish in stepping on the toes of anyone substantially thinner. Several fistfights broke out, one pugilist swinging wildly while shouting, "PEEP POLE," his chunkier adversary ducking & countering, "PROP PURTY," before landing a low blow to the other's groin. Black eyes, bloody noses & misc bruises grew more frequent. Pearl, unperturbed, weaved thru the mayhem like a fish thru familiar water. When S- & shadow pointed to the sign reading WELCOME to the MUNICIPAL PARK/NATURE OBSERVATORY, the girl happily consented to making the detour.

Their feet finding soft refuge in the waving grass, the duo marched on, their shadows happy to dash on ahead. S- winked @ the radiant blue-eyed blonde reposing in the sky, smiling thru a grove of meditating pines. Dashing twd the lake, Pearl

153

made straight for the geese & goslings, her aim to throttle any neck foolish enuff to get w/ in her grasp. The frantic fowl protested in loud honks, shrill curses & a mad thrashing of wings, prompting S- to hurriedly pursue the girl & herd her along. The entire observatory heaved a relieved sigh when the pair came to the park's end. Soon after, S- spied the familiar fresco, recalling the brightly lit labyrinth w/ its promise of infinite wisdom.

Their approach, however, was swiftly impeded by an immense density of pedestrian traffic. What earlier had been a sea of people was now a stubborn wall of milling or stationary bodies. Many were weeping, nearly everyone wiping tears from long, drawn faces. Some sobbed loudly; others blubbered or bawled unabashedly, almost as if in competition to see who could wail the longest or loudest. Every few yards vendors & hawkers shouted, offering one-day-only discounts on super-absorbent four-ply tissue or colorful two-sided souvenir handkerchiefs, tastefully stamped w/ corporate logos andor signed by famous S&M artists. Standing on tiptoe, craning his neck, S- noted someone on the topmost libary step shouting thru a megaphone, her voice barely audible over the incessant sobbing.

"Oh, i forgot what day it is," Pearl declared. "Cover your ears. We're not supposed to listen."

His books clasped in one hand, S- managed to cover but one ear, Pearl not bothering to cover either of hers. The girl instead grabbed his arm, pulling him thru the crowd, the wall of wailing bodies reluctant to part w/out the youngster prodding, poking, @ times kicking a few shins. Finally, she gave up, opting to climb a stone ledge, suggesting it might be okay to watch so long as they didn't look. "We're allowed to hear," she added, "as long as we don't listen."

Again craning his neck, S- could make out a woman of medium height & maximum weight bellowing into the megaphone. The square-jawed brunette stood @ a podium, a banner billowing behind her. The words CITIZENS FOR LARGER DONUT HOLES waved in the breeze. In crisp, sugary phrasing, the woman beseeched, cajoled & entreated, sweet-talking & buttering up the crowd; tears jig-jagged down their long faces as they ate up her dire prediction on the latent dangers baked inside currant standards in donut hole circumference. The fiery speaker sprinkled disturbing statistics into her appeal, eyes glazing over as she egged them into considering all the innocent infants, toddlers & underaged midgets living under the daily danger of choking on standard-sized donut holes. "GRANTED, IT HASN'T HAPPENED YET," she shouted, "BUT WHO HERE WOULD LIKE THEIR CHILDREN, THEIR NEIGHBORS' CHILDREN, TO BE THE FIRST TO MEET

SO UNFORTUNATE, SO UNTIMELY & ULTIMATELY SO PREVENTABLE A DEMISE?" Adding further how larger donut holes held the economic advantage of allowing donut makers to bake more donuts using less dough, the speaker gently kneaded the crowd into signing the circulating petitions & dropping a few coins in the accompanying donation buckets.

Before the bloodcurdling wailing could completely subside, a grizzled, hand-cuffed man w/ a gash above his left eye mounted the podium. A new banner waved above his scarred head: EQUAL RIGHTS for CONDEMNED KILLERS, its letters an artful arrangement of serrated knives. At first, strident boos rose from the crowd, the man's raspy voice struggling to be heard over the disapproving din. The boos however were quickly countered by shouts of "Let him speak! Let him speak!" these mainly from men in orange jumpsuits, their wrists also restrained by handcuffs.

When the hissing died down, the unshaven convict waxed philosophical, contending the indisputable fact that inalienable rights could neither be created nor destroyed. Eliciting numerous nods, he further asserted the self-evident logic that the rights of the brutally murdered—as well as their property—should naturally go to those persons closest to the victim @ the time of the victim's demise. More heads nodded; the speaker urged his audience to shout in the affirmative if they were in agreement. When the crowd responded in a unified roar, the speaker then asked, "And who is always closest to the victim @ the time of his or her ghastly demise, huh? Why isn't it he or she standing over the victim w/ the murder weapon?"

The crowd fell hushed, caught off-guard by the irrefutable logic. He assured his audience how violent criminals love life & liberty just as much as the next person, sometimes even more than their unfortunate victims. Indeed, he insisted, it was watching others squander the joys that flesh is heir to that has led many of history's most reviled mass murderers to snuff out the lives of those who failed to appreciate life & living as much as their life-loving assailants did.

S- shifted uncomfortably as faint whimpering began to erupt around him. Numerous hankerchiefs were called into service, hankerchief vendors suddenly inundated w/ new requests. The man @ the podium, rubbing the gash above his eye, recounted the secondhand crib he as an abused child had been forced to stroll around in. He recalled the silver spoon he as an adolescent could never eat from, as it would surely be used as evidence against his father, who had purloined it along w/ other misc pilfered cutlery. With tears staining his soiled cheeks, he recalled the first of his several victims: his young wife, who had served him steamed vegetables, knowing full well he was a meat & potatoes man. How was one to cope w/ such wanton insensitivity? he asked the hushed audience. By the time he completed his life's litany of gruesome circumstances leading ultimately to his brutal murder of a family of seven (along w/ their pregnant cocker spaniel), the crowd's intermittent sniveling had evolved into heart-wrenching wails. The plaintive moans & anguished groaning were accompanied by gnashing teeth & free-flowing tear ducts. Petitions were hastily signed. Coins were heard plinking into the bottom of donation buckets labeled 'Condemned Convicts for Constitutional Reform.'

So, too, when the next speaker, representing the PETTY CRIME GUILD, petitioned for lower insurance rates for embezzlers. Current rates, the speaker declared, were prohibitive, dissuading many a natural-born chiseler from even entering that once lucrative trade. The art of embezzling had suffered a serious decline, he argued, as those caught & convicted could no longer provide for their families, who, in many cases, had been bamboozled as well—thus victimized twice. When he had sufficiently picked the crowd's pockets & tugged @ their loosened purse strings, a new speaker was handed the megaphone, this one advocating the death penalty for anyone contemplating suicide.

"Let's go," Pearl yawned. "I'm bored of not listening."

The pair bulldozed their way up the crowded steps, S- twice scooping up a dropped kerchief & once pausing to lend his shoulder to cry on. As he & Pearl neared the top step, a new voice blared thru the megaphone, this one musical in timbre, the speaker's tonality modulating in alluringly rolling cadences. S- halted, intrigued & determined to listen further. The speaker spoke of a two-faced government, promising if S-elected to guarantee every hypocrite two votes. "That way their first vote would be canceled out by their second," he intoned. The crowd laughed, those around S- applauding. The speaker's sonorous inflection grew more confident as he spewed a long list of social grievances: the dire need for more progressive donut legislation; the injustices heaped upon convicted killers; the rights of shoplifters to use their own shopping bags instead of purchasing the stores'; the exponentially unfair increases in petty criminal fees—compounded by the sharp decline in their access to adequate social services; the need to restore the death penalty to those trying to kill themselves. Craning his neck, his shadow climbing onto his shoulders, S- was able to read the banner frantically billowing above the speaker's full head of dark wavy hair. VOTE FOR FILKIN GRIMSPOON, the candy-striped banner urged.

* * * * *

156

As PEARL & S- ENTERED the literary infirmary, its head libarian was peering down from his lofty office window. Neimann Gorge shook his perspicacious neocortex @ the motley assemblage of troglodytes gathered on his otherwise pristine steps. W/ hypercritical eye, he surveyed the throng of rattle-rousers: antediluvians, to his apperception. Paleolithics gathered to give voice to their ceaseless bellyaching & ballyboo-hooing—all for the sake of not hearing themselves excogitate. But then again, he reminded himself, social strife was not only natural, but necessary—even noble—human progress being a Sisyphusian struggle twd the highly improbable...if not the hopelessly impossible.

He recalled the legendary hero, Mosey ben Absolom, the historical—some would argue, hysterical—genius attributed w/ leading a group of poor slaves into a land of bilk & money. Tho ben Absolom died never tasting the fruit of his beleaguered efforts, he spurred his fellow slaves thru revolt after revolt, their first insurrection resulting in their copper chains being replaced by a sturdier bronze. A subsequent rebellion resulted in iron chains, tho, in a deal arranged behind closed curtains, those chains were alloyed w/ an ancient version of fool's gold. Generations later, those tarnished shackles were replaced by silver lockets & finally w/ the gold manacles their scattered descendants still wear to this day. Historians unanimously agree: Absolom's descend*ants* were the richest slaves in history.

Neimann resolved to not let cynicism dampen his mood. He turned to gaze fondly @ the pink carnation poised elegantly in the vase on his desk. Never before had a mere flower filled his being w/ such rapture, w/ such—dare he say it?—naked ecstasy.

His thoughts traveled back to the previous day: he had found himself inexplicably on the first floor. Being there, he thought to inquire of Mz Pritt how his loaned bookends might be faring. As he struggled to get his predicates to follow their subjects, or his verbs to conjugate w/ their nouns, his hands, propelled by their own volition, reached for one of the silky hands belonging to Mz Pritt: a hot steaming towel of a hand, he clearly recalled, soft as if soaked in lotion, pliable as if constituted of dough. But rather than pulling away, Mz Pritt promptly contributed her other hand to the pile, massaging his knuckles as if she had intuited his nervous digits' every need.

Neimann stood speechless. Yet his being tongue-tied didn't seem to matter. Mz Pritt said something w/ her eyes. His face flushed further, his ears prickled, his brain threatening to spontaneously combust. Yet in the end, it refrained from exploding. She pressed her hot cheek to his & giggled. But not a silly schoolgirl giggle. No, this giggle was constituted somehow differently. Exactly how, he would need to read up on. Nevertheless, it sent tingles trickling up his spine & made walking seem like there was no ground for his feet to tread on.

And that, Neimann mused, was only yesterday. Now, today: here he stood, the most radiant of afternoons shining thru his top floor window; larks & linnets on the outside ledge pausing from their skittering to twerp full-throated cheerful greetings. Tho any number of philosophers, empiricists, rationalists & rigorous epistemologists might question his assertion, he felt unequivocal about its verisimilitude: while he had walked to work that morning, the very clouds were smiling down @ him. Somehow he knew they knew exactly what he was feeling. And maybe he was intoxicated by this newfound joy, but he would swear on a stack of ontological dissertations that the sun kept winking @ him; winking & patting him on the shoulder in affectionate approval.

When he greeted his staff, several stopped & stared. Someone whispered either he had been drinking or had availed himself of the infirmary's stock of quaaludes. The comment didn't bother him. He chuckled, in fact. Then—when he ambled into his office—there she was! Running her finger along the spine of al-Ishrag's **Breaking Wind of Reason**. In her other hand, she fondled a carnation, pressing it to her precious button of a nose, waving it like a magic wand before using it to tickle his chin.

Neimann sighed in triumphant bliss, recalling how w/out a second thought, w/out cogitation, mastication, cerebration or the slightest equivocation, he invited her to dinner: invited her to meet his Aunty McAssar & dear little Pythagoras—in a word, to enjoy the other half of his now glorious existence. He recalled her smile, her "Yes," the kiss on his cheek as she handed him the carnation & left.

Neimann stared down @ the crowd now beginning to disperse. Checking in w/ Plato & Socrates, he remembered his book club. Speculating that a few of the bookworms would no doubt be mingling among the rabble, perhaps even semi-persuaded by its ultra-liberule nonsense, he calculated he still had time before they gathered in the basement. A whim arose in his musing & began to tickle unmercifully @ his sunny disposition.

On the wingéd shoes of Aphrodite's little brother Hermes, Neimann jaunted down to one of the basilicas, one he rarely visited: The Basilica of Harlequin Romance. Recalling his undergraduate studies @ Literary U, he struggled to recollect even one of the half dozen titles lauded as romance classics. Condemned to read a few in order to graduate, he had only browsed their liner notes, managing still to ace the final exam. Now regretting the egregious laziness of his impatient youth, he scratched his forehead, the titles of the genre's most celebrated masterpieces just beyond the tip of his beta waves.

* * * *

"GREETINGS FELLOW BOOKWORMS & lovers of elusive truths."

Neimann strutted in cheerfully, those scattered about the room immediately put on guard. Pausing from picking a scab, Heidi eyed the wide-toothed libarian mistrustfully. Sedgewick reattached a skeptical foot while Ruth ceased caressing her whip to pop her gum, emitting miniature bursts of cannon fire. Only Hector dared ask what the others were wondering: "What gives, Bub?"

"I thought i'd share something a bit different today." Neimann grinned from ear to ear, plopping a pile of paperbacks onto the lectern. The topmost volume displayed a cover whose buxom, dark-haired heroine wore a scarlet dress while being clasped around the knees by a kneeling, muscular Negroid w/ Aryan features. **The Tigress of Temple Gray**, the book's title read.

Heidi, seated closest, shivered in revulsion as she grabbed the edges of her chair. Sedgewick dropped his jaw, whispering to Heidi his gratitude @ not having brought his younger brother. Hector, on the other hand, stood up, the better to see the source of their discomfort, only to be promptly yanked back in his seat by an indignant, cannon firing Ruth.

Oblivious to the slight uproar, Neimann raced thru roll call, reading last week's minutes in a matter of seconds. He subsequently selected a paperback from the center of the stack, one boasting of being UNEXPURGATED. Prefacing his remarks w/ comments on the healing power of love & the salve Eros provided to bereft, hapless spirits, Neimann then orated the seduction of Psyche by Cupid, which, he happily concluded, begat Pleasure. He added how some scholars consider Aphrodite more powerful—certainly more crafty—than even the staid, bullishly one-dimensional Zeus. It was Helen of Troy, he reminded his audience, not Ares, who launched those thousand ships & determined the fate of the Greeks, the Trojans & all generations to follow.

But barely had Neimann finished reading the first paragraph of a selected passage—one whose alliterative & parallel structure, combined w/ sensually descriptive detail, had rendered it among Romance Literature's finest—when whip snapping, knuckle crackling & a volley of plaintive moans & groans derailed his concentration. He glanced up @ an audience of beet-red faces, violent gum smacking & flaring nostrils. He found himself gripping the edges of the lectern in stunned confusion.

"Heidi," he stammered, "s-s-surely you recognize the importance of love in the human quest for meaning & purpose, don't you?"

The red-faced rag doll fumed, her words clearly audible, her tiny teeth flashing. "Contrary to popular stereotypes, Mr Gorge, guerrilla women do not pine for fist-wielding generals to slap them into submission."

Neimann blushed, aware his temples were throbbing. "I was...i mean...guys... Heidi..."

"Hey guys. *What's up?*" Edmund interrupted, entering & immediately sensing the palpable tension.

"Mr Gorge is reading about the nasty stuff," Sedgewick groaned.

"I was not..." About to explain himself, Neimann stopped in mid-objection. A flash of insight circled the outer hemispheres of his gray matter, revealing the excerpt he had been reading (a passage beginning w/ slapping, her him, then him her, followed by passionate groping & unfettered kissing, along w/ the stripping away of what barriers remained btwn them) had not merely been metaphoric: had not been, as he had initially taken it, a passion-filled description of love's ability to remove the existential hostility btwn the sexes...but had in fact been indeed about— about the nasty stuff.

Neimann's face flushed, his stomach suddenly queasy. A rumbling deep in his bookbelly, followed by a constriction in his throat, alerted his brain that something (his lunch perhaps) was about to come up. Abandoning **The Tigress of Temple Gray**, **Lady Chatterton's Poolboy**, **Madame Ovries** & the other unexpurgated classics, he dashed from the room twd the nearest lavatory.

* * * * *

WHILE NEIMANN HAD BEEN SCOURING the Basilica of Harlequin Romance, selecting the particular passage that would prove so irksome to his digestive system, two men had sauntered into the Libary & Literary Infirmary, both put off by the bright lights & richly wrought archways that were the hallmarks of our municipal palace of higher learning.

When their narrowed eyes had sufficiently adjusted, one of them pointed an arthritic finger as they both made for the ambulatory. The shorter of the two wore a derby hat & walked w/ a cane used mostly for swatting things invisible to the patrons they passed. The taller man wore his hair piebald, patches of curly reddish-brown tufts here & there, w/ curvy patches of baldness elsewhere. His musculature just beginning to sag, his face to wrinkle, the man had no doubt been lean in his youth. Yet for occasions such as this, he had swallowed a watermelon whole, this to calm his nerves & settle his quivering stomach.

When the two reached the top floor, the shorter, older man paused, catching his breath as the taller, middle-aged man pushed thru the door marked HEAD LIBARIAN. As no one was w/in, they looked about the brightly lit rotunda, the younger w/ an expression of mild intimidation, the elder w/ sheer contempt.

The room could have been cluttered w/ rabid, disease-infected rodents as far as Sur Harry was concerned. He kicked any book w/in his foot's range, toppled a few w/ his cane, then walked about w/ his hat in one hand, cane in the other, now & then whacking an unsuspecting volume across its arrogant elitist spine.

The taller man, Counting Commissioner Donald Dicker, lifted several books from their chair, closed them gently & set them almost reverently on the coffee table. He sat in the vacated chair, his eyes wandering to the back of his head, where his mind was rumored to hang out.

The two men sat or paced respectively until, whacking the sturdy spine of a particularly uppity title, Sur Harry turned to the Commissioner—seeing only the piebald head above the chair.

"What you ought to do is burn the whole dammed blDG down."

"Can'tt do it," the Commissioner stated flatly, tripping over a t, nearly stumbling on the d as well.

"Sure you can!"

"Can't ddo it, Harry. You know we can'tt."

"No one's sayING to acTUALly strike the match. All you have to do is *threa*TEN to." Sur Harry puckered his lips. "These braiNY-ack types are moRAL weakLINGS. The guy's onLY puNY musCLE is crammed INside that skinNY skull of his. I'm telling you DonNIE, he'll coWER beFORE you can eVEN lift a hot poKER to his eyeBALL."

"There are rules, Harry."

"Don't you think I know that? It costs me an arm & someBODy's leg eVERy time I need to bend one of those rules."

"Harry, you know we need to @ least *appear* to follow the rules. Otherwwise others will use our not following the rules as an excuse to not ffollow the rules they're supposed to follow."

161

Sur Harry fell silent tho only for a moment.

"You know, DoNALD...you can always use a GOOJ card."

"Can'tt do it."

"Why not?"

"Ran out. Used my last Get-out-of-Jail card this mmorning."

The aristrocrat reached in his stuffed shirt to pull out a deck of tiny cards. Removing several from the stack, he tossed them in the Commissioner's lap. "AfTER S-elecTION you should requisTION the prinTING of more. I don't see how aNY puBLIC serVANT can funcTION w/out 'em. If I had a doLLAR for eVERytime I had to lie to DEfend the truth, I'd own half the SmoLET PeDESTal."

Sur Harry sniffed the air, scrunching his face as his nostrils detected an unfamiliar odor. "I'm telLING you, there is someTHING fesTERing in this estaBLISHment. Can't you smell it? You've heard what my INformants are rePORTing."

"Whatever you pay them to report."

"BEsides that.... I'm telLING you, DonNIE, there's a CONspiracy AFoot."

"You mean other than yours?"

"Our conspiracy is auTHORized! It's leGALly reGISTered w/ the OfFICE of CONspiraTORial CorrecTIONS. I can show you the certiFIcate, wise aLECK." Sur Harry thrust his cane like a sword, the piebald head his pretended target. "We can't have eVERy Tom, Dick & MaRY going ARound conspiRING w/OUT a liCENSE. RememBER, DonNIE: we're the rubBER, they're the glue—aNYthing they ACcuse us of bounCES off of us & sticks to their you-know-who. I swear, sometimes I don't know whose side you're on."

"Yours," the Commissioner sighed. "But you need to bear in mind, Harry: the law still allows others to have contrary ppoints of view—& to air them openly."

"As well it should! How else are we to idenTIfy the iDIots AMong us? ContraRY to what you may think of me, i'm an aVID belieVER in free speech. That way we can weed out the wrong opinIONS up front."

The Commissioner shook his head as Sur Harry narrowed his eyelids & imagined the shaking skull to be a lopsided wiffle ball. Several times the aristocrat mimicked knocking the ball out of the park w/ his cane. Bases loaded, two outs in the bottom of the tenth, the score tied four to one, Sur Harry was about to wallop a grand slam when the Commissioner leaned fwd, reaching for a book.

"CareFUL," the aristocrat cautioned. "You might catch someTHING."

Checking his swing, preparing again to clobber a grand slam, Sur Harry's victory was again thwarted when the door swung open.

"I'm sorry," a surprised, wide-eyed Neimann apologized. "I wasn't expecting—"

"Sit down, MiSTER Gorge," Sur Harry ordered.

"Harry, this is my rresponsibility," the piebald head cut in. Dropping the book, the Commissioner motioned to the libarian. "Have a seatt, Neimann."

The libarian moved to his desk cautiously, sliding slowly into his chair, not daring to remove his gaze from the piebald Commissioner or the cane-wielding aristocrat standing a few feet behind the Commissioner.

"I ddon't suppose you pparticipated in what went on tthis morning?" the Commissioner began, clutching his tummy.

"You mean the Crybaby Convention?" Neimann asked.

Sur Harry huffed. The Commissioner nodded.

Neimann swallowed, his throat constricted & unusually dry, his stomach still unsettled from his recent encounter w/ the Bookworms. "No, sir. I had medical staff to supervise. After that i had to prepare my afternoon lecture."

"You know we honor every citizen's right to sspeak their minds," the Commissioner continued.

"But don't APpreCIate it when they do."

"Harry, i said i'd handle this. He's right, tho, Neimann. Just because ppeople are ddiscontent, doesn't give them the right to bbring down those of us who aren't. Complacentness is next to Puppiness."

"But they hold these conventions every S-election season," Neimann reminded his guests. "It's tradition—guaranteed by the Constitution, intended to kick off bulloting season."

"Ttrue," Commissioner Dicker conceded, flipping one of his GOOJ cards over in his hand, "but according to rreports, the crowd this year was...how did the reports put it, Harry? Oh, yes: uncommonly hostile to established norms & long-cherished ideals, many of which date back to @ least last year.

"One speaker, we are ttold, used a slew of six syllable words, none of which our agents were familiar with. If government agents assigned to protect the common wealth can't ddecipher what these provocateurs are provocateering, how can we assure the all-too trusting ppublic that the message is acceptable to general standards of accepted ddecency? After all, Neimann—there were ttoddlers in the audience. I better not find you were behind this display of excessive syllablism."

Neimann tugged an earlobe. "I assure you, gentlemen...i would never deign to become embroiled in political imbroglio. Politics, after all, is for those who have lost faith in the human capacity to know right from wrong for themselves," Neimann eyed Sur Harry, "or those prone to restrict the behavior of others under threat of punishment, death or social disenfranchisement."

"Another six syllable word, Neimann."

Neimann fell silent, looking from the Commissioner to Sur Harry, not even bothering to correct the Counting Commissioner's math. Beads of sweat popped up along the libarian's hairline, the liquid pimples soon sliding down his sullen cheeks.

The Commissioner shifted, puckering his lips before continuing. "Several inspectors from the Dept of Kooties found indications of contaminants seeping thru the mortar of this libary's ffoundation." The Commissioner flicked the card in his hand, pulling another from his pocket & adding it to the first.

"I'm sure they are mistaken," Neimann rallied. "These pillars have withstood contaminants borne of ignorance, tyranny, superstition & even blind misguided faith—for hundreds of years. I'm certain they can withstand any threat posed by kooties."

"I wish I could bbe so sure, Neimann." The Commissioner scratched his nose w/ the cards. "Suppose a few of these ppillars were to come ttumbling down, knocking some innocent boy or Brittle girl on the noggin? Smashing someone to a bloody ppulp, guts spewing out, their internal organs oozing onto the sidewalk as the life slowly seeps out of them? That wouldn't be too smart for a ppillar of higher learning, now would it? We may have to close this libary down...just ttemporarily, of course. We can revisit the matter sometime after S-election."

"But, but..." Neimann stared wide-eyed as the Commissioner again rubbed his nose, adding a third card to his collection. Neimann looked @ the scowling aristocrat whose palsied claw clutched the top of the Commissioner's chair, reminding Neimann of the iconic portrait of the hawk-eyed Annabelle McDougal standing behind her scowling husband, Smolet the Great.

"Of course, you can always..." The Commissioner paused, smoothing a brow, patting his stomach. "You can always consult the One."

"If you eVEN BElieve in the One," Sur Harry injected.

The Commissioner paused, cocking the brow he had just smoothed. "You know what the Good PUP says: 'The ONE protects the one who protects the One.'" The Commissioner reached for the nearest book, fanning its pages & patting its smooth surface before rising.

Neimann sat dumbfounded as Commissioner & aristocrat took their leave. Volume III of **Clever Witticisms for All Occasions** gazed up sympathetically @ the libarian but Neimann could not be enticed to open its conciliatory pages. Even the pink carnation on the corner of his desk failed to brighten his now clouded disposition. He instead acknowledged the flower's inevitable demise now that it had been plucked by a human hand—even one as precious as Mz Pritt's—& placed in a man-made vase.

The Commissioner meanwhile, his fingers laced, hands cupped under his bulging belly, strolled down the ambulatory a couple of paces ahead of Sur Harry.

"I still say you were too eaSY on the eggHEAD," the aristocrat complained. "I tell you, i miss the days when you could just whack a felLA." Sur Harry smacked a Greek-Corinthian column to demonstrate how it once was done. "And if they said aNYthing, you could call the conSTAble & have the slime hanged. Those were the good ol' days."

"I know," the Commissioner sighed, relieved his belly was finally beginning to settle. "But you forget, Harry: to depose our last ttyrant, our forefathers came up w/ this demicracy thing. Now, on ppaper @ least, we're supposed to protect the rights of every dammed citizen—even their right to criticize those of us charge."

"Fiddler sticks," Sur Harry countered. "If our flounDERing farTERS had thought for one minute peoPLE would take their words liteRALly, they would neVER have writTEN them into the consTItution."

"Shhhh," several voices hissed from nearby tables. The Commissioner turned to Sur Harry, pressing a finger to his lips.

Aware his words had been echoing off the vaulted ceilings, Sur Harry grew indignant, glaring @ any pair of eyes deigning to glower in his direction. A sudden swarm of invisible flies felt the aristocrat's wrath. His tongue, however, remained immobile until the pair had exited the libary.

"Sometimes i wonDER whose side you are on, DonNIE?" he continued in the open air.

"Harry, we've been thru this. It's in my jjob description: i have to @ least appear impartial...*and*, i have to be open to taking bribes from bboth sides. This libarian was easy. So was that nephew of yours. It's fellows like this GGrimspoon who will give us a run for our One...him & that gosh-darn S-."

Sur Harry donned his hat, tapping it in place w/ his cane. A soft rumbling among a gathering of discontented clouds caught the aristocrat's attention. The scent of impending rain, accompanied by several distant strikes of lightning, sent the two pillars of the community scurrying to their horse & surrey, Commissioner Dicker taking the reins.

"Where should we go, Harry? Home?"

"How aBOUT once or twice ARound the park. I have a hankERing for lookING for peoPLE i can't see," the aristocrat tittered.

Chapter 15

As soon as S- & Pearl stepped thru the libary's double doors, Pearl took off, meandering the aisles of majestic, lofty shelves, rearranging books according to her own Dewey Decimal System. Quickly bored, she then took to sitting across from various patrons, staring @ them long & hard—until each felt compelled to glance up. Some would stare back in silence; others inquired what she might be staring @. In either case, she would slink under the table, crawl on all fours & pop up across from her next victim.

S-, meanwhile, returned his books to a gracious, dreamy-eyed Mz Pritt, who purred as she dusted her desk & assorted her paperclips, now & then stopping to fondle andor gaze lovingly @ a pair of puppy-eyed bookends.

By the time S- began to search for Pearl, the girl was zigzagging thru the infirmary, stealing pain pills & lifting books from one sleeping patient to slide into the grasp of another sleeping patron. Backtracking, she then wandered from one basilica to the next, imagining herself dodging some maniacally malevolent archenemy. Spotting S-, she gave her malicious archrival a new face. She eluded the befuddled S- for the better part of a half hour, having honed her evading-capture skills from her brother. S- searched high & low, as well as several places inbwtn, even descending into the basement where the startled Lugworts fired a volley of dirty looks—some angry, some paranoid, some reeking of sheer hatred. Quickly slamming the door, he hurried back up the elevator.

Eventually Pearl reversed tactics (another technique learned from her brother), following a few yards behind S- as he ducked btwn various bookshelves. Tho S-'s shadow caught on immediately, it chose not give the girl away. Tipped off, however, by his shadow's barely suppressed giggles, S- soon caught on as well. As thunder had begun rattling the windows & lightning flashed in the sky's darkening eyes, he opted to extend the game, leading Pearl around the entire libary/infirmary till the blackened sky cracked a faint smile. As an ever-widening yellow shaft of light poked its way thru the multi-paned rose-tinted windows, S- veered twd the exit, shrugging his shoulders & throwing up his arms as if deciding to abandon his search. Reaching the exit door, he abruptly whirled around, his shadow gleefully shouting *Gotcha!*

The tiptoeing Pearl doubled over in laughter, convinced she had been pulling the strings. The two exited hand-in-hand, agreeing to another jaunt thru the Municipal Park & Nature Observatory. S- sauntered casually as Pearl ran in figure eights among the rain-drenched beds of tulips, azaleas & daffodils. She insisted on climbing a blue spruce she called Bruce, S- standing fearfully below despite Bruce's repeated assurances he would not let the girl fall. Relieved when the girl climbed down, S- sprawled along a park bench, deciphering the incessant, often contradictory gossip of several crows who taunted a family of cuckoos & harangued a panhandling scrubjay. Pearl meanwhile stomped & shouted, jumping over rain puddles, then jumping in them. When she had sufficiently stomped the last of the puddles out of existence, she returned, wiggling her way beside S- on the bench. She removed her shoes & socks, the sun's yellow fingers enveloping her tiny toes w/ its warming massage.

S- observed a modest parade of pedestrians, many walking together tho talking to themselves. A small boy w/ a large forehead kept punching himself in the face; his twin sister sticking needles in her flesh, examining the beads of blood before tasting them w/her tongue. At a bandstand, a group of girls kept setting themselves on fire while surrounded by a gaggle of boys peeing on the bushes. S- nodded @ two Great Danes jauntily walking their two-legged companions, who huffed & puffed, struggling to keep up.

"You ever been to the zoo?" Pearl asked, watching one of the Danes pause to wait for its human to relieve itself.

S- shook his head.

"We should go. It'll be fun." Pearl smacked her socks against the bench, testing them for dryness. Pocketing the still soggy socks, she donned her shoes & rose, slipping her hand inside S-'s, pulling him along.

"It's just past the animal prison," she coaxed.

A few blocks away, they came to an ominous fortress of gray cinderblock, a steel fence surrounding the stolid concrete edifice. On select blocks of stone, carved figures had been etched herding animals away in handcuffs. Two uniformed bulldogs wearing badges, holding billy clubs & smoking cigarillos guarded the entrance.

Animal Prison

was inscribed along the gate in thick cursive letters, the capitals heightened & augmented w/ floral curlicues.

"Want to peek in?" Pearl suggested.

When S- failed to respond, Pearl pulled him in anyway, leading as they strolled the main promenade. Bobcats, pronghorn, iguanas, jackals, Irish setters, bison, caribou, impalas, giraffes & a long list of similar felons paced the iron cages & barbed mesh-wiring. Several more dangerous inmates lay shackled or strapped in decorative straitjackets. Other less intimidating convicts circled confined open spaces encased by high walls, electric fences & armed cigar-smoking bulldogs.

"Serves them right," Pearl blurted, pointing @ two glassy-eyed platypus monkeys. "If they can't behave civilized, they deserve what they get."

After meandering several winding boulevards & dodging numerous finger-pointing onlookers, S- & Pearl came to a food court bustling w/ human activity. The pedestrian rest stop was crammed beyond capacity w/ human beans, many dressed in alligator shoes, toting snakeskin briefcases & pulling legal tender from leather wallets. Snacking on alley-cat burgers & side portions of pinto chips, they chatted incessantly, milling about as if they had nowhere else to be, occasionally exchanging papers andor admiring each another's embossed letterheads.

"Animal lawyers," Pearl explained in a whisper. "By law, each prisoner is assigned an attorney by our jewish...our judas...no: our ju-dish-shell system. Should any prisoner claim human incest, no wait: an-cest...an-cest-tree," she corrected herself, "Should any prisoner claim human ancestry, they can go to a kangaroo court where, if they are deemed competent to stand trial, they can argue for the right to be declared human—provided they show a valid driver's license, D&A samples & another form of picture ID.

"Doesn't happen a lot," Pearl conceded, "but there's a baboon working in the Chamber of Commerce & several orangutans have been given the right to vote—but only to break a tie.

"C'mon. The zoo's on the next block."

Doubling back & crossing thru an AGGRAVATED ASSAULT-FREE ZONE, Pearl led S- to a saw-toothed metallic structure, its windows glazed & shaded, its steel frame spiked w/ barbed wire & decorative smiley faces. Arranged in a circular maze of halls, dimly lit latticed rooms, stairwells & terraces, the MUNICIPAL ZOO claimed to offer an educational trek thru recorded time. Visitors were encouraged to begin w/ the Prenatal Period, then follow humane evolution thru the Pavilion of Prehysteric Times & so on.

Entering the first exhibit, S- stared transfixed @ a toothless man & an equally toothless woman displayed inside a crude cave. The couple moved slowly, bent over, their faces disfigured by what a nearby placard explained was old age & the ravages of life's daily struggles. They dressed in loose-fitting fur, both hunched over a mock fireplace. One blew on the artificial fire while the other bowed to a stone altar around which lay scattered bones & the skulls of small animals.

In an adjacent display, Pearl gawked @ a similar scene, tho the cave was now the inside of a thatched-roof hut. Next they came to a house of mud, then one of stucco, followed by one of wood & finally of drywall w/ elaborate wainscoting. With each period, the human specimans acquired more teeth & stood straighter, their clothes less rough & ultimately synthetic. The fireplaces also grew less crude while the altars remained pretty much the same—save that the skulls were now of small children.

"We *have* to go in there," Pearl pointed, insisting on skipping the bronzed, ironed & steel ages to go straight to the ATRIUM OF THE BIRD-BRAINED.

S- complied, pausing momentarily to read the sign above the entrance:

ALL SPECIMANS DISPLAYED WITHIN
VANISHED DURING THE "MIDDLE" PERIOD OF HUMAN HISTORY
(which transpired circa three weeks ago)

PLEASE WATCH YOUR STEP
as specimans within will be watching yours

S- entered apprehensively, he & Pearl warned by an attendant not to get too near the specimans as the zoo assumed no responsibility for lost or damaged gallbladders. While Pearl rushed thru the exhibit, S- strolled casually, taking ample time to read the eye-catching, informative plaques. He became particularly methodical when he entered the exhibit's North American wing. He stared long & hard @ a chisel-chinned, immaculately dressed speciman pacing its cubicle, peering back @ him thru hard, devouring, watery blue eyes. S- bent low to read the corresponding placard.

170

WHITE-BREASTED MASTER-BAITER
*Also known as the 'chosen', the 'favored',
the 'righteous' andor the 'white man'.*

Master Baiters with unwavering consistency trample on the rights of others while convincing themselves they *are the ones being persecuted. This speciman shows unusual adroitness @ not batting an eye when asserting its right to push aside andor annihilate others in its unrelenting pursuit of liberty & justice 'for all.'*

After staring intensely @ the glowering speciman which seemed fond of displaying its middle fingers, S- moved to the next speciman.

RED-NECKED SELF-LOATHER
*Also called 'bigot', 'God-fearing' or, oftentimes, 'Officer'.
Note: not all SELF-LOATHERS have red necks, some being
red-eyed, others red-baiters.*

In their neurotic need to always have someone to look down on, the self-loather will strike, oppress, even kill, anyone who dares give it a glimpse into its low sense of self-worth. Members of this species are adept @ torturing, torching, andor lynching others while exalting in their own unstained, god-fearing, peace-loving purity.

(CAUTION: Do not feed their wounded egos).

At the next display, S- gawked @ a tight-knit family whispering among themselves as the children pointed accusing fingers @ him. As the young boy showed S- his tongue, the girl hid sheepishly behind her mother's dress. S- stepped closer to read the corresponding plaque.

YELLOW-BELLIED SAPSUCKER
Often called 'model citizen', 'here boy' or, during times of war, 'loyal patriot'.

Ignorance is indeed bliss for this speciman, consistently behaving as it believes will net its greatest advantage. Clinging to a peace-loving nature, the sapsucker is easily drawn into armed conflict approx. every 11 years. Unable to admit fault, it perpetually climbs up the wrong tree, stubbornly refusing to descend even when said tree is being chopped, disease-ridden, andor has burst into flames.

S- continued to gawk @ the complacent family, the mother wrapped in soft mink, the father hunkered over a game board, the children competing for their parents' attention, resorting to smacking each other should all else fail.

"Over here!" Pearl called, running in to drag S- to another wing of the pavilion. She pointed excitedly to a threadbare, underfed speciman w/ a scraggly tuft of hair & deep-set brooding eyes. "He kinda looks like you," she exclaimed. "Only meaner."

Tho S- failed to see the resemblance, he read the decorative plaque.

PIGEON-CHESTED FREEDUM-FIGHTER
Known also as 'anarchist', 'radical' andor 'liberator'.

Motivated by an unrelenting desire to live unrestricted lives, Freedumbers advocate absolute freedom for all, slaughtering anyone who disagrees with or impedes their quest. Given power, Freedumbers evolve into paragons of despotism, insisting @ gunpoint that all resultant oppression and slaughter be for 'the sake of the greater good'.

As S- studied the sad-eyed speciman, its five o'clock shadow well past midnight, Pearl announced she needed to use a bathroom. As she dashed off, S- poked his head into a pavilion honoring 'The Hero thruout History.' Disappointed the exhibit had little to do w/ sandwiches, he ambled back to the main corridor, spotting Pearl skipping twd him, a cone of cotton candy wrapped in her tiny fist. Before she reached him, a bedraggled figure stepped btwn them, looming like a dark shadow. The man, his complexion jaundiced, his thin, wiry beard infested w/ flies, peered probingly into S-'s face, their two noses nearly touching. S- stepped back, vaguely recognizing the crooked teeth & centipede-like stitches. The floor beneath him wobbled as familiar words echoed in his memory: YOU KNOW NOT WHAT YOU DO.

"Don't worry," the man reassured him, holding up both palms as if surrendering @ gunpoint. "I'm not here to harm you." The man peered deep into S-'s eyes, his own eyes bright & delirious. Pearl stepped btwn the two men. Looking into the haggard face of Erle Greaves, she extended her cotton candy. "Want some?" she asked.

* * * * *

THE EMACIATED ERLE devoured half the cotton candy in one gulp.

"Hey!" Pearl screeched, eyeing him w/ contempt before graciously handing him

172

the rest. She dashed back to the concession stand, returning w/ an alley-cat burger & a weaselschnitzel, both generously smothered w/ sourcrop & horseradix. The former seminary student blessed the girl as he devoured both, licking every last remnant of juice trickling down his forearm. Pearl returned again w/ a king-size bag of barbecue cowchips & the three strolled twd the Nature Observatory, Erle feebly apologizing for his previous behavior, unable to explain even to himself what had possessed him.

The two man sat on a park bench within sight of the towering oak tree, who eyed Erle w/ bemused compassion. Pearl, surrendering the bag of cowchips, ran off to join a raucous swarm of children wielding bats & chasing squawking geese. S- gazed into the knobby, wizened face of his silent friend as Erle examined his own garment, obsessed w/ several rips & gaping holes in his soiled muslin vestment.

"Have you ever seen anything more holy?" Erle asked, inspecting one particular slit @ length. He looked up @ S-, his eyes clear & sadly serious. "I know you think you've come to save us," he said, "but there's little left to salvage. And what there is to save must first be destroyed. You know that, don't you?"

S- looked twd the shimmering lake. A blond boy was waving a baseball bat while chasing a family of baby ducks. The mother duck, frantic to the point of quacking shrill obscenities, fluttered her feathers, the boy holding his ground, threatening to pummel her as well.

"Or maybe you don't," Erle continued. "Forgive me. I presume too much. Truth is, i haven't been myself much lately." He indicated the scars & haphazard stitching crisscrossing his half-starved body. He held up a thumb sewn on backward & a foot realigned crookedly such that his two feet seemed @ cross-purposes.

"To think it was only a few months ago," he reminisced. "I was cramming for the final exam before my ordination. I was studying so hard, my eyes began to cross. I struggled as hard as i could to uncross them. But sometimes our eyes have a mind of their own. When i picked up THE GOOD BOOK & began to read despite my blurry condition, i noticed THE BOOK we claim to be sacred—the one we worship as the very WORD OF PUP—was full of typographical errors. And it all made sense. See, most of PUP's disciples never went to school or had any formal education. Not only that, none of them could type. Add to that, they recorded PUP's wisdom on a used, secondhand typewriter—a typewriter missing the letter A."

As S- listened, his shadow observed the mistress in the sky, her radiant lips a brilliant ruby as she lounged across her blue sofa, fluffing & rearranging the pillowy clouds, blowing on a few or shoving them along w/ her tapered fingers.

She frowned momentarily, perturbed by the piercing honks & frenzied squawking of ducks & geese. Children swinging bats & tossing rocks ran in circles, screeching w/ laughter as they chased the scuttling flock, who managed just barely to evade their menacing reach.

"That's why the ancient alphabet begins w/ the letter B," Erle continued, his sparkling, delirious eyes oblivious to the mounting pandemonium. "That's why the original scribes assert how in the beginning, there was no beginning...since w/ out an A there was no way to begin. Once i realized that, it all made perfect sense: the truths we are taught to parrot as gospel are nothing but perfect NONsense."

S- caught a glimpse of Pearl. Having originally sided w/ the children, the youngster had taken pity on the ducks. Retrieving the very stones the kids threw, she tossed them back @ the children, her aim considerably more accurate than theirs. S- pictured her @ the dining room table, meticulously practicing her aim. As the children scurried away, several crying, he turned his attention back to Erle.

"That's why the first Puppians banned the letter A from all speech. It used to be that to use an A in a sentence was a mortal sin. Even today, some Verbatums believe to give a Dreg or a Canaan an A on a school exam is a sacrilege."

A dark cloud abruptly hovered over the pair. A chill coursed thru S- as he gazed up @ the menacing shadow, stern eyes & arched brows of Police Chief Willoughby, the officer's face red as a fresh pimple, his displeased lips clamped tight.

"Humph," the C of P humphed, tracing the scar atop his scalp before pulling out his billy club.

"You know, there's a stiff penalty...I SAID THERE'S A STIFF PENALTY FOR VAGRANCY," he drawled, his eyeballs appraising both Erle & S- as he shook his rotund head. "AND THERE IS AN EVEN STIFFER PENALTY FOR PROPHETEERING W/OUT A LICENSE. I suggest you run along," he ordered Erle, using his club to point out a recommended route.

Erle stood unwillingly. "And there is less profit in false prophets," he quipped, pivoting & shuffling away. "Even the One won't save your ONE," he shouted over his shoulder. "No one can...not even him." He pointed to S-.

The Police Chief pretend-hurled his club, Erle flinching, then quickening his pace. As the former seminary student disappeared w/in a grove of bowing beech trees, the C of P tapped his club in his upturned hand.

He glared @ S-, his eyes rolling as if traversing a rollercoaster as he shook his head. "You can feign ignorance," he cautioned, the barrel of his club aimed btwn

S-'s eyes. "YOU CAN FEIGN INGORANCE but...EITHER YOU ARE W/ US...
or against us. Sooner or later, YOU'LL HAVE TO CHOOSE."

* * * * *

THAT EVENING S- SLOUCHED across his loveseat, his camera limp around his
neck, its lens capped & sleeping. His brows wrestled like competing inchworms
as he puzzled over Buck's recent change in demeanor. Clearly the man-child was
painfully uncomfortable in S-'s presence. S- shrugged off his shadow's suggestion
that Buck seemed equally uncomfortable in everyone's presence, even giving Pearl
a stiff shoulder. S- recalled the several occasions he had watched big brother &
baby sister roughhousing like wild tigers, knocking over statuary, dislodging
wall-hangings & shattering defenseless bric-a-brac—Buck ostensibly practicing
his hogtieing technique, Pearl dutifully giving her mother something to clean up
afterward. Brother & sister @ such times were inseparable. Yet recently, Buck
hardly acknowledged his little sister.

See, it's not just you, his shadow concluded.

Man & shadow compared notes on that evening's dinner. Buck's (aka Bill's)
dimples had gone on hiatus, his troops negligent in their duty. Even the rare coin
tumbling from the man-child's pockets did so listlessly, as if hardly caring if it fell
to the floor or not.

Buck's being barely talkative stood in stark contrast to Mr Smolet, who was full
of probing questions, mostly aimed @ S-. Where had he been that day? Who did he
talk to? Was he exercising his voting finger? S- squirmed, thankful Pearl answered
the tuffer questions, even diverting her father's attention by firing mashed potatoes
@ any object the banker called out, the girl's aim & distance greatly improved.

And to everyone's surprise, Mrs Smolet made a rare appearance. Tho she neither
touched her food nor rubbed S-'s knee under the table (something he was beginning
to miss), she sat @ rigid attention, engaging in whatever light conversation the
family could muster. S- found himself feeling slighted by her refusing to look his
way, finding solace however in the smiling glances she slipped her husband, her
glossed lips busily chewing on something.

As he slouched in his loveseat, his shadow in the rocker opposite him, S- recalled
Penny's late arrival to the table, her hair a category six hurricane. The girl shuffled
in, gauze wrapped around every inch of her body, save her eyes, lips & navel.
Determined not to bat an eyelash, she struggled w/ each utensil. She spilled every

glass of lemming-aid her grumbling brother poured for her. Complaining about her attorney & her chatterbox of a cosmetologist, she pushed aside her buzzers & bells, begrudgingly answering her mother's inquiries w/ curt guttural grunts & groans.

S- recalled the secret passage Pearl had shown him. He imagined slipping secretly into Penny's room, replacing her light bulbs w/ a few of his own. While the girl slept, he could then do a photo study of her shadow. He imagined developing the negatives thru the nite such that in the morning, she would awake to a stack of fresh prints on her nitestand.

It's worth a try, his shadow concurred.

While the two debated what grade film to use, what shutter speed to try, a light tapping rattled the windowpane. A head of scraggly hair poked its way in.

"It's me," Erle whispered, grimacing as he pulled his skeletal figure inside. "I know who you are!" he exclaimed excitedly. "I know where you come from! I know your whole history!"

Erle stood, whisking around to grab two books he had lugged along. The smaller, a worn, tattered volume, had its spine reinforced w/ duct tape. Its bold lettering professed THE BOO, its last letter worn to near invisibility. The larger, heftier book proved to be a brand new dictionary, its cover unblemished, its pages crisp & virginal.

"I didn't see it @ first," Erle declared, his words popping like stray firecrackers. "I'm sorry i doubted you. It's all in the BOOK. Once you cross your eyes, it explains everything clearly."

Erle plopped into the rocking chair, dropping both books in his lap. Just as quickly, he was on his feet, pacing the length of the room, his shadow remaining in the rocker, cradling both books while flipping thru THE BOO's onion-thin pages.

"It says in the BOOK," Erle proclaimed: "'HE shall be born of a man & a woman.'" He stared @ S- as if the sentence made all else self-evident. "Don't you see...all births here, @ least among the Brittles & the Baums, the Dumpletons & the Smolets, are *virgin* births. But *this* man," his shadow pointed to the text, "this man will be born of a man & a woman. A man will actually...actually do the nasty thing, you know...that thing w/ a woman." Again Erle paused, allowing S- time to digest the obvious implication.

"Think of the horror, the disgrace of begetting a child by...you know. So they cast the baby out. Suck out its memories. Attempt to destroy its higher consciousness. Leave it to wander alone in the wilderness."

176

Erle's shadow, as animated as Erle himself, waved THE BOO's in S-'s face, encouraging him to read the passage for himself.

"But in the BOOK, he returns. In fact, there have been a number of you thruout history. Going all the way back to B-: 'cause, see, PUP himself was A-, the missing beginning. You come back. As long as we transgress, guys like you come back. You come back inexplicably drawn to the very people, the very parents, who cast you out." Erle paused again, his eyes piercing so deeply into S-'s, S- imagined them inspecting the back of his skull.

"You are the bastard son of Mr Smolet," Erle blurted. "He & Mrs Smolet are your parents!"

While Erle waited for a reaction, his shadow scanned the next verse.

"In the next verse," Erle continued, "it says you return to, quote, 'cut the pig open.'" Pausing, his brows slightly furrowed, Erle pondered the words, his shadow consulting the dictionary. Pausing a second, the shadow reread the verse, finally nodding w/ renewed confidence.

Erle continued. "It says you will slice the pig open & from its entrails trees will sprout flowers, grass will grow green & people shall thirst w/out going hungry. This shall reign for a thousand & thirty-six years, thirteen days & twelve minutes (give or take a nanosecond or two—it's hard to be precise).

"Don't you see? You have returned to kill Mr Smolet so the rest of us can enter paradise. You are the ONE!"

S- stared back @ his visitor in blank disbelief. His tongue remained stationary, his eyelids refusing to blink.

"Oh, i know you doubt it. Of course you doubt it. It took years for your cognizance to even function. You walked around like a lost sheep. For decades you were a catatonic, in a PUP-induced daze. But slowly things will come back to you. They have been coming back to you, am i right? Whether you want to or not, you slay that overstuffed banker for the sake of the rest of us. And the stronger you resist, the more PUP's angles..." Erle again paused, his shadow poring over the dictionary. "The more PUP's angels," he corrected himself, pausing as his shadow rose to whisper in his ear, "the more the voices in your head lead you to it. You can't help yourself," Erle concluded. "The will of PUP is final."

Again Erle stared @ the silent, dumbfounded S-. Again he broke the strained silence. "And i'll tell you something else." Erle peered deeply into S-'s eyes, his shadow closing THE BOO w/ a thump of triumphant finality. "That marionette, sitting in the temple, on his gilded throne...is an imposter. He's nothing but a puppet!

The other day in synachurch, instead of bowing my head, i opened my eyes. I sneaked a peek @ the O mighty ONE. And I noticed someone was pulling his strings!"

Erle plopped into the rocker, his shadow barely escaping being crushed. "I'm guessing he who controls the One controls the puppet's strings. It's called 'greasing the church's psalms': psalms, according to that book," he pointed to the dictionary, "is a derivative—a misspelling actually—of 'palms.'

"It's all in the BOOK!" Erle railed, both he & his shadow pointing to the dictionary. "I'll prove it to you. Come to synachurch temple tomorrow. You'll see for yourself." Erle rubbed his scabs, S- noting the calm agitation in the ex-student's eyes. Several scars on his face had healed since that afternoon, the stitches flaking off & fluttering to the floor.

"See, what happens," Erle continued, his shadow again fondling THE BOO, "is over generations PUP inevitably becomes the mouthpiece of those who control his strings, particularly his purse strings. Till someone like you descends to turn things back to their rightful order. No wonder the Tower of Power trembles @ your arrival. You've come to retune PUP's strings to their rightful chord."

Erle leaned back in the rocker, staring ahead, his thoughts light years into a brighter future, one w/ no pain or suffering, when everyone would be seated on the right hand of PUP & extra chairs brought in to accommodate even the lowliest of the low—including a Canaan or two. His shadow, having abandoned THE BOO, seemed now intent on scavenging for food. Having little success, it turned to scrounging the few coins tucked in the battered folds of the loveseat. "At first i thought you had come to destroy the old order," Erle said, more to himself than anyone in the room. "But now i understand: you are here to restore it."

Chapter 16

CLAD IN SHIMMERING SILK PAJAMAS, hoisted by velvet-lined suede platform slippers, Sur Harry paced the carpeted cubbyhole he mockingly called his STUDY. "Who needs to stuDY," he was often heard to quip, "when one alreaDY knows all there is to know?" The half-pint of an aristocrat listened w/ amused contempt—contempt tinged w/ envy—@ the peaceful chirping coming from the adjoining room. There his wife, Beulah, slept soundly. Snug as a bug, he mused, picturing his wife beneath several layers of cashmere comforter, a mere bump in a king-size bed they hadn't shared for years. "Who needs sleep?" he scoffed, kicking the wastebasket before it dared contradict him. He, after all, had perfected the art of catnapping: quick, frequent dozings-off that came in handy during contentious Bored of Directors meetings. Only that afternoon, he had awoken refreshed & rejuvenated after an intense labor-management dispute, his Louisville slugger poised in case anyone dare accuse him of having not paid attention.

"NitWITS!" he grumbled. "Nose-picks & dipsticks." Grabbing an umbrella, he began to parry & thrust @ his own image in a full-length mirror. He recalled advice his paternal grandfather had once given him: "Remember, Harry, today's assistant will be tomorrow's assassin. They always turn on you. Soon as you cut their wages or rescind their benefits, they're on you like flies @ a corpse's banquet."

The aristocrat again kicked the wastebasket, then smacked the baseboard w/ the umbrella. He whacked the doorjamb so it wouldn't feel left out. As he parried again before the mirror, he pictured dicing the turned-up nose of that librarian fellow. He wondered if these goodytwoshoers would ever learn that loving one's neighbor is akin to fiscal suicide. Loving *some* of your neighbors, sure—like those graced w/ a corrugated forehead, for instance; or a finely chiseled Romanesque snout; or, like his paternal grandpupa, w/ a cleft foot. But *all* your neighbors? Ballshoot! You needed people to step over. And a few to step on. How else was one to reach the top shelves in the pantry?

Feeling exasperated, Sur Harry collapsed in his desk chair, reaching for his prized seventy-ninth revised edition of THE BOOK, an original first printing, autographed by its Author. He paused, admiring the crinkly parchment, reinforced by non-yellowing scotch tape—tape only someone w/ his annual income could afford. He ran a rheumatic finger along the gold-leaf edging & toyed w/ the silver-tasseled bookmark. Next he grabbed a dictionary, one Beulah must have bought, so new were its pages, its ink still damp. Sur Harry could smell the fresh glue.

Biting his lower lip, he dove headlong into his task. He opened both BOOK & dictionary, the entire fate of civilization—not to mention his tobacco stock, his candy stores & bedbug emporium—rested on what he was about to pen. He shuttled from BOOK to dictionary to BOOK again, transcribing, lifting passages, always careful to include each word before rearranging the order.

He smirked as he whacked his umbrella against the side of his desk. "VerbaTUMS," he sneered, referring to that fringe group of zealots—iconoclastic fundamentalists who advocated leaving the holy text intact. He spit in the wastebasket. "Twits." He spat again. THE BOOK, after all, had been divinely inspired. Its crumbling parchment contained the sum total of all the words in PUP's divine vocabulary, each word a sacred gift—a gift PUP encouraged those who understood Him to reuse, rearrange, even reverse, to get to the truer, deeper meaning @ the heart of His indisputable wisdom.

Sur Harry sat back, reminiscing fondly on his first encounter w/ a then much younger Reverend Hickey. Here was a man of the loincloth: a man who understood the holy text, who understood not only were the *words* sacred but their divine letters doubly so. Neither the Reverend nor Sur Harry had any qualms about rearranging a word like *evil* to read *live*. Neither did Sur Harry hesitate to spell *Satan, Santa*. The aristocrat, in fact, considered converting *Satan's claws* to *Santa Claus*, a stroke of insightful genius—PUP inspired, even if he said so himself, which only he did.

Tho his eyes tired quickly, Sur Harry's brain was on fire, the aristocrat struggling w/ certain inconsistencies in PUP's antiquated verbiage. Obscure in their usage, words like *mountain* or *truth*, *compassion* or *charity*, proved perplexing. But that's what the dictionary was for. He turned to the hefty tome, pleased not only w/ the smooth, cool feel of its unsullied cover, but even more so w/ the appealing scent of its barely dried glue. He sniffed the binding before & after each word search, scouring the virginal white pages for more contemporary synonyms to words rarely used anymore. The task proved slow going, but as the waning moon moved east to west, he transcribed & revised, PUP's irrefutable purpose beginning to shine thru. With each successful line translated, Sur Harry grew more certain this would be the sermon to top all sermons.

The nite wore on, Sur Harry crossing thru words like *mountaintop, truth, visage & believer* to substitute the dictionary's more colorful, contemporary synonyms: *camel heap, puke, horse's snout, sex-slave, etc.* He scribbled feverishly, now & then sword-stabbing the wastebasket or sniffing the dictionary to rekindle his feisty spirit. He wrote, revived & rearranged till the ~~truth~~ puke he knew to be the very backbone of PUP's sacred will cascaded like a ~~waterfall~~ urinal, tumbling forth ~~majestically~~ masochistically into the ~~lake~~ cesspool of ultimate ~~truth~~ puke.

Eventually dawn awoke & stretched her rosy limbs. Like a Peeping Tom, she peered thru the narrow crack in Sur Harry's drawn curtain. His fountain pen snug in its inkwell, Sur Harry snored contently, his skinny head a paperweight stuck to the top page of his masterpiece. From the adjoining room, Mrs T'leBaum began to crow, causing her husband to stir drowsily. Showering & dressing, Sur Harry donned an extra layer of stuffed shirt, selecting shoes of extra height, these w/ stylish stiletto heels. Wrapping several promissory notes around a plump cigar, adding a pair of GOOJ cards for good measure, he tucked the generous tithe inside his coat pocket. Head high, heels higher & clicking w/ renewed confidence, Sur Harry practically tap danced twd the TEMPLE OF PERPETUAL PUPPINESS. Declining breakfast, he gulped instead a bloody Mary—one the cook assured him had been squeezed from a fresh supply of Mary Janes.

* * * * *

THAT SAME MORNING, S- half-awoke to shadows dancing along the far wall. Animated shadow-figures built a fire, its smoke billowing till its black cloud engulfed the ceiling. S- rolled over, falling back asleep.

Moments later, a noise stirred him. Groggily he looked on as more shadows, galloping on horseback, sliced each other w/ swords or jabbed one another w/ lances. He saw his own shadow hovering in a corner, protecting a pigtailed infant, clasping it in terror. Turning his back to the harrowing scene, S- rolled over again, swiftly falling back asleep.

Till another noise stirred him. Shadows were now gathered in small clusters. Some stood below a massive mulberry, gazing up @ one of their number dangling by its twisted neck. Others marched in a circle, each stabbing the one in front of it in the back. Another band of shadows was kicking & stomping a cringing figure curled in a fetal position, clutching its head. Shaken by the vision, S- ducked under the covers.

A hand—more like a monkey's paw—removed the cover. The shadow being kicked, stretched its hand, reaching for him, its cheeks turning pale, its eyes pleading, its wan smile encased in a small head w/ long, flowing hair. A more menacing shadow loomed large, stomping its female victim, whose small hand grew gnarled & wart-ridden. S- bolted upright, his heart pounding, his neck & forehead sopped w/ sweat.

The room lay quiet & shadowless save his own shadow, snoring beside him. As the pounding in his ribcage subsided, S- recalled the previous evening, envisioning the animated & emaciated former seminary student. He recounted the fatal prophecy & Erle's unshakeable insistence that everything writ in the pages of THE BOO was true. The words "cut the pig open" hovered in the recesses of S-'s imagination.

As dawn climbed the horizon, donning a flamingo morning gown, S- cowered in his pajamas, his shadow yawning & stretching, insisting Erle was deranged—divinely inspired, perhaps, but even so, the man's thumbs were on backward. S-, however, was not convinced. Despite dawn revealing her sultry thighs as she changed into a bright yellow diaphanous miniskirt, her seductive blue eye playfully winking @ him, S- was reluctant to climb out of bed. The cheerful chirping of cicadas seemed only to mock him as he pictured himself slashing open his employer, his landlord, his partner & possibly—assuming Erle was correct—his own father.

S-'s shadow rose w/out him, curling in the rocking chair as it thumbed thru the newest installment of **Rules for the Rode**. Nothing in the manual advocated violence, the shadow pointed out. In fact, almost every instruction resulted in S- being the one stepped on or over. As long as S- stuck to the rules, his shadow reasoned, he would be fine. *By the way*, the shadow added, *according to this paragraph here, we're late for breakfast*.

The two raced to the dining room, the shadow struggling w/ S-'s shirt buttons, fumbling to tie his shoes as they were descending both staircases. S- found the family gathered around the dining table, each gazing up @ him, nothing in their faces indicating they even suspected the fate looming on the bleak horizon.

Mr Smolet stroked his false beard, engrossed in a Sunday morning comic book. INVESTMENT MAN graced the glossy cover: an Italian-suited, square-jawed hero flew thru the air w/ an attaché case in one hand; wrapped in his other arm was a woman of ample cleaving, wearing a pearl necklace. Buck sat across from his father, painstakingly avoiding all eye contact. His few deployed troops stood lackadaisically, having abandoned their posts. His placemat, the salt & pepper shakers, the sugar bowl, the entire dining room set stood utterly defenseless. Pearl half-ate, half-played w/ her food while Penny poked @ her pancakes, her placemat conspicuously absent of buzzers & gong. Mrs Smolet, donned in praying-nun slippers, hummed snatches of what S- suspected to be a church hymn. Recalling Erle's invitation that he attend morning service, S- broached the subject, his comment meeting w/ several surprised glances, Buck's gaze tinged w/ contempt.

Mr Smolet set down his comic. "You sure about that?" He smoothed his beard before reaching for his glasses.

Buck snarled, "You're kidding, right?"

"I'll take him," Pearl offered.

"Finish your oatmeal," Mrs Sticky Buns instructed. "You & your sister can both take him."

"Mummy!" Penny protested.

"I think it would be a good idea if Bill accompanied them, too," the banker added.

"Oh, geez!"

"Now, now." The banker waved his glasses. "Remember what you & Uncle Harry discussed. It will be a wise gesture; show your uncle you really mean business."

"If Buck goes, then i don't have to, right?" Penny interjected.

"Bill! My name is *Bill*."

"Sorry."

Mr & Mrs Smolet exchanged looks, the latter glancing disapprovingly @ the girl's hair, teased into elephant ears, her bangs braided into a limp trunk.

"Actually, dear," Mrs Smolet suggested, "there will be lots of very handsome Brittle men there. Illegible bachelors. It wouldn't hurt if you let them get a peek @ you. You know what they say: 'Pretty is power.' But honestly, dear, if you're going to wear burlap w/ those leather pantaloons, for PUP's sake, @ least pick colors that match."

Penny scrunched her face, registering her protest in silence.

Buck leaned back, several coins spilling onto the dining room floor. One coin rolled noisily in drunken loops, finally colliding into S-'s chair leg. As S- bent to retrieve it, he noted Mrs Smolet's hand playfully patting her husband's knee. As he placed the coin on the table, the lady of the house announced she & Mr Smolet could not accompany them as they had a highly personal matter to attend to, her husband vaguely nodding his assent. Thereafter Mrs Sticky Buns continued to hum as she toyed w/ her hair, looking occasionally to her husband, visibly pleased as he approached the final pages of INVESTMENT MAN in *Attack of the Accruing Forfeitures.*

* * * * *

"THIS IS GONNA BE FUN," Pearl assured her brother & sister as the foursome promenaded along the Sunday morning streets. A clear-eyed sky smiled down as the sidewalk began to fill w/ plump, paunchy & pleasantly corpulent churchgoers, all in seemingly staunch competition to outdress one another. One minute Pearl would grab S-'s hand; the next she would dash off for a quick round of Ninja hopscotch on an unsuspecting sidewalk. Her older siblings, however, declined to display any enthusiasm. A grumbling Buck marched several steps ahead while Penny held up the rear, dragging her hobnailed boots, sneering every time her younger sister tried to goad her into hurrying up. The closer the quartet come to their destination, the farther Penny fell behind. Yet, as the flying buttresses & towering turrets came into view, the teen sidled up to S-, grabbing his hand & lacing her fingers w/in his. When the surprised S- glanced @ the girl, she smiled feebly, her cheeks flushed, her eyes quickly darting away like frightened mice.

The growing congregation of churchgoers soon engulfed the foursome. The lean & lanky were swiftly outnumbered by the thick & burly, the chunky & tubby, the dumpy & stout, the beefy & pudgy, the big-bellied & buxom, the elephantine & gargantuan: all lumbering up the stone stairs & thru the double doors of the synachurch-temple w/ its adjoining mosque & coin laundromat. Buck walked in front of his sisters, w/ S- wedged btwn the pigtailed Pearl clinging to one hand & the elephant-haired Penny clutching the other. S- grew increasingly self-conscious as heads turned, some seeming to almost jerk off, so abrupt were the sudden double-takes. A vague sense of peril bristled the hair on his neck as the quartet wound their way thru the parting, suddenly quiet crowd. Buck bounded up the steps leading to the Smolets' honorary box, S- & company following @ a slower pace. After they sat, an irritated Ester arrived, ordering them to stand again.

"Attending two months in a row," she huffed, "as if every other month isn't sufficient to be told PUP loves you more than the rest of us." She assaulted their seats w/ a dust rag as if blaming the pew, or maybe the dust, for some gross transgression. "Go ahead," she snapped, "sit your wealthy butts down."

"So very glad to see you again," a smiling Reverend Hickey approached, his longer arm already extended. The man of the cloth adjusted a crooked collar before greasing his palm in preparation of several lightning-slick handshakes. He stared long & hard @ S-. "Two months in a row; this is indeed a great day for genuflectors everywhere," he smiled. As he turned to Buck, Penny & Pearl, he placed his longer arm behind his back, palm turned upward. The fingers writhed like impatient earthworms, each vying for S-'s attention. S- stared @ the wiggling digits, unable to decipher their intention. After patting Buck's shoulder, stroking Penny's hair & tugging Pearl's ear, the religious leader scuttled away, mumbling vague predictions about someone or other burning eternally in hell-fire.

Finally seated, S- looked over the milling congregation, noticing a piebald-headed man seated in the box opposite them. Next to him sat the bug-eyed woman who liked to spit, multiple umbrellas already opened below. He fidgeted as more & more pudgy faces stared up @ him, their sagging jowls quivering as they whispered to one another, now & then a fat finger pointing in his direction. He spotted the wild-eyed Erle, waving from the balcony & flashing him a crooked thumbs-up. A few rows behind the seminary student sat the doctor who had verified, clarified, certified & rarified S- to vote. Seated next to that docter was the MD who had sedated Erle in the confession booth.

The organ began, its heavy chords rolling into a hauntingly sustained melody suggestive of an angelic horror movie. S- listened, easily picturing a virgin angel skipping innocently along under a clear blue sky. As the organ chords grew more menacing, a secular railroad track entered S-'s imagination. The virgin, hesitating to cross said track, was suddenly, violently snatched up by a wingèd demon, who, in S-'s imagination looked like a fanged Hector. The demon tied the struggling virgin to the rails just as a change in chords signaled a massive train, hell-bound for evil, coming around the bend.

S- looked over @ Ester leaning heavily into the organ, her body hunched, her purple hair now a bluish halo. He envisioned the innocent angel pleading for mercy as the sideburned demon rubbed his hands like a devious fly lording over fresh fecal matter. S- pictured saliva dribbling down the demon's cleft chin as the demon gave the knots he had learned as a misunderstood boy scout one final tug. As Ester pressed into the organ keys, her body writhing as if having a seizure, the locomotive gained momentum, mere seconds separating the helpless virgin from the steel wheels of pounding, relentless evil. S- squeezed Pearl & Penny's hands, his own hands clammy w/ sweat. Closing his eyes, he feared the worst for the virgin angel, relieved when the harrowing chords subsided, replaced by a sustained tremor. The church lights dimmed, one remaining spotlight focused on the pulpit. The throne descended, a listless PUP bent fwd on the plush upholstery, His head btwn His knees.

Quicker than a heartbeat, PUP jerked Himself alive. He looked from left to right w/ an air of piercing disapproval before jumping to His feet & clicking His heels before balancing on the back of His regal chair.

Great day in the morNING, PUP greeted, one of His eyes having trouble staying open. I am glad to see so maNY of you here TOday. Woe to him who is not TOday here for he shall sureLY feel my wrath as will his sons & daughTERS unto the 6.235th geNERaTION.

PUP somersaulted, landing on the chair arm, clasping both hands behind His back.

There are maNY in this muniCIpaliTY, a few eVEN in this room... (PUP looked around suspiciously, His good eye scrutinizing the deaf, dumb & dumbfounded among the congregation.) *...EVEN in the great halls of this our eterNAL PupPIness who would lay claim that PUP is dead. Do i look dead?*

A sea of faces shook their heads, half the assembly shouting a defiant "NO!" Reassured, PUP continued.

Yet, they do lay claim that PUP is dead; that PUP does not hear your cries of pain; does not hear your pleas for merCY; does not eVEN know what you want for pupMAS.

But you, all you seaTED here TOday know the puke: that I am your liVING PupPET & shall be w/ you all the days of your eVILS from the first sigNING of your birth certiFIcate to the reaDING of your last spill of tesTICles, when you turn your life saVINGS oVER to the One...in My name. I ASsure you, I...SEE...ALL.

PUP pirouetted as He jumped to the floor, landing in a graceful split before masterfully coming to a full stand. He struggled to open His defective eye by rubbing it w/ one hand as the other reached behind to scratch an itch.

I see what you eat for breakFAST. I see inTO the fuTURE. I know how & when what you have eaTEN for breakFAST will come out in the end. I see now, as I will two months from now, how you will vote in the forthcoMING S-elecTION.

PUP ceased rubbing His posterior to point w/ both hands @ His audience.

Now some would say I am not a poliTICal PUP. That I would stay my nose firmLY from the unsaVORy stench of poliTICal wrangLING. And it is true, for the realm of poLItics is BEneath the cowPIE of my DIvine inteRESTS.

But how you vote is not. For is it not said that SanTA is a red-faced poliTICian? SanTA Claus, that black-sootED PURveyor of chaOS, that gleaNER of OneNESS into smaLLER & smaLLER & thus weaKER & more vulNERable parts—OneNESS the necTAR that all PUP's chilDREN are DEcreed the right to sucKLE UPon. Where the deVIL irks so lurks eVIL. For the deVIL is eVIL—eVIL w/ a capITal D...the D he got in grade school for not stuDYing THE GOOD BOOK hard ENuff.

PUP strutted to the edge of the stage, playfully threatening to lunge into the laps of any suspected evildoer in the front row. He reached in a pocket, extracted a kerchief, blew His nose, replaced the kerchief & placed His hands on His hips.

You think you are saved! You think BEcause you come to viSIT me but this one day a week, for an hour & twenty-three odd MInutes (miNUS the commerCIALS), that BEcause you saCRIfice your hard-wrenched One & illiCITly PROcured proFITS to the syNAgong cofFERS, that PUP will neVER DEsert you. PUP crossed His arms & leered @ the hushed audience. *Well, you are right!*

His defective eye suddenly opened only to just as suddenly slam shut w/ the finality of a guillotine. Undeterred, PUP continued, uncrossing His arms.

The otHER day I oVERhead a child, a mere oVERgrown lad, too big for his britCHES, barely aBLE to graDUate the hoLIer-than-thou insTItute of GlaDIaTOR U. And this lad said to me that eVIL is just someTHING we self-righTEOUS call other peoPLE to jusTIfy our right to do eVIL UNto them.

HorseraDISH! HorseraDISH, I say (which by they way is on sale this week @ Pete's Dry Goods & BaBY BOUtique). I immediATEly washed that child's mouth out w/ three parts soap & two parts lye (which alSO hapPENS to be on sale @ Pete's thru next week).

PUP scratched Himself btwn His legs

Then I proceeDED to tell the lad the stoRY of ESAYAH. How ESAYAH went up to the caMEL heap w/ his staff, which he did jerk & jerk & jerked off UNtil the Word of PUP cascaDED down like puke shaped inTO bread loaves.

ESAYAH did pick up the loaved puke & did take a bite thereof. And lo, PUP did APpear. And did have the fair horse's snout of a BritTLEbaum: & PUP alSO had the softNESS of spaghetTI hair that hung off eVERy PROportion eVEN UNto the fat ass of a BritTLEbaum.

Thus did ESAYAH know the springs & founTAINS of bullDUNG, the oCEANS, the riVERS w/ its winDING farts, the tiNY male peePEES that did span the land in ABundance were all gifts of PUP & that BritTLEbaums were PUP's true sex-slaves.

Titters began to echo from the rear of the church. Rustling could be heard in the balcony & among the less obese worshippers. Mothers reached to cover children's ears. Eyelids, which had been drooping, suddenly popped open to full alert as parishioners sat on the edge of their seats. Some leaned fwd, eyes wide in disbelief. Others nodded in total agreement, amening & hallelujahing every time PUP affected a pregnant pause. PUP, meanwhile, continued to scratch Himself in holy places.

But do you think this child would unDERstand what you & I, oVER-grown flat-nosed BAboons, know? Of course not. For he, this boy weaRING SanTA's jockSTRAP, then proceeDED to SUGgest our flounDERing farTERS & the tiRED, peace-loVING PUP-feaRING settLERS who folLOWED them, were eVIL in the way we ran the NiBIan off this land so we could unsetTLE this terRItoRY.

What you & I know to be canniBALizing, maKING-whooPEE-in-the-backSEAT-of-used-carRIages, picKING-their-noSES-&-eaTING-it-too saVAges, this child called peace-loVING chilDREN-of-PUP...peoPLE who onLY wanTED to eVIL & let eVIL...onLY wanTED to PROtect the land their anceSTORS had eVIL'd on for 10.937 geNERations.

But how can you be peaceFUL & PROtect your land @ the same time? It can't be done! But I did not try to CONfuse the boy w/ loGIC.

I oPENED to the Book of Bob, chapTER 11, verSES 1-14. FootNOTE †, coROlary 16-34: 'nd lo, PUP s'id to his B'boons of the fl't-nosed, I sh'll bring your eNEmies ripe w/ w'TERmeLONS where your moTHERS sp't. And ye sh'll P'Rt'ke of the uRIn'l cup & e't of the pig's feet BEtwixt the groin of PUP, 's they would THEMselves. Do not sufFER this peoPLE's gisSUM in the c'rRI'ges of the lord for they sh'll pick their noSES & wipe it unDER PUP's pew.'

And thus I poinTED out UNto this child, do you not see what the GOOD BOOK did PREdict 29 bilLION, 227 milLION & 18 years ago to the day...BEfore we setTLED in this cowPIE? PUP did PREdict the eVIL that is the NiBIan as He had the CAnaan. EaTING of PUP as they would THEMselves; picKING their noSES; foreplayING in the backs of parked carRIages.

PUP leaped to his throne & spread his arms wide.

For PUP knew they were eVIL, knew they would corRUPT us w/ their twitCHY finGERS, knew they would inFILtrate, marRY our pretTIer house-sluts, INsist on the vote & weekENDS off w/ pay. PUP knew they would drag us INto the quagMIRE of their canNIbal picNICS. And we would be forEVer stripped of the chasted love PUP BEstows on onLY those of the flat-nose & spaghetTI-haired, BAboon-faced.

Executing a perfect backflip, PUP landed seated on the back of his throne chair, crossing his legs & folding both hands on his knee.

So I BEgan to spank the child & whip the boy for tho it pains PUP to pumMEL his peoPLE, were I to sufFER one false sex-slave to think ill of me there would then folLOW anoTHER & anoTHER till no one sex-slaved & nay, I said as I smote the child, betTER I not to spare the rod then alLOW the deVIL's dilDO to pleaSURE said child. And when I was done, the child saw the light. He bowed & said UNto me 'Oh wonDERous PUP of the BAboon-faced, what can I do to make MYself worTHY of your great OneDERfulNESS.'

And so I spoke to him of the upcoMING S-elecTION.

Unbeknownst to the all-knowing PUP, by the time He launched into how the enlightened might cast their bullots, half those in the balcony had poured out of the temple & onto a hot angry street. So too the rear seats of the lower level. Meanwhile, those parishioners aroused from their snoring awoke abruptly, unsure what had been happening but shouting "amen" & "PUP be praised" w/ the rest of the remaining congregation, these prompted by cue cards the church deacons systematically waved.

S-, Penny, Pearl & Buck remained seated, Buck struggling to subdue his dimples as S- stared @ PUP's strings, unsure if said strings controlled PUP or PUP controlled said strings. When PUP ended His sermon w/ a particularly difficult somersault triple-twist split, the house roared in spontaneous, rapturous applause. Prompted by cue cards, they jumped to their feet, bellowing, "Bravo, Bravo" & calling for an encore. The exhausted PUP collapsed on his chair, rising slowly to the ceiling into which He disappeared.

Only a few faces remained in the balcony, among them the doctors & a perturbed Police Chief, out of breath from having dashed up the stairs. Some in the balcony shook their heads in dismay while others smiled profusely. Erle's thin face had grown thoughtful as he tugged the split ends of his unkempt beard. Most who filed out of the Temple of Perpetual Puppiness did so in complete silence. Even those stirred by the rousing sermon to renew their commitment to 'the ONE who protects the one who protects the One' had little to say once they had fully rubbed the sleep from their eyes.

According to the dozens of reports flooding headquarters, Woodbees thruout the community had suddenly grown emboldened. Even those who had graced the synachurch-temple in order to hedge their bets had swiftly resolved to no longer waste their hard-earned One on the temple collection plate. Some sarcastically quipped how they may as well put their One in the pockets of the clothesless. Upon hearing this, the Grimspoon camp swiftly issued campaign buttons to that very same effect.

Sur Harry, Counting Commissioner Dicker & others pillars among the parished community placed the blame squarely on S-. His unexpected presence @ temple that day was cited as irrefutable proof. Several pointed to his sordid menagè á trois w/ the Smolet girls as a gross distraction, this undoubtedly rankling the more overly sensitive upstanding congregators, sending many scurrying in disgust to the nearest puke hole. What other explanation could there be? they unanimously decried.

Meanwhile, in Woodbee Supurbia, in many a residential suite, tubs of fresh raccoon, squirrel & kids' feet were fed in abundance to voracious, insatiable feeding ducts. Friends & acquaintances, butchers & bologna kings, barrel-chested barbers & antiquated antique dealers gathered to discuss new strategies. Soda jerks & cryogeneticists, coroners & child molesters, homeopaths, psychopaths & floorists weighed in w/ fresh, bold opinions. Inferior decorators, druggists & their dealers, invalids, paralegals, hairdressers & paraillegals seconded motions while handymen, euclideans, geriatrics, chimney sweeps, contractors, cartoonists, ovulators, obstinantricians, flight attendants all joined in open discussions. Junk bond dealers, curators, ophthalmologists, trash collectors, embalmers, appraisers, auditors, caterers contributed their two & a half sense while accountants, probate officers, acupuncturists & not-so-acupuncturists had even more to say. Predictions of a new era (where Woodbees would finally control their own destiny) were voted on & passed unanimously—this further confirmed by a science teacher/part-time astrologist who forecasted the coming year as that of the Woodpecker, which she affirmed was close enuff to Woodbee & Peckerhead to be of high significance.

"The hail w/ that," the more pragmatic Ira Fuse bellowed. "I say we beg, borrow & steal all the One we can scrounge. It's time we pulled the rug from under their Brittle butts. I say we clean their clocks!"

"Here, here," the Union of Watch Repairmen seconded, leading those present in a boisterous chorus of *Hickory-Dickory Dock*, those singing unaware of a pair of high-powered binoculars peering down from a lone, phallic-shaped tower.

Chapter 17

THAT AFTERNOON, while ransacking the kitchen cabinets, Mr Smolet was interrupted by the trumpet blare, siren wail & slow fading gong of the manor doorbell. He waddled thru the front doors, opening the final door to a lean, medium-height Dreg. Swiftly, the banker slipped on his glasses, squinting as he struggled to see what was in front of him. His blue enlarged irises searched & searched, looking everywhere save @ the doughboy calling his name.

"Mr Smolat. Mr Smolat, sir."

The banker shrugged, closing the door & retreating to his cocoon. Removing his glasses & sighing heavily, he leaned against his office door, latching it to make doubly sure no one deigned to disturb him. When the trumpet blared again, he called for someone—anyone—to please, please get the dammed door.

A moment later Penny trudged down the steps, her elephant bang bouncing against her forehead as she traipsed thru each front door. When she opened the final door, a pair of olive-green eyes widened in delight.

"Aftanoon, Mz Peny."

"Oh, hi, Weed. How are you?"

"Fine. Thanx fer asing. Hafn't seen yu n yeers."

"I know. No offense, but to tell the truth, i've gotten pretty sick of pizza. How's your spelling?"

"O, it comes & goez. Seams ta git betta on reiny dayz, yu no."

"What brings you here?"

"Well, i'm hare ta cee S-."

Penny turned & called for S-, straightening her burlap blouse & wiping the

191

smudge from one of her combat boots w/ the heel of the other. Hearing no response, she led Weed to the foyer, then trudged off. She called from the second floor landing; that call also received no response. She moved below the trapdoor, staring up @ its rough unfinished surface, finally willing herself to climb the rickety stairs, raise the door & enter the garret.

She looked around, aware this was her first visit to S-'s private quarters. She puzzled over the faint red-tinted lighting. She examined the living room w/ its mismatched furniture & veritable forest of scattered rule books. She tiptoed to the bedroom, peeking in curiously, startled when S- suddenly materialized behind her, drying his hands w/ a towel.

"You have a visitor," she stammered, blushing as she willed herself to look directly in his face. To her surprise, his eyes were nowhere as frightening as she had let her imagination believe. They were dark—a murky black chocolate— yet w/ a warm gentle texture. The brows were nearly knit together—almost in a perpetual state of confused curiosity. But this rendered his gaze vulnerable, even endearing, she concluded. Before she could stop herself, her hands reached out & took his.

S- accepted the tender gesture as he observed the girl's shadow lower its glance, then hide its face inside a wall crevice. His own shadow dashed to reassure it. Only after some coaxing did the girl's shadow pull its head out, its gaze still averted. Penny slid her hands deeper into S-'s, smiling wanly as she squeezed his palms. As she repeated he had a visitor, her shadow took his shadow's hand to rub against its cheek before clasping it confidently & leading the way down the stairwell.

"Reidy?" Weed asked, a slight wheeze in his breathing. S- nodded as Penny pulled her hand from his. He felt an abrupt shock: the loss of the soft hand w/ its comforting warmth sending a sudden feeling of emptiness coursing thru him.

"Will you be back for supper?" she asked, removing her bang from one eye. S- turned to Weed, who shook his head. He shook his head in kind, pained by the hint of disappointment in the girl's lowered glance. Penny stood on the porch, leaning on the doorframe, absentmindedly twisting the doorknob as she watched the two figures fade from view. Sighing, she turned, her shadow lingering a moment before following her & closing each door.

S- glanced up, bemused by the middle-aged bag lady pacing the late afternoon sky. Strands of stringy gray hair, twisted in a bun, stretched from horizon to horizon, the spinster rolling a noiseless shopping cart made of thin clouds. Her back hunched, a frayed pale blue shawl proved the only sign of her faded glory. Mumbling mainly to herself, she kicked a few bushes, sending the aroma of jasmine, honeysuckle & spearmint wafting in the air.

Weed led S- first thru a neighborhood of brownstone houses, the doors carelessly dabbed w/ face paint & faded lipstick. Houses of tin or aluminum-alloy were smeared w/ cheap rouge, purple or pink mascara lining the sagging eaves in a vain attempt to make cheery the dull grimy windows staring out @ nothing in particular. Now & then a gaudy structure leaned on a street corner, smoking a cigarette, advertising something vague & mildly suggestive. Tho intrigued, even titillated, S- felt something ominous & threatening about the dark, alluring entryways & the scents of musk, sweat & cheap perfume curling out the upstairs windows.

That neighborhood soon dissolved into what Weed called the "endustriel districk." Towering metallic insects became the norm: barrel-shaped, bloated bellies chugging, gurgling, burping andor breaking wind as they spewed billows of greenish-yellow cloud into the bag lady's choking cheeks. The metal spiders, cockroaches, beetles & caterpillars hovered on thin wiry legs, their precarious limbs eaten by rust & corrosion, their knees bent under as if about to give way. S- walked by cautiously, fearing any moment one might topple, sending plumes of dust & billowing cloud into the already foul atmosphere.

"Dis iz Crooked Tawn," Weed announced as they entered a new neighborhood. One-story rundown shanties & boarded-up bungalows devoid of any gaudy makeup stretched in every direction. Most slumped crookedly @ obtuse angles. As S- & Weed strolled the uneven sidewalks, S- spied several residents, their bodies awry, a head or an arm off-kilter, chests sunken, buttocks protruding & unevenly aligned. One emerged from the back of a house, dressed in black & wearing a ski mask. Prancing on tiptoe to the bungalow next door, it used a crowbar to bust out a window & climb inside. No sooner had he crawled thru than someone emerged from the bungalow's front door, crowbar in hand, only to tiptoe to the bungalow a couple of doors over.

As S- & Weed entered still another neighborhood, Weed whispered, "Nibiaans lif hear. Cee howe deas houses haf no fondation. Thats becuz de Poweres that DO keep makin Nibiaans move." When S- raised an eyebrow, Weed explained how every time Nibians found a new home or tried to settle down, someone would discover gold on their land...or think to build a railroad thru it...or elect to erect a shopping maul. "Lass year, "a coople of keds found a few courters inn a Nibiann sandbox... soo thay had ta relocade agin.

"Stay awey frum deas poeple," Weed then warned, cocking his head twd a group of teenage boys, their smiles tilted, their teeth awry. "Thay call demselves Dixstickss. Cee dose clubs thay carrie, de wans cumin outa there pants. Thay wate till thay git yu alon—den thay cum awl ovah yu." Moving cautiously, aware they were being eyeballed, S- & Weed strolled on, arriving next @ a series of rowhouses & ramshackles. "Mostly Handpanlers lif hear," Weed explained. "Thay descented frum de Canaans."

The front lawns of the teetering abodes were comprised of withered shrubs, a few raggedy weeds & sprigs of dead grass. Families had gathered outside, the elders teaching their scaly-skinned children to "sit" & "roll over" then "beg."

"Job trainin," Weed whispered. Then, "Heir we ar." Weed stopped in front a two-story cottage looking like a couple of ramshackles pulled together & held in place by loose thread, paperclips & super-adhesive chewing gum. S- followed his host thru a warped screen door that clattered as it closed behind them. The semi-spacious living room was dark & musty, fresh air having apparently been banned from the premises. Week-old odors lethargically raised their heads, eyed the two arrivals, then settled back down to continue snoozing.

A cow resembling a woman emerged from the shadows, wringing her hands in a threadbare apron. Two gigantic curlers crowned the woman's square, elongated face on either side of her head. Her wide gaping nostrils flared every time she bellowed "Mooove, mooove" to a small herd of children trailing in her wake. S- counted only two toddlers, tho they seemed triple that number as they circled the woman, lassoing her knees, climbing her dress, attempting every route imaginable in their relentless pursuit of her ample breasts.

"Maw, dis iz S-," Weed announced as he dodged a tumbling toddler. He gently lifted the child, brushing off its bottom before sending it off, the tot quickly about-facing twd the object of its oral desires.

"Mooove, mooove," Mrs Farrago insisted, negotiating her way to a cluttered table. With one clean sweep of her arm, she cleared the table surface. She dumped the contents piled atop three of four chairs, retaining one chair for herself, one for Weed, & one she urged S- to make himself @ home in. "Mooove, mooove," she ordered her relentless fan club, each vying to climb the chairs offered to Weed & S-.

Smiling @ S-, Mrs Farrago plucked from the surrounding clutter a bag of yarn, several knitting needles protruding like antennae. She pulled out something that could have been a gigantic sock w/ arms, or an octopus's sweater, or perhaps a pair of unipants for Siamese quintuplets. As Weed's mother spoke, the knitting needles

194

were set into mesmerizing motion, the yarn, the needles, her fingers all moving as one—that is until she noticed S- watching.

"It's just a little habit of mine," she explained, putting the needles aside. "Mooove, mooove," she urged an undeterred toddler. "Not that i actually aspire to actually knit," she added, smacking one of the children, sending it off crying. "I'm @ least a hundred generations removed from even the slightest hint of Brittle blood. To actually knit would be an exercise in futility. Mooove," she snapped, raising the back of her hand to threaten the crying infant.

"Still, it gives my hands something to do." She retrieved the needles & continued knitting. "Plus, it cuts down on the number of times i slap the children. Mooove, i told you."

"Would you like a glass of stewjuice?" she offered. "Weed, get you & our guest a glass...i know about you men & your stewjuice." She winked @ S-, the needles in her fingers a blur of motion accompanied by rapid, rhythmic clicking. "A keg after work, two on weekends, all you can drink on Sundays."

Weed returned w/ two glasses of an amber liquid topped to the rim w/ orange bubbling foam. Weed took a deep swig from his glass, then licked the liquid fuzz from above his upper lip. S- examined his drink, amused by the distorted reflection of everything in the room.

"S- wurks w/ Paw," Weed informed his mother, wiping his lips w/ one hand, pushing away a suddenly-thirsty toddler w/ the other.

"Mr Farrago is a good man," Mrs Farrago stated. "Except, of course, when he's frightened...which, regrettably, is most of the time." The lady of the house sighed.

S- watched the needles as Mrs Farrago recounted her husband's lists of phobias, adding she had given up counting the countless times her husband would wake her in the middle of the nite.

"Why, just the other nite he woke me @ three in the morning. I turned on the light & there he was, huddled in the corner. I went all around the room, lifting covers, looking under the bed, opening the closets. 'See, there's nothing,' i told him. 'It's probably just shadows.' But he just shivered like a Canaan in a Turkey Shoot. Finally i suggested we have another baby. That's the only thing that seems to calm him."

Mrs Farrago rose, announcing it was probably time to start dinner. "Sit, sit," she insisted of S-. "Mooove, mooove," she instructed the children. "Margaret, come help me peel some ragweed."

Several older children had entered the room. The tallest girl, her belly swollen,

195

had just squatted on the floor, pulling the youngest of the toddlers to her. "Ah, maw," she protested, struggling to raise herself again.

"I'll peel the ragweed," a younger sibling offered, following her mother into the kitchen. No sooner was the girl gone when the other toddler began to cry. The girl promptly returned, tickling the toddler's chin until he smiled. Asking the child if he'd like to help peel ragweed, she steered him twd the kitchen, challenging him in a race to see who could make it there first.

The child stumbled away. S- looked about the poorly lit room as Weed introduced the remaining siblings. He nodded to Margaret, the oldest sister, who, S- was told, dropped out of hirer school to give birth to the child currently in her lap, two-year-old Tasha. Orson, seated @ the bottom of a stairwell, was sixeen, here for the weekend, by leave of his probation officer. jj, thirteen, brooded higher up on the staircase, whittling something from a pair of long sticks, occasionally tossing his penknife into the woodwork w/ deadly accuracy. Eve, who had turned six a couple of years ago, was the girl helping their mother in the kitchen along w/ Josh, four, who sometimes mistook Eve for his real mother. Missing, Weed added, was Martha, who was babysitting a neighbor's children & Joseph who had run away from home but would most likely be back by suppertime.

As Weed & S- returned to sipping stewjuice, the door abruptly opened & the screen door cursed. A gruff voice announced it was home. Margaret gathered young Tasha to her chest. Orson stared @ his returning father, unmoved, while jj jabbed his knife into the baseboard. Several odors scurried to the far corners of room as the man of the house stomped across the threadbare carpet, dropping his tool belt in his wake.

* * * * *

As THE SAVORY AROMA OF RAGWEED permeated the Farrago ramshackle, Penny Smolet lay across her princess-size bed, staring @ the ceiling fan, her head cradled in her small interlaced hands. The warm, dry touch of S-'s palm nestled snugly in her memory.

She recalled their walk to church. A strange impulse—like a voice whispering in her ear—had prompted her to take his hand. A ploy @ first, or so she told herself, intended to make others think she & S- were, well.... As simple as he was, w/ his unkempt appearance, his gaunt expression, his @ times penetrating stare, S- seemed to command this influence over others. They moved out of his way, avoided his toes.

They distrusted & hated him, of course...but it was more than that: they feared him... or something about him. Feared him enuff to stay out of his way. No one dared say anything or pull them apart. Perhaps they would fear him enuff to not auction her off.

Holding his hand like that had been a ruse...but today, in his apartment, when she took his hand w/out a second thought, it was all she could do not to fall on her knees & smother his rough dry hand w/ kisses. She recalled the look in his dark, fathomless eyes: part confusion, perhaps a little frightened...yet there was also something harmless...& tender too.

Penny brushed her bang aside as she pictured herself & S- walking—somewhere, anywhere, everywhere—hand in hand, together...not as make-believe but as true....

She hesitated to complete the thought.

If she could just get him to dress better...& tie his shoes. In the proper attire, he might actually command people's respect. And if she wore his ring, she would also command respect...if not fear. She could get rid of her stringbean of a lawyer w/ his annoying habit of stroking her hair every time he used some fancy legal term he knew she wouldn't understand.

Lost in such thoughts, Penny rose, walking zombie-like to her closet. She pushed aside the burlap trousers, the panda fatigues, the zebra jumpsuits & leopard vests. She reached for a white blouse w/ puffed sleeves, its draped-neck collar laced down its edges. These & a pair of burlap pantaloons, she thought. She would wear these tomorrow. He would be sure to notice. She fell on the bed, imagining his eyes widening as she entered the dining room—eyes following her as she sat next to him @ breakfast.

Her shadow, meanwhile, remained in the closet, trying on different shoes & imagining accessories. Penny, prone across her bed, thought back to their first encounter: he entering the dining room, head bowed so low she actually felt pity for him, imagining him unduly fascinated or perhaps confused by his poorly tied shoes. She recalled stifling a giggle, struggling not to smile, hoping her parents would interpret the curl of her lips as a disapproving smirk.

Up from her bed in a flash, she rummaged thru her closet, ferreting for just the right pair of shoes to match the burlap pants. She frowned @ the army boots, grimaced @ the raccoon pumps, searching for something...something dainty. She nearly cringed @ the thought, but bolstered herself. Then there came that other word: the one she dare not say out loud. Afraid to admit it—even to herself—she was looking for something her mother would call 'feminine.'

197

She stumbled upon a pair of black T-straps, ones that might accent her feet—her ankles & shins being among her best features...or so her school councilors had told her (the male ones anyway). But the T-straps called for different pantaloons. Burlap would clash. Normally she liked clash. But would he?

Meanwhile the girl's shadow slipped on a pair of black cotton knickers. The slacks hugged tightly @ its hip, the pant legs traveling down to just above the shadow's shapely calves.

Penny collapsed in a chair, staring despondently into her vanity. She mussed her hair, unplaited her bang, uncurled the elephant-ears, experimenting w/ piling her hair on top, tying it back, or spreading it full width across her shoulders. She remembered a pair of cotton knickers, ones that matched the shoes. She dashed to the closet, grabbing the knickers from her shadow's grasp & holding it @ arm's length. Clutching the slacks to her chest, she closed her eyes, imagining S- entering the dining room, his pupils alighting on her in delight, his dark serious gaze opening wide as he recognized here was the girl—no, here was the woman—of his dreams. She fell back on the bed in a dreamy ecstasy. As she lay there, eyes closed, her shadow slid onto the vanity chair, staring into the mirror, tinkering w/ various hairdos.

Penny reached twd the nitestand, picking up her rule book, subtitled FISHING WITH HOOPS. She flipped thru its pages, scanning several chapter titles: *Using the Right Bait, Sinking in your Hook, Reeling Him In, Gutting & Filleting.* She skimmed the preface, sitting up straight as she turned to Chapter One. Her shadow, meanwhile, had settled on a ponytail, then walked into the closet where it organized every dress, skirt & blouse—first according to color, then by tightness of fit, finally by how much skin each would expose.

* * * * *

"WAD DE SAM CREEK HE DOIN' HERE?" Stubbs Farrago sneered, stumbling over his children as they & he poured into the kitchen.

Weed announced he had invited S- to Sunday supper.

"Wad fur?" Stubbs barked, pumping a mug's worth of stewjuice from a barrel near the sink.

"Now dear, leave the boy alone," Mrs Farrago interceded. "It's Sunday. And as THE GOOD BOOK says, even PUP took a day off from abusing His wife & children. Sit down. Dinner's almost ready."

Standing on tiptoe @ the stove, Eve was expertly overturning the artificial loin-chops sizzling in a frying pan. Next to her Mrs Farrago lifted the lid of a bubbling stockpot. Seemingly surprised when a billow of steam made a hasty escape, the bovine matron froze, screwing up her face in confusion. Her hand trembled. Still on tiptoe, Eve looked into the boiling pot, then reached for a wooden spoon, stirring the pot's contents. She took the lid from her mother's hand, Mrs Farrago sighing w/ relief & drying her hands on her apron before ordering one of the kids to "mooove" & chiming in a cheerful manner: "Who's ready to eat?"

Weed motioned for S- to sit @ the big persons' table, the shorter table being reserved for the children. Margaret, Orson & jj sat w/ S- along w/ Weed & their father. As the older children were finding their chairs, the back door suddenly opened. A thin-faced lad, his nose identical to Stubbs's, entered, walking w/out a word to the smaller table.

"Joseph, where you been?" Mrs Farrago chided, her eyes studying a bowl of steamed ragweed Eve promptly commandeered & began dishing out. The boy froze, saying nothing. Mrs Farrago continued scolding. "Mooove," she ordered a toddler as she approached Joseph, hands on her hips. "You ran away, didn't you?"

The boy fidgeted in humbled silence.

"How many times have i told you to bring one of your older brothers in case you have to cross a busy street?"

Joseph stood, his hands listless @ his sides. His guilt-ridden eyes followed Eve, serving his younger siblings child-size portions of boiled dandelion.

"You never know when a T'Baum or a D'Brittle might be out on a Sunday drive!" his mother continued. "I've a good mind to send you to bed w/ no supper."

Joseph stared @ the floor, occasionally stealing glances @ Eve, now serving the loin-chops. He watched her deftly cut Josh's meat into bite-size pieces, periodically negotiating w/ the rambunctious Tasha, who insisted bibs should be worn atop the head instead of under the chin.

S- found himself empathizing w/ the berated Joseph, himself being scrutinized by the piercing stare of Mr Farrago. His supervisor masticated bitterly on a tuff piece of loin-chop, washing down each swallow w/ a swig of stewjuice.

"You think youse betta den PUP's wee-wee people, don't ya?" Stubbs wiped his lips. "Anythin' i can't stand, it's a uppity social climber," he muttered low enuff to still be heard.

"Paw, don't," Weed pleaded, touching S- on the arm in comforting solidarity.

"Don't 'paw don't' me. Don't ya see?" Stubbs sat back, including all his children in the conversation. "Da way it's suppose t' work is dat you start from de bottom & works your way up. Sure ol' Stubbs is @ da bottom. Seventeen years it took me t' make it t' head janitor. Now i's even got an ass-sis-*ant* workin' under me. 'Nother ten or fifteen years, i'll be managin' de janitorial dept, wearin' a tie & drinking coffee spiked wid a little Crandy, smokin' an 'xpensive T'leBaum cigar—while i watch others prespire. 'Nother five or ten years & ya brother, Weed, will not only be makin' dough—he'll be mixing da secret sauce, too...maybe even in charge a countin' de pepperoni & mushrooms. We Farragos work hard t' get where someday we's goin' t' be. Weed, git me another glass a stewjuice, will ya? We works hard."

The janitor handed Weed his mug & spit out a dandelion seed. "Now dis guy," he pointed to S-, "dis guy comes int' town wid his blank stare, his shoes untied, his zipper practicly down t'his knees & starts takin' ovah the company."

"Now honey, don't get yourself riled." Mrs Farrago passed the glass of stewjuice she had taken from Weed. "I'm sure he don't mean to take your job from you."

"Paw, he's hartly takin ova de cumpany," Weed tried to reason.

"Da hail he ain't. I seen it b'fore. Mark my word: afta de S-election, afta he sells 'em his vote, they'll promote him t' carriage driver. You kids don't have enuff scrapes & bruises, dodging dem dammed Brittle carriages. Now som'one sittin' @ my own table is goin' t' be draggin' you six-n'a-half feet under." Stubbs slammed his mug to the table, sending the dinnerware clattering. At the smaller table, Josh began to holler.

"Now you've done it!" Mrs Farrago snapped, rising from her seat. "Joseph, sit down before your supper gets cold. You can go to bed w/out your supper later. And tomorrow, young man, you take a jacket in case it starts raining."

Mrs Farrago leaned over the hollering Josh only to stop just as she reached for him. Her brows knitted as she stared blankly @ the tears streaming down the child's face, her countenance even more confused as Josh increased in decibel level. As Mrs Farrago looked around, Eve set her fork down & slid from her seat. She picked up the child, then sat, placing little Josh on her lap. The holler quickly subsided to a whimper. She jabbed a bite-size morsel of loin-chop & pretended it was a bee buzzing before Josh's eyes. The bee began to playfully poke his tear-stained cheeks, from the left, then the right—until Josh, wising up to the bee's maneuvers, opened his mouth @ the perfect moment. The bee flew in, upon which the gleeful child promptly chewed it to death.

Stubbs called to his wife. "Sit down 'enrietta."

As the Mrs sat, Mr Farrago stumbled to his feet, wobbling as he pumped himself another mugful of stewjuice. Instead of returning to his seat, he stepped behind Weed, placing one weather-beaten hand on his eldest's shoulder.

"You see dis boy," Stubbs addressed S-, spilling some stewjuice as he waved his glass. "Dis boy a mine is a lousy spella."

"Paw," Weed whimpered.

"A lousy spella. He couldn't spell his way outa a M&M factory. But when it comes t' making dough," Stubbs clucked his tongue, "he's de best. He could win de Peable Nobody Prize for his dough.

"And ya know what else?" Stubbs wobbled sideways, spilling his drink tho catching his balance. "He's a great friggin' arteased. It's true. It's true...dis boy can paint a blue sky like ya wouldn't believe. His clouds are as white as clouds. And his reds: hail, fire would blush wid embarrassment t' be seen anywhere near his reds."

"That's not realy tru," Weed protested.

"Hush, boy." Mr Farrago stumbled backward, the kitchen countertop breaking his fall. "Youse a photographer." Stubbs pointed his half-empty glass @ S-. "You want t' take a great pitcha, you jest take a pitcha of my son's pitchas. Dat's what ya need t' do." Stubbs turned, reaching to replenish his mug, swearing @ the mug for refusing to hold steady.

"Honey, remember how we used to dance?" Mrs Farrago was on her feet & @ her husband's side. She pried the glass from his grip & coaxed his unsteady feet into an even less steady tango. She glanced over her shoulder @ S-. "Stubbs & i use to wear out the dance floor. We were the envy of the Dreg Ball."

Despite her husband's attempts to lead, Mrs Farrago took charge. "Mooove, moove," she directed her children—this time the older ones—as she steered her husband out of the kitchen. A few minutes later she returned, cheerfully announcing Mr Farrago had decided to retire early. She cautioned the children to keep their voices down as they finished their meal.

"Martha's not back yet," one of the older boys observed.

"Her supper's getting cold," Margaret added.

"Maw," Weed suggested, "lit Margareet haf Marta's fude; she's eting fur too."

"Nah. Martha will be walking thru the door any minute," their mother argued.

"That's what you said yesterday...& the day before that," jj reminded her.

"She's out babysitting, i tell you."

"Maw, a corse she is. But itz dark. Yu no she'l wate till mornin befor cuming hoam."

"You're right," Mrs Farrago conceded, slumping in her chair, slowly picking @

201

her ragweed. "Martha's a clever girl. She'll wait till morning." Mrs Farrago looked @ S-. "She's only making a little extra One to help the family out."

Mrs Farrago repeated the last sentence several times, the kids rising one by one as Eve took their empty plates & carried the dishes to the sink. Margaret remained longest, finishing Martha's meal while Mrs Farrago stared from pot to pan to spatula to serving spoon, relieved when Eve delicately pried each from her fingers. Weed poured himself half a glass of stewjuice & led S- back into the living room.

On their return walk, he apologized to S-. "Yu mustnt lissen ta my ol man." He picked up a bulky stick & wielded it threateningly as they passed thru Dixsticks territory. "He thinx i spit betta thin anywan to—but no wan spits lik a Britlebum."

Coaxed by his shadow, S- invited Weed to paint in his attic some nite. Weed could paint, he suggested, & he would snap pictures.

"Will Mz Peny be dere?"

Despite the poor illumination, S- could see Weed blush. An awkward silence loomed until Weed explained, "Itz jest dat whin eva sumone maid fun a me 'cos a my closes, she wuz nise ta me. Not in fron a anyon a' course. But in pryvit. Onze she even trided ta help me soun out wurds...til Mr Smalot had my paw sespended. Paw sed i wuzn't ta tolk ta her no moor. An de necks dey, he got hiz job back. Say hallo ta her fore me @ lease."

When they neared the Smolet Manor, S- bid Weed goodnite, watching as the man-child faded into the shadows. The lightly salted nite sky gently rocked a near-full moon in its navy-blue hammock. An owl hooted, announcing curfew for all creatures wearing feathers. As S- stared into the sultry cheeks of the moonlit evening, his shadow took note of nearby shrubs rustling despite the absence of a breeze. S- strolled around the side of the house, greeted by the humming mulberry, who promptly lowered a welcoming bough. S- climbed cautiously, his shadow leaping from branch to branch, both squeezing thru the open window together.

Chapter 18

THE FOLLOWING WEEK CAME & WENT. The fair-haired mistress lounging in the sky wore pale pinks & lavender in the morning; blue & aqua & lacy white during the day; scarlet, peach & crimson around sunset. Most mornings found Mrs Smolet singing to the Boston fern, serenading the African Violet, cooing Aloe Vera or teasingly chastising Mr Rubber Plant for being such a sourpuss. Clad in kangaroo slippers, the lady of the house romped from room to room, gleefully cleaning every surface to impress the hired help.

Mr Smolet, btwn rummaging thru the garage or upsetting the laundry room shelves, frequented the family den, rustling the financial pages of the *ONE & Only Times*. Bustling about him, pruning the touch-me-nots, watering the baby's breath & scolding the wandering jew for its tendency to migrate, Mrs Sticky Buns would once or twice waltz her fingers along her husband's shoulders; Mr Smolet rolled his eyes, chomping on his unlit cigar or stroking his false beard.

S-'s days slipped into something Weed called a "rooteen." He came to tread delicately thruout the house, almost grateful when no one was around...especially Penny, who seemed to seek him out. The girl frequently brushed past him in the hall or popped her head out of her room to flash him a smile. At mealtimes, she appeared in frilly, bright-colored blouses, her hair a roiling ocean of bangs & curls, her cheeks marred by red splotches S- initially took as a sign the girl was ill. Her chin & forehead secreted a thick, pinkish powder that caked & flaked off as the day wore on. By week's end, however, the red & pink discoloring had toned down & the girl's attire became less flamboyant, tho still riveting his attention. Her hair settled into resting jauntily on her exposed shoulders.

One evening, in fact, Mrs Sticky Buns stumbled upon her eldest daughter teaching her youngest how to apply makeup. Initially stunned, the matron stood in the doorway, dizzy w/ delight @ her Penny not only preparing herself for auction, but prepping her little sister to one day walk in those very same high-heeled shoes. The rest of the week Mrs Sticky Buns divvied out extra nitrate tablets to all houseplants (including the wandering jew), excessively spraying lemon water on every frond in sight, kissing petals, massaging roots, pinching the cheeks of a gaunt Mz Gardenia, who soon blushed w/ renewed self-worth.

By week's end, however, Mrs Smolet had again descended under a black cloud. Come Friday, snapping turtles adorned her feet. She accosted S- in the hallway, entreating him to water Camellia & Rhoda Dendron as she was too depressed & wished not to inflict her beloved friends w/ her soured mood. The lady of the manor nevertheless tagged behind him, sighing heavily as she wished out loud for someone to meet her in some secluded theatre balcony, preferably w/ a box of dark chocolates, which she asserted to be the well-known secret pathway to any woman's lonely parts.

Even more morose than the lady of the house was the sullen, foot-dragging, passive-aggressive Buck (aka Bill). The blue-eyed man-child had not cracked a dimple all week. He sulked @ the dining table, barely raising an eyebrow should Penny, Pearl, or anyone present encroach on his territory. Hoping to regain the boy's favor, S- developed some of Buck's more eye-catching photos. He included several of the pimple faced girl Buck had been so taken by. The man-child glanced @ the snapshots half-heartedly, more preoccupied w/ looking about as if to see around corners. He shrugged as he flipped thru the pictures, hardly bothering to glance @ the last few.

"Nice," he offered, handing the collection back.

Saturday morning, S- stood outside Buck's relocated bedroom, his shadow bolstering S-'s nerve, chiding him for being such a scaredy cat. S- stared @ the flat-faced bedroom door, which seemed to glower @ him. He knocked gently. Hearing what might have been a voice, he cautiously entered. Buck lay stretched across his bed, two plastic soldiers in either hand, their rifles locked in mortal combat.

Mumbling, his phrases confused, S- conveyed as best he could that he was low on DEVELOPER & in need of more STOPPER & FIXER as well. Buck frowned, sitting up to search for a pencil & a scrap of paper. He scribbled an address & handed it to S-. He then maneuvered S- out of the room, closing the door in S-'s face before S- could suggest he (Buck) tag along.

While Buck continued to sulk, S-, accompanied by Weed, strolled to PERMAN'S SWITCH, BAIT, TACKLE THEN SNAP A PHOTO SHOP. Winding their way among the rods, reels & fishing nets & passing the cameras, strobes & tripods, the two were soon accosted by a friendly "May i help you?" Perman Radcliffe stepped from behind a counter, scratching his burly side-whiskers & peering @ S- thru wire-rimmed spectacles. S- immediately recognized the bare-shouldered girl standing nearby. Clad in a lacy bra & matching panties, the girl Buck called Jasmine was doling out change to a bucktoothed customer. Pinned to the girl's bra was an eye-catching campaign button proclaiming:

UNDRESS HYPOCRISY;
VOTE FOR FILKIN GRIMSPOON

Below that, in a smaller font was the promise:

HE'LL CLAD THE CLOTHESLESS

Stating his purpose, S- was led past the angleworms, lures & specialty hooks, Mr Radcliffe proudly displaying a vast selection of photographic chemicals. The store owner recommended one of two brand names: one whose bottles whistled a catchy jingle when lifted off their shelf; the other promising to also cure athlete's foot, dry mouth & whooping cough—in addition to preventing erectile dysfunction—all while guaranteeing the clearest, sharpest, most vivid pictures imaginable. When S- turned to Perman, hoping for a final endorsement, the store owner abruptly flashed a broad smile, his eyes no longer trained on S- but on something outside. Perman raised a palm as if waving to someone, tho when S- turned to see who, no one was there.

"I'd be most interested in seeing some of your work," the store owner smiled, turning to S-. "Every year i rent a gallery. I like to showcase some of the finer achievements of our many talented snapshooters. I've no doubt you can offer this year's exhibit a unique perspective."

After probing S- on matters of personal technique, previous training, preferred shutter speeds & theories on resolution, double-exposure & solarization, Perman grabbed three of the whistling bottles, steering S- & Weed twd the cash register.

"You know, certain primitives—the Wignuts & Erstwilders for instance—believe that taking their picture would trap their souls inside the photo." The store owner chuckled. "My son doesn't believe in the soul, but i gotta tell ya, when i look @ photos of the late Mrs Radcliffe—whenever i see that arresting smile, that glimmer in her periwinkle eyes—i'm sorry, but i can't help feeling maybe the Wignuts are right: a little bit of her soul is left behind."

"Say that too loud & they'll start non-taxing us for Mom's spirit."

From seemingly out of nowhere Edmund appeared, his russet hair disheveled, his shirt tail outside his pants. *I see you met Paps*, he addressed S-, one eye scrutinizing Weed suspiciously.

"You know my son!" Perman exclaimed, his eyes widening as a warm smile stretched his thin lips. "I'm not surprised. Maybe you'll use him as one of your disciples. I hear the Tower of Power is trembling in its jackboots. What you did @ Temple is the talk of the town. I never believed I would live long enuff to see it."

"Listen Paps, S- & i have some business to discuss." Placing a bony hand around S-'s shoulder, Edmund pulled S- to him as if they were recently reunited Siamese twins. "It's no easy task giving birth to a new age, you know. *Imagining a day when Dregs, Woodbees & Brittlebaums can sit @ the same table & receive equal service from the Nibian & Canaan wait-staff...that's easy.* But bringing forth that day...well, that requires a lot of masterminding, not to mention some pre-calculus."

The store owner beamed. He rubbed his sideburns, smoothed his thick brows & removed his spectacles to wipe his watering eyes. "Of course, son. Certainly. Absolutely. You fellows go on up. I'll ring up these supplies & have Jasmine bring them to you. Nice to meet you, both of you." Perman shook S-'s & Weed's hands.

Edmund led the duo upstairs. Out of earshot of his old man, he mumbled a few curses, raking his fingers thru his hair. Entering his apartment, he closed the door behind his guests & latched a shiny new deadbolt, bidding S- & Weed be seated.

Weed introduced himself, shaking Edmund's hand before making his way to the sofa. As he & S- sat, Edmund shook his head despondently, his cheeks going into sudden convulsions. His right jaw moaned in dire concern over some vague disaster looming in Buck's future. The left jaw sympathetically inquired into what that disaster might be? The right shrugged its corresponding shoulder, not @ all certain of said disaster's exact nature, yet absolutely convinced it was coming—even more certain that, whatever it was, it would be *terrible, terrible, just absolutely terrible*.

"He's like a brother to me," Edmund confided to S-. "Hail, i'd auction my own sister off to him—@ *half price*—but," Edmund clucked his tongue, "he knows our plan...& the others don't know him like i do." Edmund paused, his right nostril involuntarily sniffling, struggling to keep its corresponding eye from tearing up as his left jaw attempted to console it. Both eyes looked around mournfully—in opposite directions—till they alighted on S- & Weed, both seated across from him.

"The others," he continued, "especially Hector, take this revolution stuff, this overthrowing the establishment, too seriously. *I'm only in it till summer ends. After that i've got to start learning my Pappy's business so i can take over* should he get so senile we'll need to put him to sleep."

Edmund studied his guests, unsure from S-'s blank stare if his words were getting thru. He turned to Weed, who was listening intently, the Dreg's worried brows displaying signs of sincere concern. "I need to warn him—Buck i mean. *If i could talk to him for a few minutes.* Just a few minutes. If i knew what his intentions were, maybe i could reassure the others. Plus—"

Startled by a sharp knock on the door, Edmund jolted in mid-sentence. His shadow also bolted, searching frantically for the best escape route. The doorknob rattled. A female voice called thru the door, "Edmund. Edmund, it's me."

Edmund rose, unlatching the deadbolt & stepping back to allow his sister entry. Carrying a paper sack, Jasmine strode into the room, her figure supple, her large head, bright eyes & acned face lighting up the room. She introduced herself & handed S- the sack. "You can pay on your way out," she instructed. While S- perused the invoice, the girl produced two campaign buttons, offering one to S-, the other to Weed. Weed's glance, until that moment, had been riveted to the button btwn the girl's breasts. Noticing the boy blush, Edmund suggested his sister join them.

"I can't, Eddy. I'm helping Pappy."

"Just a couple of minutes, Jas. *I'm sure these guys would love to hear anything you could tell 'em 'bout Grimspoon.* Weed here seems particularly interested."

His sister turned eagerly to both guests. "You decided who you're bulloting for yet?" she asked. "We're gonna win," she added, pointing to Filkin Grimspoon's name, bending fwd to help Weed & S- read all the better. "We're getting all kinds of donations down @ headquarters. The One keeps pouring in. Look...the champagne committee was even able to buy all clothesless volunteers underwear." The girl turned to model her panties & brassiere, snapping the band of her panties to demonstrate its snug fit. "Now we have a place to hang our buttons. Think of it," she insisted, her bright gray eyes brimming w/ optimism. "After we win, decent, hard-working people may never have to lose their shirts again."

"I'll voat fore hem," Weed promised as he pinned his button to his shirt.

"*You know who else would probably vote for Grimspoon?*" Edmund suggested, "maybe even convince others to sell their votes?" Edmund looked from his sister to S- to Weed & back to his sister.

"*Buck Smolet.*"

Jasmine huffed.

"No, i'm serious. *He's already rubbed elbows w/ the Bookworms Illegitima.* I know for a fact he's looking for a change—he's as tired of the static quo as we are. *He's even mentioned to me personally how unfair it is to have someone w/ your shapely contours running around one cool breeze away from catching pneumonia.* He said if he had it his way, *everyone would be guaranteed @ least a pair of used military briefs.* Just think: if we can get that son-of-a-banker to sell his vote, *that's one crucial bullot* snatched out of the greedy paws of those Brittlebaum baboons."

As Edmund speculated, S- observed Jasmine's eyes go into overdrive. The vague possibility of a Smolet endorsement became something @ least likely in the girl's mind...which, in turn, morphed into something vaguely possible...which then grew into a distinct probability. The image of a new dawn glowed in the girl's widening eyes. Her imagination fired off volleys of rocketing fireworks, heralding forth a new dawn just w/in inches of being the new reality. "How can we win him over for sure?" she entreated.

Edmund turned to S-, his left jaw humbly pleading. "Just a few minutes. Tell Buck, Jasmine & i need to see him—tonite if he likes. We'll come to your place."

"*Just a few minutes,*" Edmund's other jaw repeated. "*That's all we ask.*"

* * * * *

THAT EVENING, shortly after the Smolets had gobbled & guzzled their supper, the front doorbell rang. S- answered; Weed entered, accompanied by jj, who hobbled in on a crude pair of hand-carved crutches.

"I hoop u don't mine," Weed entreated, referring to his brother. As S- didn't mind, the three lugged a canvas, an easel & a small sack of paints & brushes up to the garret. After some coaxing, Weed set up the easel & canvas, positioning himself as close as he could to the faint red light. "I'm wornin' yu," he apologized. "Don't expeck munch."

As Weed hemmed & hawed, jj plopped onto the futon, using his penknife to carve symbols from the Periodic Table on his crutches. S- retrieved his camera, assuring Weed he was more interested in taking pictures of Weed drawing than in what Weed might draw. Vaguely hesitant, Weed spread out his brushes & opened his paint kit, wiping the sweat from his unsteady hands. At first snapping a few photos of Weed inspecting his brushes, S- soon turned to snapping shots of Weed's shadow. Whereas Weed squeezed paint tubes cautiously, as if fearing to make a mess, his shadow squeezed exuberantly, gushing paint from its shadow tubes, stirring the black colors together as if mixing a multihued stew. As Weed dabbed conservatively, the shadow swung its arms in broad flourishes. Within a few short minutes, however, Weed & shadow coalesced. Weed's hunched shoulders relaxed, his breathing steadied & the faint wheeze that typically accompanied his breathing vanished.

S- aimed his camera @ jj's shadow, which had climbed into the rocker & set it in silent motion. The shadow, bent on contorting its every limb, twisted its arms & legs into excruciatingly painful positions, punching itself in its face & trying to pluck out its eyeballs. When it noticed the camera lens w/ its shutter wide open, it paused in annoyance. Finally, it rose to whisper in jj's ear; jj scowled @ S-.

S- set aside the camera to join jj, sitting on the loveseat as the two of them watched Weed lost in his task. S- marveled as a quick, confident, unselfconscious hand created crudely majestic trees & a swirling ocean threatened by rumbling storm clouds. In the foreground, faint figures in bright dresses danced across a dark, lush meadow, all birthed from the globs of colored paint smearing Weed's palette.

Upon hearing the trapdoor stir, jj turned. S- also turned, spying the suppressed dimples of Buck, the icy blue stare surveying the attic before the man-child fully committed himself to entering. S- jumped up in delight. Weed, pulled from his trance, set down his brush.

"Who are they?" Buck demanded, pulling S- aside & hissing in a low whisper. "You shouldn't have invited them."

S- nodded tho making no attempt to ask Weed or jj to leave. Buck continued in a whisper, "Look, I'm sorry i haven't been able to talk to you. I've wanted to...you don't know how badly...but you also don't know what they have planned. I only know little bits & pieces...but believe me, it isn't pretty."

A light tapping on the windowpane caused Buck to jump, his shadow immediately diving for the rafters.

Edmund poked his rusty, freckled head thru the open window. Climbing thru, he turned to assist his sister. Buck's face, initially cautious & annoyed, flushed w/ fear as he watched the sparsely clad Jasmine enter w/ her brother's assistance. His shadow reemerged, unable to take its frightened eyes off the acned figure w/ her confident breasts & short-cropped chestnut hair. Edmund stepped btwn Buck & his sister, half his mouth smiling, the other half scowling. "So what's been going on?" the smiling half queried.

Buck shh'd Edmund, looking @ the others in wide-eyed terror.

"Don't sshh me, you sorry—"

"Shh," Edmund's other half hissed. "Give the man a chance to speak!"

"I can't stay long," Buck blurted in an urgent whisper. "I'm only here to tell you to stop what you're planning; you defy the Powers that DO & it'll be the last thing you do do."

"What is this?" Edmund spoke from both sides of his mouth. He turned, strafing the eyes of everyone in the room. "Are you suggesting we turn back after we've gotten further in the past few months than we've been in decades? You heard what happened @ the Temple of Perpetual Puppiness. Rumor has it they're remodeling the laundromat, hoping to make up their lost revenue."

"I was there!" Buck hissed.

Ignoring Buck's comment, Edmund continued, "The Brittlebaums & their cronies made complete jackashes of themselves. *I'll tell you, i had my doubts...but Heidi & Sedgewick really knew what they were doing. Score one for the Lugworts,* zero for the Brittlebaums. They've exposed themselves for the idiots they truly are."

"They've done no such thing!" Buck countered, no longer whispering. "You think the Brittlebaums talk their babel to pull one over on you? They don't. They talk their babel cause they really believe it. They believe every word of it!"

"You watch," Edmund addressed the others. "As S-election nears *they will spout even more of their absurdly asinine NONsense. In blind obedience to their belly-aching entrails, they will spew forth more flatulent gibberish...*exposing their peanut brains for the frightened frauds they truly are. Even the naive sheep they call 'loyal citizens' *will one by one turn away, refusing to listen any longer to their Brittle, self-serving delusions.* And for the first time in their corrupt history *they will know how the rest of us feel.*"

As Edmund proclaimed the death of the Powers that DO, S- snapped an extensive photographic study of Edmund's shadow. Pontificating among the rafters, like an actor portraying a battle-weary general delivering a final speech before sending his troops into apocalyptic glory, Edmund's shadow crisscrossed the length of the ceiling, hands clasped behind its back, nose pointed twd the clouds, eyes aimed @ a distant heaven, taking its curtain call long before Edmund had finished the accompanying monologue.

Buck, however, remained unmoved. "They will never know how the rest of you feel. Listen to me, guys. I've taken three semesters of War & Annihilation, majored in Civil Atrocities, minored in Revolutionary Tale Spins. For PUP's sake, i even won runner-up for my thesis, *Lies & the Truths They Reveal*. The entire course of history shows the more you attempt to expose them, especially to themselves, the more desperately & unrepentantly, the more mercilessly, they will move to stamp you out!" As Buck pleaded, his shadow knelt before Jasmine's shadow, its hands folded in supplication, occasionally wiping away a dark tear. "They would rather destroy you than see themselves thru your eyes."

Buck turned to S-. "The martyrs they worship today are the ones they crucified yesterday. That's the way it's always been." Buck glanced around him, desperately seeking a sympathetic face.

"Jasmine," he begged, "i'll buy you all the clothes you could ever hope to wear. Don't suffer from naked exposure in the vain hope anything will ever change."

"*And what about the rest of the naked masses?*" Edmund challenged. "*Is she to forget about them?*"

"When i'm S-elected, i'll introduce legislation to get everyone socks...& after that, shoes—"

"When you're what?"

Buck froze, his shadow clamping its shut mouth.

"You're running for City Council?" Jasmine asked.

Buck said nothing, his eyes downcast, his teeth pressed to his lower lip.

Edmund moved to w/in an inch of Buck's nose. "So the rat is out of the bag," he proclaimed, both sides of his mouth quivering w/ spite.

"Don't you see?" Buck forged on. "One day i'll control the One. My Pupa, Uncle Harry, all the Brits currently in control will be dead. We can change things then...peacefully."

"Righhht. We can change things then...*peacefully*," Edmund mocked. "We've been hearing that mantra ever since Cain invited his little brother over for pork chops."

"Jasmine," Buck pleaded. "Talk some sense into your brother. You must know this very room is crawling w/ spies."

As the others looked to each other, Buck pointed to Weed & jj. "You don't think they're here just for their health, do you? Their father works for my father. And look who invited them." Buck looked accusingly @ S-. All eyes followed suit.

"They have him eating out of their trough." Buck pushed on, looking @ Edmund & Jasmine. "He doesn't know it. He's too...he's too trusting to know it. But they do."

Buck again pointed to jj & Weed. "And always, just as you commonists are about to grasp the hand of true equality, these turncoats, these sons of cheap britches, descendants of humble pie, will sell you out for a few unkept promises: an extra bushel of ragweed or a prominent place of employment for their virgin daughters— usually under the tutorage of some slippery-tongued professor @ Housekeepers U.

"Edmund, Jasmine, for the love of a warm blouse & clean cotton jeans, somewhere along the line you will sell each other out—& if you don't, they will." Buck pointed a third time @ Weed. "And if by some vague fluke of history, you & they stand united, the Tower of Power, w/out flinching, will destroy you both—w/ PUP's snuff-sniffing blessing."

"Well, *well*, well," Edmund sneered, pretending to stroke the moustache he as yet was unable to sprout. "I guess we know what Buck will be shooting for come S-election day.

"As to you," Edmund turned to S-, both jaws snarling in unison, "You & your spies haven't begun to see what tricks Edmund Radcliffe has up his sleaze. *One way or another the Lugworts of this world will emerge victorious. And if we don't,*" Edmund turned to Buck, his narrowed eyes unflinching, "no one will."

Chapter 19

WHEN IN THE COURSE OF HUMANE EVENTS it becomes necessary for one community, deeming itself more civilized than all others...when it becomes necessary for said community to pass laws to ensure its further advancement—said community will render said laws in pencil such that w/ dependable eraser said laws may easily be amended to the personal advantage of more elite segments of that same said community. Thus it had become firmly established policy w/in our micropolis that no law enforcement agent be compelled to work weekends or during holidays.

In fact, so sacrosanct were SaturSundays in the corridors of our municipal police headquarters—reserved as it were for relaxing, recreating & domestic quarreling—it was deemed in extreme poor taste for any citizen to commit a crime more serious than jay or kaywalking while said law enforcement agents were home abusing their spouses & neglecting their offspring. Fully anticipating our more hardened miscreants might purposely ignore so consecrated an ordinance, a subsequent ordinance was passed rendering all crimes committed on weekends *missed demeanors*. Thus, those hired to serve, protect & perpetrate the citizenry of our fair micropolis were not in the habit of reporting to the Municipal Police Station on weekends.

However, w/ so highly contentious a S-election rapidly approaching, an exception to even this law was declared necessary. Thus, on one particularly sweltering Saturday afternoon—the mistress in the sky sporting sunglasses, applying suntan & moisturizer, wearing a scant two-piece that all but snarled the sluggish traffic—all law enforcement agents (be they dressed in blue, in gray, in plain clothes or clown suits) were summoned to our tiny municipal auditorium where the honorable Police Chief William Willoughby stood @ the podium, tapping on the microphone.

213

"Is this mic on?" (tap, tap) "Can you hear me?" (tap, tap) "Can i have your attention, please? Good afternoon officers, agents, double agents & misc turncoats." (tap, tap) "Can you hear me? We all need to be seated. Everyone please, take your seats."

To the right of the Police Chief, his Deputy Ass't, Lt. Helen Shewes, sat @ a long rectangular table rubbing her seriously pugged nose. Newly appointed, the Deputy Ass't filled out her uniform w/ a confident, muscular grace, her short blonde hair protruding like yellow wings from the sides of her police cap. Seated to her right, Counting Commissioner Donald Dicker shuffled & reshuffled his note cards, his piebald head immaculately manicured for the occasion. The gold-plated brass knuckles awarded the Commissioner for outstanding service while Minister of Kid Glove Interrogations was prominently displayed on his right hand. Dressed in a triple-breasted dark blue uniform, Dicker had made doubly sure to polish its buttons to a near incandescent glow.

"Can we all be seated?" the Police Chief repeated, drumming his fingers on the podium as he waited on last-minute stragglers. "Can i have your attention?" He pounded a gavel. (Rap, rap.) "I want to welcome you here today." (Rap, rap.) "I know most of you...most of you have second jobs spying on your neighbors or surveiling each other, but we would not have called this meeting had it not been deemed urgent."

As Chief Willoughby spoke, members of the audience clicked pens & flipped open notepads. Several stealthily snapped photos, some thru their tie clasps, some from coat buttons, some from fake cigars. The younger recruits, fresh out of ICU Academy, whipped out the increasingly popular 35mm's, these cleverly disguised as tourist cameras.

"At this time i'd like to have Commissioner Dicker address you. As most of you know, the Commissioner has an important announcement we will no doubt wish to discuss. Commissioner."

Donald Dicker rose to tepid applause, those applauding mainly midgets with similar piebald hairstyles & dark blue triple-breasted uniforms. The audience grew quiet as the Commissioner approached the podium. Thanking Police Chief Willoughby & Lt Shewes, (whom he complimented for looking equally enticing & intimidating in her tight-fitting, spiffy uniform), then thanking the members of the audience & those on the Counting Commission staff & all the men & she-males who put themselves daily in alarm's way so his children & grandchildren could safely go to bed @ nite knowing the sun would indeed rise the next morning, the

Commissioner promised to get right to the point. Rubbing the back of his neck, he paused, looking around, his nervous eyes finally spotting his note cards still lying on the table.

"Chief, would you mmind?" He pointed to said cards.

Lt Shewes scooped up the cards & handed them to the Chief, who in turn passed them to the Commissioner. The Commissioner took another moment to loosen his belt in homage to the two watermelons he had swallowed prior to arriving. He undid the lower buttons of his uniform, also in homage to said watermelons.

"Men, women, & those of you still trying to decide, we are in the ddawn of a new age; an age ddifferent from any age that may have hitherto ddawned before it; an age thatt can gloriously shine for all ages to cccome—or, an age that can sputter & ddie; that can tripp over its own shoelaces & bring to its ddemise the whole march of civilization up to this heretofore ppoint." The Commissioner paused, his lips moving as he silently counted to ten (a technique he had mastered @ Executive Training School to affect a pregnant pause).

"I have stood among you more than twenty-seven years—thirty-one if you count the nnervous breakdown & the ttedious recovery period—during which ttime, in the hearts of many of you, i was still Counting Commissioner even tho i couldn't, & thus didn't, count." (Tepid applause.) "Those of you who know me, know i have always shot from the hip, even if sometimes shooting in the bback...but let he who has not made a mistake or ttwo—shot a few innocent citizens, accepted a bbribe in marked bills, or lied on the stand to save his own sorry ash—let anyone who has not been caught w/ his hands in Mz Demeanor's proverbial cookie jar be first to sslap me in handcuffs."

No one moved to cuff the Commissioner. He dabbed a few beads of sweat from his forehead & continued. "S-election is upon us—the height of our ddemicratic ideals: that season where we reshuffle the pecking order, that those in the middle may risk experiencing what it is like to slip twd the bbottom; that those on the bottom might hope to experience the exhilarating joy of rising a few rungs on the ladder of misplaced jjustice; & that those @ the top can remix their martinis & pposition their lawn chairs that they might gaze down @ those less superiorly endowed & perhaps see them in a new light, if only till the sun goes ddown.

"Such a time—rife with ppossibilities—is, as you are all aware, also ffraught with ddanger." A modest volley of applause rang out, this accompanied by low murmuring as well as a restless shifting of chairs & intermittent coughing.

"This is when the Dregs of our society come out in full fforce, insisting to be heard

215

if not seen. The Canaan. The Nibian. The Nattyhead & AntiPhants. The Diphthongs. Leghuns & Dibildogs. The Erstwilders & Doodle Dix. The Suite Idlelynes. When unDOers & *ant*agonists insist on challenging our right not to give them a second thoughtt. And this is when the sneakiest snake of them all—you all know who i mean—bores his way into our complacent contentment, challenging the vaults of our single-minded Oneness...w/ only one ppurpose on his forkedd, two-faced empty stare: to undermine everything our ggreat civilization stands against." ("No, no," several chants rang out.) "And so this is the ttime we must be super-vigilant in our pursuit of truth, jjustice & greater health benefits w/ more comprehensive retirement pensions—for all agents, double agents, tturncoats, cross-dressers & budding espionage engineers."

As applause rose amid hoots & whistles, the Commissioner paused, running his hand across his forehead before scratching his neck w/ his note cards.

"Of course, this will mean sacrifice." The Commissioner paused as someone booed. "Oneness, as we all know, is nnever everlasting...or @ least can not be everlasting if we don't take ppains to replenish it now & again...& rrestore it to the hands of those most capable of knowing whatt to do w/ it. And what better way to ensure that everlastingness than by each of us ppaying a fairly substantial nontax to its health & well-being."

Several boos rang out. Again the Commissioner counted, tho only making it to five before a small assortment of wilted vegetables flew past him, splattering across the stage.

"Thanks to the current administration, an administration i've been pproud to serve all forty-nine of my twenty-seven years, we have maintained our ever-tightening vise-grip on the forces that corrode our hold on a ffickle citizenry. In addition to employing/deploying the finest ppolice force any One can buy, we have created opportunities over the past twenty & seven years for more than forty percent of our citizenry to find ggainful employment in the espionage industry: becoming agents, double agents, undercover circus clowns & the highly revered ttriple agent, each as your conscience or lack thereof has allowed. But this success, this growth in the turn-your-neighbor-in-for-a-cash-reward industry, has not bbeen w/out serious cost—severe cost to our municipal budget & to the hhallowed vaults of our esteemed Oneness, the very vaults that keep the wheels of pprogress grinding down our enemies while greasing our collective ppalms."

"Here it comes," Lt Shewes leaned in & whispered to Chief Willoughby.

"How best are we to ensure the One prevails in the days, years & ddecades to come?" The Commissioner paused, his lips moving as he made it to seven & a half before more vegetables flew. "Why, by giving back to the very vaults that have given so generously to us all."

Boos broke out from all corners of the auditorium. Shouting quickly followed, the shouters being shouted back @, mostly by the piebald members of the audience who insisted the Commissioner be allowed to finish. These in turn were shouted down. Fists began to form, waved threateningly in the reddened faces of anyone who refused to be silent. The Police Chief rose hesitantly, scuttling to the podium & rapping the gavel.

"Gentlemen, ladies, please." Tho facing the audience, Chief Willoughby directed his remarks @ the Commissioner. "I'm sure, Commissioner Dicker...i'm sure there is no one here unwilling to share in the lofty task of preserving our precious fountain of Oneness, may its golden waters flow forever." (Several amens rang out.) "Several of us, myself included, Deputy Ass't Shewes & other senior officers of our laudable staff, have read your ambitious—& might we suggest, ambiguous—proposal. We applaud the rather creative attempt to levy a 'special privilege' Sir-tax on all double agents..." ("No, no, no!" numerous cries echoed.)

The Commissioner wedged himself btwn the Police Chief & the microphone. "Now, now. We all acknowledge & admire the self-evident fact that ddouble agents do twice the surveillance of a regular agentt. We simply recommend you be entitled to contribute to the One accordingly." ("No, no, no," more cries echoed.)

The Police Chief leaned into the mic, his head nearly colliding into that of the Commissioner. "And, for those of you who have excelled to triple agent status, the Counting Commission has seen fit to delay implementing your Sir-tax." (Mild, skeptical applause.) "Your Sir-tax will be implemented gradually, over a period of several days." (Boos, hisses & chair-smacking.)

"What the Police Chief is not ttelling you," the Commissioner broke in, "is that valued employees & all double & triple agents will be eligible to accumulate bbonus points. By year's end you can have earnedd enuff points to acquire a free juice blender, a twelve-cup coffeemaker or a deluxe salad mixing bbowl!"

The nos, boos & boo-hoos quickly rose to feverish pitch, half the audience leaping to their feet, flailing their arms & brandishing fists.

"However..." The Police Chief cut in, out of the corner of his eye noting a piebald midget snapping his picture, then jotting down what the C of P assumed to be his badge number. "However...." he repeated, catching another piebald midget snapping still more pictures of him, jotting down additional notes & aiming his tie clasp tape recorder directly @ the Chief.

The C of P froze, scratching the scab atop his head as he tried to recover his derailed train of thought. Several undercover officers, smoothing the collars of their clown suits, crossed their arms disapprovingly, one drawing a line across his throat w/ his forefinger, then pointing @ the C of P. As the Police Chief swallowed saliva, he felt himself shoved aside.

Lt Shewes commanded the microphone. "However," her thick, husky voice echoed thruout the hall, bringing the entire auditorium to attention, "the senior staff would prefer discussing your lofty proposal *after* this year's S-election..." (Several cheers went out.) "...after we have a better idea of just what administration we will be dealing with & whose Oneness we will be called upon to replenish." Thunderous applause broke out, peppered w/ hoots & hollers, whistles & foot-stomping. Hats flew in the air as several agents, including those assigned to spy on each other, hugged one another.

Red-faced & flustered, his watermelons unsettling in his stomach, Commissioner Dicker shoved both Lt Shewes & Chief Willoughby out of his way, twisting the microphone neck in his direction.

"You are making a mistake," he shouted, flailing his arms & brandishing his brass knuckles. "How many of you have even bothered to read the reports you've been turning in? If you have, you know none of you are to be ttrusted. Think about it, agents! We can't even trust the ppeople we hire to trust! No one is safe or above suspicion."

Pandemonium erupted as numerous agents charged the stage, some to rough-handle the Commissioner, others to save said Commissioner from being rough-handled.

"I'll tell you what you have," the Commissioner continued, his volume significantly diminished as he was shoved farther from the mic. "You have *ant*archy; you have unDOers in positions of power; you have aliens demanding inalienable rights—equal rights, no less, as if there are enuff to go around. You have..."

While he ranted, the Commissioner was pushed & shoved, angry faces challenging him on all sides. A herd of piebald midgets wedged themselves btwn the Commissioner & his antagonists. On the opposite side of the stage, the Police Chief & his Lt were barraged w/ backslaps, shoulder rubs & a few unfinished milkshakes. Milling about angrily near the exit door, the Commissioner waited as the crowd began to dwindle. Gradually regaining his composure, he finally ordered the barricade of midgets to move aside as he approached the Police Chief.

"You pplanned this, Willoughby," he fumed. "Don't think we haven't bbeen

watching you. You & your mal-practicing physician friends are going ddown."
Before the Commissioner could display his brass knuckles, Lt Shewes stepped btwn
the two men, her buxom chest defiantly demanding the Commissioner stand down...
or else.

"You're on the wrong side of this one, sir," she challenged the Commissioner,
her deep, throaty timbre calm & confident. "You know as well as i do there's plenty
of One to go around—provided no one takes too much. Keep in mind, sir, for months
now we've asked these agents to go home every nite to face their families after
turning their next door neighbors in. What's next? Turning in their family's friends?
Or their family members themselves?"

"Tuff love, Lt," the Commissioner barked back. "We call that tuff love. I love
you Woodbees. I really do. You know i'm more Woodbee than i'll ever be Brittle.
But you defy the Brits & they win...& they *will* win—by hook or by crook, they
always win—you defy the Brits & they'll be barbequing roast police chief & stuffed
lieutenant @ their victory celebration."

Commissioner Dicker stormed away, trampling several midgets unable to move
aside in time. One midget, eyeing the Police Chief, jotted a few notes, dotting his i's,
crisscrossing his t's before adding a last period w/ an air of finality. Turning away,
the midget thumbed his nose @ a fellow midget jotting notes on him w/ a similar
air of finality.

"Well," the C of P sighed, he & only a few other officers remaining. "I guess
there's no turning back. I SAID...I said there is no turning back now."

"You were great, Willie." The lieutenant kissed her superior on the cheek.
Placing her gloved hand on his shoulder, she gave him an encouraging squeeze.
"Don't worry about Donald. He's caught btwn a rock & a brittle place. Right now
he's too scared to even trust his own shadow.

"Think of it, Chief," she added as the two were turning off lights. "The people in
control of their own destiny. The poor no longer having to turn to crime to eke out a
miserable living. Lugworts no longer needing to conspire against a system that has
all but forgotten them."

"You're a dreamer, lieutenant." The Police Chief sighed, closing the exit door &
double checking the lock. "YOU'RE A DREAMER." As he descended the outside
steps, several camera bulbs flashed. An equal number of hedges rustled. The patter
of multiple feet scurried away, their fading footsteps replaced by the twittering of
magpies, swallows & an occasional screech owl. "There's no turning back now," the
Chief assured himself. "THERE'S NO...turning back."

* * * * *

THAT SAME AFTERNOON S- slouched across the battered futon, his legs stretched onto the footstool. His shadow stood over him, slowly flipping thru a selection of snapshots it had come to favor—several of which S- also liked. As each in turn commented on the framing, the composition, the subtle glint in this person's eye or the laughter in that person's smile, neither heard the timid tapping on the trapdoor. Only when they paused to contemplate a photo of a copper-headed, smirking Edmund brashly displaying a middle finger did they catch the faint sound of the trapdoor raising. His shadow slipped S- the photos.

Both turned as a freshly scrubbed, shining strawberry of a face poked its way in, a pair of hazel eyes looking around almost shyly. Penny's cascading hair was parted on the right, her bangs sweeping to the left. Her petite figure climbed into the room guardedly, meekly closing the door as if in mortal fear of disturbing any dust.

S- stood, momentarily dazzled by the modest cream-colored blouse, the plaid pleated skirt, the simple elegance of her stockings & shoes. The girl flashed a bright smile as she let fall a gym bag slung across her shoulder. When she noticed him holding pictures, she pointed. "May i?" she asked, hooking a lock of hair behind one ear before accepting the photos he extended. When she sat in the rocker, S- returning to the futon.

"These are...interesting," the girl offered, a ring of surprise lilting her voice. "I've never seen Buck so...so...what?" She gazed up, her eyes a pair of sparkling question marks. His throat constricted, S- shrugged.

"I see you tried to tie your shoes," the girl changed the subject. Handing S- the photos, she dropped to her knees. After rectifying his shadow's shoddy handiwork, she gazed up @ him. "Guess what i have?"

Retrieving the bag, she pulled out a black leather pouch. "It's a shaving kit," she explained, unzipping its contents & pulling out a razor, scissors, a small comb & hairbrush. "You wait. I'll make you so handsome, people will mistake you for a blue-bloodied Brittlebaum."

Offering no resistance, S- allowed himself to be maneuvered to the footstool. Sit still, he was ordered. Penny reached in her bag, extracting a long towel she placed over his shoulders & pinned around his throat. A few minutes later she was humming, alternating btwn clipping his hair & brushing or combing it. On occasion she would step back to study her progress. At other times she walked methodically around him, biting her lower lip as her eyes grew lost in thought.

"You know," she mused, staring twd S-'s shadow, who stood next to her, its arms folded, admiring her precision. "Underneath it all—you're not a bad-looking fellow. You need a little meat on these cheeks, tho. A bit more muscle on these shoulders. Maybe some surgery to bolster that sunken chest...but you keep yourself clean & your clothes tidy...."

"Who knows?" she added after a long pause. "Pupa might even let you propose to me." Penny began playfully running her fingers thru his hair.

S- reddened, confused & frightened, yet feeling a tinge of delight. Something in him stirred. He noted the girl's shadow retrieving the broom & dust mop, beginning to tidy up. He closed his eyes, aware of Penny humming in time to her shadow's sweeping. His own shadow sat on the loveseat, thumbing thru the most recent edition of **Rules for the Rode**, not finding what it was searching for.

Vague fears began to intrude on his musing. Images of Mr Smolet discovering them together flooded his imagination—displaced by a tingling sensation each time Penny's warm fingers touched his skin. He savored the brush of her blouse against his shoulder, the occasional puff of her breath tickling his neck. He delighted in the scale of notes she hummed, their vague melody occasionally broken by her gentle, soft-spoken banter. When he opened his eyes, he saw his shadow a few feet away, snapping photographs—pausing repeatedly to flirt w/ the girl's shadow.

That evening, in the bedroom directly below, Mr & Mrs Smolet sat engaged in silent communication. The master of the house chewed unmercifully on a few stray thoughts as his better half doused herself w/ Mz Aloe's special lotion.

It's less than a week away, Mrs Sticky Buns confided w/out moving her lips, her husband nodding w/out moving his head. And she is doing everything in the rule book, his wife added. The lady of the house sighed, her eyes wandering about the room in complacent wonder. Who would have believed it? she continued. Our little lamb chop about to step up on the auction block of matrimony.

A month ago i wouldn't have believed it myself, her husband's silence offered, removing his shirt & dropping it in the laundry hamper. But then, a month ago i wouldn't have believed our Bill—

A light bulb suddenly clicked on. Not so much in the room but in the banker's head. Grabbing his wife by her chin, he kissed her startled nose, an act so spontaneous, so tinged w/ unabashed rapture, Mrs Sticky Buns braced herself for a full, no-holds-barred ravishing.

She plopped across the bed, her arms & legs prepared to fly open. The banker, however, dashed into the master bathroom, rummaging thru the medicine cabinet. Pushing aside the lotions & moisturizers, the talcum powder & hairspray, the nail polish & polish remover, the tweezers & eyebrow pencils...then onto the next shelf, reaching past the aspirin, antacids, antidepressants, rubber cement & barbiturates, he snatched up a gold cuff link.

"Found it!" he shouted, practically dancing as he returned to the bedroom. "That's one down & two to go!" The banker stopped mid-joy, his jaw nearly dropping as he observed his wife disrobing.

"Just think, dear." Her voice soft & sultry, Mrs Sticky Buns kicked off her nun slippers & unsnapped her bodice. "In less than a week, our precious pumpkin auctioned off to some handsome Brittle stud, repunishing the Smolet lifeblood even more. And after that..." (Her skirt fell to the floor, her diaphanous slip revealing pliable portions of white thigh.) "After that, our Bill seated on the City Council, insecuring your big, strong, manly Oneness will carry on forever. What more could a man ask?" Mrs Smolet's slip cascaded to the floor as if the answer to that question lay somewhere in the vicinity of where she stood.

"The other cuff link...& its matching tie clasp," the banker rejoined, waving the one cuff link, then turning to the dresser to attack his wife's jewelry box.

"You know, dear," Mrs Sticky Buns murmured softly as she approached him, stroking the fine hairs on her husband's back, rubbing her pelvis against his buttocks, "according to some Myst Sticks, the surest way to find what we're looking for is to turn our attention elsewhere..." She blew in her husband's ear, her tongue tracing the contours of his earlobe. "Somewhere plea-sur-a-ble," she cooed.

Almost swatting @ his wife, the banker slipped away, opening dresser drawers, checking the tops of shelves, standing on tiptoe as he disemboweled the top shelf of the walk-in closet. Undeterred, Mrs Sticky Buns shadowed him, grappling to unbuckle his belt, even suggesting a place the other cuff link might be, insisting her husband feel inside—just to be sure.

"Why are you strutting around like one of those clothesless?" her husband finally chided. "Have you no shame!"

Mrs Sticky Buns stepped back. "No shame @ all!" she conceded, pushing her husband away as if staving off a bully. "Doesn't that make you mad? This shameless huzzy..." (She played w/ her breasts, brandishing them like ripe mangoes.) "...in your very own home...protesting the plight of the clothesless. Doesn't that just burn your gut?" Spittle spurted from Mrs Smolet's mouth as she taunted her husband.

"Stop it, Eleanore! What if the kids hear?"

"What if they did?" his wife challenged. "Imagine hearing their mother was for the clothesless. Even campaigning for that miserable Filkin Whatsitzface. Marching thru town shouting 'STOP THE NAKED LIES, STOP THE NAKED LIES.' What if your kids did hear? In fact, let's call them. Hey, kids!"

Mrs Smolet bolted for the door, her panicked husband lightning quick in blocking her exit. As she tried to squeeze past, the banker stood his ground, manhandling her where he dare, her supple, moisturized flesh defying a solid grip. The wafting aroma of Aloe Vera wreaked havoc on his olfactory glands. His only hope lay in pinning his wife against a wall or on the bed. As he wrestled her away from the door, Mrs Sticky Buns managed finally to loosen his belt, his pants falling around his knees.

The banker tumbled fwd, taking his wife w/ him, the pair toppling onto the floor. At the top of her lungs, Mrs Sticky Buns declared Filkin Grimyspoon her savior, insisting shirts, shoes & most especially underwear were tools of the devil.

Mr Smolet grappled to stifle his wife's screeching. The hanging wisteria & potted pansies turned their petals, the latter secretly delighted by what they surmised was about to transpire. While one of the banker's hands covered his wife's mouth, his other fell into his wife's deft command. She guided it till her muffled screeches dissolved into muted murmurings, her calls for Filkin Grimyspoon transforming into soft cooing mixed w/ pleas of yes, yes, oh yes. Encouraged by the desired result, the banker applied his dexterous frankfurters w/ even greater diligence, his wife's fingers finding a place on him that produced a similar response. Soon a pair of dueling murmurings competed in topping the pleasure scale: this one moaning while insisting there, there; the other imploring yes, yes, don't stop...then faster, faster.

When they finally lay exhausted, their chests heaving, their breathing slowly coming back under control, the banker kissed his wife in several places before rolling onto his back. "No fair, Eleanore," he sighed, "that was hardly in the rule book."

Chapter 20

AUNTIE MCASSER, AS NEIMANN CALLED his mother's half-sister, stomped around their small two-bedroom condo, her bottom lip protruding in its permanent pout. Glazed braised rabbit bubbled on the stove, a peach-cheery cobbler baking in the oven, its thick, sticky aroma tiptoeing into every nook of their modest apartment. Under her breath, the silver-haired matron shouted silent barbs, stuffed w/ curses, as she listened to the hissing of the shower & the off-key singing of her ingrate of a nephew. The nerve of him, she thought—after all, hadn't she given him everything?

She stormed about the kitchen, grabbing a knife & imagining the neck of a red-headed huzzy as she sliced & diced the defenseless shallots & garlic cloves. The task executed w/ military precision, she then looked about as if for a place to bury the body. She settled for folding the garlic & company into her secret sauce. Neimann, she reminded herself, said he wanted his absolute favorites tonite—practically insisted on it. Here she had given him the best years of her life—the second half of it anyway. And now here he was, planning to replace her—& using her own culinary skills to do so.

She brushed her hair back, catching a glimpse of her plump, admittedly overripe, figure in the mirror. Gone were her glory days. Then, too, gone were those years of abject humiliation, the errors of her youth all but forgotten. True, Neimann had been a dear to offer his spare bedroom. But then again, she had repaid him w/ years of loyalty—not to mention the culinary masterpieces she prepared for him nite after nite. She even put up w/ his irrepressible naiveté, tolerated his ultra-liberule conceits, smiling thru headaches as she listened to his highfalutin verbal gibberish.

Still, his oversized cerebral cortex, for all its syntactic gymnastics & seditious assaults on common, pragmatic sense, was too refined for the likes of some libarian ass't—some sorry excuse for a mere Woodbee. No doubt this woman, this Kate, was nothing but a huzzy bent on stripping away any hope Neimann had of bettering himself.

The fool, she snapped, hearing the off-pitch crooning over the running water & hiss of steam. The stupid fool! Didn't he know how ridiculous he looked, grinning from ear to stupid ear like that, staring into empty space? He had been like that for weeks. So much so, she had even come to miss the way he would diplomatically ignore her, hanging out instead w/ his book buddies or secretly flirting w/ those glossy periodicals he filed under his mattress. These days he preferred staring @ the woodwork or smiling stupidly @ candlelight flickering. The other day he spent a full half-hour fiddling w/ her antique music box, listening over & over to the chime's endless refrain of *Love is a Many Resplendent Ding-a-Ling*. And he completely brushed aside her comments on which vegetables sauté best @ which temperatures & which oven cleaner leaves the least residue & can double as toenail polish remover in a pinch.

Ignoring *her* was one thing...but ignoring Pythagoras! That dog doted on the ingrate: lived for Neimann to come home, fill her bowl, add food coloring to her milk, scratch behind her ears & fluff her pillow when she was ready to retire.

As if on cue, a four-legged Bratwurst sauntered into the kitchen, its droopy ears scraping the floor as it made its way to an empty bowl. Looking about, seeing no one dashing to replenish said bowl, the Bratwurst emitted a muted woe-is-me, pity-the-helpless whine.

"Wait your turn," the old woman snapped, her hands presently covered w/ a speckled pasty substance. Methodically she stuffed the pasty mash into several multicolored lobster shells. Pythagoras looked on sad-eyed as the matron rinsed, then wiped her hands w/ a kitchen cloth. Seemingly oblivious to the dog's persistent whine, the woman proceeded to brush the shells lightly w/ sesame oil, after which she carried the pan of stuffed lobster to the oven, sliding it next to the peach-cheery cobbler.

Another woeful whine was met w/ the matron's brusque kick: not hard but abrupt enuff to make its point. The old woman ordered the Bratwurst to move. Demoralized, Pythagoras turned, sulking away only to be called back by the repentant matron. Auntie McAsser stooped, scooping up the Bratwurst, rubbing its head & kissing behind both ears. She explained thru pursed lips how "mummy's just upset because another bitch is planning to destroy the life the three of us have built together." To show the Bratwurst there were no hard feelings, she reached in the oven & pulled out one of the stuffed lobsters. Removing the shell, she scraped the remains into the dog's bowl.

Both woman & Bratwurst perked their ears @ the sound of the shower stopping. Neimann's singing rang out all the more clearly, accompanied soon by a rap-tap-tapping on his dresser followed by the clattering of clothes hangers. As he always left his door cracked, his aunt could even distinguish the one-two one-two slapping of aftershave being briskly applied.

The spindly legged matron shook her head. Neimann's sudden fondness for aftershave said it all. She sighed, acknowledging she had long feared this moment. She told herself to be grateful it hadn't happened sooner. But still, she argued, why did it have to happen now, less than a week before the Smolet girl goes up for auction? You'd think PUP was deliberately out to thwart her.

"I'll get it!" Neimann called, his aunt only then aware the doorbell had rung.

She glanced @ Neimann poking his ridiculously smiling face into the kitchen. His clean, shaved, cologned, wiry figure was a slap to her face. How could he be so insensitive?

Her nephew dashed away, this time his singing on pitch as he approached the front door.

His aunt turned, determined to concentrate on her next task—heating her special crandy-cream sauce. She hummed...or tried to, her insincere harmonizing swiftly drowned out by the lilting musicality of two high-pitched voices enraptured to see each other. Her stomach wrenched @ the warble of a feminine voice telling her Neimann how handsome he looked. His response—remarking how every time he thought she could not get more beautiful, she continued to prove him wrong—did not help his aunt's disposition. When the profusion of complimentary horseradish was followed by a lingering silence, the old woman imagined two sets of lips puckered & pressed against each other. She wondered if Neimann had read up on what to do w/ his tongue. Nearly tripping over Pythagoras, she clutched the edges of the sink to compose herself.

When her equilibrium returned, the matron plucked a wooden spoon from a basket & stirred the sauce bubbling on the stove. She sighed, watching the sauce thicken, recalling how this very sauce once stole a young man's heart: a young man who in turn stole a younger girl's honor.

She stirred w/ increasing vigor, wincing each time she heard that high-pitched squeak call something "absolutely adorable": their small modest apartment—

"absolutely adorable"; her gold-inlaid eighteenth century music box—"absolutely adorable"; the family heirlooms cluttering the end table—"absolutely adorable"; the simulated fire in the cardboard fireplace—"absolutely adorable"; the Neimann Hall-of-Fame, a hidden cranny off the living room crammed w/ Neimann's childhood etchings, old report cards, his surrealistic finger paintings & abstract nudes (Neimann having never seen an actual nude)—all "absolutely adorable."

As the two voices drew closer, the embittered matron stirred more vigorously.

"And this is my Auntie McAsser," Neimann announced proudly. He stepped across the kitchen threshold, moving to one side to allow the lithe willow of a woman thru. Wrapped snuggly in a shimmering black dress, Mz Prit towered over Neimann's tiny aunt, the old woman reminding herself 'the taller they come, the farther they fall.'

"Auntie is the greatest gourmet chef this side of Puppiland," Neimann boasted. "Hush, Pythagoras. That's Pythagoras, our Polish Bratwurst."

The dog, ears scraping the floor, emitted a low, hostile growl, baring its molars. The old woman looked on w/ an approving smile.

"Auntie...this is Kate Pritt, the Kate i've been telling you about."

"Howdy-do," his aunt returned, turning her back as she pretended to adjust the stove burner.

"Everything smells absolutely delightful," Mz Pritt chimed.

"Appetizers will be ready in a minute," the old woman offered matter-of-factly. "Help yourself to a glass of D'leBaum crandy. You'll have to forgive Pythagoras," she added as the dog continued to snarl. "You know how Bratwursts are—never afraid to speak their minds. They say dogs are actually good judges of character." She glanced over her shoulder, eyeing her house guest.

Mz Pritt, however, was ogling Neimann as he poured crandy into two fluted glasses. He offered to pour one for his auntie but the old woman waved him off, pointing to a stein brimming w/ homemade stewjuice. Having forgotten she had poured it, she swiftly made up for lost time.

"Sit," she ordered, wiping her lips w/ the back of her hand.

"Pritt? Pritt?" the old woman repeated, her brows rubbing together as she savored the name. She puckered her lips as she brushed away several cobwebs clogging her memory. "Are you by any chance...oh, what was her name? Dorothy...Doughty... Dortie! Dortie Pritt!"

Mz Pritt eyes widened as she flashed a pleased smile. "You knew my mother?"

"Then Donald Dicker must be...."

"He's my great-uncle."

"Really?" the matron added, smacking her lips before downing another gulp of stewjuice. She spun around twd the oven, nearly kicking the growling Pythagoras in the snout. Grabbing two oven mitts, she opened the oven door, pulling out a bubbling pan of stuffed lobster oozing a cornucopia of aromas which quickly filled every corner of the kitchen. Finding a ladle, she doused the lobster w/ crandy-cream, garnishing the concoction w/ basil & jives.

"Eat," she bade her nephew & guest. "The rabbit won't be ready for another twenty minutes.

"I remember Don Dicker when he was in his prime," she continued.

As Mz Pritt proclaimed the stuffed lobster absolutely delicious, the pint-size master chef replenished her stein. "Such a fine, upstanding young man in those days...handsome as a devil...a real catch. I knew from the start what that Rosetta Whatzername?—the one who later married that Radcliffe fellow...i knew what she was after, what all her kind are after. I don't fault Donald one bit, refusing to marry her after they—"

"Auntie has rubbed elbows w/ most of the upper-crust Woodbees," Neimann cut in.

"Who are we," the matriarch continued, raising her stein as if about to drink, "who are we to demand the privileged behave w/ the mere common decency & moral integrity the lowly are compelled by law to adhere to?" The matron chugged from her stein, even Pythagoras pausing in her growl to admire the tiny woman's imbibing capacity.

"Auntie was @ the head of her class @ Waitress Tech," Neimann informed Mz Pritt. "Won a scholarship to spend a summer @ the Brittle Shake'n'Bake Camp. Didn't you almost marry the head chef, Auntie?" he asked. "Anyway, she got him to divulge many of his choicest recipes...some he never shared w/ any of his other students. Auntie must have charmed his pants off," he teased.

"Not @ the supper table," his aunt chastised, clunking her stein down. "Kate, Pythagoras is addressing you."

The ass't libarian turned to see the Bratwurst hoisted on its haunches, its front paws raised, a slobbering pink tongue dangling from its mouth. Mz Pritt looked to Neimann, then to the aunt, her confused expression begging for a translation.

"He wants you to share some of your lobster," Neimann's aunt informed her.

"Here, give him some of mine," Neimann suggested.

"No, he wants some of Kate's," his aunt insisted. "Kate's our guest. And this is her opportunity to get on Pythagoras's good side. Go ahead, Kate. Show her she's just like one of the family."

Gingerly Mz Pritt plucked some lobster out of its shell. Encouraged by the matron to drench the morsel in crandy-cream, the ass't libarian did so, offering the dripping sample to the dog. Pythagoras advanced, boldly licking the contents off the fork, then barking for more. Needing no translator, Mz Pritt forked over another morsel. Soon she & Pythagoras were the best of friends—so long as she kept the lobster coming.

Meanwhile Neimann's aunt had risen, busying herself @ the stove. Turning off the pot of sizzling braised rabbit, she tested the peeled asparagus before spooning it into a serving bowl. A thick dish of banana au gratin was pulled from a second oven, followed by a steaming-hot pan of peach-cheery cobbler.

Everything on the table being blessed as "absolutely delightful," seconded by Neimann's rapturous whiffs of approval, the matron sat down, immediately rising again to refill her stein. As Neimann chewed, he shared his vast warehouse of knowledge on modern culinary practices, sidetracking down the evolution of the human taste bud into the invention of the tater-tot by the ancient Aztecs. Both aunt & visitor smiled & nodded, the latter sincerely fascinated w/ the little-known & even-less-cared-about facts her Neimann showered on her. From the corner of her eye, the aunt noticed Pythagoras managing to scarf up the bulk of Mz Pritt's dinner, mildly offended when the dog declined any of the peeled asparagus.

An hour or so later, Mz Pritt & Neimann were @ the front door, Neimann preparing to walk Mz Pritt home. As Neimann bent to grab Mz Pritt's purse, his aunt complained of feeling faint. "Why is the room spinning?" she asked, suddenly staggering backward, the secondhand chesterfield managing—almost miraculously—to catch her fall.

Neimann & Mz Pritt dashed to the elderly woman's aid. Mz Pritt grabbed a nearby pamphlet, fanning the matron while Neimann gathered bottles of bleach, Dreg repellent & ammonia in an attempt to revive the fainted woman via an assault on her olfactory nerves.

Mz Pritt was spraying the repellent when the matron opened her eyes, coughing, choking & cursing, swearing the button-nosed witch was trying to kill her. Together Neimann & Mz Pritt helped his aunt sit. When the old woman had regained her composure, Neimann suggested he remain to ensure she was okay.

"Oh, you two go on," his aunt rejoined. "Don't worry about poor old sickly dying me."

"No, you stay," Mz Pritt insisted, looking @ Neimann. She assured them both she was a big girl who could find her way home alone.

"I had a lovely evening," she cooed as Neimann walked her thru his condo hallway.

"I hope you had enuff to eat," Neimann said. "Sometimes Pythagoras can be such a pig."

"What i did taste was absolutely delicious," she assured him, kissing his cheek.

Neimann hesitated, recalling his recent perusing of several Harlequin Classics. Tho he knew what should come next, not a single muscle would move in that direction. Thankfully, Mz Pritt came to his rescue, leaning in closer, her head zeroing in on his, his eyes closing, his lips experiencing a wet burning softness he had yet to find adequately described in any of those classics.

Her arms slid under his, clamping around his shoulders. His arms, compelled by their own volition, clasped her around the waist, tugging her closer. He felt her pliant contours & curves, marveling @ how her body fit into his like two pieces of a human puzzle.

When the pair released, he held onto the hallway banister until the swimming in his head subsided & his feet were able to stand again on their own. He stood dazed, elated as he waved to the figure descending the stairwell. When she turned back, flashing a smile & blowing a kiss, heat gushed to his face, his ears burning; his immediate impulse was to search for the nearest fire extinguisher. He turned hesitantly twd his apartment, sensing that in opening the door he would destroy a moment he wanted to last forever.

"'Bout time that huzzy left," his aunt sneered as soon as Neimann reentered. The old woman sat in her favorite chair, throw pillows propping her up on all sides. A family album lay in her lap, its stiff pages creaking as she turned them. Pythagoras curled in Neimann's favorite chair, her dark eyes focused sadly on her master as if she too felt betrayed.

"She's up to no good," his aunt spoke sharply.

Neimann looked away so as to not endure her bitter gaze. He plunked onto the chesterfield, reaching for the pamphlet still pungent w/ Mz Pritt's perfume. The pamphlet offered socially accepted swear words to hurl @ political opponents. Below each epithet was a corresponding apology to explain what one 'really meant' should the political winds change & one find oneself on the same side as one's former adversary.

"She's after our One," his aunt pursued. "Somehow she knows about the trust fund. You didn't tell her, did you?" His aunt glanced up, rubbing her nose as if to relieve a persistent itch.

Neimann set the pamphlet down, dropping his head into his hands.

"Her uncle, or great-uncle, or whatever Don Dicker is...he's on to us. He knows we've had our hearts set on getting you the best catch in town. He's set this niece on you to distract you from pursuing your better interests."

"Why are you doing this?" Neimann turned on his aunt, the veins in his neck pulsing. He struggled to reconcile the two conflicting images: the tender, burning feel of Mz Pritt's body pressed perfectly into his—against the harsh embittered worrywart of a woman seated before him. He recalled in dazzling detail the sensation of Mz Pritt's moist lips pressed against his, her hair tickling his neck, her skin soft & supple; & now his aunt's contemptuous crow's-feet, her mouth's bitter sneer, the snarl in her every syllable. And what was all this jabber about the One? She knew how little he cared for that false idol. Commissioner Dicker's words came back to him: "You can always consult the One"—a phrase the Powers that DO often resorted to to reel in those who stray too far.

"Look here," his aunt harped, reaching for the daily *ONE & Only Times*, handing the paper to Neimann. Folded to the society page, the newspaper showed a photo of an adolescent girl w/ freckles, dark curly tresses & gigantic brown eyes. PENELOPE SMOLET, the header announced. Neimann read the caption: "Penny Smolet, shown here @ age 11, oldest daughter of the honorable Mr & Mrs Charles Dinero Smolet, turns 17 next week. She will be joined by the rest of her graduating class @ this Friday's Grad-fest ala Auction."

"So?" Neimann hissed.

"So? This is as good as it gets." His aunt snatched the paper, smacking the newsprint w/ the back of her hand. "Sure, she's not pure Brittle stock, but what she lacks in rich blood, she makes up in being bloody rich. In two or three generations your offspring will be sharp as rulers, nearly full-blooded Brittlebaums...@ least for commercial purposes. You & i both know how a little One can bolster any birth certificate."

Neimann stood up in exasperation. "I don't believe this!" Again grabbing his aunt's pamphlet & opening its flap, he wondered if he might find a few choice epithets to hurl @ her.

"I've worked & scraped my whole life for this moment," his aunt pursued.

"This is why you were disgraced in the first place." Neimann's lips quivered as he broached what had heretofore been restricted territory. "One would think you'd have learned your lesson. Nothing good ever comes from conniving."

"And nothing good comes from marrying below your station!"

"What station!" Neimann screamed, turning away & entering the Neimann Hall of Fame. Bewildered, he stared @ the childhood photos, the crude drawings, his higher school diploma, his college thesis—all staring back @ him. The shrine to his modest accomplishments had been erected by his aunt—the same aunt who was fond of telling perfect strangers how her nephew was destined for greatness, how greatness itself would reach a new zenith once the world recognized his vast reservoir of hidden genius. Now that same aunt was determined to strip away something that made him happier than he had ever imagined happiness could reach. "Why, why?" he asked the innocent, adolescent two-dimensional face peering back @ him w/ schoolboy wonder.

"Think about the libary," he heard his aunt call.

"What about the libary?"

"You said they were threatening to close it. Do you think they would dare close any doors you chose to open if you were married to the prize possession of the great Smolet dynasty?"

Neimann stood in thoughtful silence.

"Do you?" his aunt taunted, reaching to rub Pythagoras's head. Her lips moved in silence as she counted. When she reached fifteen, she repeated the question. "Well, do you?"

* * * * *

ON ANOTHER SIDE OF TOWN, Pearl popped her mischievous eyes thru the garret trapdoor to find S- quietly snoring. The rocker he slouched in also napped. When she tickled his nose, S- swatted @ her, his snore but briefly interrupted. As S- refused to stir, the girl began exploring the apartment. She investigated the darkroom, its pictures scattered in disarray, its faint chemical odors making her slightly queasy. His bedroom had rule books piled or dropped in every corner. The bed was neatly made tho the sheet & blanket were reversed, the sheet on top. His pillow rested @ the foot of the bed.

She began to scavenge the apartment for whatever source of fun she & her shadow might find. They climbed the cedar chest & made faces in the mirror. They tiptoed around the floor, pretending it was full of landmines, each creak representing a fatal explosion. They were blown to smithereens several times, one particular explosion waking S-'s shadow, who immediately joined in the fun.

Locating the mop, Pearl promptly mounted as if riding on horseback. Chased by land-bound enemies, her horse grew wings & flew around the apartment. When safe @ last, she dismounted, turning the mop into a sword—tho no ordinary sword. This sword drew moustaches, befuddling her adversaries, completely disarming them. Thus was the floor lamp subdued, then the footstool, even the mulberry spying on her thru the open window. Pearl's giggling grew louder when she imagined each assailant a woman & the sword not only swashing on moustaches but beards as well.

Prevailing against the futon & defeating the loveseat, the girl turned the fatal weapon on the sleeping S-. Startled, S- jolted awake, his initial surprise quickly replaced by grumbling grogginess.

"Wake up, sleepyhead," Pearl taunted, her freckles dancing w/ delight. She stood on tiptoe, lurching twds him. "Guess who likes you?" she teased, a bright beam of mischievousness sparkling in her eyes.

S- blinked & frowned as his brain wrestled w/ the question.

"My sister, silly." Pearl plopped onto the futon, pulling @ the hem of her dress. "Haven't you noticed? She's been trying on all different kinds of clothes, mostly girly stuff. She's wearing makeup. Yesterday she came in my room & took back all the necklaces & earrings she lets my dolls use."

Pearl peered into S-'s dark eyes.

"Don't you see? Girls wear earrings & makeup & put on girly clothes when they want a boy to notice them. I even caught her reading her rule book, tho she made me promise not to tell. So you can't tell her i told you, okay?"

S- nodded as Pearl jumped to her feet & tugged @ his arm, insisting he follow her to the mirror.

"My sister put this here, didn't she?"

S- nodded again, recalling Penny's visit. "This is so you can see yourself as you pass by," Penny had explained, tucking a lock of her hair behind one ear. "If you walk past it & your hair looks a mess, or your shirt is misbuttoned—you know to fix it."

The instructions were simple enuff, S- fully understanding them; he & his shadow also aware it would bring him one step closer to the dreaded inevitable.

"Are you saving up for auction day?" Pearl asked. S- looked into the eyes of the girl's mirrored reflection. The real Pearl looked up @ him.

"Your One," she explained. "Have you been saving your One?" Getting no response, she explained further, "The One Pupa gives you for working @ the bank?"

S- stared blankly @ both girl & reflection.

"You haven't been picking up your pay, have you? Don't worry. Pupa's probably just holding it for you...so you don't spend it on anything frivolush like Penny does, or lose it all the time like Buck."

Pearl reached under the bed, pulling out S-'s shoes. "You should go down & ask him," she suggested. "I don't know how much you need to bid...but it's usually everything you've got. Which is why you need to start saving now."

She sat S- on the edge of the bed as the two of them negotiated which sock & which shoe went best on which foot. S- looked on, impressed the girl could tie a lace on the first try. He listened attentively as she explained the convolution of rules—rules, she informed him, evolved over centuries of amendments & addendumdums.

As Pearl understood it, anyone could bid but it almost always went to the highest bidder—"except," she qualified herself, "when the highest bidder dies... usually of rat poisoning during the wedding reception. This means the second-highest bidder could marry the prize—unless, of course, he too dies on his way to the altar."

Pearl steered S- to the mirror as her shadow dashed to retrieve the footstool. She adjusted his collar & struggled to untangle his hair. As she combed, she recounted one legendary wedding—one mentioned in her school textbook. The wedding was said to have gone thru thirteen grooms before the lucky bride had one who managed to survive beyond the pre-nubtials.

"The moral of the legend," she concluded, "is that no matter how hopeless things may seem, you still have a chance. I'll tell you what." The girl's hazel eyes widened. "I have some One hidden away. I'll loan it to you to help you get started."

Pearl stood back, examining S- from head to foot, her shadow doing the same. She led him downstairs, ignoring the DO NOT DISTURB sign dangling on the doorknob of her father's cocoon. She knocked unabashedly. When she heard a grunt from w/in, she opened the door & pushed S- inside, whispering, "Don't be afraid" as she swiftly closed the door behind him.

S- stood, momentarily dazed, his eyes adjusting to the poor illumination.

Mr Smolet, his shock of bright white hair in mild disarray, was on his knees, feeling as far behind the credenza as his pudgy arms could reach. Marshalling considerable effort, he rose to his knees, then his feet as he shuffled to his desk. He collapsed in his seat, motioning for S- to also sit. A smile tickled its way across the banker's slack jaws as he sized up his tenant. S- sat attentive, smartly groomed, seated respectfully—looking, in fact, like a potential investor ready to deposit his hard-earned life savings into the secure vaults of the Smolet First Pedestal.

"Son, i'm delighted to see you." The banker beamed, about to don his glasses, then thinking better of it. "Who'd of thunk it? When you first arrived, looking for nothing more than a roof over your head, who'd have thought you'd be my savior?

"That's right: my savior," Smolet repeated, aiming one of his frankfurters. "Two of my greatest possessions—my son & my most eligible daughter—have, thanks to you, taken up the cup of their filial responsibility." The banker leaned fwd, opening his cigar box. "They have swallowed the bitter pill of sacrifice & abandoned all self-interest to submit themselves fully to society's higher will. And all this @ a most critical time in the history of this great micropolis."

S- fidgeted as the banker stood, walking around his desk & plopping in the chair adjacent to S-'s. "And to think i was warned that you...you would be nothing but trouble. Some called you my doom, my demise just waiting for the right moment to drop the anvil of destruction onto my benevolent, over-generous skull." Smolet reached over to embrace S-, his clammy hand heavy on S-'s shoulder. "But you & me...we're *part-ners*, right?"

S- forced a smile.

"Now what can i do for you?"

S- spoke carefully, his shadow feeding him words as he articulated his having heard a certain rumor: something about being paid for the services he rendered the Smolet First Pedestal Bank & Pizzeria.

"Hmpph!" Mr Smolet hmpphed. "I see someone's been opening their big mouth. Stay away from those w/ big mouths," the banker warned, wagging the cigar he held. "The bigger the mouth, the more likely you'll fall in & get chewed up by a set of rotten crooked teeth.

"Now correct me if i am wrong," Mr Smolet rubbed his three chins, "but i don't recall any mention of financial remuneration when we first shook hands & agreed to be partners. Do you?"

S- shook his head.

"I thought not. Now let me explain the way the system works." Mr Smolet snapped the cigar in half, handing the smaller half to S-.

"You & me, we are the guardians of the One. I may be the bank's president &

chief CEOO & you may be a lowly ass't janitor, but you, me, the bank's tellers, the bookkeepers, desk clerks, secretaries, managers & VP's, extortionists & loan officers, all the way down to the lowliest pizza boy assigned to find new ways to get more crust using less dough—we are all soldiers fighting for the same cause. You get me?"

Mr Smolet plopped his cigar half into his mouth, rising as he paced one corner of his cocoon. He stopped directly beneath the portrait of Smolet the Grating. Avoiding S-'s eyes, the banker continued. "Now suppose if for your services—hypothetically speaking, of course—suppose for your services, i would take some One & say, on a weekly basis, dispense some of that One to you?"

S- glanced up @ the stern eyes of Smolet the Grating, eyes seeming to frown down on him.

"Would i not then have to dispense some to each of our soldiers? Pretty soon there would be no One for any of our soldiers to guard. You, me, the other employees would be out of a job—& then where would any of us be? This is why those few employees we do pay, we make sure to generously underpay."

The banker again took the chair next to S-. He raised S-'s hand—the hand still holding the cigar half—& moved it twd S-'s mouth. S- reluctantly placed the cigar btwn his lips as the banker demonstrated how to puff.

"I used to light them," the banker remarked. "Till my doctor warned me how lighting them increases the risk of smoke. Now i just puff them plain."

The town's leading financier then sat back, he & S- practicing their puffing. When the banker leaned fwd, he patted S- on the knee. "You & me, we have an unspoken deal. Right...partner?"

What deal? S-'s shadow asked.

"It's unspoken, remember...but, since you're a promising young lad, we'll speak about it just this once." Mr Smolet sat back, removing his cigar before continuing. "In exchange for you mopping floors, vacuuming, dusting the furniture & taking out the trash, i let you live in the garret rent-free. I let you fraternize w/ my children— despite the risk of them contracting fleas or being susceptible to lugworts. I let you sit @ our table, savoring not only the sweet smells of our meals, but the equally delectable aromas of my wife & daughter.

"But i'll tell you what," the banker offered, struggling to stand before waddling to his desk. "Because you're one to never complain—& because you have done me a great favor by helping straighten out my Bill & my Penny—i'm going to promote you to..."

236

The banker paused, first flipping thru a rolodex, then fanning the pages of a crisp new rule book, "to ass't to the ass't ass't vice president." The banker slipped on his glasses, his magnified blue eyes blinking profusely. "The position even comes w/ an additional key," he smiled.

Mr Smolet opened a drawer, pulled out a key & tossed it to S-. "Best of all, your promotion will allow you to continue to live in the garret & to fraternize w/ any new children me & Mrs Sticky Buns might choose to have. What do you say to that?"

Wincing @ the nasty taste in his mouth, S- removed his cigar. He gazed up @ the portrait of Smolet the Great & the hawkeyed Annabelle McDougal. "What do you say to that?" the couple echoed in silence.

S- nodded & rose, moving twd the door. The banker also rose, assisting S- in exiting, gently pushing when S- seemed to hesitate. As S- stepped thru the doorway, the banker grabbed S-'s cigar half, shaking S-'s empty hand & wishing him a good day.

Behind his closed door, Mr Smolet looked @ the cigar half, popping the unchewed side in his mouth. He removed his glasses & looked about his cocoon, unable to decide where to begin next.

Chapter 21

THE FOLLOWING MORNING our town's chief financial officer lumbered wearily into his First Pedestal & Pizzeria. He waddled thru the front door oblivious to the blatant lack of hellos & good mornings which (according to section 6, paragraph 3 of the First PB&P application form as well as chapter 8, subdivision 9, verses 27-31 of the employee handbook) were mandatory for all employees. For weeks, in fact, the banker had entered his home-away-from-home unmindful of the fewer & fewer obligatory greetings, himself even failing to return salute when his chief investment manager called "ten-hut!" & his entire staff rose & snapped to attention.

As in previous days—days stretching into weeks—the banker was preoccupied w/ matters we @ headquarters had been desperately trying to decipher. According to our reports, he chewed/paced/rummaged as if his time on Earth might be coming to a close. We were sure his interview w/ S- had unnerved him—not that he couldn't handle the starry-eyed do-do bird. For a man like Smolet, handling the anomaly known as S- was easier than tripping a blind man or stealing a trust fund from a baby. Yet, as Smolet reminded himself, the fool had the gall to expect a paycheck: one more sign the banker's delicate dealings were on the verge of collapsing. If things didn't turn around, he might have little choice but to tear the whole dammed bank down, brick by brick.

Smolet tossed his hat on the credenza & hung his jacket on the coatrack. He rounded his desk, debating where to begin, acknowledging how he had disemboweled both his offices @ least half a dozen times each. He was staring up @ the heating duct, considering removing its grating to feel around inside, when his office door opened.

Sur Harry stood in the doorway, one palsied hand clutching the doorknob, the other choking his cane. The aristocrat's hat drooped on his elfish head, the rippling of the corrugated forehead a sure sign the town's leading Brittlebaum was not @ all happy.

"CD," the patriarch huffed. Removing his hat, Sur Harry approached, perching on the edge of the nearest chair. Reaching in his vest pocket, he pulled out a soiled stack of neatly banded legal tender, which he tossed on the desk.

His nephew sat down cautiously, carefully counting the bills w/out removing the band.

"EVEN less than last SunDAY," Sur Harry grumbled, looking around as he burped his derby. "If it weren't for upgradING the coin launDROmat, we might as well close the TemPLE doors. Thank PUP both our clerGY & the conGREgation have a lot of dirTY launDRY.

"I don't understand it, CharLIE. A couPLE of weeks aGO, PUP gave the most impasSIONED serMON of His eterNAL life. I couldN'T have said it betTER myself. EVEN the sociETy page of the *ONE & OnLY Times* acknowLEDGED feWER peoPLE were snorING than @ aNY other serMON in syNOgongual hiSTORy."

The aristocrat looked around as the banker finished counting & recorded the total in a ledger. "Capital O, lower n, even lower e," Smolet mumbled as he wrote. In a smaller booklet, the banker dashed off the amount & signed the receipt.

"These are peRILous times," Sur Harry frowned, leaning fwd to receive the promissory note. He shook his head as he studied the written amount. "A mere pitTANCE," he muttered. Folding the receipt, he slipped it in his vest pocket. "You hear 'bout DonALD & the Turncoat UnION?"

His nephew nodded, the enlarged blues eyes apprehensive.

"And those inferNAL town criERS are all up in tears. I tell you, CD, sometimes it makes you want to give up oppresSING peoPLE. Maybe then the inGRATES wouldn't be so REsentful."

The banker fanned the bills before slipping them in a burlap sack stamped FOR DEPOSIT ONLY. When Smolet stood, his uncle also rose.

"Good thing we've been stockpiLING the bulk of this town's One," the old man offered. "AccorDING to DonNIE's calCUlations, our oppoNENTs will be lucKY to accuMULate eVEN a tenth of what we've stashed aWAY."

Ushering Sur Harry out of his cocoon, Smolet closed the door behind the aristocrat, silently latching the lock & counting on his fingers to a hundred & one. Ear pressed to the door, listening until satisfied, the banker cautiously opened the door & poked his head thru. Again satisfied, he lugged himself, burlap sack in hand, down into the basement. He looked both ways & several times behind him as he tiptoed to the door marked:

PRIVATE
FOR NO ONE ONLY
KEEP OUT
THIS MEANS YOU!

Pulling out the key slung around his neck, the banker looked around once more, craning his neck as if to see around corners. Apparently satisfied, he slipped the key into the lock. Cautiously opening the door, he flicked on the light switch & slid inside. He stepped gingerly among the scattered stacks of stuffed bags, banded bills & rolls of coins. Removing his glasses, he tossed the sack of bills onto the pile, dislodging a small avalanche. He stooped to retrieve the sack, preparing to reorganize the haphazard piles when a sudden loud banging sent him scrambling from the room. He slammed the door shut, clutching his pounding chest as beads of sweat popped up across his startled forehead.

He spied S- @ the bottom of the staircase, wrestling w/ a mop & giant metal bucket, suds dripping down the bucket's sides & onto the floor.

"Oh," the bank president gasped, using the sack still in his hand to wipe his forehead. "It's only you," he sighed.

The banker stared @ S- a long moment, then looked @ the door & back @ S-.

"What are you doing w/ that?" he asked, pointing @ the mop & bucket. "Have you forgotten? I promoted you, remember? You are now ass't to the ass't ass't vice president—in the non-managerial dept. I'd introduce you to your boss but we haven't hired him yet. We do, however, have your office ready. Here, let me show you."

S- abandoned the bucket & mop to follow his employer/partner to the third floor. Just off the fire escape was a door labeled BROOM CLOSET, tho an X had been crossed over the words w/ a magic marker. The banker waved S- in, clicking on a bare dingy lightbulb & standing next to S- as they both surveyed the cobwebs & considered the dust devils. A cockroach, apparently caught w/ its pants down, scurried thru a crack in the baseboard. The banker chewed on something, his three chins jiggling furiously as he studied S- out of the corner of his eye.

"Come w/ me, son," he ordered, leading S- back to the main floor. After passing the tellers (as well as those hired *not* to tell), the banker turned to S-. "I bet you don't know what the ass't to the ass't ass't vice president does, do you?"

S- shook his head.

The banker reached in his coat pocket. "Your job is to look for things. You see this here cufflink?" Having reached his office door, Smolet stopped. He opened his palm. S- examined the shiny cufflink, its gold embossed w/ the engraving, R24.

"Somewhere in this bank, or maybe @ the house, or maybe even in one of the billion & one places in this micropolis...somewhere there's another cufflink just like it. Only the number will be different & the letter will be an L. Plus, there is a tie clasp w/ a similar engraving, except again w/ a different number & another R. Your job as ass't to the ass't ass't is to find them—& find them in a hurry."

S- studied the cufflink.

"Of course," the banker whispered, leaning in so only S- could hear. "Like always, this will be our little secret...right...partner?"

The banker winked, looking @ the burlap sack in his hand. He unzipped the bag, pulled the bills from their binding & handed half to S-.

"Here, that's your advance." The banker explained how the Bored of Directors had that very morning voted to increase all vice ass't's salaries by however much S- was holding in his hand.

"Not only that," the banker elaborated, "you get the rest here if you can find both the cufflink & tie clasp *before* S-election Day."

On the banker's advice, S- began his search immediately. He returned to his new office, again surprising the cockroach as well as a few of its friends. He then scoured the entire third floor, to the annoyance of the numerous clerks, bookkeepers & loan officers contending w/ several irate harlots apparently upset over some early withdrawals. He then made his way to the second floor to the additional annoyance of the accountants & CPAs assigned to compound interests, freeze assets & cook some books w/out benefit of either stove or matches.

The banker, meanwhile, slipped back to the basement, revisiting the PRIVATE: FOR NO ONE ONLY room. He quickly tossed the rest of the bills onto the appropriate pile. He turned off the light & locked the door, double-checking the deadbolt was secure.

As he slipped the key back down his shirt, he almost smiled like he hadn't almost smiled in days. "Maybe, just maybe," he told himself, "I'll open that vault yet."

* * * * *

MEANWHILE, IN THE MUNICIPAL WATERING HOLE for unemployable intellectuals (aka the libary&literary infirmary), Neimann Gorge slouched in his office chair, his eyes focused on the ceiling, his meditative cerebration beleaguered by images of inevitable doom. Numerous classics lay scattered where he had abandoned them, several absentmindedly making their way back to their bookshelves according to the Luey or Huey, rather than the Dewey, decimal system.

His neglected book-buddies grew increasingly concerned, dismayed by Neimann's growing preoccupation w/ staring out the window. Even Mz Pritt sensed something was amiss. Neimann's usual grin had failed to burst across his face @ first sight of seeing her that morning. Instead, a dark rainbow lingered btwn his lips. He immediately turned away, pretending not to have seen her. When she approached, slipping her hand into his, giving his palm that playful squeeze that usually sent his ears into spasms, his responding squeeze was tepid @ best. Had she done something wrong?

She recalled the long sighs of the previous evening. When she first stepped into his apartment she fell naturally, instinctively, into his arms. Nothing had ever felt more natural. She rubbed her nose against his, brushed her cheek against his fragrant chin. She even whispered for him to take her: right there. She was his, she sighed into his ear. Was that it? Had she moved too quickly?

Maybe she should have given Pythagoras more braised rabbit, she considered. She shook her head: that couldn't be it. Perhaps she had somehow insulted his aunt. The old lush did grow meaner the more the woman drank. Had she not praised the woman's cooking enuff? Neimann had proved the consummate master in spouting all kinds of superlatives to describe the woman's cooking: comestible, gustatory, titillative, paradisiacal, nectarous, bitchin'. Her own vocabulary meanwhile was woefully limited to hackneyed phrases like delicious, delectable, scrumptious & absolutely divine.

Lost in her internal debate, the ass't libarian/nurse barely registered a voice inquiring into books on sacrificial son-rearing & father/daughter incest. Apologizing profusely when the voice persisted, she directed Reverend Hickey to the appropriate basilica before returning to reshuffling the same pencils & papers she had shuffled earlier. Absentmindedly reviewing the same applications from the same applicants she had reviewed previously, Mz Pritt finally rose, heading for the LADIES ONLY room.

Standing before the mirror, she pulled several safety pins from inside her waistband. Deftly she began tucking her skirt's waistband under her belt, the hem rising so as to reveal just a hint of the lacy silk slip underneath. She dropped first

242

one of her top's straps, then the other, opting to leave the left strap dangling as it tended to reveal slightly more skin. For a moment she pondered doing away w/ her bra altogether.

When a coworker/nurse walked in, she hastily returned the left strap to its upright position. She about-faced, storming out & up the elevator till she reached the Conclave of Sordid Affairs. Her index finger guiding her eye, she surveyed the shelves, her lips moving as she devoured each successive title, finally pulling down Paige Turner's **Seduction by the Numbers:** *Have Him Eating from More Than Your Hand.* She skimmed several pages, chewing a cuticle as she reviewed material she once knew by heart. Finally she slammed the book shut, kicking off her pumps & artfully removing her brassiere w/out disturbing her blouse. She turned, walking barefoot to the top floor of the ambulatory.

As she reached the landing, a piebald midget hobbled in front of her, blocking her path. "Forget it, Katie." The midget removed the toothpick pressed bwtn his lips. "Save yourself. I'll handle things from here."

The immaculately dressed midget smoothed the lapels of his zebra-striped suit & hobbled up to Neimann's closed door. He pretended to knock three times, then threw the door open.

The daydreaming Neimann bolted to attention as the miniature replica of Commissioner Dicker waddled into his office & rapped a threatening knuckle on one of Neimann's favorite books. The midget reached in his zebra-striped pocket & pulled out what he called a half-a-david, slapping the folded document on Neimann's desk. Neimann stared @ the midget as he reached for the legal parchment.

"I think we both know what it says," the midget sneered, removing the toothpick from his mouth. "It's from the Dept of Offensive Odors. According to the study they're about to conduct, something around here stinks." He sniffed about, lifting his nose & turning his head as if gathering preliminary evidence. "This establishment is to be shut down immediately—if not sooner." Flicking his toothpick @ Neimann's chest, the midget hobbled away, leaving Neimann's chin to slump to his breast, his languid hands to clasp the arms of his chair.

Neimann's first thought was to recollect where he had relocated the books on suicide. While struggling to marshal his disoriented thought processes, he heard the door open again. The midget poked its piebald head inside. "I almost forgot. A message from the Commissioner. He told me to tell you, & i quote: 'The ONE protects the one who protects the One.' Comprendez?" Without awaiting a reply, the midget was gone.

Neimann stared @ the half-a-david, dreading the day the authorities were sure to deliver the second half. He rose, moving to the window, where he gazed down @ a cruel & indifferent micropolis. His eyes glazed over, his thoughts an entangled web, he stared out @ nothing in particular. A red cardinal sporting a black Mohawk landed on the outside ledge, chirping tidbits of various facts passed down since antiquity. Neimann ignored the deep-throated warbler, hearing not a single chirp, much less caring what the winged messenger seemed to suggest.

Finally he gazed @ a book face down on the floor. For days he had not bothered to retrieve the fallen volume. Stooping to pick it up, he ran his palm along its smooth lambskin. These books were innocent, he reminded himself, recalling the hours of delight he had honed even from this peculiar collection of lowbrow haiku. These books w/ their many creeds & colors, their varying texts & textures, their ageless insights, their grappling to make sense of the world continually overrun by sticky, disease-infested, self-serving NONsense—these innocent lambs had done nothing wrong. They longed for nothing more than to be held, cradled in someone's lap, their pages spread-eagle to the universe. They longed solely for someone's curious nose to poke around inside till the mind opened & the eyes grew wider, the brain wiser.

Kissing the artificial lambskin before returning it to its rightful shelf, Neimann plucked down a heftier volume from an adjacent shelf. He parted the book's stiff shoulders, the words on its title page identical in font to those emblazoned on its rugged, threadbare cover: **The Courage to Do**: *Moving Mountains in a Time of Mounting Molehills*. Neimann sped-read the stout, heavily footnoted volume, his eyes frequently arrested as he digested its author's timeless advice.

In its introduction, Ryuichi Yamuzaki warned how moving mountains was never easy. Mountains, after all, persisted for thousands of years, so dismantling one would seem to take just as long. Success, the author emphasized, required stubbornness, persistence, fearless courage & unshakeable resolve in the face of numerous setbacks, as well as patience beyond all measure—not to mention self-sacrifice. The author detailed every mountain's determination to last forever & how fundamental change, the kind that truly lasted, would @ first be tediously slow— usually a one-step fwd, two-steps back rollicking ocean of a process—all this in the face of relentless, granite-cheeked, bone-chilling, stony, snow-capped resistance. The most successful mountain movers, the author noted, were almost always preceded by cemeteries full of defeated forerunners who laid the groundwork thru their blood, sweat, tears & massacred relatives—their combined endeavors taking decades to come to only modest fruition.

Neimann looked @ his watch, Socrates & Plato assuring him he had less time than that to save his many friends from impending exile. Ignoring the cardinal hopping about, insistently chirping as if it had some crucial insight to contribute to Neimann's dilemma, Neimann recalled the Commissioner's final message: "The ONE protects the one who protects the One. Comprendez?"

"Yes," Neimann muttered out loud, "I comprendez."

Tossing **Courage** aside, Neimann fumbled for another volume, one lurking on the farthest shelf. He pulled down the flimsy dusty paperback. *Rumple P. Stilkskin,* the author's name read, stitched in lazy, flowery cursives that flaked off should one rub too hard. Below the author's name was the book's title: **The Midas Touch:** *the Shortest Cut to Fabulous Riches, Dam the Cost.*

* * * * *

"*WHAT DO YOU WANT?*" Edmund called to a shadow milling about the dark alley. The rusty-headed revolutionary strained his eyes, wondering who the lurking figure might be. He had been up late, a dog-eared copy of **The Science of Free Radicals** balanced in his lap when a soft persistent rattling on a downstairs window had interrupted his nearly nodding off. Cautiously, he stepped out his back door & onto the fire escape, spotting a figure on crutches standing in the shadows. He trotted down the stairs, his leather pajamas squeaking as he approached a boy whose dark hair glistened when the boy stepped in the lamplight. The sickeningly sweet smell of imitation Nibian oil wafted thru the air as the boy drew nearer.

"What do you want?" the left side of Edmund's mouth repeated.

"I want to join," the boy whispered, leaning in conspiratorially, his eyes shifting as he looked around the deserted alley.

Edmund stared @ the boy. "*You're jj, right?*"

jj nodded.

Edmund rubbed his chin, then smoothed his left eyebrow. "Why should i trust you?"

jj sneered. "Who wants to be trusted? I just want to join."

Edmund's left cheek was about to order the boy away when his right cheek cracked a half smile. His right hand gestured for jj to follow. "*C'mon up,*" he said, reaching the fire escape & bounding up the steps two @ a time.

jj also bounded up two steps @ a time, holding both crutches in one hand till he reached the top landing. Returning his crutches under his arms, he hobbled into the dimly lit, poorly furnished apartment, closing the door behind him. At Edmund's instruction, he hobbled to an empty chair, looking around a room shrouded in thick shadows, cobwebs lined like hammocks around the furniture's legs. A single reading lamp provided the only source of light.

When Edmund reached for **The Science of Free Radicals**, a comic book fell from its center. Recognizing the buxom contours of the heroine on the glossy cover as Princess Photon, jj pointed.

"Isn't she great?" he enthused, adding his favorite part of that episode was when Princess Photon zapped her electromagnetic radiation on the Positronic Leptons. "My all-time favorite issue," he added, "is *The Corporate Quarks Eat Their Just Desserts*."

Ignoring the burst of boyish enthusiasm, Edmund tossed the comic book aside. "*So what do you know about us?*" he asked.

"Nothing," jj confessed. "Only that i want to help take down the ONE."

Edmund sized the boy up, his left jaw twitching w/ uncertainty, his right equally suspicious, yet intrigued. Something about the boy reminded Edmund of himself.

jj picked up Princess Photon. "So what have you got planned?" he asked.

Edmund retrieved **The Science of Free Radicals**, its subtitle promising *101 ways to subvert the laws of physics*. "You any good @ science?" he inquired.

jj lowered his head. "I never was much good @ school."

"*That's always a good start,*" Edmund encouraged, sitting on the edge of the sofa. "No true genius ever is. *Me & the Lugworts are planning to conduct a number of scientific experiments.* I've a number of hypotheses we wanna test out."

"What kind of experiments?"

Edmund worked both jaws in unison. "First we want to see *if two objects maybe can* occupy the same space *@ the same time.* Like suppose one of those objects is a flying anvil...& the other: *the soft, receding hairline of a Brittlebaum head?*"

jj's eyes widened as his lips curled upward.

"There's another interesting experiment in here." Edmund opened the book, flipping back & forth until finding the appropriate page. "Here it is. This one involves *meeting a deadly force* w/ an equal *but doubly deadly* counterforce."

jj sat up, his hands clasped in silent approval.

Encouraged by so receptive an audience, Edmund continued, fanning the pages of the textbook as he spoke. "*According to what they told us in school,* matter can't be created, *but we intend to prove conclusively* that it can most definitely be destroyed. *And after that*—you know that pish-posh about objects in motion tending to stay in motion?"

"Yeah,"

"*Suppose the object in motion is a 300-pound, PUP-worshipping, butt-licking genuflector falling from a ten-story bldg?...&* suppose the object determined to stop its motion is a concrete pavement?"

jj lurched further fwd. "I wanna help."

"Maybe." Edmund wagged a cautionary finger. "*Maybe.* We're also planning to conduct a few chemical experiments. *You know how to strike a match?*"

jj nodded, barely able to contain himself.

Welcoming jj into the Lugworts as a full member-in-training, Edmund initiated the teen w/ the secret handshake he that very moment made up. He then rose, opening a closet from which he pulled out his entire collection on *The Adventures of Princess Photon.* As he & jj reviewed their favorite episodes, Edmund's right side goaded jj w/ seemingly innocent questions. With unrestrained enthusiasm, jj confessed a secret fantasy to one day meet Princess Photon in person—maybe even ask her out. The two conspirators found themselves in complete agreement that one day the Princess' arch-nemeses, the Capitilipstic Oinkers, would be microwaved to critical density, then fed to the poor starving galaxies who would never again have to retreat to their black holes w/out supper. After reconfirming their mutual belief in the goodness of all things unBrittle, Edmund affected a yawn, hinting it was time for jj to leave.

"Don't go out the back," he warned. "*Never leave the same way you came.* Here, go thru the front door."

Edmund led jj down into his father's shop, cautioning the boy to watch his step. "*Wait a few minutes,*" he whispered. "I'll stand out back. *If someone followed you,* that'll distract them long enuff for you to get away. *Just make sure you latch the door behind you.*" Edmund again executed the secret handshake—or @ least a close enuff approximation—before returning to his room. As promised, he stood on the fire escape long enuff for jj to elude any pursuer.

jj stood momentarily in the shop, waiting for his eyes to adjust. He looked about, gradually discerning the narrow aisles. The racks of photography & fishing equipment were soon distinguishable, illuminated slightly by outside street lights. As he hobbled thru the maze, he caught the reflection of light bouncing off the cash register. Turning, he hobbled twd the large metallic box. As pressing its keys had little effect, he reached for his pocketknife. Applying equal measures of force & finesse, he managed to pop the lock & slide the drawer open. Even in the dark, he could discern several denominations of legal tender smiling up @ him. Sundry coins seemed to whisper his initials. After helping them climb into his pockets, he closed the drawer cautiously, hobbling to the front door. Stepping out into the cool nite air, he sighed heavily & cracked a broad smile: the evening had proved more profitable than he had even imagined.

Chapter 22

MANY WERE THE SHE-MALES in our micropolis taking issue w/ our time-honored traditions. Some, for instance, objected to PUP-sanctioned sacraments such as: all males inherit the earth while she-males inherit the right to sweep, dust & vacuum the dirt thereof. Others took issue w/ males getting to write, revise, edit & doodle in the margins of all rule books while she-males were limited to attaching the self-adhesive smiley-faces adorning each chapter heading—these adding the attractive panache that made such books a big hit @ yard sales.

In truth, our hallowed forefounders—as well as all their descendants, down to the contemporary Diddlethrum, Ritt'lbass, T De'um, et al—maintained emphatically that men & women be treated equally (except of course where equal treatment might challenge male superiority). Never content to merely contain their dissatisfaction (like our more model citizens), said she-males w/ increasing vehemence came to attack several icons of our revered traditions: one of these being our Grad-fest & Auction.

Each year families gathered religiously in one of our more affluent high school gymnasiums to talk, laugh, backslap, hoot, holler, salivate & gloat over our budding population of seventeen-year-olds—our fe-males @ least. Adverse to these celebrations, the abovementioned she-male agitators had lobbied aggressively to ban graduating females from stepping onto the papier-mâchéd pedestals doubling as their auction blocks.

According to most historians, the auction ritual was a by-product of late-mid-current-century Brits. Fearing their precious bloodstock too rapidly thinning, innovative Brittlebaums designed a process by which those w/ some Brittle-blood might legally fornicate w/ others of more Brittle-blood. Calling said process 'marriage,' they further devised a bring-the-whole-family-to-observe-&-celebrate ceremony during which female Brittle-blood bearers might simultaneously generate an increasing flow of greater Oneness in their quest to snag a Brittle Buck, a handsome Bob or @ least a lumbering Leroy.

Of course, no sooner does someone announce a party than those not invited begin to cry foul. Woodbees, who came to outnumber Brittlebaums three to one (thus gaining nearly 50% of the popular vote), came to insist *their* sons be allowed to bid on what few waning drops of precious Brittle-stock remained. Decades of bickering, threats, war, food fights & voluntary abductions eventually led to what our history books call 'The Grate Compromise': Woodbee boys, financed by vast quantities of the One, or in possession of Special Merit Scholarships (also acquired via vast quantities of One), would also be allowed to bid—provided they registered in the prescribed manner. Thus it was that despite she-male protests, gradu-auctions continue to this day. And thus it was that on one particular sunny day in early June, four human honeysuckles— Penny Smolet & three other semi-Brittle debutantes—were to step onto the auction block of matrimony, offering up their tender loins to the highest bidder.

To extend the festivities & create some suspense, all graduating seventeen year olds, including those w/ less than no Brittle-blood, were also honored w/ certificates of lesser merit. Bussed in from less affluent districts (most attending vocational Hirer Schools), they came w/ their unruly families, donning new dresses & eating all the finger food (w/ their fingers no less). They milled about the ballooned, festooned & festively pantalooned gymnasium in myriad shapes & mediocre sizes. They came tall & thin or short & plump. They came pudgy w/ red hair & splotchy skin. They came mousey w/ pig-noses & bony knees. Some were pointy-chinned & all elbows. Others came round-faced & lazy-eyed. The more modest among them stood around cocky & conceited while the cuter they were, the more churlish they became when our resident lechers tried to cop a feel.

Heidi Kilborn milled among them, her dun-color hair teased in an attractive coiffure her nervous hands seemed intent on undoing. Having washed her knees & trimmed her moustache, the girl felt uneasy, habitually smoothing her flower-patterned sundress & glancing down @ her first ever pair of matching shoes. Never had she experienced such a phenomenal feeling as having shoes that matched. She blushed when acknowledging the numerous double-takes from admiring male classmates. As she considered her stockinged, shapely legs, she even resolved henceforth to wash her knees more often.

Sedgewick, sans nose, & his younger twin, Rheum, stood on either side of their fidgeting friend. Quoting one of Heidi's more recent published works, Sedgewick declared her attire "a sellout: a blatant capitulation to the ritualistic circus of homo-semi-sapian vanity," his disapproval voiced in a nasally whine. Heidi, however, stood her ground, her gaze darting around the room, her neck craning to see around taller heads as if she were looking for someone.

Several feet to her left stood Jasmine Radcliffe, the girl's brassiere & panties clearly visible thru the pink diaphanous slip her father insisted she wear on so special an occasion. White frilly lace lined the slip's collar & hem while a scarlet sash was draped across her chest, hand embroidered with the campaign slogan STOP THE NAKED LIES. Her acne a minor constellation, the pumpkin-faced radical stood on the periphery of a group surrounding the magnetic Filkin Grimspoon. Jasmine watched w/ admiration as the politician's hired consultants altered his attire & reworked his casual banter as fast as the charismatic leader could size up each approaching constituent.

Also looking on in mutual respect was Belinda Grimspoon, a corsage of campaign buttons dominating her chest. As her uncle nodded, smiled & shook hands, lisping to the lispers & developing a nervous tick should the person he addressed have one, his statuesque niece gazed out @ the sea of smartly dressed Brittle bodies w/ their powdered cheeks & slick faces. She but half-tuned in to the master of ceremonies praising the organizing committee & their paid staff of volunteers, none of whom appeared to weigh under 295 pounds. After kudos & self-praise were heartily handed out to all those who had made such an auspicious occasion possible, the Hirer School graduates were called onto stage one by one—the order partly alphabetical, partly according to final test scores & partly according to services rendered the school administration andor janitorial staff.

Among the first called was Jasmine, the acne lighting her face aglow w/ defiance. After accepting her Certificate of Graduation, she snapped off her panties, tossing it into the crowd, shouting "Long Live the Clothesless." Scores of Bucks, Bobs & Leroys, as well as a dozen or so Johns, Jims & Janes leaped for the flying treasure. Weed & jj Farrago jumped into the fray only to collide into an immovable object they subsequently recognized as Bill Smolet. jj scrambled to gather his crutches as Bill & Weed rubbed their respective heads. All three looked on w/ disappointment as the panties were whisked away by the school's Viceroy of Student Affairs.

When Heidi's name was called, Sedgewick & Rheum expected a similar display—sans the panties, Rheum prayed, tho Sedgewick hoped otherwise. The flat-chested rag doll of a girl mounted the stage balling her fists, striding w/ determination—until her eyes alighted on a crop of platinum hair piled high into a double-decker ice cream cone highlighted w/ sprinkles & a crowning dab of chocolate syrup. Tho her mouth opened, her tongue flopped like a fish out of water, her words so soft even she could not hear them.

Cheered on by her uncle's entire entourage, Belinda Grimspoon was among the last called to the stage. She & a few other girls were handed special certificates, entitling those so honored w/ a full free week @ the university of their choice: Waitress U, Babies R Us, Dungeons & Drudgery, Old Maid Prep, or the nationally accredited Femme Fatale Academy.

After the final girl had mounted the stage & descended, family & friends hugged, cheered & backslapped the graduating girls while backstabbing the reputation of any graduate prettier or better endowed than their own. At some point a gavel banged. A 400-pound officiator drawled into a microphone, announcing the second half of the ceremony approaching. "Tonite's auction will begin in about ten minutes," she advised.

* * * * *

EARLIER THAT MORNING, even before the golden-haired sun had wrapped its pale arms around the dew-drenched morning, excitement percolated thruout the Smolet household. Penny loitered before her closet, trying everything on twice. She had packed away her men's fashion, retired her army boots & denounced forever her contemporary line of burlap apparel, stuffing them in boxes & storing them inside the secret corridor leading to S-'s garret. Now, on the morning of her gradu-auction, she couldn't decide what to wear.

Pearl ran btwn her sister's room & S-'s apartment, ostensibly to help them both get ready. Her older sister had spent the entire morning grooming S-, cutting & styling his hair, selecting clothes from both her discarded wardrobe & what she could wrest from her "Don't-call-me-Buck-my-name-is-Bill!" brother. When Penny left S- to get herself ready, her younger sibling stepped in, polishing his wingtips, selecting argyle socks & spraying his tied shoelaces w/ Lock-tite.

Then she sprinted downstairs, advising her older sister to wear red. "S- doesn't know it," the girl assured the bewildered Penny, "but red is his favorite color." She concurred w/ her older sibling's tactic of applying a subtle hint of makeup over the preponderance of heavy powder accented by two gaudy lakes of bright rouge advocated by that morning's rule book.

"Yes, but can he afford to bid?" the despondent Penny beseeched her little sister.

"I gave him all our cash," Pearl counseled. "Plus Pupa must have paid him. I saw a whole lot of One in his shirt pocket."

"Do you think he can win? I mean, *really* win?"

"Oh, he'll win," Pearl assured her sister, her comment rife w/ the unquestioned certainty only a child would cling to. She helped her older sibling into a navy-blue skirt & scarlet V-neck blouse tight enuff to draw attention to Penny's tiny but expressive breasts.

Again she assured her doubting Thomas of a sister, who slumped before her vanity mirror. "According to his rule book, they don't kill him till after he consums... consummes...whatever that word is."

The proud parents, meanwhile, were doubly excited. The thought of their ripening peach of a daughter being auctioned off bubbled thru their casual banter & tickled their toes as they bounded thru their getting ready rituals. Mrs Smolet aka Mrs Sticky Buns, formerly Eleanore T D'baum, sighed thruout her morning. She recalled her own beleaguered youth, the thrill & excitement of her own gradu-auction denied her, she & her Charlie having celebrated their nuptials prematurely.

"It's the only way to guarantee he'll be the one," she recalled her parents parroting each other, her Uncle Harry standing somewhere in the room, cane poised, the imminent arrival of swarming flies looming heavily in the air. "You lead him to the guest house," they instructed. "We'll slip in the back door. Your Uncle Harry will bring the camera. When the act is consums...consummes...whatever that word is, we'll jump out w/ this here rule book." Her mother pinched Eleanore's tearstained cheek, assuring her daughter everything would be for the best.

But tonite, Mrs Sticky Buns assured herself, shirking off the painful memory, she would experience all the excitement, all the exhaleration of being unctioned off to the highest bidder, even if only vicarriagely thru her Penny.

And her Charlie agreed. Charles D Smolet hummed as he clipped his toenails. The banker had resolved that for @ least this one day, he would forget his personal trials. Surely, w/ S- also searching, it was only a matter of time before the missing items were found. And maybe, just maybe, if tonite's bidding proved lucrative, it would placate his uncle, the Commissioner & the Powers that DO just long enuff. Perhaps, he thought further, if the Tower of Power proved successful in securing Bill first chair on the City Council, all his worries would be over. With Bill in his corner, even Sur Harry might think twice before raising his cane @ any fly that might inadvertently wander in the vicinity of the banker's nose.

"If the earth was in the sky," the confident banker told his reflection in the mirror, "i'd be walking on air."

By early evening the Smolet family, minus Bill, were gathered in the living room. S- had to be dragged down last, Pearl firmly clasping his arm, tenaciously pulling & tugging as if dealing w/ a stubborn mule.

Mr Smolet raised an eyebrow of curiosity. "Why is he coming?"

Waiting momentarily for her sister to respond—which didn't happen—Pearl took the initiative: "He needs to see the ceremony. So he can better understand our cust, our crustems, whatever that word is."

"Let him come, Charlie. He looks so handsome," Mrs Sticky Buns gushed. "He'll fit in so well, most people won't even notice he's there."

"Alright," the banker conceded, pulling out a fresh cigar. "But there's not enuff room in the carriage. Bill had to go on ahead. This one will have to walk alongside."

Together the entire family, sans Bill, traipsed out the back door to the family garage, the reluctant S- trailing several steps behind.

* * * * *

EARLIER STILL, THAT SAME MORNING, S- had awoken to a wrenching pain in his gut. He sat on his bed, across from his shadow as they watched dawn crack open like a rotten egg oozing slowly across the town's zigzaging skyline.

Maybe you won't really... the shadow began.

S- gazed @ his shaded friend.

Maybe you'll lose... You could lose on purpose.

S- sat motionless, unconvinced. When Penny, then Pearl, arrived to tame his hair & select his outfit, he submitted like a prisoner being prepped for the death chamber. So intent were the two, their shadows in perfect sync w/ their persons, he lacked the heart, never mind the will, to resist them. Even the triumph of finally tying his shoes on the first try rang hollow.

"Now you mustn't tell anyone," Pearl had cautioned. "If Pupa finds out, it will ruin everything. You read the rule book, didn't you?"

S- nodded, imagining his landlord/employer/partner/friend fuming w/ anger, the banker's tense frankfurters clasped mercilessly around S-'s throat. Tho perfectly willing to be throttled to death, S- feared an involuntary impulse to defend himself

254

might inadvertently cause him to strike back, thus landing the fatal blow to the very man to whom he owed everything—perhaps even his birth.

As he trotted alongside the Smolet coach, S- began to falter, weighed down by ominous misgivings. As the carriage turned a sharp curve & pedestrians dove helter-skelter out of its way, S- slowed his pace, the carriage pulling so far ahead no one seemed concerned when he ceased running altogether. He stood catching his breath as pedestrians dusted themselves off & went about their business. He glanced around @ the cheerful waving of young alders, @ the aromas of lilac, lavender & sage giggling as they tossed themselves into the wind w/ fearless abandon. He stared @ the sensuous tango of the evening breeze, a reddish-orange sunset exploding in the background. Many of the shops & storefronts had shut down early, displaying signs like CLOSED FOR GRADU-AUCTION & GONE TO THE GRAD-FEST. Several surrounding bldgs had begun to doze off; those few w/ their eyes still lit nevertheless began to yawn.

S- turned, unable to determine the shortest route out of town. Choosing a direction @ random, he hastened his steps, fearing the carriage might return @ any moment. Should anyone approach, he altered his direction, his greatest fear being some perfect stranger might slip him a note insisting he turn back to fulfill his mission. Avoiding human contact, however, sent him in circles, leading him down back alleys & onto side roads offering no exit. Nevertheless he held fast to his resolve, barely aware of a slightly bowlegged Schnauzer sidling up to him. Emitting a low growl, like it was mumbling to itself, the Schnauzer fell into step, its tiny legs pumping like pistons as it worked to keep up w/ S-'s hurried gait. From time to time, the dog would dash off to sniff out something, then dash back in a huff, muttering something that sounded like "God dam eat."

S- continued @ a brisk clip, wary of all approaching pedestrians. The Schnauzer occasionally plunged its black nose into discarded debris or dying grass, each time shaking its head & huffing, "God dam eet."

S- noted its bushy beard & twitching moustache, its thick brows rising & falling, its head shaking as if it could barely contain a boiling anger. When it dashed off to bark @ a STOP sign, S- veered away in an attempt to lose it. But the Schnauzer bounded back alongside him, its clipped ears perked up like antennae, its rump held high as if immensely pleased w/ itself.

"Nozing vill pleeze me more zen tu shake zee dust a zis place off me paws," it muttered, a few seconds later adding, "God dam eet."

Focused on an approaching pedestrian, S- failed to register the remark.

When he heard a carriage approach, S- braced himself, fearing to turn around & look. The Schnauzer, however, charged immediately, barking ferociously, snapping @ the wheels & baring its teeth as the carriage bounded by. Even after horse & passenger had passed, the dog continued to bark, growl & mutter. Relieved, S- felt grateful, even reassured by the Schnauzer's fierce vigilance.

"Zey nevah look vere dey is goink, do zey?" the dog complained. "God dam eet." Struggling to catch its breath, the Schnauzer muttered a long string of epithets, the words 'God' & 'dam' sprinkled generously therein.

S- walked on in silence. When he came to a DO NOT YIELD sign, he paused to ponder its suggestion, sensing more than seeing the Schnauzer trot off, this time to sniff a newly painted fire hydrant. S- continued on. A few blocks later, the Schnauzer returned.

"I zee yoo haff finely had enuff a zis place, too," the Schnauzer huffed as together they stepped off a curb. S- felt a mild tug, turning to notice his shadow lagging behind, its widening eyes lasered in on the Schnauzer.

"Zings @ first vere very tuff for me as vell," the dog continued. "Jest to zervive, i haff to learn ven to beg, venz to roll over, venz to play dead. You von't beleaf vut a four-legged guy haff to do juz to get a god dam bone." The Schnauzer paused, dropping on its haunches to scratch behind an ear.

S- slowed, allowing the Schnauzer to keep pace, his shadow finally catching up.

Ask him his shadow whispered.

His shadow egging him on, S- halted, turned & asked, "Who is this God fellow you keep mentioning?"

The Schnauzer snorted, shaking its head as its tail rose, stiff & rigid. "At your serveace," it barked, tipping its head in a slight bow. Pausing to dislodge a flea from behind its other ear, the dog continued on, cantering along as now S- trailed slightly behind. "I come for a liddle vizit," it muttered over its shoulder. "Tu zee how zincs iz goink. Zees humen beanz...zey need checkink in on from time to time. Only zay alvays make zis beeg fuzz ven zey zee me...so i tink i dizguise mezelf. And vy not as a dog? i decide. Zat way I jest spell me name backwads, zincing diz is preety clevah, no?

"Pluz, i like ze zymbolism—i'z alvays bean a suckur for zymbolism. But, ze god dam joke vuz on me. From zee very first zese humen beanz, zey treat me like a...oh, vats de point complainink? Nevah yoo mind."

The Schnauzer bounded on ahead, momentarily fascinated by a withered sunflower suffering its last death throes btwn a crack in the sidewalk. After a curious sniff, the dog lifted its leg, showering the drooping stem w/ steaming yellow liquid. S- continued on, deliberately slowing his walk until his four-legged companion caught up.

"Sew yoo like ze camera I send yoo, no? Funny zing 'bout zee lens. Yoo can viden it to infinitee vunce yoo know how." The Schnauzer halted, casting its bright gray eyes up @ S-. "Yoo evah figure out zat dream? Ze one wid ze girl reaching for yoo to zave her?"

S-'s knees buckled, the sidewalk wobbling as he lunged for the nearest lamppost. The surrounding bldgs swayed as S-, clinging to the lamppost, crumbled to his knees, his eyes clamped shut while he begged for the swirling around him to subside. He heard his heart pound, felt his face flush, his head floating like steam from a boiling pot. As the sidewalk & bldgs slowly regained their footing, his own sense of equilibrium returned. He glanced around, the street eerily deserted. He saw no sign of anyone. Even the Schnauzer was gone. More eerily still, there seemed no evidence the dog had ever been there.

S- struggled to his feet, his knees unsteady, his heart still pounding as he recalled the dream. In the same instant, he remembered Penny, only a half hour earlier seated in the carriage, her hand reaching out to him, her father brusque in insisting, "NO!" & closing the door, ordering S- to walk along side.

S- whirled around, both he & his shadow looking in all directions, scrounging for some clue as to which way to run. A bee hovering over a radiant sunflower offered its suggestion. Several strands of lilac & lavender threw in their two scents. S- sprinted down several streets, the DO NOT YIELD sign & a fire hydrant waving him on. A wren reported having recently flown over the gymnasium in question, pointing him farther. S- raced thru the more affluent sector of town, detouring into cul-de-sac after cul-de-sac after cul-de-sac, his shadow dismayed @ the city's plethora of well-manicured dead-ends. After following a gully @ the behest of a trickling stream & stumbling over a set of indifferent railroad tracks, S- & shadow found themselves on the outskirts of Crooked Town. Turning to retrace their steps, they heard a cackling voice, echoed by a small chorus of similar cackling.

"Well, lookee what we got here."

A shabbily dressed teenager stepped from behind a dumpster. Another, caressing a crooked smile, popped up from inside another dumpster. Others emerged, hidden behind lampposts, abandoned furniture & a carriage stripped of its wheels. S- was soon surrounded by a pack of snickering Dixsticks. One by one they reached down their pants as they moved in closer.

"Looks like Little Bo' Peep done lost his sheep," their leader bleated.

"Yeah, & he don't know where to find them!"

* * * * *

THE EVENING PREVIOUS, jj scrambled home from Perman's Switch, Bait, Tackle, Then Snap a Photo Shop, his pockets jingling w/ a music he rarely heard. He crept mouse-like up the squeaking stairs to the bedroom he shared w/ his male siblings. As he quietly negotiated the covers, sliding into bed, he heard faint whimpering. He lay motionless, listening to the intermittent sound of someone sniffling. When he reached twd its source, he felt his hand slapped.

"What's the matter, Weed?" he whispered.

"Nuthin," his older sibling snapped.

Undeterred, jj gently coaxed Weed into explaining the sobs. In grossly misspelled sentence fragments, punctuated by occasional whimpering, Weed unburdened his woeful tale. As near as jj could make out, it had something to do w/ a penny & that this penny was maybe a person, a girl perhaps. There was also something about a gradu-auction & this penny slipping away, perhaps to be lost forever.

Despite his failure in hirer education, his untried youth & what his teachers predicted would surely be a steady decline into abject Dreghood, jj managed to assemble his brother's broken puzzle pieces into a coherent narrative. Even more fully, he understood—again w/out the aid of a formal education—there was always one sure cure to fix just about anything that ailed man, beast or humble Dreg. He reached in his pockets, instructing his brother to hold out both hands.

Weed felt the warm, greasy, crumpled bills. He heard the tinkling of coins & felt their weight as his cupped palms proved barely able to hold it all. He could little guess how much he held. He puzzled a moment—his brother being notorious for the holes in his pockets. How could jj have accumulated so much Oneness? jj shushed him, confiding he had been saving up for just such an emergency. Despite his doubts, Weed ceased to question the source. He imagined instead Penny Smolet standing like a precious pearl on her auction block, him placing his bid. He could hear the ringing of bells, see the flashing of lights, picture a gargantuan auctioneer removing his/her D'leBaum cigar to pronounce Weed Farrago THE WINNER!

Weed lay back, caressing the legal tender. He slept poorly the rest of the nite, grateful @ the coming of dawn, which allowed him to count the treasure & proceed w/ his day. By afternoon he had scrounged up a secondhand suit. He doused his

258

head w/ generous portions of antibacterial imitation Nibian oil & patted his chin w/ an equally generous portion of his father's imitation aftershave. He powdered & preened as he imagined Brittle boys did to look so debonair & refined. Accepting jj's company for moral support, he arrived an hour before the doors opened so as to ensure he would be among the first to place his bid.

* * * * *

MEANWHILE NEIMANN GORGE was also splashing himself generously w/ aftershave. His mood, however, was the complete antithesis of Weed's. The recently deposed libarian pulled on his powder-blue shirt, straightened the billowy, salmon-colored cravat & slipped into his dark-blue tweed jacket w/ the demeanor of one headed for a chopping rather than an auction block.

His Aunty McAsser fussed & fidgeted, hurrying him along as Pythagoras yipped, snapped & woofed @ his heels. "He's sure to be the handsomest 210 IQ in the gymnasium," his aunt assured the excited Bratwurst. "And if the auctioneers are half as smart as their forged diplomas claim," she addressed her nephew, rearranging his cravat, "they would stop the bidding as soon as you arrive & immediately hand over the booty."

When Neimann stood ready, sweat trickling down his forehead, his palms moist & sticky, his Aunt fished thru her purse, pulling out a promissory note. The note, stamped w/ the seal of the Smolet First Pedestal Bank & Pizzeria & signed by the great Smolet himself, pronounced the sum total of her entire savings. It guaranteed its bearer entitled to a grand total of oNe. She handed Neimann the flimsy slip of paper, kissed his drooping cheek & promised she would wait up: this in case her assistance was needed in helping him w/ the mechanics of consums...consummes... whatever-that-word-was...his marriage.

Neimann arrived just as the Woodbee portion of the ceremony had ended. The graduating girls, their families & friends were leaving en masse, having little interest in watching the auctioning of their feminine superiors. Neimann glanced around @ the men-children in razor-sharp creased trousers huddled about their families, receiving last minute instructions as proud paters & doting maters handed them blue-ribboned promissory notes. Other boys, these dressed in wrinkled slacks, their hair slicked back & smelling sweet with genuine Nibian oil, similarly gathered around their less prominent families. Here too he noted the similar exchange of promissory notes, these w/out the blue ribbon his note also lacked. Neimann gazed

259

@ his promissory receipt—the capital N beginning to sag—then marched w/ feigned confidence twd the bidding booth.

With each step, however, he collided w/ a whale or an elephant or a hippopotamus—or so the officiating staff seemed to the libarian. Toting clipboards & wielding monogrammed pens, the registering officials seemed bent on crushing him btwn them, mercilessly stomping on his toes. Each spoke unnecessarily loud when w/in his hearing as they welcomed the more smartly dressed Brittle boys, jotting down their names & verifying their pedigrees. They gleefully examined all premium promissory notes (those w/ @ least two capital letters) & wrote out receipts, wishing each bidder the best of luck.

Neimann, along w/ the lesser dressed, found his toes perpetually squashed by huge-bellied men & bull-necked women teetering precariously on stiletto heels. Oftentimes he was shoved into a corner, his pleas for common courtesy, mutual respect, or just mere recognition completely ignored.

Weed too found himself summarily shoved & stepped over. Tho jj brandished both crutches—pounding, striking, even tripping a myopic official or two—the officials merely stood up again, brushed themselves off & gathered their clipboards. Looking over his or Weed's head, their beady eyes searched till a corrugated forehead or a pair of sharply creased trousers caught their attention. They then bulldozed their way around, over or thru any Dreg or Woodbee foolish enuff to remain in their way.

By the time the last of the promissory notes had been gathered, Neimann & half the Woodbee bidders were seeking medical attention. The other half, including Weed, had been corralled & ushered away, the officiating bouncers oblivious to any pleads for fairness or justice. Said victims disposed of, the bouncers closed & barricaded the gymnasium doors. Finally, the officiating auctioneer rapped her gavel, announcing the bidding would now begin.

A long rectangular box, part maze, part obstacle course, was rolled onto stage, its contents encased in thick plexiglass. The twenty or so Brittle candidates rushed the box, each vying for a better look. Inside another box was a near equal number of gophers, each blindfolded & shaved such that their only remaining fur designated a number from one to twenty. Someone distributed pamphlets to each contestant, the pamphlets containing the name, pedigree & history of each gopher. As instructed, the highest bidder selected his gopher first. The second highest bidder followed suit & so on. When all but one gopher had been selected—that gopher prone to epileptic fits, according to the pamphlet—the auctioneer raised her gavel, about to pronounce the gopher-selection process officially closed.

She paused, however, her attention distracted by commotion in the back of the gym. Despite the barricade, the gymnasium door had flung open. In tumbled a disheveled S-, his hair resembling a raging fire, his body bloodied & bruised, his clothes ripped & tattered much as they had been when he first entered town. Try as they might, the 310-pound officiators, the 295-pound bouncers, the 350-pound auctioneer, could not ignore the sight. No one dare impede the staggering/stumbling apparition as it struggled to approach the stage.

Pearl alone dashed to the aid of the dazed & befuddled S-, leading him to the glass tank & pointing to the lone gopher, @ that moment rolling over & scratching its belly after a pleasant snooze. She removed S-'s shoes, revealing a sight rarely seen among the uppermost strata of Brittlebaum society: hard, cold cash.

As eyes gawked & mouths gasped, the flabbergasted auctioneer searched the faces of her confused staff. Their tongues tied, their eyes blinded by the glare & glitter of cold cash, her staff stood dumb, several scratching themselves or each other. The auctioneer felt little choice but to accept the last-minute bid, assigning S- the last gopher.

A bell rang, officially ringing in the next phase of the ceremony. Four female tulips appeared in succession, each in turn parading down a long plank, pirouetting & sashaying back before stepping onto their assigned pedestal. A short, cross-eyed strawberry blonde walked the plank first. A pudgy brunette nervously chewing on a braid followed. A third girl w/ harsh, piercing eyes & shiny new braces repeated the routine. After she stepped onto her pedestal, a hush fell over the crowd.

Penny Smolet stepped out, nervously straightening her dark skirt & smoothing the collar of her scarlet blouse. She walked w/ her head high, her eyes focused above the crowd. Mrs Smolet gasped as she dug her nails into her husband's arm. To their right, Pearl tugged @ S-'s hand, gazing up & smiling into his confused expression.

When bidding on the strawberry blonde began, several boys had their gophers herded into a round wire cage. An officiator—the very hippopotamus who earlier had plagued Neimann's toes—rapidly spun the cage by a metal crank. With the gophers sufficiently disoriented, the cage door was flung open & the dizzy, blindfolded rodents tumbled onto the hazardous obstacle course. An electric current spit yellowish-blue sparks as the gophers stumbled, staggered, barged, blundered, jostled, flailed, groveled, lunged & leapfrogged—generally panicking their way to the finish line.

The audience meanwhile shouted & cheered, jeered & hurrayed, booed & hurrahed, cursed & prayed. They gestured frantically, hoping that by pointing, shouting & swearing their chosen gopher might gain some advantage. Side bets were wagered & leftover promissory notes exchanged hands, officials demanding a share of the cut for looking the other way. With each girl auctioned, the excitement grew, some so taken by a favorite gopher they no longer cared who the frazzled critter represented.

"And now, for the prize catch of the year," the auctioneer pronounced after the bony-kneed girl w/ braces had been auctioned off. The spotlight moved onto Penny as the remaining gophers were crammed into the crowded cage. The wheel spun, the hippopotamus giving the crank extra spins to prolong the suspense. Seventeen disoriented gophers plopped onto the electrified obstacle course, drunk w/ vertigo as the floor beneath them snapped, crackled & spit. The roar of the crowd proved deafening as the bulkier gophers trampled their smaller kindred, clawing @ anything & everything w/in range. When gopher nineteen stumbled over gopher eight, nineteen clawed furiously, drawing blood as it inadvertently ripped off eight's blindfold. Quickly assessing the situation, oblivious to the shouting around it, eight made its way helter-skelter to the most likely exit, collapsing in exhausted relief as it fell to safety.

An ominous hush filled the gymnasium. Jaw after jaw dropped w/ a silent thud, broken only by a single "Hurray!" as Pearl jumped up & down & squeezed S-'s limp hand. Anyone listening closely might have also heard another sound: this a heavy sigh of relief. Penny shifted her weight as she waited to be helped down from her papier-mâchéd pedestal.

Chapter 23

EVEN BEFORE THE EPILEPTIC RODENT crossed the finish line, Charles D Smolet had yanked off his glasses, firing a glacial stare @ his tenant/employee/soon-to-be ex-partner. Noting the fists quaking @ the end of the banker's arms, accompanied by veins pulsing across the crimson forehead, S- avoided the laser beam of bulging blue eyes zeroed in on him. He gazed instead @ the vague reassurance in Pearl's glistening eyes, the fidgeting youngster barely able to contain her enthusiasm.

Over the PA, the master of ceremonies' voice cracked & wavered as she struggled to regain some semblance of composure. In faltering phrases, she instructed the families & uh friends of the uh um brides & grooms to uh locate their um assigned locker room. "The uh receptions, followed by the um nuptial ceremonies, are uh about to um commence. Please proceed in uh um orderly uh fashion."

Mrs Smolet clung to her husband's arm, @ times pulling, @ times pushing the near-catatonic financial officer as she steered him twd their designated reception area. Despite her own disappointment, Mrs Sticky Buns heeded her maternal instincts, which told her to always look on the bright side—& if there wasn't a bright side, to pretend there was anyway.

"Just think," she reassured her husband, rummaging thru her purse for a handkerchief, "since Penny will only be moving upstairs, we won't need to hire a moving van." Mrs Smolet sniffled & blew her nose. "Plus, once the honeymoon is over, you can double his rent." The matron dabbed one eye, then the other. "Not only that: as a married couple, they'll only need one rule book btwn them—@ least until Penny starts having affairs. Think of all the One we'll save."

His disbelieving eyes focused blankly ahead of him, the banker allowed himself to be herded into the GIRLS' LOCKER ROOM. He winced upon glimpsing his daughter's name scrawled in festive paper streamers, cursing S-'s misspelled initial crudely written in gold glitter. Failing to heed his wife's warning to duck, Smolet swiftly became enmeshed in a spider web of low hanging, multicolored decorations. His arms flailing, his heart swearing, the banker grimaced @ the red & purple valentines plastered along the metal lockers & dotting the pewter walls. 'Congratulations' some read; others proclaimed, 'First comes the One' or 'Then comes marriage.' Still others: 'What PUP hath joined let no man push under a moving carriage.'

As the prospective bride & groom had been whisked away for last minute preparations, the Smolets joined the other guests, comingling w/ friends, acquaintances, curious onlookers & gossip columnists vying for a juicy exclusive. The pair graciously weathered the barrage of heavy sighs, cautious congratulations, sincere condolences & overly polite well-wishing. Mrs Smolet, who resolved to accept the entire matter philodendronically, located a can of disinfectant/Dreg repellent, busying herself by attacking the room's foul odors. While her husband deflected the pitying smiles & averted glances, she removed the musty towels & sweat-laden gym trunks lying about the floor & benches, tossing them down the decorated laundry chute.

Having dashed ahead of her parents, Pearl skipped around the locker room, racing up & down each aisle. She came to a screeching halt, however, after nearly colliding w/ a towering wedding cake. To the cake's right was a mechanical priest, a life-size replica of the honorable Reverend Hickey. Pearl circled the replica, marveling @ the realistic detail, right down to the greasy upturned palm & lopsided grin. She sounded out the words on the priest's lapel: *2 quart-ers per 15 min-utes.*

"Hey, Bill. Com'ere," she shouted. "Bill," she repeated, looking about. Getting no response, she yelled louder. "BUCK, COM'ERE. YOU NEED TO SEE THIS!" After still no response, she shrugged, concluding her brother must have dashed home to get his shotgun.

As a crowd gathered to gawk @ the cake, Pearl ran her finger across the curlicued frosting & popped it into her mouth; her eyes challenged those staring @ her to do something about it. She waved when her mother appeared, accompanied by a human prune toting a parasol & wearing a festive trench coat. Pearl recognized the prune immediately.

"Aunt Beulah—watch this." She scooped a second then third finger full of icing, each time checking to see if Sur Harry's better half might die of a heart attack—or @

264

least have her cardiac arrested. Her great aunt merely pursed her shriveled lips, once or twice spitting @ an unpolished shoe or a poorly creased pair of pants.

Upping the ante, Pearl snatched one of the replicas of a bride & groom, about to bite off its marshmallow head when the crowd's low murmur chilled suddenly, swiftly dissolving into hushed silence. Turning her head, Pearl spotted S- tucked into an ill-fitted white tuxedo, his bowtie askew, his hair partially parted in three places. She bounded over to greet him, adjusting his tie before taking his hand & pulling him over to the smiling replica of Reverend Hickey.

"This is the fun part," she enthused. "First the bride & the groom are handcuffed, to symbolize something or other. Then everybody rips the petals off their flowers & tosses them on the floor for everyone else to step on. Mummy says it's an old futility custom. Then the father of the bride...hey, where's Pupa?" Pearl looked about, her excited eyes momentarily clouded w/ concern.

Abandoning her search, she shrugged. "Anyway, someone pumps the priest here full of quarters & you & Penny are pronounced husbanded & wived. The bride gets a megaphone & you get a set of earplugs w/ a lifetime warranty."

Before Pearl finished, the lockers began to rattle, the floor quivering beneath them. The cake wobbled on its table while the mechanical priest vibrated, its forced smile seeming to panic. The 350-pound auctioneer rounded the corner, gruffly squeezing her way thru the dense crowd of curious spectators. Behind her, Penny appeared in a rustling, regally festooned gown, a frilly sash strapped diagonally across her bosom announcing where similar gowns could be purchased & @ what price range.

The auctioneer cleared the phlegm in her throat, demanding everyone's attention. She produced a pitch pipe, blew a B-flat & proceeded to conduct as the audience hummed a tepid rendition of a wedding dirge. Within the first few bars, however, she grew aware w/ increasing annoyance of a new commotion drawing the hummers further & further off-key.

All eyes & ears turned as Sur Harry appeared, brandishing his cane, smacking a locker here, a wooden bench there & a wedding guest or two for good measure. Behind the pouting aristocrat waddled the Counting Commissioner, clutching his stomach after a near overdose of watermelon. Behind the Commissioner, Pearl's father appeared.

"Hold up," Commissioner Dicker exhorted, barging past the auctioneer. Pulling out half-a-david & smacking it into S-'s palm, the Commissioner pronounced the wedding as one that would never ever take place—not if he, the honorable members of the City Council, their staff & secretaries, maids, interns, janitorial staff & indentured servants had anything to say about it.

The crowd stared in astonishment as a trio of men toting briefcases shimmied their way thru. Their leader, sporting a perfect ski slope of a nose, informed S- of his right to remain silent, adding that if he (S-) knew what was good for him, he (S-) dam well better exercise that right.

"Just a minute," another voice shouted, this one also turning heads. The crowd separated further as Filkin Grimspoon squeezed thru. Pearl jumped to attention when she spotted her brother. Just as quickly, however, Buck was gone.

Dressed elegantly from head to waist & casually from waist to foot, one shoe neatly tied, the other blatantly missing its shoelace, the town's leading opposition candidate barreled his way twd the big-bellied Commissioner. "I'll have you know i represent this, this..." After looking S- over & strip-searching his vocabulary, the politician finally settled on the word "man." He balanced his briefcase on the upturned palm of Reverend Hickey, snapped it open, then slammed it shut in a menacing gesture.

Unperturbed, Commissioner Dicker eyed the politician/lawyer. "Why ddoesn't that surprise me, Grimspoon?" The Commissioner snapped his fingers, upon which his own lawyers snapped open their briefcases & simultaneously slammed them shut. Gesturing to his entourage, the Commissioner turned, bulldozing his way thru the crowd; his lawyers, Sur Harry & Smolet followed as they all exited together.

S- stared @ the half-a-david in his hand. When Grimspoon patted him on the shoulder, a shiver ran first up, then down S-'s spine. When the lawyer assured S- not to worry, S-'s entire body went into spasms

* * * * *

"DIDN'T I WARN YOU HE COULDN'T BE TRUSTED?" Sur Harry hissed, thrusting his cane mere inches from Smolet's trembling jowls. "'It's awwwl unDER CONtrol,'" the old man sneered, recalling their previous conversation. "'He's like putTY in my hand.' I'd like to smack the putTY in your head."

"Now, now, Harry," Commissioner Dicker cautioned. "We can't afford to turn on each other. I'm sure Chuck had our bbest interests in mind."

The three community stalwarts were gathered in the game room of Sur Harry's mansion. Also present: Professor Major-Lieutenant General Armstrong Cody, who held lifelong tenure as Dean of Gladiator U & its sister campus, Academy

266

I. The Professor-General reclined in a double-padded La-Z-Boy, puffing a top-of-the-line D'leBaum cigar. All four pillars of the community were engaged in a puff-a-thon.

The Professor's hawkish eyes followed Sur Harry as the aristocrat paced a small area of carpet, using his cane sometimes as a bat, sometimes a sword, sometimes a golf club, tho always aimed @ the banker's jittery nose. Averting his gaze, Smolet cowered on the nearby sofa, an unlit cigar crushed in his clamped jaw. Now & then, on the sly, the banker plunged his fingers btwn sofa cushions to feel around. Seated in the adjacent La-Z-Boy, Commissioner Dicker blew smoke rings, expertly circular as now & again he studied his cigar as if its elegant contours were the very definition of perfection.

"What if she marRIES that freak of naTURE?" Sur Harry smacked the sofa arm inches from Smolet's dangling hand. "That's my preCIOUS bloodstock he'll be suckLING on!"

The aristocrat gazed up, his eyes meeting those of his first wife, her lopsided head expertly mounted on the far wall. He browsed the other heads mounted @ equal distances around the room, proud of his numerous conquests. Ever since his thirteenth birthday, Sur Harry had come to relish the thrill of the hunt. Born as he was, however, w/ a delicate constitution—one always in need of amending—he had come to prefer hunting indoors. As Treasurer for the Temple of Eternal Puppiness (thus overseeing the church, mosque & synagong coffers), he had palmed enuff excess alms to import rare & exotic animals from all corners of the animal prison. The ferocious beasts, mildly sedated, of course, were let loose to roam his game room, hiding behind the La-Z-Boys & sofa, the divan & end tables while Sur Harry crouched in a hidden compartment, his double-barrel bazooka poised & loaded, his butler ready to pull the trigger on command. To date, the fearless aristocrat had bagged three tigers, two lions, half a bear cub, a cross-eyed gazelle, a cocker spaniel, two burglars & his first wife. The aristocrat sighed, certain that had Matilda lived past their first argument, she would have been so proud of him.

"Wê can havê this marriagê tiêd up in litigation till this grandniecê of yours is an old woman w/ a dozên grandchildrên," the Professor-General counseled, displaying his predilection to cover his e's w/ pup tents in homage to his fond memories as a young cadet camping outdoors. He exhaled smoke thru his nostrils. "Wê havê biggêr problêms @ thê momênt."

"I say let the ceREmony contiNUE," Sur Harry asserted. "I've still a few botTLES of toXIC bubBLY. That & a litTLE rat poiSON sprinKLED in his wedDING cake will prove BEyond a doubt the guy is noTHING but a roDENT. No juRY would dare CONvict us...espeCIALly one on our payROLL!"

The Commissioner fondled his cigar. "Harry, we ddon't even know if this guy imbibes...or eats. Do we, Chuck?"

Removing the soggy cigar from his tense jaw, Smolet shook his head.

Sur Harry swished his cane, glowering @ the banker. "The man sits @ your taBLE eveRY day...for weeks, no less. And you neVER think to ofFER him aNYthing to eat?"

The banker shrugged, averting his glance as all other eyes bore into him.

"Thê Acadêmy is hurting, gêntlêmên," the Professor-General interjected, heaving a sigh of impatience. "Nêêd i rêmind you, our ovêrhêad is skyrockêting."

"We know, Professor. But the source of the problem is this S-." Commissioner Dicker stared @ his cigar. "It's a historical fact, whenever one of these...these guys appear, the disagreeable elements of society band together & make a big stinkk. The downtrodden, the ddisenfranchised all suddenly decide they're tired of being stepped over—even tho it never seemed to bbother them before. I ttell you, we let this guy marry & there'll be lots of little sons of s-'s running around causing even more hhavoc. Then where would your Tower of Power be? This marriage is something none of us can afford."

"To hail w/ the downtrodDEN," Sur Harry barked, swinging his cane as if suddenly beset by an onslaught of gadflies. "The downtrodDEN is just some ruMOR those gooDYtwoshoERS made up to make our wine taste bitTER. I say we FORget ABout them. We need to conCENtrate on the onLY One that truLY matTERS—which the GOOD BOOK clearLY states is U, S, us: the spaghetTI-haired!"

The Commissioner shifted in his chair. "It's your call, Professor. Think it's time to pull out the bbig guns?"

A pensive Professor-General puffed his cigar, holding his breath before blowing smoke out his nose. "Pêrhaps. Nêêd i rêmind you, gêntlêmên, thê bigger thê guns, thê grêatêr thê ONê?"

Sur Harry ceased swinging, leaning on his cane for support. Both the Commissioner & Smolet removed their cigars, all the better to listen as Armstrong Cody ran his fingers thru the medals lining his chest. The soft tinkling, like wind chimes, filled the ensuing silence. The Professor rubbed his bullet-shaped head as he pontificated on the foolhardy march of human inclination twd the twin abysses of world peace & universal brotherhood. Said march, the Professor-General argued, fails to acknowledge how such a pursuit undermines the very pillars upon which all great civilizations are built & precariously balanced.

"Inêxorably," the Professor espoused, "thê wêll-fêd grow contênt & thus wêak—as wêll as lazy up herê." The Professor tapped his bald skull w/ the barrel of his finger. "Thêy bêcomê soft, pronê to fits of amnêsia. Thêy forgêt that to sêcurê frêêdom, wê had to êxêrcisê tyranny; to protêct pêacê, wê had to wagê war; to promotê dêmicracy, wê had to silêncê thosê wê prêfêrrêd not to listên to." The Professor paused, allowing the chiming of his medals to add a musical refrain.

"Nêêd i rêmind you of thê first indisputablê law of Capital-I-ism?" he continued, wrinkling an eyebrow as if to solicit a response.

"Profit is everything," the Commissioner offered, staring @ his cigar held @ arm's length. "Without pprofit, there can be no growth. No growth…things eventually wither & ddie: the One soon reverts into the None."

"Êxactly. And thê sêcond irrêfutablê law? Harry?"

"The cheaPER the laBOR, the maXImum the proFIT," Sur Harry chimed in.

"Prêcisêly. Thê sad rêality, gêntlêmên, is nobody is willing to work for slavê-wagês anymorê—@ lêast not for frêê. Êconomic êxploitation must bê compulsory—êspêcially now that it's gêtting hardêr & hardêr to find voluntêêrs."

The Professor-General proceeded to support his thesis w/ a battalion of footnoted crossed references, the other three pillars of the community nodding in contemplative silence. The Commissioner & Sur Harry puffed their respective cigars @ their respective paces. The banker meanwhile twisted his cigar as he chewed on several tuff thoughts, his eyes lasered in on the nearby statuettes, straining as if to see what lay behind them. Several times his nervous frankfurters dove btwn the sofa cushions, once purposely dropping his cigar as an excuse to glance under said sofa.

The ride home that evening proved one of the worst in the fiscal officer's memory. As Smolet bounced atop his buggy, he pictured Donald Dicker's cold, calculating glare trained on him, one piebald brow raised in mild suspicion. In slow, deliberate phrases, pretending to speak to his cigar, the Commissioner assured the others that defeat @ the bullot bbox was highly unlikely. The Powers that do DO, the Commissioner contended, supported by the town's more vital institutions—its church/temple/mosque/synagongs, its City Council, the business community, the Water & Sewage Treatment Facility, the Chambers of Commerce—were all campaigning to ensure the sound ddefeat of any & all rivals. "Besides," the Counting Commissioner affirmed, "the vast majority of the town's hard ccurrency has been systematically amassed &

secured inside the vaults of the First Smolet Pedestal Bank & Pizzeria. There is enuff One to bbuy the best weapons, the best votes, the best judges & bypass the peskiest laws should the latter prove necessary—tho it probably in all likelihood wwouldn't.

"All our hopes," the Commissioner concluded, "rest now w/ you, Chuck. Hope you remember tthat combination," he snickered.

It was a joke, the banker had to remind himself, recalling Sur Harry & the Professor also chuckling, each attempting to match the perfect smoke rings the Commissioner blew w/ seemingly no effort. Still, the banker could not shake the vision of Sur Harry's beady eyes riveted on him, the black cane quivering in his great uncle's palsied grip. So vivid the image, Smolet neglected to rein in his horse as he entered the garage. He screeched to a halt, barely averting disaster, his heart racing as he alighted from the carriage.

He yanked each doorknob he encountered, slammed every door he passed thru. Despite the ruckus, the manor slept peacefully, nothing daring to stir as the banker stomped & cursed. The ancient grandfather clock held its breath, refusing to tick till the banker was mounting the stairs. The upstairs houseplants hunkered & cowered till he passed. Several dust devils dove for cover while a lone spider, building a modest cathedral on a ceiling corner, abandoned construction, opting a short time later to collect its suitcase & relocate elsewhere.

When the banker entered the master bedroom, slamming its door, Mrs Sticky Buns lay sprawled under the covers. Tho awakened by the commotion, the lady of the house pretended to sleep. She lay still, one eye cracked as her husband collapsed in a chair, throwing off his shoes, cursing each one as it landed. Plodding twd the bathroom, he stubbed his toe, cursing the baseboard. When he returned, tripping over a shoe, Eleanore Smolet pretended to awake, stretching & yawning as she *Hello, dear*'d him. Throwing off the covers, she came to her husband's aid, steering him to the edge of the bed & rubbing his throbbing toe before helping him undress.

Tho the banker protested, insisting he was old enuff to undress himself, he nonetheless submitted as his wife undid his belt, slid down his zipper & tugged @ his pants. Unbuttoning his shirt, she pulled his arms thru. After yanking his undershirt over his head, she playfully waltzed two fingers thru his chest hair. She removed his watch & the key around his neck, ignoring the steady stream of expletives he muttered under his breath. She *Yes, dear*'d him as he grumbled on about a piebald idiot, a derby-headed oxymoron & a metal-headed lewdten*ant*.

The banker continued to vent as his wife turned off each light. She *Yes, dear*'d

& *You're absolutely right, dear'*d him as she went. When all but one light glowed & that light but dimly, she climbed onto the bed, kneeling behind him, gently kneading his shoulder & neck muscles.

Shortly thereafter he ceased venting. Lying back per his wife's instructions, the banker began to purr, his eyes popping open when his wife suddenly straddled him. She kissed his chest hair, nuzzled his belly button, licked his nipples, cooing as she bade him to tell Mummy where it hurt. Lacking all will, too exhausted to resist, Smolet submitted to his wife's command. Surprising even himself, his energy quickly rebounded. When the couple were done, the banker rolled over, purring contentedly, his wife kissing his cheek & wishing him sweet dreams as the two dozed off.

Sometime later, the banker bolted awake, Mrs Smolet peacefully snoring beside him. Within seconds he was up, dashing to his wife's side of their walk-in closet. Sliding the door open, clicking on the overhead light, he stepped inside. He stooped low, scooping up a gold cufflink. Its engraved 'L73' smiled up @ him, glistening @ his grateful expression as if inquiring what had taken him so long?

* * * * *

AFTER WEED HAD BEEN EJECTED from the Gradfest, the dejected Dreg hobbled home in such a despondent manner, jj felt compelled to offer the use of his crutches. Weed shook his head, hiding his tears & handing back the cash. As the two trudged home, Weed insisted on kicking every can, throwing every stone & snapping in two every stick stupid enuff to cross his path. Arriving home, he skulked up to his room, jj opting to join his siblings lounging in the living room, mostly sprawled about the floor. For several weeks the Farrago children had been enjoying front row seats to a live action drama.

An anthill had sprung up bwtn the floorboards, providing several evenings of free entertainment. Joseph had been first to notice the budding new metropolis. He spotted the early scouts, two tiny black explorers intently searching for a new promised land. Soon thereafter, troops arrived—worker ants & army ants—united in a common mission to build a sand temple for their Missus. Barely a week after the crude temple's completion, Margaret remarked the worker ants seemed agitated, as if refusing to lug another sand boulder. The army ants then attacked the workers but were soon fighting amongst themselves. Too busy killing each other off, they proved totally unprepared when a platoon of red ants, followed swiftly by reinforcements, toppled the anthill, enslaving the black ants & erecting another temple—one which by ant standards might have been comparable to a Taj Mahal.

Then, only a couple days ago, Orson observed a red ant & a black ant scurrying from the premises, the boy swearing up & down the two seemed pretty fond of each other. Together they built a more modest anthill while the Taj Mahal seemed to disintegrate of its own volition. Excited by recent developments, Joseph & Orson pointed out to jj how there were now ants w/ red heads & black bottoms & ants w/ black heads & red bottoms working in lockstep to build yet another pyramid from the shifting sands.

The Farrago family, gathered in the living room, watched intently as the continuing saga unfolded. Mrs Farrago sat @ the table knitting another sweater, this one apparently for a two-headed octopus. Periodically, btwn knit ones & purl twos, she would order young Josh to moove. jj's father leaned back in a rocking chair, little Tasha perched on his jiggling knee. From the kitchen came the sound of running water & sweeping. jj imagined Eve cleaning up, Margaret most likely seated @ the table, finishing Martha's supper before it got cold.

"How was the Gradfest?" his mother inquired. "Moove," she ordered Josh, the infant halfway up her leg. When jj failed to answer, she repeated the question; jj shrugged, reluctantly offering a tepid "Alright, i guess." He pulled out his pocketknife & began tossing it @ the ruins of the Taj Mahal.

"Moove," Mrs Farrago again ordered Josh. "This could have been Margaret's Gradfest if she hadn't..." The matron's mind traveled, her eyes going blank till the persistent Josh brought her back to reality. "Go watch the ants," she urged, setting him on the floor. "Watch real close. See if you can tell which ant is planning the next coup d'état."

jj paused from throwing his knife, watching his father play w/ young Tasha. "You're granddad's little girl, yeah, you are," his father cooed. "You're granddad's little girl." Mr Farrago repeatedly counted Tasha's wiggling toes, sometimes finding only nine, sometimes eleven or twelve, wondering w/ exaggerated astonishment where the missing toe had gone or from whence the extra toe(s) had come. Tasha squirmed in delight @ her grandfather's unlimited array of flabbergasted expressions & corresponding vocal effects.

Leaning twd jj, Joseph pointed to the empty mug @ their father's feet. "Eve accidentally brought home a keg of prune juice," he whispered. "Again."

Btwn amused smiles @ her husband & her totally engaged children, Mrs Farrago called to Eve, urging the girl to forget about cleaning & join them. The matron hummed softly as her deft fingers took on a life of their own. She even failed to notice Josh's successful climb into her lap. Thus was she unprepared to catch his fall when Weed came bounding down the steps sounding like a herd of runaway Brittlebaums.

"Thay've sirrounded tha house!" he shouted, his urgent footsteps shaking the floorboards, his eyes wider than she'd ever seen them.

"Whooo?" Mrs Farrago called out as Eve ran in from the kitchen. Stubbs ceased rocking, clinging to his granddaughter as loud banging rattled the front door & windows. Similar banging came from the kitchen.

"Open up," a bellowing voice commanded. "This is the police! OPEN UP, I SAY. THIS IS THE POLICE!"

Chapter 24

PROFESSOR MAJOR-LIEUTENANT GENERAL CODY rubbed his bullet-shaped skull as he strolled the narrow corridor of Academy I. He repeated the gesture ritualistically. Tho by no means superstitious, the Professor nonetheless found the habitual maneuver always brought good luck. Born w/ a painfully flat, rather lopsided cranium (for which he was brutally teased as a child), Armstrong Cody as a young upstart lieutenant had undergone hours of surgery to reshape his skull—this to pay homage to the two items most responsible for his cataclysmic climb to success. Not only was he a 6.45-star major-lieutenant general & Dean of Academy I, but chief occupant of the Tower of Power which overlooked Gladiator U & guarded everything beyond.

As was his routine, the Professor-General spent his morning in boxing gloves, sparring several of the community's professional dummies. Still @ the peak of his prowess, he delivered six black eyes, four bloody noses (two of these broken) & numerous cuts & bruises. He, on the other hand, suffered only one minor bruise, this when one of the dummies forgot her instructions & swung back. After soundly sending each dummy to the campus infirmary, the Professor was off to the academic torture chambers. There, mingling among his more eager cadets, he calmly observed myriad enemies-of-the-state get their just desserts.

As was also his routine, the Professor heaved many a heavy sigh as he peered thru his binoculars, lamenting the good ol' days: days when the art deco, acoustically enhanced chambers of torture would reverberate w/ the shrill shrieks of *true* enemies-of-state. These days, random citizens had to be pulled off the street or dragged from their homes: some for having a bad hair day, some for dipping the wrong end of their donut in their chai, still others for having the gall to order chai in the first place. Such

274

citizens had little to confess beyond cheating @ solitaire, forcing the Commission on Homeland Insecurity to use whatever worthless drivel each tortureé spewed forth to construct compellingly convoluted yet convincingly cohesive conspiracies so as to keep the private donations & public funding rolling in.

And then, much to the Professor's chagrin, there were the unions. Only the other day, a new report had reached his desk, this one detailing the TORTURERS' 190 demanding a wage increase—rising mental health costs being cited:

> "...brought on by the inability of current standard-issue earplugs to adequately diffuse the piercing screams & shrill pleas for mercy—which too often reach deleterious decibel levels..."

the report read. The report further documented several scientific studies suggesting innocent citizens scream longer & louder than their guilt-ridden counterparts.

"Wimps," the Professor-General grumbled as he wound his way thru the enraptured cluster of onlooking cadets. Shaking his head, he vacated the chamber.

He ran a calloused hand thru his medals, the soft tinkling soothing his troubled disposition as he made his way to the conference room abutting his office. Entering, he paused by the wide window, staring down into the empty stadium dotted w/ mounds of packed dirt & grassy hills. In a few short weeks, the stadium would be filled to capacity w/ cheers, jeers, foot-stomping & ricocheting bullots. He observed the groundskeepers in their concerted effort to revitalize the bloodied grass, where five days a week aspiring cadets played King of the Hill, perfecting the requisite skills of mutilation, rape & slaughter.

"Git 'êm whilê thêir hormonês arê raging," he reminded himself, citing his dog-eared military training manual, specifically the verse on how to forge a lean, mean mutilation machine. For months the Professor had been observing his boys hone their rape skills, shaking his head @ the hysterical women screaming in vain, their soon-to-be-orphaned children looking on, bawling their terrified little eyes out. A controversial policy to say the least, the Professor had had to muster all his powers of persuasion—even threatening to take his expertise elsewhere—before the Powers that DO finally acquiesced to his insistence the games be as realistic as possible.

"Wê can't havê our soldiêrs gang raping random civilians w/out propêr military training," he had ranted, resorting to jumping on the conference table & brandishing his fists. "Rapê is rêprêhênsiblê ênough, gêntlêmên, w/out our bravê boys in uniform complêtêly botching thê manêuver." He recalled glaring down angrily @ the balding, frightened-eyed university chancellors. "Nêêd i rêmind you, gêntlêmên...thê mastêr classês may start our wars, but it is thê horny working classês who fight thêm—your Dixsticks, your Cockortwos, your Dibildogs."

Savoring the memory of that battle won, the Professor-General failed to hear the doorknob jiggle. He turned slowly, nodding to a pint-size albino entering in a plaid skirt & billowing blouse, pink lipstick & purple mascara applied to an otherwise chalk-white complexion.

"Morris," he acknowledged the stocky man whose security badge identified him as Mr Code, DIRECTOR OF PERCEPTION MANAGEMENT. The man entered confidently, hiked up on purple pumps, lugging a hefty, color-coordinated, accordion-style briefcase.

Behind the Director, a gray-haired human crab scuttled in, bowlegged & bent @ the back & knees, her pointed, upturned chin & hooked nose nearly touching @ their tips. Hauling a notebook & oversized purse in one claw, in the other she lugged a device resembling a double-barreled saxophone. A portly, ample-chested blonde assisted her from the rear. The crab-lady nodded when the Professor addressed her first as Barb, then as Mz Wire. Setting the device down, she readjusted her security badge, which read Barbra Wire, SECRETARY TO THE DEPT FROM HISTORICAL FACT.

The bowlegged spinster promptly introduced her plump companion as Mz Rosie B Guile, the dept's newest intern, adding its previous intern was on unexpected maternity leave. "Rosie comes to us from the Ministry of Proper Gander & will be handling our research," she explained. "Rosie, help me w/ this myth-o-lizer, will you? These newfangled models clog so easily." Together the two women blew, sucked on & adjusted the device until one barrel began to bubble while the other clouded w/ a sallow-greenish mist. Mz Wire motioned for her intern to sit & found her own seat as well.

The three visitors gathered around a gutted-out armored tank fully equipped w/ pens, paper & cup holders, a tanning lamp, gun sights, complimentary cosmetic kits & a rotating paperclip/staple dispenser. As the Director of Perception Management extracted several reports from his briefcase & spread them about the tank's top, adjusting the tanning lamp & reaching for one of the cosmetic kits, Mz Wire opened her notebook, flipping thru several pages before settling on one that seemed to please her. Nodding to the Professor-General, she took a quick hit from the myth-o-lizer as she waited for the meeting to commence.

His council ready, Professor Cody stepped to the head of the tank. Tinkling his medals, he flexed his biceps. Next he flexed his triceps, followed by his deltoids, his pectorals & finally his gluteus maximus. As no one rose to challenge him—their eyes lowered, their heads bowed—the Professor assumed full command, calling the conference to order.

"I'vê givên our currênt situation a grêat dêal of thought," he began, pausing to rub his bullet. He stepped behind Mz Guile, arching fwd on his tiptoes, his binoculars aimed down the bleach blonde's open blouse. Planting his feet firmly again, he turned to Mz Wire. "Barb, rêad that back."

Taking a hefty pull from the myth-o-lizer, Mz Wire scanned the notes she had just scribbled. "Aftêrz szêriöus dêliberatiönq," she read, "cönfêrring w/ my chiêfz öf staffq & öthêrq militarily & möral lêadqêrs..."

"That's good," the Professor lauded. "I likê thê êxtra z's & q's. Makês mê sound a bit êxotic, don't you think, Mz Guilê?" Again the Professor-General stood on tiptoe, binoculars poised.

The intern nodded, blushing as she sat up straight & played w/ her bangs.

"Noticê how thê cannonballs abovê the o's give my words additional authority. I trust Barb has instructêd you how whên writing my autobiography you should includê @ lêast one anêcdotê pêr chaptêr rêgaling my rathêr quaint êccêntricitiês."

Again the intern nodded.

"And rêadêrs nêvêr tirê of hêaring how whên i rub my skull, ladiês tênd to swoon—êvên thê happily marriêd onês bêing pronê to slip mê thêir addrêssês... which i politêly accêpt but nêvêr act upon...@ lêast not till thêir husbands havê bêên sêcurêly slaughtêrêd in battlê." The Professor winked @ the young intern, who giggled, her plump cheeks turning scarlet when he rubbed his bullet.

"And most important," he continued, wagging a finger, "undêr no circumstancês must you rêvêal any rêal intêlligêncê. Êxpêriêncê has taught thosê of us in thê military sciêncês that whênevêr wê êxposê our truê intêlligêncê, thê common massês want to add thêir worthlêss two cênts. Thêy start applying all sorts of moral impêrativês; impêrativês any sêlf-rêspêcting êmpirê submits to only as a last rêsort—whên wê havê no othêr choicê. I trust, Barb, you havê alrêady briêfed this buxom bêauty on thêse mattêrs?"

The Secretary From Historical Fact nodded as she took a healthy drag from the myth-o-lizer before passing it to her ass't. Taking an aggressive pull, Mz Guile began to cough, then wheeze, her mentor slapping the girl on the back until her breathing came under control.

"Good," the Professor concluded, capping his binoculars & returning to the head of the tank. "Now whêrê was i?"

"You were cönferring w/ yöur militarily & möral leadqers, sir."

"Right. Thanks, Morris. Which rêminds mê...havê you that rêport on this whatzhisfacê, this Grimspoon?"

"I have, sir." The Director of Perception Management paused from penciling his eyebrows to rifle thru his papers. "I've even managed to secure a copy of a speech he gave. I must say, you were right, sir; he does indeed tend to exhibit certain, shall we say, common liberule tendencies...like that idea we are *all* somehow equal."

"Cockamamiê nonsênsê," the Professor scoffed, kicking an invisible seeing-eye dog. "How can wê bê a grêat pêoplê if wê'rê êqual to êvêryonê êlsê? Têll mê that." He flexed his biceps, rubbed his bullet & winked @ Mz Guile. Wheeling around to grant the intern an unobstructed view of his gluteus maximus, the Professor-General began to shadow box an apparently formidable foe.

"I think this Grimspoon could prove a worthy opponent," Mr Code added, readjusting his tanning lamp before applying blush to his cheeks. "Doomed, of course, but worthy."

"Bring him on," the Professor commanded, panting slightly as he delivered a left & right jab to his shadow, followed by a wicked uppercut.

"I'm sure you'll agree, sir, he's quite skillful @ manipulating such rhetorical devices as logic & reason. He also seems fond of referring to what he calls our 'common wealth.'"

"Drivêl. Shêêr drivêl," the General sparred. "Thêre is nothing common about wêalth. Hêêd my word, Barb. Mz Guilê. You sprêad wêalth too êvênly & it's no longêr wêalth, is it? Duh!"

"I agree, sir. But the poor, the undereducated, the starving masses eat that sort of thing up. Listen to this." Squinting his beady eyes, following the painted nail of his stubby forefinger, the Director began reading, "'Everyone—not just your D'leBaum, your Dumpleton, your Rittl'baus—has a right to share in our common wealth; everyone has the PUP-given right to grow thick around the middle as well as btwn the ears & in the buttocks.' Rather clever argument, wouldn't you say, sir?"

The Director continued, "'Imagine a time when all of us—Brittlebaum & Woodbee, Menial & Dreg, Scarburrow & even the clothesless—not only not see our own feet, but not see the feet of those we inadvertently step on.'"

The Professor hissed, pausing after giving his shadow a sound throttling. "You hêar that, Barb? Mz Guilê? Writê this down: If êvêryonê wêre obêse, who would bê lêft to êat? Makê no mistakê, Mz Guilê; wê havê bêen since thê bêginning of timê dêvouring êach othêr: big fish swallowing up thêir puniêr nêighbors. Why do you think thê morê privilêgêd classês suffêr from so much indigêstion? Duh."

Turning away briefly to pummel his shadow, the Professor again reared around to his face his council. "Think how this would cripplê thê bullot box. Fat pêoplê arê too êasy a targêt. Skinny pêoplê arê much hardêr to hit. Thêy run fastêr, too. Not only that, for your avêragê Brittlêbaum, thê poor & undêrnourishêd arê hardêr to sêê—giving your Woodbêê a dêcisivê advantagê: all of which translatês to a morê êxciting, crowd-rousing, nail-biting Turkêy Shoot. I têll you this: thêrê will bê a sêvêrê drop in S-êlêction tickêt salês if this Grimspoon gêts his way. What elsê doês this intêllêctual pipsquêak say?"

Pausing from attaching a false eyelash, the Director scanned the speech again. "Here's something interesting: he claims ages ago—as far back as when our great-great & even our not-so-great great-grandparents were still in diapers—that demicracy was spelled w/ an *o*. 'Who took the circular *o* out of democracy?' he rants. 'Who removed the all-encompassing *o* & replaced it w/ the selfish, self-centered *i*? And ask yourselves,' he continues, 'who writes your rule books? I bet most of you think they come from the ONE? Am i right?'

"Here he usually pauses for a count of ten." The Director rubbed his own bullet before readjusting his toupee & reading on.

"'Most of you, all your lives have been assured they come from the divine hand of PUP. You've sat in Sunday school, hearing over & over how PUP writes these rules in His spare time, when He's not out ruffling the oceans, stirring up the winds or directing the stars. Likê you, i too once accepted w/out question that PUP dictates His infinite will to semi-divine, low-wage elves who faithfully record His every word—albeit grossly misspelling many of His most important pronouncements. I too once believed He chose inconsequential, uneducated elves as a clear demonstration of His divine solidarity w/ His little people, who despite their imperfections can still aspire to sniff @ His divine feet, take out His garbiage & clean His latrines while He reads the Sunday edition of *The ONE & Only Times*.'"

"Thê blasphêmê!" the Professor fumed, knocking his shadow to the floor w/ a solid one-two followed by a vicious kick to the groin. "Blasphêmy, i say. Thosê êlvês spêll bêttêr than half my cadêts!"

Suddenly gyrating as if on the verge of an epileptic fit, Mz Wire struggled w/ her handbag, which crashed to the floor & spilled its guts as she & Mz Guile fumbled w/ a replacement cartridge for the depleted myth-o-lizer. Upon attaching the fresh cartridge, Mz Wire again inhaled the soothing, jaundiced mist as she beheld the Professor-General fight off an entire battalion of phantasmagoric demons. She scribbled feverishly, recording in minute detailz the Major-Lt General single-handedly demölishing the six-headed fire-breathqing liberule-leanzing debils, many of whöm had illicitly secured the right tö cast an illegal bullöt.

Undaunted by his invisible shape-shifting enemies, the Professor-General paused to catch his breath. "This is morê sêrious than i thought," he huffed, applying an interminable bout of head rubbing while teetering dangerously high on his tiptoes & peering thru his binoculars. "Morris, takê this down. Barb, Mz Guilê. Bê surê to includê thêsê as êxamplês of my astutê ability to act dêcisivêly in timês of crisês. Add thê rêquisitê z's, q's & cannonballs—maybê êvên a fêw w's whêrêvêr you sêê fit.

"First & forêmost, Morris, instruct all appropriatê pêrsonnêl to confiscatê thê town's êntirê supply of Monopoly gamês. Wê nêêd all availablê GOOJ cards @ our disposal. I will not havê my officêrs arrêstêd êvêry timê thêy sidêstêp a law thêy havê sworn to protêct." The Professor played w/ his medals as he observed Mz Guile's bosom jiggle the more vigorously the intern scribbled.

"Sêcond. Morê rulê books. Wê nêed more rulê books. Inform your staff, Morris, no mattêr if thê nêw rulês contradict thê old. Thê days of a consistênt, unambiguous mêssagê arê long gonê. Our goal now is to propagatê *conflicting* mêssagês. Our objêctivê: to makê it so your avêragê Joê Blow doêsn't know his hêad from his mass. That goês for êvêry Janê Dow, too. Thêy mustn't know *what* to think. Wê don't want thêm thinking; wê want thêm *fêêling*: prêfêrably confusêd & frustratêd. So frustratêd thêy start to panic. Oncê thêy panic & grow fêarful, thêy'll turn to thêir s-êlêctêd lêadêrs for answêrs thêir littlê pêê brains can't êvên bêgin to comprêndêz. Barb, rêmind Mz Guilê hêrê what you so brilliantly oncê quotêd mê as saying."

The Secretary to the Dept From Historical Fact set the myth-o-lizer aside. "Cönfusiönq is thê yöungêr siblingz öf fêarq," she reiterated, "& fêarq is first cöusinz tö hatrêd."

Reassured by Mz Wire's quick & accurate response, the Professor resumed shadow boxing @ a more measured pace. He glanced out the window while his three advisors continued to jot notes, their pens scratching feverishly.

"Nasty namês," he blurted, pausing as the new suggestion took shape. "That's what wê'vê bêên missing. Nasty namês. Wê nêêd morê nasty namês. Sadly, wê'vê bêên too hasty killing off thê pêoplê wê dismiss. Wê should havê allowêd a littlê morê brêêding room. Our Nibian population is down to a tricklê. Thêrê's talk of putting Canaans on thê êndangêrêd spêciês list. No onê wants to point a fingêr @ thê Drêgs on account of thêy do such a good job w/ our laundry & ironing our undêrwêar. Whêrê does that lêavê us? Thê lêft-handêd? Thê Scarburrows? A' fêw Lugworts? Thosê nasty Nabors nêxt door? Wê nêêd nêwêr, êvên nastiêr namês for any & all pêoplê wê can afford to discard.

"This timê wê'll comê up w/ thê namês first...thên find pêoplê to attach thêm to. Pêoplê who likê polkas. Or thosê who buttêr thêir toast on thê wrong sidê of thêir brêad. Barb, Mz Guilê, this sêêms likê a task for your agêncy. Scour thê dictionary. Sêê what you comê up with. Any unplêasant namê; êvên namês that only sound unplêasant. If you gêt stuck, take a plêasant word & add 'anti-' to it...or bêttêr still, stick 'êxtrêmist' @ thê ênd of it—that nêvêr fails."

As he gazed out the window, his back to his advisors, the Professor asserted that hatred was not just a science, but an art—one finely honed thru the torturous chambers of history. He recommended each reviled group be assigned a color. Red, he cautioned, was overused, citing redskins & communists, redcoats, rednecks, red turbans, redshirts, red herrings, even red snot chili peepers. He insisted on more creative hue-baiting: trying chartreuse, ocher, aqua, sienna or cerulean, for example. He further instructed they focus on physical attributes: snotty noses, knobby knees, tennis elbow, Parkinson's disease, double-jointedness—even the inability to roll one's r's or to not pronounce the t in "often."

Citing how human beans have never proved more creative than in devising reasons to despise one another, the Professor-General brainstormed other reasons to hate one's neighbor. As the Professor displayed a near encyclopedic knowledge of time-honored reasons for displacing the weak & seizing their land while utilizing their skills as housekeepers & cooks, Morris Code, Barb Wire & Rosie B Guile silently tiptoed from the room. Having heard the same tirade on countless occasions, Mr Code & Mz Wire were fully cognizant of the expectation placed upon them. They further understood that should they fall short of said expectation, the 6.45-star Major-Lieutenant General would have no trouble devising nasty names for them.

* * * * *

WHILE PROFESSOR CODY RETURNED to vigorously rubbing his bullets, Buck Smolet crouched Nibian-style @ the foot of his bed. Balanced in the man-child's lap was a tattered copy of the military classic **My Way** (or The Highway). Except for his sister's Gradfest & to attend classes, Buck now rarely left his room. A celebrity among his classmates & professors, a hero among the cooks & secretarial staff, he had quickly tired of the accolades, backslaps & butt pinching. He would wince when reminded the entire fate of civilizing civilization rested on his trigger finger. The more his professors praised his instinctive resolve to inflict maximum damage before even deigning to negotiate; the more they touted his intuitive grasp when negotiating to ignore any terms agreed upon & do whatever he felt like doing anyway—the more self-conscious he grew & the more he came to question his own motives as well as the motives of those praising him.

Less from instinct & more from experience, Buck also understood the danger in expressing his doubts—even in the privacy of his own bedroom. Someone was always watching, perhaps even listening in on his own thought process. The authors of **My Way** devoted half their masterpiece to the paramount importance of surveillance—not only on one's enemies but on one's friends, particularly one's best friends.

He struggled to keep his eyelids open. He read & reread the same pages till his eyes hurt: till he knew key passages by heart. His brain fatigued, his entire body ached, his muscles exhausted from excessive hours tossing hand grenades. In intense preparation for S-election day, his bruised shoulders were suffering a serious case of what the Academy called bazooka burn.

As he massaged his shoulders, he thought back to the evening his entire life had changed. He could still picture his Uncle Harry seated on the chesterfield, his father snoring in the bergère. He recalled the small granules floating to the bottom of his father's glass of crandy. At the time, he had failed to register their significance. His own head, after all, had been swimming in a drunken fog, his brain struggling to keep up w/ his stupid tongue as he expounded on some theory from that pamphlet Heidi had handed him. Before he knew what was happening, a cane came crashing down on him. Several stinging lashes later, his uncle had him by the ear, dragging him from the sofa. There came kicks & more cane-lashing...& curses, lots & lots of curses as the old man corralled him into the game room. At first he feared his was about to be another head lining his uncle's wall. Kicked to the floor, he found himself kneeling before the military-issue loafers of the Dean of Gladiator U. His uncle, joined by Commissioner Dicker, yanked him to his feet, shoving him into a recliner.

A bright light aimed directly in his face blinded him. The rest of the room was shrouded in darkness. His welts throbbing, his every nerve on edge, Buck could distinguish nothing save the soft tinkling of the Dean's medals. A match was struck, a cigar lit, its orange glow pulsating as Professor Cody puffed, exhaled, puffed & exhaled again. The match was extinguished. His thoughts still reeling, Buck watched in surreal disbelief as his favorite professor, his mentor, in fact—or so he thought—leaned fwd, pressing the burning cigar into Buck's arm. Buck yelped, cursing as he yanked his arm away.

"So, what's this i hêar 'bout you turncoating, soldiêr boy?"

Instantly Buck sobered up. Instinctively he followed the recommended protocol every cadet learns by sophomore year. He stiffened his back, gazed out defiantly & displayed a stiff upper lip. His bottom lip, however, had a mind of its own. As his thoughts raced, Buck suspected it was all a test. When @ war, always expect the unexpected. How often had he been told that? He resolved to remain placid. Should he w/stand the interrogation, it would give his grade point average just the boost his sagging report card sorely needed.

As he waited for his eyes to adjust, Buck had listened carefully, determined to establish exactly where his uncle & the Commissioner were standing—& if anyone else was in the room. All he heard was the Dean shifting in his chair while reaching for what proved to be a large envelope. The cigar clamped tight in his jaw, the Professor-General unsealed the envelope & slid out its contents.

Buck shook off the painful memory, gazing up from **My Way** (or The Highway). On the bed behind him was the book's sequel, **My Way** (or the Bye-Bye Way). Tho not nearly as lauded as its predecessor, the sequel was nonetheless touted for its detailed descriptions on how to pummel an opponent w/out leaving incriminating bruises. The Dean, however, had seemed unconcerned w/ that—as the tiny scar on Buck's arm attested.

"Hêar you bêên taking up photography," he recalled the Professor saying.

Buck could still hear the snicker as the Professor-General removed his cigar & flicked ashes twd Buck's feet. "Wêll, wê'vê takên somê picturês of our own." Returning the cigar to his mouth, the Dean dropped a seven-by-nine glossy into Buck's lap. Buck glanced @ a photo of himself. There he was, smiling as if posing for the camera. He sat perched on a wooden fence, wearing a yellow sundress, a pair of hoop earrings dangling from his ears.

"It's a forgery," Buck scoffed. "See here: the dress strap isn't really hanging on anything. Same thing w/ this earring. Anyone can tell you doctored this up. Besides, yellow isn't even my color."

"Pêoplê bêliêvê what thêy want to bêliêvê, son. You know that. Thê mass assês always assumê thêir trustêd lêadêrs would nêvêr liê to thêm."

283

"General I.C. Redmud," Buck name-dropped, recalling his junior year textbook. **"Ignorance, the Smart Leader's Bestest Friend,"** he added, hoping the reference might earn him extra credit.

"Bravo...you *havê* bêên paying attêntion."

His eyes having adjusted, Buck could distinguish the Professor-General's grinning dentures. He heard his uncle cough, calculated Sur Harry to be standing just behind him, cane no doubt poised & scanning for flies.

"Okay, wisê guy," the Dean challenged, "talk your way out of this onê."

Another glossy fell into Buck's lap. The camera angle was ill-chosen, the composition amateurish, the focus leaving much to be desired, but the subject matter sent Buck's heart racing. There he was again, this time leaning against an embankment. A few feet away sat Jasmine, her legs crossed @ the ankles, her feet dangling happily as she smiled, completely @ ease in her nakedness.

Buck recalled the occasion, the animation in Jasmine's eyes as she rambled on & on about Filkin Grimspoon & how every injustice would go away w/in the first few weeks of a Grimspoon administration. Buck had scoffed, deeply skeptical. In truth, he found himself wishing he were Grimspoon, painfully jealous of another male held so high in Jasmine's esteem.

"So what?" Buck taunted, feigning defiance, wondering if, after he passed the interrogation, it would be kosher to request a copy of the photo.

"And what about this onê?" The Professor-General tossed a third photo into his lap. This time Buck was straddling a chair backward, his arms dangling over the chair's back. The back of a blurred head dominated the photo. In the background, among the piles of disorganized books, were several of the Lugworts. The blurred head, Buck realized, had to be S-.

Show no surprise, he cautioned himself, his heart suddenly pounding so loud he feared everyone in the room heard it. Re-stiffening his back, he marshalled control over both upper & lower lips.

"Just as i thought," Professor Cody sneered. The Dean sat back, rubbing his bullet as the burning cigar gyrated in his mouth. "Hêrê's an intêrêsting scênario," he ventured after a silent count of ten, lurching fwd to snatch up the photos. "Supposê, instêad of S-êlêction officials picking up thê usual assortmênt of Canaans, Nibians, Dibildogs, Wêtlandêrs & whatnot...supposê thêy—accidêntally, mind you—pickêd up a fêw of your so-callêd friênds...pêrhaps êvên this lovêly lady, hêrê? My, what striking êyês shê has, don't you think?"

"That's illegal," Buck protested.

284

"Êxplain for mê, son, how an accidênt can bê illêgal? You hêar that, Harry? Donald?"

Buck heard snickering behind him.

"Funny thing about that word 'illêgal,'" the Professor continued, pretending to examine his cigar. "What doês it rêally actually mêan? I was pêrusing my dictionary thê othêr day & thêrê wêre a numbêr of words i thought i knêw thê mêaning of but discovêrêd i rêally didn't. Takê that word 'illêgal,' for êxamplê." The Dean rose, disappearing into the darkness. When he returned, he adjusted the light to shine on a hefty book cradled in his lap. He flipped briskly thru the crisp pages until finding his place.

"Hêrê it is; 'illegal: any act committed for PUP andor country.' Hm." He paused to allow Buck time to absorb the meaning. "Intêrêsting, don't you think? Hêrê's a sêcond dêfinition: 'Any act in which an individual, heeding the stupidity of the mass asses andor the arrogance of outdated rule books, strikes out in pursuit of the greater ONE.'

"You might bê intêrêstêd to know," the Dean added parenthetically, "that thê grêatêr ONE is dêfinêd as synonymous w/ thê lêssêr onê, i.ê., onê's sêlf.

"And hêrê's the final dêfinition: 'A legal act for one's own benefit, which, by definition, will benefit all others w/ the possible exception of those it doesn't.'" The Professor-General slammed the book shut with triumph.

"Yês, it sêêms it would bê *illêgal*," he concluded. "So, oncê again, lêt us considêr. Supposê this girl, this..."

"Jasmine," the Commissioner inserted.

"Yês, Jasminê. Lovêly namê. Supposê this lovêly girl, this Jasminê—ill-clad tho shê bê—should somêhow ênd up part of a Turkêy Shoot. That would bê a tragêdy, wouldn't it?"

Buck refused to answer.

"And supposê thêse friênds of yours should also ênd up trying to dodgê thê bullot box?" The Professor held up the last photo. "And how would you fêêl about this guy, thê onê w/ thê blurry hêad—how would you fêêl if this onê winds up caught in thê sights of a loadêd bazooka?"

Buck shuddered. He could still see the orange glow of the gyrating cigar as the Professor chewed more than puffed.

Now he rose from his bed, one leg having fallen asleep, his head throbbing.

"Of coursê," he could still hear the Professor saying, "thêre is always a sêcond option. Lêt's say you yoursêlf ran for City Council. An intêrêsting idêa, no?" The

Professor removed the cigar, wielding it like a wand. "Think about it. With your marksmanship skills, your lack of êmpathy, that hêightênêd sênse of ênlightênêd sêlfish intêrêst you'vê bêên blêssêd with...you could êasily win—êvên capturê first chair if you put your gun sights to it. You win...i win...your unclê wins...your fathêr wins—wê all win. And you, my boy, gêt to walk in thê soft silkên slippêrs of your forêfathêrs, Smolêt thê Grêat, Smolêt thê Grating, Smolêt thê Sêmi-Grêat & thê currênt Smolêt, your fathêr, Smolêt thê Gratêfully Rich."

Buck dared not flinch, his expression as noncommittal as he could make it.

"If all that should happên," the Dean speculated, his free hand jiggling his medals, "i would fêêl prêtty cêrtain thêsê finê young pêople—êxcêpt maybê this onê—" he pointed to Edmund, "wouldn't accidêntally find thêmsêlvês in thê wrong arêna comê S-êlêcting day. Wouldn't you think so, Harry?"

"I would be pretTY cerTAIN of it."

"So would i," the Commissioner added.

Buck nodded to acknowledge the two voices behind him. Prompted by a bony claw digging into his shoulder, Buck dropped to one knee & bowed his head before the Professor-General. He reached for the Professor's hand & kissed its ring before taking a puff on the proffered cigar.

"Good," the Professor-General concluded. He signaled for the Commissioner to switch on the overhead light. "I think wê undêrstand êach othêr, soldiêr. You may rêport back to duty."

The four exited together, Buck sandwiched btwn his uncle & the Commissioner, his former mentor commanding the rear.

"Oh, & anothêr thing." The Professor stopped, pulling from the envelope the third photo. "As far as this fêllow goês, thê onê who's hêrê to sêducê your sistêr, stay away from him...his fatê is nonnêgotiablê. If you so much as brêathê nêar him, i guarantêê you, you & hê will bê thê first onês out of thê pên. If i have to, i'll cast thê dêcisivê bullet mysêlf. Got mê, soldiêr?"

* * * * *

WHILE BUCK WAS WRESTLING w/ memories he'd rather forget, Edmund piddled about his room, a bottle of root dangling in one hand. His hair in a state of rebellion, the rust-headed radical stood hunched over a table. Atop its waterlogged surface was what @ first glance looked to be a rollercoaster but upon closer inspection proved a veritable amusement park of chemical fomentation: glass tubes, beakers, funnels, flasks & bell jars; the beakers heating over Bunsen burners. Liquids bubbled & chemicals changed colors, emitting gasses that traveled along the glass tubing, condensing farther on, to be mixed w/ other liquids & reheated to begin the fomenting process again.

Edmund measured carefully, oblivious to the moaning of creaking stairs. Neither did he hear his door latch being expertly picked...or the slow mournful squeal of the backdoor opening. While he adjusted the flame below a bubbling beaker, Ruth & Hector crept twd him, careful not to rattle their chains. The sudden snap of a cat-o'-nine tails, its caustic tongue cracking inches from his ear, sent Edmund's shadow scurrying for the ceiling. Edmund dropped to his knees, his face flushed upon realizing he had been had. "Dam you," he snapped.

"Gotcha, Bub."

Hector plunked a liter-size bottle onto the table as Ruth coiled her whip & clipped it to her belt. Reaching btwn her breasts, she produced a key, unlocking Hector's leg-iron before plopping onto the sofa, her arms spread wide, her thighs even wider.

Edmund inspected the bottle, reading the label: LIQUID COW MANURE (CONCENTRATED). "Excellent." His right jaw grinning, he removed the cap & inhaled. He nearly retched, gagging & coughing as he returned the cap, smiling from his left jaw.

"*Help yourself*," he offered his guests, pointing to an eight-pack of root with three bottles missing.

Hector grabbed two, handing one to Ruth. Uncorking his root, he tossed the cap in a corner before plopping to the floor btwn Ruth's legs. Ruth in turn used her teeth to unscrew her cap, spitting it in the general vicinity of Hector's cap. After each guzzle, she balanced her bottle on Hector's head, Hector all the while fondling her leg iron.

Soon after, Sedgewick hobbled in, the bottom half of his left leg missing.

"How could you forget your leg?" Ruth teased, shaking her head before taking another swig of root.

Sedgewick hopped to the nearest chair. "I didn't." He was about to elaborate when a faint knock drew their attention.

"*Who is it?*" Edmund called.

Heidi entered, half a leg slumped over her shoulder. Her clothes better coordinated than in the past, she tossed the limb to Sedgewick before slumping onto the floor next to him.

"See anyone?" he asked.

"Nada," she replied. "No one."

Twisting his limb back in place, Sedgewick explained he'd intentionally left his leg behind in case someone was following. Heidi, he added, had circled back to catch anyone in the act of trailing them.

"I think the rumor is true," Heidi offered.

"What rumor, Bub?"

"Our boys in blue are on strike. And their spies are refusing to turn in their next-door neighbors."

"The Powers that DO have been severely crippled," Sedgewick declared. "The Powers that do DO are now on their own."

As the other Lugworts digested the news, yet another knock startled the conspirators, several shivers slithering up several spines as heads turned twd the front door.

"*Who's there?*" Edmund called in defiant annoyance.

"Eddy, it's me."

"What do you want?"

"That package you ordered is here."

Edmund signaled to the others, who quickly rose, gathering around the table so as to obscure anyone's view of the bubbling amusement center. He raked his hand thru his hair as he approached the door, opening it but slightly.

Satisfied, he stepped back, allowing his sister entrance. A paper bag in one hand, Jasmine stepped in, her graceful, well-toned figure causing Heidi to glower. Heidi fiddled w/ her own limp curls, noting how Jasmine's brassiere & matching panties brought out the sparkling gray of the girl's riveting eyes. Jasmine waved, handed her brother the bag, turned & left, leaving Ruth to smirk & Sedgewick & Hector to ogle, Ruth violently plucking a few hairs of Hector's sideburns.

"Great," Edmund exclaimed. "*This is the last ingredient.*"

While Ruth & Hector returned to their seats, Heidi & Sedgewick inspected the amusement park. Edmund ripped open the bag & tore into the enclosed box. He double-checked the label against the ingredients listed in his pocket-size manual before indulging Heidi, who insisted on inspecting the book's jacket.

"He looks a little like Mr Gorge," she noted, pointing to the goateed author who wore a chef's hat & smiled under an arc of letters formed from sticks of dynamite. "Cooking up Mischief," she read aloud.

Edmund grabbed the book, flipping to the chapter *Explosive Cocktails*, mumbling as he read, measuring the prescribed amounts of ammonium nitrate, hydrogen peroxide, sodium bicarbonate, linseed oil & super-concentrated cow manure, adding last a dash of paprika. Oblivious to the banter around him, he poured carefully, his tongue tracing his upper lip as he delicately added each ingredient. Only @ hearing the names Weed & jj did he stop, wheeling around.

"What? *Arrested?* When?"

"Last nite," Heidi reported.

Edmund's left jaw froze, his right cheek twitching spasmodically. He looked to each face in the room. "They may know about us, then. That kid, jj; *he came over the other nite*, wanting to join us."

The others looked @ each other in turn.

Sedgewick removed an elbow, using it to scratch his chin. "Think he'll give us away?"

"We haven't done anything wrong, Bub." Hector pointed to the rollercoaster. "Not yet, anyway."

"Since when does not doing anything wrong stop the Powers that do DO?" Heidi countered.

"She's right," Sedgewick inserted. "All they need do is claim 'desperate times demand desperate measures.'"

"Or 'if you're not w/ us, you're against us,'" Heidi offered.

"Or 'it's a matter of municipal security,'" Ruth chimed in.

Edmund took a pull from his bottle of root. "They'll torture him for sure. *Hail, he'll probably fold the moment they offer to replace his homemade crutches w/ an aluminum alloy*." Edmund bit his lower lip, both sides.

"We need to step up our plan, Bub. We can't afford to wait."

All heads nodded. Hector cracked a few knuckles as Ruth downed her root. Finishing his bottle, Edmund reached for another, offering the remaining two to Heidi & Sedgewick. While Sedgewick acquiesced, Heidi declined, giving her bottle to a blurry-eyed Ruth, who burped in gratitude.

* * * * *

THE DAY FOLLOWING HER GRADU-AUCTION, Penny lay sprawled across her comforter, her head resting in her hands as she stared @ the twirling ceiling fan. Clad only in a flimsy blue satin slip, her bare legs dangled over the side of her bed. Had the agent assigned to her not been on strike, no doubt said agent would have reported her as exhibiting dangerous leanings twd supporting the plight of the clothesless.

The events of the Gradfest had shipwrecked any sense of the teen's equilibrium. Nerve-racked, her future uncertain, Penny had tossed & turned the previous nite, unable to sleep or make sense of her conflicted feelings. She recalled what was @ first exhilaration—knowing she & S- would be wed—which then somersaulted into confusion, tinged w/ a scary sort of curiosity. What now emerged was mostly fear. How strange, she thought, to go from feeling excited & relieved—realizing she'd narrowly escaped the Brittle grasp of some boring, most likely overbearing, aristocratic apechild—to feeling hopeful, won by someone she thought she truly loved, to then feeling even more relieved upon hearing their nuptials would be postponed. The culminating ritual, the one involving the sacrificial surrendering of her tenderloins while news cameras flashed behind the two-way mirrors, might be held up for weeks, possibly years. Litigation, as everyone knew, was far too One-generating for any attorney, judge or legal institution to keep simple or resolve quickly.

Penny looked about her room, overwhelmed w/ the sense she was looking @ the world thru newly opened eyes. She studied the portraitures covering her walls: portraits she had created from many an uneaten breakfast, lunch, or dinner. She looked @ the crude rendering of horses & puppies: products of her adolescent period. She frowned as she examined the abstract, boldly suggestive busts & gentlementalia she had fantasized about during her naïve pubescence. The full-bodied, bare-chested, muscular men of her teenage years now sent shivers of revulsion thru her mind. She jumped from her bed, dragging her vanity chair to the closest portrait. She climbed on the chair, lifting the portrait from its nail.

As she removed each portrait, she thought of S-, his dark, morose yet kindly eyes—kind @ least when they looked on her. Behind their blankness she suspected a clarity she had yet to fully fathom. His lanky, wiry physique looked nothing like the bodies & busts of her portraits. Yet he was tolerable to the eye—in some vague, exotic way, especially when she herself dressed him. Admittedly, his hair was a tangled mess, but w/ the right gel even that could be tamed, somewhat. Plus, there were signs he could master grooming, even dress himself. He was, ultimately, trainable. And as everyone—her father, mother, Bill, even Pearl had proved—he was infinitely malleable. He could one day be molded into the perfect husband—if she had the patience.

After removing the final portrait, Penny reached to pull down her hula hoop display. She recalled her mother years ago encouraging her in their use, insisting that the more boys she got to jump thru them then—she was, what, ten?—the easier it would be to get them to jump thru later.

"Would it be all that bad...?" she asked herself out loud, stopping before completing the sentence. Would it be all that bad, she asked again silently, if she & S- were never conjugaled? She understood, of course, that should S- lose in litigation—or be accidentally poisoned—there would be a special auction & she'd still end up sold to the highest bidder, tho @ a ten-percent-reduced rate. But should the litigation drag on...& on...& on & on...who's to say how long she'd be free to be her own person? She might even come to like it—once she got over the scariness.

Tossing the hoop display on top of the portraits, she fell backward onto her bed, lying prone while staring first @ the ceiling, then @ the bare walls. Shadow outlines of the removed portraits remained, staring back @ her. Penny propped herself on her elbows, her pupils widening as a new thought circled her brainwaves.

She recalled several pictures she had seen in S-'s apartment: one striking photo of Buck, his dimples dancing like they hadn't since he was maybe four years old, & photos of Pearl lost in her mischievous antics. Photos of people she'd seen on the street but never really noticed—or @ least hadn't noticed the way S- seemed to notice them. She leapt from her bed, rummaging inside her closet, her shadow pointing to a bright summer dress & a pair of flower-patterned slippers. Once dressed, the teen stepped deeper into her closest, opening the hidden panel & squeezing past the stacked boxes of her former wardrobe.

Chapter 25

THE INFORMAL MEETING BETWIXT the community stalwarts—Mssrs Cody, D'leBaum, Dicker & Smolet—proved woefully inadequate in addressing the beehive of concerns buzzing amongst the feverish antennae of every Brittlebaum once-, twice-, thrice-, or even more-times-removed from authentic Brittle-blood stock.

Thus a second meeting was called, trumpeted forth by none other than PUP Himself from the catacombs of His struggling Temple of Perpetual Puppiness & Coin Laundromat. So large the expectant crowd—if not in number, certainly in combined weight—PUP even sanctioned the expansion of the D'leBaum Mansion's west wing.

A miniature stadium was decreed, said stadium to include suede-cushioned bleachers, adjustable footrests, cupholders, cigar lighters, ashtrays, straw dispensers & trapdoors such that each seat could convert to a convenient commode should the necessity arise—which it almost certainly would. A weight room was added for those wishing to strengthen their arguments & a kiddie pool provided for those Brits unable to swim w/ the big boys.

CD Smolet, also by divine decree, was to report to his First Pedestal earlier than usual that Monday morning. Before any nosey staff arrived, the banker was to dash off several premium promissory notes, to be slipped under some table about which would be seated representatives from the Depts of Concrete, Coercion & Collusion; Laissez Faire Bookkeeping; & False Pretenses Synonymous. Tho the Directors of said Depts had initially petitioned for hard cold cash, the banker (via his persuasive skill @ subordinating clauses & misplacing any pesky modifiers amongst intransient verbs & indefinite pronouns) managed to convince said Directors to pay their foremen & crews in cold slices of leftover pizza—w/ unlimited toppings, of course.

Thus the new wing was added, the bleachers installed, the weight room & swimming pool completed just as a throng of corpulent Rittl'baus, D'baums, D'leBaums, Dumpletons, et al arrived. Mingled among the menagerie of Brits, Baums & honorary Woodbees were both the steamed & esteemed members of the City Council.

City Council Chairperson Ollie Garky sat @ the presiding throne. The palsied, shriveled octogenarian-times-two wheezed & coughed as if he had barely managed to extract himself from his deathbed—which was indeed the case. To Mssr Garky's right: the Honorable Clarence Sayles, dressed to the hilt in high hat, midriff & low bottoms. Everything he wore displayed its original price tag—including the recent nose job. To Ollie Garky's left: retired Admiral Warron Peece, his many medals artistically arrayed to resemble a loose cannon.

Nearby: Sur Harry, Commissioner Dicker & Professor-General Cody conferred, Sur Harry hiked up on several thick phone books. The anxious aristocrat looked about, straining his nervous eyes, craning his neck, scrunching his face in a vain attempt to locate what under his breath he referred to as "my confounded nephew." Tho countless human beach balls lumbered thru the milling crowd, filling the stadium seating, spilling mustard & sauerkraut as they juggled their jumbo hotdogs, not one possessed the bulging blue eyes, the quivering triple chin or the thick tuft of brilliant white hair of the town's chief guardian of the One that protects the ONE. Upon the meeting being called to order, Sur Harry abandoned his search, smacking a few invisible flies in retaliation for his nephew's tardiness.

Calling for the crowd's attention, Mssr Garky hacked & wheezed some more, hawking up what those in polite society call a 'fur ball.' His hands shaking, his sibilants whistling & sending the guard dogs into a frenzy, the man who held first chair on the City Council for more years than anyone was allowed to count, began w/ an impassioned plea. Italicizing his s's, inverting a few e's & drawing x's over his o's, he begged those in attendance to nevər fŏrgət the Primə Dirəctive ŏf Thə Tŏwer ŏf Pŏwər: eithər yŏu are in chargə, təlling evəryŏne elsə what tŏ dŏ—ŏr sŏmeŏnə elsə is in chargə, telling yŏu what tŏ dŏ.

"Here, here!" Mal Feisance called from the crowd, tho whether in agreement w/ the octogenarian-plus or merely to call over a hotdog vendor was anyone's guess.

Addressing the recent strike, Mssr Garky assured the crowd that the Uniŏn ŏf Spiəs, Dŏuble Agənts & Turncŏats was bəhaving irrəspŏnsibly—illəgally, in fact, dəspitə what thəir dictiðnaries might say. "What is mõrə," he added, moistening his cracked lips & pounding his chest to get his lungs going, "the strikə had cõmə @ a suspiciðusly inðppõrtune timə, crippling law enfõrcemənt's effõrts tõ herd thə requisitə Nibians, Diphthõngs, Dimlets & ðthər miscreants necəssary tõ ensurə a smõõth, safə, səcure S-eləctiðn."

Amid the ensuing applause, the octogenarian-plus keeled over, his head kerplunking into the mic before slamming onto the table. An enclave of medics raced over to give him mouth-to-mouth & shock his lack of any heart into beating again.

While the paramedics worked feverishly, the Honorable Clarence Sayles manned the microphone, urged by the medics to stall for time. "I know i preach to the converted converted," he began, waving his prodigious digits, each adorned w/ an opulent ring polished to a blinding sheen, "when i remind you that ours is the greatest greatest civilization ever ever built by man, beast & indentured servitude. A civilization so perfectly perfect that naturally those envious of our dominating dominance would seek to tear us down, to wear us out, to contaminate all the all we have accumulated w/ their superior inferiority complexes. Such persons are redundant in their redundancy & in denying the fair fairness of our just justice." The Councilperson waved his hands, intentionally blinding his audience w/ the reflective glare bouncing off his massive rings.

"What is it that rankles our rankled enemies so?" he continued, pausing to tug an earlobe to test whether its ruby earring created the same effect. "What causes our adversarial adversaries to devise such convoluted convolutions & irreverent irreverences in their vainly vain attempt to make you & me feel guilty over our successful successes? Isn't their free freedom enuff? They are, after all, freely free to go any anywhere they please—so long as they stay out of our gated communities. But is that enuff?"

"No!" several in the crowd shouted.

"They are free to say any anything they want—so long as they use appropriate language & don't go ballistic each time we exercise our PUP-given right to wear state-of-the-art earplugs. But is that enuff?"

"No!" even more of the crowd shouted.

"Of course not. Instead their bellies bellyache just because we own 95% of every everything—which happens just by happenstance to be more than 300% of what they'll never own. But don't let these devious numbers deceive you."

"Here, here!" several more in the crowd shouted, myriad peanut & pretzel vendors scurrying to meet the sudden upsurge in demand.

As the Hon. Mssr Sayles again flashed his rings, the 800-pound gorilla in the room stood up, primping her curls. As she spoke, half the audience ignored her while the other half paid no attention. "I remember before i was born when everythin' was purr-fect," she iterated, dropping her g's to the annoyance of the couple seated in front of her. "Seems to me it was that J- fella startin' all the ruckus: comin' round advocatin' sharin' w/ the less fortunate. Seems to me 'less fortunate' is one a dem dere code words for 'lazy degenerates.' Seems all you hear these days is these commonists talkin' bout equal rights."

"Yeah, as if there's enuff to go around!" Emma Glutton shouted from several rows behind the primate.

Shouts & foot-stomping erupted, vibrating the bleachers as more & more Brittlebaums vied for the attention of the understaffed concessionaires. Only gradually did a hush fall over the crowd as the dyslexic Admiral Peece reached for the mircopohne.

"Bülly for üs, my fellow cizitens," he began, adjusting his monocle & chewing the tips of his walrus moustache. "Need i remind yoü that freemod is never cheap. And I say, bülly for that! The preporty you rightfülly horad müst be procteted @ all cotss. And that's no büll.

"As one who has flolowed the visicsdütes of hitsory, I müst remidn yoü of what we in the bülly-for-üs büisness call the P.P. Principle. Since time immotral, donimant powers got to be so manily by trapmling on the rigths of the less mitilarily endowed—those more ignonart or considrebly less devioüs. Bülly for us, I say! Eventülaly every süch süccesfsül society has had to come to a crossroad where those @ the pot müst decide which is of more valüe: Pepole...or Propetry."

The entire stadium fell hushed as several more 800-pound gorillas, strategically scattered about the stadium, echoed the Admiral's words: "Pepole. Or propetry. Pepole. Or propetry." At first a whisper, increasing gradually in volume, the throng joined in the chant, stomping their feet until the bleachers threatened to capsize. Only when Mssr Sayles used his rings to mesmerize the audience did the crowd simmer down.

"To my mind, the bloody naswer is quiet ovbioüs," the Admiral continued, pulling the mircopohne closer to his lisp. "Wars have been, & are to this revy day, foüght based on the P.P. Pricniple. And I say, bülly for that. Millions if not blilions of pepole have been slaügtherde over the centüries. And still, pepole keep making more people—making more people being smoething most of them do pretty well." The Admiral paused, using his monocle to silently count the fingers of both hands.

"Land, on the other nahd," he huffed, "is finite. Land, in fact, can never be created no matter how namy times we derstoy it. Ckech your maps, your atlases, your globse. You'll dicsover hünamkind has been fighting over the same swathes of landmass ever since war was invetned as a means to güanartee paece. I personally have sialed the 8½ seas thosünads of tiems to wrest land form those woh wrets the land from thoes who rwest the land from those febore them—ad naüseam. Today we parcel land in masses so msall, we've balery room to büry all those we've had to slaügther to secüre a serüce foohtold. By the revy laws of the free makret, which my fellow coüncilpesron, the Hon. Mssr Salyes, who knows better than I, will attest: that which is most scarce becomes by defitinion most valüde. To which I say, bülly for that."

"Has Anyone Noticed How Those With The Least Property Make The Most People?" Geri Mander stood & shouted, capitalizing her words to give them more weight. "The Only Ones We Have Left To Take Land Away From Is Ourselves."

"noT thaT wE caN eveN dO thaT!" Donnie Brook countered, capitalizing his last letters just to be contrary. "noW thaT thE workinG classlesS arE throwinG theiR weighT—oR lacK thereof—arounD, eveN ouR spieS & doublE agentS arE havinG seconD thoughtS."

"Who AllOweD ThoSe ScouNdRels SeCond THouGhts In The FiRst PlaCe?" Geri challenged, capitalizing even more letters. Numerous heads nodded in agreement.

"See what hapPENS when you let peoPLE think for THEMselves!" Sur Harry added, pulverizing a few flies w/ his cane.

"Nevertheless..." Commissioner Dicker stood, commanding everyone's attention as the Admiral passed down the microphone. "Nevertheless, they *are* having second thoughts. And other city workers are jjoining them, refusing to cross the ppicket line."

"whaT tHe SaMuel T Hill Is happNing to DeCent sociEty?" several voices shouted from various sections of the stadium as chaos erupted. Distraught citizens began capitalizing letters @ random, some x'ing out their more offensive vowels, still others parenthetically minding their p's & q's.

"wE shoUld firE tHe whoLe loT oF 'Em!"

"String thxm up by thx pensions we've bxxn promisxng thxm!"

"(P)ay them more inade(q)uately than we already have!"

"Drag thêm to thê acadêmic torturê chambêrs!"

"RepLace thE whOle kiT'n'caBooDle!"

Amid the mayhem someone suggested calling up the reserves. One voice lauded the Dept of Incompetence, currently overstaffed, while others endorsed the Ministry of Oxy Morons, purportedly on standby, waiting to be called up for active dereliction of duty. Foot-stomping, clapping & cheers rendered both suggestions unanimous.

As the rabble quieted, Commissioner Dicker again assumed command of the microphone. Rubbing his neck, he cautioned the audience that replacing law enforcement workers w/ inexperienced staff—even such venerable veterans as those in the Dept of Incompetence—might increase instances of non-Nibians, even the nicer Woodbees & perhaps a Brittlebaum or two, being inadvertently hauled away as a public enmity. "It is one thing to accidentally-on-ppurpose shove someone in the pen," the Commissioner warned, "but to accidentally not-on-purpose do so may well rruffle some Brittle feathers."

Counter-arguments quickly ensued. Someone prone to spit his b's riled the rancor of those seated directly in front of him. Fist fights nearly broke out when several 800-pound gorillas dropped their g's on several persons attempting to catch some z's. One such Brittlebaum awoke abruptly & began swinging, no amount of apologizing placating him till he had punched a few i's & knocked out a few t's.

"wheRe aRe thE poLice wHen You neEd theM?" several exasperated Brittlebaums cried out, some referring to the fisticuffs, others objecting to the sudden price hike in caramelized pupcorn.

By the time tempers finally settled, Ollie Garky had been revived. Still a bit blue in the lips & gaunt in the cheekbones, the council chairperson nevertheless demanded the microphone. His fellow councilpeople apprised him of all that had transpired during his demise. After consulting himself & reaching a consensus, the octogenarian-plus announced nð ðne prəsent wðuld mind shðuld a nəighbðr ðr twð be accidəntally sacrificəd tð the bullðt bðx...sð lðng as it wasn't ðne of thəm.

"Here, here!" someone shouted, waving a promissory note. The hotdog, pretzel & pupcorn vendors once again scurried to meet the demand.

As the debate continued, the town's more prosperous, prominent & prodigious citizens resolved several further matters: among thəse that anyone whð writes a law shoůld be allowed to bbrəak said law on the ggrounds that in having Writtən Such A Law, onE musT haVe alrəady bbeən above that laW in the first pplace; that all bribês bê tax-dêdüctiblê so long as said bribês bê for a wqorthy causzê; that hefTY finəs be leVIED on all acts of kindNESS twd those who don't DEsərve said kindNESS; & that vðting əligibility be dêtərminəd accðrding tð wəight rathêr than agê, as wəight is hêaviər & age was wwhat Adm Peece called "ehpemelar." These & other resolutions still to be written were rubberstamped in advance so as to save time, each to be enforced retroactively after their landslide victory @ the bullot box, something the arriving CD Smolet assured the crowd was "in the bag," tho deliberately not specifying which bag.

Commissioner Dicker & Professor Cody exchanged smiles, both patting the banker on his billfold as Smolet took a seat among them. The Professor-General flexed his deltoids as the Commissioner pursed his lips & rubbed his settling tummy. Sur Harry, having sufficiently burped his derby, pulled out a case of cigars, which he began breaking in half & passing around. Campaign buttons were also distributed: black & white lettering on an orange & purple background reading *Vôte för thə ÖNÊ htat c'ant bə bêat*. The button showed a round, pudgy, smiley face, flexing a bicep & sporting a handlebar moustache above a triple-chin just barely discernible behind its drooping whiskers.

* * * * *

SINCE THE POSTPONEMENT of his wedding & his clash w/ the Powers that DO, S- had sought refuge in keeping himself occupied. Demoted @ the bank, when not mopping floors or dodging Stubb Farrago's snide remarks, he spent most of his time in his darkroom. Barely able to store his growing stockpile of snapshots & seven-by-nines, he nevertheless developed more. He thought frequently of Buck's initial enthusiasm in helping assemble the darkroom. S- pictured Buck & Buck's shadow, working separately yet in unison, the two @ times disagreeing as to where to mount the enlarger or position the timer, yet managing always to reach a compromise both agreed to be the better solution.

He was recalling Buck's meticulous endeavor to develop immaculate headshots of the girl, Jasmine—making sure every precious pimple received its due—when his shadow perked its ears.

Someone's in the living room, it cautioned.

Peering thru the curtain, S- spied a petite figure in a bright dress & colorful slippers. Penny was examining a stack of photos left on the footstool. She glanced up as he entered, her eyes smiling, her lips sullen & serious. She held out the photos, asking if she might borrow a few. "I need something to put on my walls," she explained.

When S- nodded, she returned to examining the photos, both he & his shadow entranced by the slight tilt of her head as she concentrated. A vague twinkle appeared in her eyes every time she alighted on a photo she liked. As she looked thru the photos, careful not to leave smudges from her slender fingers, S- stood baffled. The photos she held were rejects, ones he had separated out in hopes that by examining his failures he might improve his successes.

Maybe she's just being polite, his shadow whispered.

But the girl's shadow suggested otherwise. It pointed to each photo's strengths while also noting any flaws. Together, Penny & her shadow whittled down the number of favorites, her shadow grabbing the additional snapshots S- held in his hand, then rising to retrieve a fresh batch from the darkroom.

Soon all four were seated, Penny, her shadow & his shadow debating the pros & cons of each photo. Dazzled by the sunlight bouncing playfully off the part in Penny's hair, S- felt himself increasingly enamored each time she hooked a lock of hair behind one ear. She held each print delicately, biting her lower lip in concentration, her eyes glazing over each time a particular photo sparked a pleasant thought or memory.

Among the final selections was one of Mrs Smolet smiling serenely, her head haloed by a jungle of houseplants, Mz Aloe Vera & Mrs Coleus smiling into the camera. There were several of Pearl devilishly romping about town as if she owned the streets. And one of Mr Smolet playing w/ Pearl, his watering blue eyes laughing merrily as two cigars protruded from his jowls, he on all fours pretending to be a walrus. Among her absolute favorites were two of Buck: in one his eyes sadly serious, his dimples almost timid; in the other those same dimples seeming barely able to contain themselves from jumping off his face.

Wincing each time she encountered her own image, she quickly shuffled past most of these. But one in particular prompted a double-, then a triple-take. She had brushed past it but kept returning, reexamining it, finally staring long & hard @ the unfamiliar version of herself. There she was in his attic, her slight figure nonetheless womanly in its bearing, her back straight, her head held high, her hair haloed in confidence. She was teasing his stubbornly rebellious curls, her expression suggesting a poise & intelligence well beyond her seventeen years.

Still she balked when S- suggested she take the photo. Only when S-, his shadow & her shadow all insisted did she finally acquiesce.

Moments later S- & Penny sat staring past each other, their shadows awkwardly engaged in a cautious embrace. When Penny rose, disappearing down the secret passage, S- felt her absence as something palpable, even painful. A tinge of regret cast its shadow around his suddenly empty apartment, that tinge but slightly abated

299

when the girl's shadow returned, kissed his cheek & squeezed his hand before its final departure.

S- leaned back in the rocking chair, his shadow joining him as they set the chair in motion. As they rocked, their heads nodded to the rhythm of the creaking floorboards, their minds humming the same tune as the overhead rafters.

Listen, his shadow whispered, *hear that*?

A soft, somewhat distant thump-thump, thump-thump, thump-thump kept repeating @ regular intervals.

"What is it?" S- whispered.

Neither answered, their combined ears straining to identify the source.

* * * * *

HAD S- ENTERED OUR MICROPOLIS a month or two sooner, had he stumbled up the libary steps & lumbered down into the basement for one particular lecture dispensed to the overeager ears of the BOOKWORMS ILLEGITIMA, he would have heard Neimann Gorge pontificate on that medium-rare phenomenon known as the 'human institution.'

"Institutions..." Neimann informed the timid-eyed Heidi, the knuckle-cracking Hector, the skeptical Ruth, the snoring Rheum & the fidgeting Sedgewick (searching that particular day for his belly button), "...institutions are a curious animal. Human institutions inevitably subvert themselves. Becoming more concerned w/ preserving 'The Institution,' they eventually embrace principles antithetical to the very ideals they profess to champion.

"Take the institution of the now-defunct Christianity," he used as an example. "That antiquated religion was originally intended to unite all mankind under one divine deity: to lead all humankind onto the blessed path of universal brotherhood.

"Yet no sooner did Christianity institutionalize than they began dividing humanity: into Hebrews & Greeks, into Christians & pagans. Soon they were dividing people w/ swords & axes & later w/ machine guns & finally into teeny-weeny pieces w/ their bombs. Not content to merely divide Christians from non-Christians; they divided this type of Christian from that type of Christian; they even divided within their own families, split over one interpretation of a particular verse in their holy scripture against another." Neimann went on, espousing how this phenomenon was not the sole domain of Christianity but repeated itself ad infinitum within all the once-great religions during that ill-fated middle-period of human history.

"Now take the institution of marriage," he continued, stepping from behind the lectern. "An institution forged originally to unite a man & a woman in what was called a 'holy bond of matrimony.' That holy bond has now evolved into prenuptial, postnuptial & antinuptial contractual arrangements where emotions must be removed from the equation, since emotions can get sticky & are prone to cloud good, sound, passionless judgment. Those benefiting most from the current institution of marriage are marriage counselors, who enjoy unprecedented job security, as do the divorce lawyers who rely on these marriage counselors for lucrative referrals."

S- would have heard the libarian cite further examples: hospitals, which, originally designed to heal patients, now focused on what was called the 'bottom line.' The Institution of Medical Care had subsequently divided into factions called 'doctors, nurses & administrators,' who quarreled & quibbled incessantly, far more concerned w/ keeping their doors open & their salaries healthy than w/ the sick who came thru said doors. Neimann cited several examples of staff quarrels so bitter that when an ailing patient raised his throbbing head to request a painkiller, one faction, then the other, ordered the patient to shut his trap, stating they would get to him when they felt good & ready.

"How common nowadays," Neimann asserted, "for the supposed healer to yank the cord to a patient's lifeline, muttering 'It served the sick bastard right,' this before returning to a bitter negotiation, cordially passing the donuts in the process."

By the time Edmund, in his usual late fashion, arrived, Neimann had moved onto The Institution of Education, which, originally established to teach & promote knowledge, was now embroiled in teacher/administration negotiations & budget allocations & how to increase test scores while administering as little monetary sacrifice as possible.

Had S- sat in on that lecture, he would have also learned a bit or two about the human institution called Law. According to legal historians (w/ which Neimann's research concurred), the legal system was initially established to ferret out Truth, then mete out Justice. But the evolution of said institution quickly led magistrates & judges, lawyers & attorneys, bailiffs, litigators, prosecutors for the defense, prostituters for the offense, law clerks, mediators, legal councilors & their illegal counterparts to become more concerned w/ salaries, procedural loopholes, public opinion, political expediency & bribes not easily traceable. Thus words like 'Truth' & 'Justice' had often to be looked up in antiquated lexicons, while attorneys &

prosecutors were more inclined to dress in their finest & spout words in Greek andor Pigs' Latin, such that juries & opposing councils would assume said lawyers knew far more than they actually did.

"In short," Neimann summarized, "the Institution of Law is now all about winning. What is more, the preponderance of litigation by trial eventually led to the realization that said juries were won over not by being bored out of their skulls, but rather by being entertained, amused, seduced as it were into voting for *this* version of Truth as opposed to *that* version of Truth.

"And, just by historical coincidence," the libarian pointed out, "the Institution of Art—originally intended to inspire & enlighten—had also evolved into realizing its mission was mainly to draw crowds, i.e. to entertain...since thru entertaining, the artist might earn enuff income to support his/her agent & to stifle the incessant whining of his/her muse (which in most cases meant his/her spouse). Thus the two institutions—the Institution of Law & the Institution of Art—merged."

By the time S- had wandered into our community, the Institutions of Law & Art had melded perfectly, further recognizing their ultimate purpose lay in the promotion & nurturing of that greatest of all Institutes: The Institution of the One.

Jurors nowadays clamored to sit on the juicier murder trials, the more wanton burglaries, grand larcenies & extortion cases. Bitter divorces were also in high demand: the more irreconcilable the differences, the more expensive the free popcorn. Everything from parking tickets to unpaid libary fines drew crowds of prospective jurors. And why not, when one enjoyed a front row seat to view some of the most highly esteemed actors, musicians, jugglers, con artists & clowns in the business?

And so, when S- entered courtside for the first of his preliminary hearings, the three rings comprising the courtroom were humming w/ court clerks & legal carpenters positioning poles, erecting tents, stringing the tightropes & securing the nets. Hawkers were selling gourmet pupcorn & offering free balloons for a dollar, said balloons skillfully twisted & contorted to resemble some of the town's most notorious criminal elements. Legal advisors w/ colorful briefs shouted orders & jotted down last-minute motions to the show's itinerary, all the while expertly stepping out of the way of prosecutors sweeping the elephant dung left from the previous trial.

Mssrs Booth, Daily & Ivans—the same ski-slope-nosed lawyers who had accosted S- in the gymnasium locker room—were gathered in one ring: stretching, practicing their scales & reviewing the lyrics to their opening number. Their clients,

Sur Harry & CD Smolet, handed them towels, passed around bottles of Alligator-Aide & distributed a white powdery substance which when snorted was said to improve performance—or @ least one's perception of one's performance.

Filkin Grimspoon consulted S- in the second ring. As S-'s self-appointed attorney, Grimspoon donned a black leotard; a pink & white candy-striped tutu hugged his slender hips. His strategy, he informed S-, was to begin w/ a brief ballet vignette followed by a monologue from a well-known tragedy of a grizzled old man who kills his entire family, then frames it on their German shepherd.

"Don't worry," Grimspoon assured S-. "Juries love dogs. Besides, i'm a master of the sad, puppy-eyed look." When the lawyer demonstrated, S- had to stifle a sniffle.

Centered in the third ring was a large blackjack table, the presiding judge serving as dealer as the members of the potential jury called out either "hit me" or "stay." Thus the 7¾ main members of the jury were selected along w/ 3¾ alternates—responsible mainly for going out for coffee & sandwiches…that & making faces to distract opposing counsel.

"This is only the preliminary preliminary hearing," Grimspoon informed S-. "Which side wins the most applause not only gets the plusher seats, but also decides if closing arguments are to be done in dramatic monologue, an abstract modern dance piece, or an operatic aria. If we win & i select the modern dance piece, we've won—none of the opposing attorneys know beans about modern dance.

"Unless, of course," he added after doing a quick plié, "they hire additional counsel. But not to worry. I have the One on our side. We can appeal & hire more dancers ourselves. Plus, i know a choreographer who has done wonders w/ hung juries."

S- glanced around the courtroom. The man he had come to know as Sur Harry leered @ him, brandishing his cane & sticking out his tongue. Mr Smolet—who had renounced their secret partnership—did everything in his nervous power not to glance in S-'s direction. The banker had further forbidden Penny to attend the hearing, on the grounds no one of importance would be listening anyway.

As the final round of blackjack ended, the presiding judge rapped his gavel & the jury rearranged their chairs. The lights dimmed save for two roving spotlights shining from the ceiling. The yellow beams searched, then steadied on the rings for the defense & the prosecution. The judge instructed the defendant & the suing parties to find their seats. Once S- & his opponents were seated, an orchestra rose from a hidden stage illuminated by floor lights.

The judge then ordered the bailiff to proceed. The bailiff, wigged & coat-tailed, rapped his baton on the legal stand, raised both hands w/ an affected flourish & waved his arms, prompting the orchestra to begin.

The overture brought tears & then warm smiles to the jury's eyes. Following the opening came the three-part harmony of Mssrs Booth, Dailey & Ivans, replete w/ twirling canes, kicking heels & a climax in which their identical straw hats rolled up their arms, bounced off their biceps & landed simultaneously atop their swollen heads. The maneuver drew rapt applause as well as beads of sweat on S-'s forehead. No sooner did the applause die down than the lights dimmed & the orchestra began again.

Grimspoon stood motionless, head bowed, hands @ his sides. Just as unexpectedly, he suddenly pirouettéd into action, flying hither & thither about the full perimeter of the ring. One moment his body tense & despairing, the next it was filled w/ flight & exhilaration. The entire courtroom sat hushed, completely entranced. S- felt his muscles relax.

As he glanced around the audience, his eyes alighted on a figure in the bleachers. Tho no taller than any of those around her, the figure, w/ her elegant neck & serene presence, seemed to tower above all others. A halo emanated around the woman's head, or so it seemed to S-, his lashes suddenly fluttering uncontrollably. A tingling ran down his spine as he clutched the arms of his chair. The room wobbled & the two spotlights engaged in a spiraling dance, a dance S- suspected only he could see. He felt about to keel over when the room erupted in thunderous applause. His heart pounding, his face on fire, he watched the figure rise as everyone in the courtroom rose in a standing ovation. The woman looked over @ him, casting a thin smile. His head continued to swim as his throat constricted & he gasped for air.

Just as quickly, the lights came up. His lawyer, along w/ his lawyer's champagne manager & other supporters, hovered around him, shaking his uncertain hand & patting him on the shoulder. They congratulated him, tho for what S- wasn't sure. He staggered to his feet, his eyes searching as the crowd pressed in on him. Finally, his gaze locked onto the tall, long-necked woman approaching him.

"Mouse, come here," his lawyer called out. "Belinda-Rose, I want you to meet the infamous S-.

"S-, say hello to my niece."

Chapter 26

FOR THREE DAYS, rain mixed w/ drizzle pelted the head of anyone leaving his/her cocoon w/out benefit of hat or umbrella. Each morning a dreary fog clung to the city streets, giving way to drizzle by early afternoon, followed by a steady downpour. One flock of sorrowful clouds would break & move on only to make room for the next sorrowful wave.

From the vantage point of his bedroom, S- gazed out @ the scurrying umbrellas, the splashing of galoshes & the sheen of wet raincoats. He peered into the sky's swollen cheeks, his head pressed against the cold windowpane. In the living room, when not gazing past the hunched shoulders of the mulberry, he moped about, the floorboards whimpering under the weight of his feet; even the rafters seemed to ache of some unspoken melancholy. Despite not descending his attic stairs, he knew a similar mood permeated the entire Smolet household. All drapes were drawn, all doors closed, most latched. No one spoke more than necessary.

While S- stalked his apartment, Mrs Smolet fidgeted about the master bedroom, @ pains to find the perfect slipper to mirror her chameleon mood. She searched in vain for something resembling a rollercoaster—something w/ steep hills & deep valleys, sharp corners & unexpected curves. She sat before her vanity, staring long & hard @ her elongated face, studying her corrugated forehead & the now permanent crow's-feet twinkling w/ hard-earned maturity, her pallid cheeks beginning to sag. During the days previous, she had imagined the worst. Yet, as she examined a few gray strands of her thinning hair, she pondered how the worst was actually not all that bad.

Thus the lady of the manor opted to prance about in bare feet. She traipsed into the hallway, gathering her watering can & filling a spray bottle w/ rosewater. Humming as she misted a blossoming fuchsia, she ignored the tsk-tsk of the devil's ivy. The overgrown vine cocked a condescending eyebrow, quoting passages from her rule book, one in particular relating to the slippery slope she would no doubt tumble down by giving way to spontaneous humming. Momentarily repentant, Eleanore Smolet ceased & desisted, unaware as she moved on to the angel's trumpet & the flowering bird of paradise that her lips & larynx were @ it again.

Returning upstairs, she paused as she passed Buck's bedroom, pressing a curious ear to the silent, dour-faced door. She wondered what her morose son might be doing. Had she the ability to see thru walls, she would have found her eldest slumped in a beanbag chair, his once proud brows caved in, weighed down by a losing battle w/ gravity. She would have noted his baby blues in a state of perpetual brooding, his dimples on vacation as the gray matter btwn his ears wrestled w/ what seemed the bleakest of all possible futures. She would have been taken aback by the legions of plastic soldiers covering every surface of his battle-scarred room.

Buck's troops, tanks, planes & airstrips had been arranged in a battle to end all battles. Their deployment would have been deemed a masterpiece by his professors, as well as subsequent military scholars. Even the Dean of Gladiator U would have (albeit reluctantly) conceded Buck's genius as a military mastermind superseded his own. By carefully calculating the inclinations of each individual soldier—who would fight, who would run, who would do something heroic, who was prone to do something stupid—& balancing that w/ the differentiated military strength & aptitude or lack thereof of each commissioned officer, Buck had constructed a battle in which @ first one side would gain advantage, then the other, followed by several unexpected breakings-thru of enemy lines. After a last-ditch suicidal thrust into the jaws of victorious death, only one soldier, one lone victor, would emerge to tell the tale. This was his master stroke: w/ only one soldier remaining it would be completely unnecessary, nay impossible, for said sole survivor to ever go to war again. It would be the coveted War to End All War: the Holy Grail of all military conquests since the forces of peace had come up w/ war as the best means of imposing said peace on an unwilling populace.

But Buck's triumph—the A++ he was sure to merit—rang hollow. The man-child brooded on his beanbag, staring into his worn shag carpet. Were he able to see thru floors, he would have seen his beanbag of a father pacing the length of a dim-lit office. He would have seen the bookshelves, the credenza & souvenir case, the desk drawers, including their secret compartments, completely gutted.

He would have watched his father sit, rise, pace the fireplace, plunk down in a different chair, then pace the fireplace again. He would have seen the banker chew unmercifully, an unlit cigar crushed in one hand, the other hand rubbing the sagging layers of a troubled chin. "Maybe i was wrong," he would have heard his father say out loud.

The brooding banker removed his glasses, his watering eyes looking inward while staring out @ nothing in particular. Smolet thought back to the Gradfest, recalling the frantic fluttering in his ribcage as he watched that infernal lazy-eyed gopher cross the finish line, his worst fear suddenly a stark reality. Yet...what was it he had feared exactly? And why? Both these questions he wasn't sure how to answer. Was it the thought of...of S- possessing his Penny? Caressing her? The two of them doing the nasty thing? Or was it....?

As he paced, he recalled being yanked from the locker room, exiting the gym into the warm nite air. The scowling eyes of Sur Harry & Commissioner Dicker met his, poisoning what otherwise was a strikingly brilliant sunset. The two men barked & brayed like angry hyenas, Sur Harry swishing his cane, the Commissioner swallowing watermelon after watermelon, firing orders no one seemed to pay any attention to. Finally someone did run off, returning soon after w/ a legal council flanked by an entourage of character assassins & petty officers. Thus reinforced, Sur Harry & the Commissioner stormed the school steps, ordering the banker, the lawyers & the others to follow.

Smolet again sat, this time @ his desk, staring up into the cross eyes of Smolet the Grating. "How come you never thought to feed him?" his shrewd Grampupa's gaze kept asking. "You let him sit @ your table. You let him savor your wife's perfume, contemplate your daughter. Yet it never occurred to you to offer him something to eat?"

The banker lowered his eyes, burying his head in his hands. Reluctantly, he acknowledged S-'s peculiar influence on his headstrong household. Bill, after befriending the doe-eyed stranger, now willingly attended War classes. Only recently Smolet had glowed w/ pride @ reports of his firstborn again excelling beyond all expectations in *Mayhem, Massacre & Cover-Up*, demonstrating an unquestioning willingness to obliterate any target pointed out to the boy. Bill had even jumped @ the chance to run for City Council, where he would get to decide which public enmities to loath immediately & which could be tolerated for another S-election or two. Before S-, Bill had all but lost the thrill of watching someone bleed to death—the boy had been that bored.

And then there was Penny's complete transformation. Before S-, she was an obstinate bundle of defiance, bound & determined to drive down her price w/ her outlandish hairstyles & endless line of burlap haberdashery. As it turned out, his precious Penny had netted enuff cash of the hard, cold kind to placate not only the Powers that DO but the Powers that do DO—@ least a little longer. And all because of that...because of...all because of S-.

Exactly how, the banker was hard pressed to explain, never mind fathom. It wasn't as if the lad did anything, exactly. As it was, S- barely spoke. And yet...now even he & Eleanore had rekindled some of their... He wasn't sure why, or how... but he strongly suspected S- had something to do w/ that, too.

"So why didn't i think to feed him?" the banker asked himself, rising to pace the fireplace. "How come it never even... How come it never even occurred to me?"

The banker knit his brow. Looking @ the crumpled cigar in his fist, he scuttled over to the overturned trash can, righted it & threw the remains in. Plopping into the same chair he had interviewed S- in, he surveyed his disheveled cocoon, gazing @ pile after pile of books, documents & other scraps of paper which had lately come to define his existence. He looked @ his sleeves, @ the two cufflinks glistening despite the dim lighting. He felt his chest, imagined fingering a tie where a tie clasp would be. As he did so, he pictured himself bent over the cold, indifferent bank vault. He saw the tumblers refusing to cooperate, his sweaty fingers nervous & clumsy as a sea of angry faces—among them Sur Harry, Donald Dicker, Ruben Samwish, Armstrong Cody, Carl Buncle & Ira Fuse—all shouting, brandishing their furious red fists.

He checked his watch as he chewed on another question: Should he? Could he? Did he dare? It would mean apologizing. Even coming clean. Could he swallow that much pride? The banker leaned back in his chair, chewing on the matter as his shadow struggled to detach itself.

Pacing beneath the portrait of Smolet the Great, his shadow gazed up, pausing to study each portrait in turn. What about the lawsuit? the banker asked himself. *Withdraw it*, his shadow suggested. Can I do that? *Of course you can*. "But what about Sur Harry?" the banker asked aloud. *What about him?* his shadow whispered.

Smolet's shadow wheeled around, moving twd the box of new cigars. Before it reached the box, the banker leaned fwd, sweeping the box's entire contents into the trash. Smolet chewed a moment, thinking to call the Mrs.

Rising, he opted to empty the trash himself.

* * * * *

THE SAME GRAY-HAIRED MISTRESS in the sky frowning in the windows of the Smolet household was also dampening spirits inside our libary & literary infirmary. Somber droplets trickled down the panes of the permanently latched bay windows. Our head libarian, his laid-off staff, the doctors, surgeons & nurses all gathered to bid one another goodbye. Neimann shook the solemn hand of Dr Oswald, embraced Dr Buncle as an old & trusted friend, wished Drs Cataract & Scurvy the best of luck in whatever endeavors each chose to pursue. He wished each staff member the appropriate farewell—troubled as he struggled to remember names he had never bothered to learn.

As the dejected staff dispersed, a few stragglers milled among their favorite basilicas, fondling a favorite spine, caressing a familiar book jacket. Neimann trudged despondently up the ambulatory for the last time. Scattered about his office rotunda were four suitcases, their gaping mouths begging to be fed. Two had already been stuffed beyond their brims, many of Neimann's dearest friends crammed inside. Neimann hesitated, estimating the two empty cases' cubic footage against the many books still calling to him from the half-depleted shelves.

"You can't do this," he could still hear his aunt bawling thru her tears. "You can't treat Pythagoras like this! That's her room!" But Neimann held fast: the Bratwurst didn't need an entire room to herself. All he was asking was a place to put a few additional bookcases.

To his disbelief his aunt held fast. "Pythagoras is as much a member of this family as you & me," she countered, brandishing a crooked finger. "I suppose next you'll be demanding i sleep in the bathroom while your over-pampered lambskins lounge in my bed!" When Neimann made no reply, his aunt huffed away, her spindly legs threatening to give way under the weight of her foot-stomping anger.

Neimann shrugged off the memory as he cleared more shelves, debating who he could take & those he'd be forced to leave behind. He failed to hear the soft patter of despondent feet or discern the rustle of hip-hugging dress slacks. He turned only @ the whiff of a familiar perfume, one that once upon a time intoxicated him.

"I guess this is goodbye," Mz Pritt pronounced, her sad chin nearly pinned to her chest.

Neimann avoided the teary eyes, the button-nose, the adorable chin. He had, after all, betrayed her. He had sold out. Despite all those lectures warning his Bookworms to steer clear of its insidious temptations, he had himself knelt to the god of Oneness.

Tho Kate never suspected his plan to abandon her & marry Penny Smolet, his fall from grace was inexcusable, his guilt rendering it too painful to ever look again into Mz Pritt's innocent, all-trusting face.

He stuck to his task, cramming all he could into the remaining suitcases, twice having to rearrange the books, all the while pretending Mz Pritt was not standing there, that her beautiful trusting gray eyes—the purest, most pristine eyes in the world—were not lasered in on his every move.

Meanwhile, the most pristine eyes in the world were welling up w/ tears. The mind governing those eyes cried out in silent agony, aware the magic btwn he & she was gone. "Neimann," the lips spoke, the throat choking, the chin quivering. "I have something i need to tell you."

"I'm not worthy of you, Kate," Neimann interrupted. "I've behaved despicably."

"No, no. Not you. It was me. It was my fault."

Neimann stopped, pained by the sound of Mz Pritt's constricted syllables, confused even more by the misplaced confession. "Don't be ridiculous. You've been a perfect angel."

"I've been a wicked devil." Mz Pritt slumped against his desk, her arms listless @ her sides. "I'm not really a libarian...or a nurse," she confessed, swiping a sudden stream of tears. "I took a four-hour seminar in libary science. Even then my test scores were doctored so you would hire me. I'm really a graduate of Femme Fatale Academy."

"I don't under—"

"I was hired by the Powers that do DO...recommended by my uncle."

Neimann hiked an eyebrow.

"Hired to distract you...even seduce you, if necessary."

Neimann dropped a book, barely missing his big toe. "But."

"I'm sorry. I didn't know you before we met." She reached for him but thought better of it. Beginning to cry, she buried her face in her hands.

Neimann raced to her comfort. "Don't," he begged. "Whatever your motives, these past few months have been the best of my life."

"Mine, too," Mz Pritt sniffled. "You were so happy; like a puppy you were. I became happy just watching you. Just knowing i could make someone that happy made me feel so good. I never knew i could feel that way." Mz Pritt sniffled again, using a thumb to wipe her tears.

Sensing his damsel in need of a tissue, Neimann looked around, opting to sacrifice the title page of a battered paperback. Mz Pritt waved him off, insiting he needn't, as she knew what his friends meant to him. She detailed having gone to her uncle, saying she couldn't/wouldn't do it, that she wouldn't/couldn't betray him. But her uncle grew angry, intimidating her w/ threats of old maid-hood. He even threatened to w/hold her GOOJ card should a scandal break out. When she said she didn't care, her uncle threatened to have Neimann's name penciled in for the Turkey Shoot.

"I didn't know they planned to close the libary." She began crying again, offering no resistance as Neimann pulled her into his arms.

He shushed her, kissing her tears until she smiled, if only wanly. He forged a trail of kisses along her cheek, ending finally @ her ear, causing a girlish giggle despite her continued sniffles. When he pecked @ her lips, she shook her head. "No, no," she protested. "I don't deserve—"

As his lips pressed into hers, refusing to be dislodged, she submitted, pulling him closer, gasping for breath finally as he released her lips to kiss her chin, moving in quarter inches down her neck.

"We're not licked yet," he assured her btwn puckerings. "I've still an ace...up my sleeve.... I haven't been reading...all these books...for nothing." The more they kissed, the less he spoke, the tighter they clung.

Rain continued to pelt the windows even as a ray of sunshine poked a timid finger thru the persistent gray. The lone yellow ray stood transfixed, calling on several fellow rays to take a peek. Together a widening shaft of light peered down on a sight never before witnessed in the penthouse of our literary infirmary. As shoes, socks & other articles of apparel flew helter-skelter about the room, Neimann thanked his lucky stars @ having recently reviewed those glossy magazines secretly filed under his mattress.

* * * * *

S- HAD LEFT HIS PRELIMINARY preliminary hearing more dazed than when he had walked in. In truth, the trial w/ its rotating spotlights, its orchestrated fanfare, the free balloons & gourmet pupcorn had left him unfazed. The tall willow tree of a girl, however, the lawyer's niece, had thoroughly disconcerted him. He had stood waiting, his eyes fluttering like dragonflies, his stomach roiling like an upset ocean. Yet the woman-child said little, slipped him no note, gave no instructions. She merely smiled, bid him a gentle *hello* & a *pleased to meet you.*

Her uncle, on the other hand, had grabbed him by a shoulder, maneuvering him

311

twd the exit. The lawyer explained in Pigs' Latin—interspersed w/ bits of Greek, Yiddish & charades—the next phase of his trials, stating there were to be many.

S- nodded obediently, struggling to pay attention despite an all-consuming impulse to turn around & gawk @ the tall, unassuming niece. Those few times he managed to steal a peek, he saw the lanky, long-necked giraffe of a woman patiently tolerating the sundry bodies, myriad faces & multiple hands congratulating the lawyer, many pleading for one last flash of his sad puppy eyes. Most assured the politician they'd be mailing in their One as soon as they cashed in their promissory notes.

When the crowd dispersed, Grimspoon & his niece bade S- goodnite, the girl saying nothing further, merely touching his hand & whispering "sweet dreams." S- stood baffled, stunned by the timid handshake, which was more the mere placing of her burning fingertips in his palm, removing them almost immediately. He staggered home, his shadow needing several times to redirect him.

And now, three drizzly days later, he stood staring out his window. The thick, overcast, gray-haired sky was slowly giving way to a thin sliver of smiling sunlight. Watching the yellow shaft gradually expand, S- opened the window, a cool gust of moist air titillating his cheeks. He crawled onto the ample arms of the mulberry, its muscular boughs, its sinewy branches shifting to receive him. Refreshed by the lengthy downpour, the mulberry protruded its wet, rough-barked chest, its lobed & unlobed papery leaves shining, its fruit clusters beaded w/ rainwater, its roots invigorated after the long, healthy dousing.

Sheltered under the green canopy, S- recounted his disappointments: his friendship w/ Buck gone awry, his partnership w/ Mr Smolet dissolved. He contemplated his supposed destiny, now seemingly inevitable: to marry the daughter & kill the father, possibly his own father...both acts taking shape before his unwilling eyes. His thoughts drifted back to the handshake that wasn't a handshake, the girl's soft, moist fingertips searing a hole somewhere deep inside him. He grew restless, unable to get comfortable despite the mulberry's adjusting to accommodate him. Finally he shimmied down the tree, planting his feet uncertainly on the soggy earth. Initially, he headed nowhere, little suspecting his shadow had already charted their course.

As if wide awake, the Farrago ramshackle had every light flickering thru its unwashed windows. S- mounted the creaking steps & rang the anemic doorbell, the house eerily silent. Getting no response, he rang the doorbell several times. While his shadow ran around back, S- peered thru the porch window, glimpsing Stubbs seated mannequin-like in a motionless rocking chair. The janitor's eyes stared ahead blankly, seeming to look @ nothing in particular. When his shadow gave a shrill whistle, S- strolled around back, knocking gently on the kitchen door. His shadow tested the knob, opening the door as S- peeked inside.

Mrs Farrago, along w/ Margaret, Orson & Joseph, was seated @ the grown-up table, the matron clutching an unfinished piece of something she had knitted, using it as a handkerchief. Margaret too had active tear ducts, wiping her eyes periodically w/ the back of her hand. Meanwhile Orson & Joseph tried everything in their power to hold their sobs in, settling on an occasional sniffle & wiping their respective noses w/ the ends of their sleeves. Seated @ the smaller table, Josh & Tasha wielded toy blocks, attempting to bash each other's heads in. Eve alone stood, hovering near the stove where she heated two bottles of a milky liquid. When S- entered, all faces turned twd him.

Without a word, Eve approached, taking his hand & pulling him to Mrs Farrago. The girl wrapped his hand around her mother's before returning to the stove. After squeezing small droplets of milk on her wrist, she handed one bottle to Josh, the other to Tasha. Both infants dropped their blocks to immediately bash each other w/ their bottles.

Mrs Farrago, meanwhile, choked on her words as she recounted recent events. Margaret & Eve translated as their mother described the rattling of windows & the banging of doors as a police raid erupted out of nowhere. There were sirens & flashing lights, the clicking of handcuffs & the dragging away of her precious Weed & poor, crippled jj. The charges included stealing & impersonating a Brittlebaum. "Weed would never do such a thing," Mrs Farrago bawled, blowing her nose & squeezing S-'s hand.

Momentarily disappearing, Eve swiftly returned, half-pushing half-pulling her shell-shocked father. "Papa has something to ask you," she announced, holding her father's hand, shaking his arm as if that might coax the janitor's mouth into moving.

Stubbs stared wide-eyed over the heads of those looking up @ him. Occasionally, his eyes darted to the spot where his keg of stewjuice once resided. When his lips finally moved, no sound came out.

"Papa's always been afraid of the police," Eve explained. "Ever since they once penciled his name on the turkey list."

"Weed is innocent," Margaret blurted. "He would never steal. He gives most of what he earns to Mama."

Mrs Farrago began to bawl, squeezing S-'s hand till S- nearly bawled in turn.

"jj is just a cripple," Orson added.

"What Papa wants to ask," Eve continued, "is if you would go w/ him to the police station. He thinks maybe they'll respect you in a kinda-being-scared-of-you kind of way. Maybe w/ you there, they'll let Weed & jj go."

S- inquired where the station was, upon which Orson stood, volunteering to show the way. The boy grabbed his father's hand, instructing S- to grab the other. Eve stood behind as the three pushed/pulled/coaxed & cajoled the janitor into the living room & thru its door.

Stubbs stepped over the threshold & squeezed S-'s hand. Stubbs glanced from S- to Orson to S- again, a vague flicker of gratitude gracing his otherwise catatonic face. His feet ceased resisting & began to move of their own volition as the three stepped into the humid, starless nite.

S- sighed, relishing the sensation of the cool air tingling his cheeks. For three days he had watched the gray-haired matron in the sky shedding an avalanche of tears. For three days he had huddled in his room, uncertain the rain would ever cease. Now the air bristled w/ electricity. Something in the way of a moon hung low on the horizon, its placid face more red than white or yellow. Something's about to give, it suggested. What exactly that something was, S- hadn't a clue.

Chapter 27

ORSON HAD NO TROUBLE LOCATING our municipal police sanctuary, this mainly from his having taken up residence there once upon a crime. It had been a childish dare, actually—instigated by his former best friend, Skunk. The two teens had come upon an unhitched Brittle carriage suffering a broken wheel, said carriage left unguarded outside a used-carriage lot. Coaxed by his buck-toothed companion, Orson climbed aboard, seizing the reins as off they went.

The carriage being balanced on cinder blocks, Orson & Skunk had to employ their youthful imaginations, steering their four rather rambunctious steeds to far-off lands. Orson imagined waving to many a friendly, smiling face & tipping his cap to young, bright-eyed Brittle girls who glanced his way shyly as he giddyup'd by. Not content to travel by road, he envisioned the horses' heels growing wings, the carriage leaving the ground to soar above treetops. Egged on by the whoo-hoo'ing Skunk riding shotgun, Orson did figure eights around the clouds as the golden-maned mistress in the sky ran her sultry fingers thru his dirty blond hair. When Skunk abruptly bolted from the carriage, Orson barely had time to turn his head before several rough & tumble hands grabbed him by his arms & neck, yanking him back to earth. Two huffing officers snapped him in handcuffs, read him his rights, documented his wrongs, then dragged him thru the slamming doors of the station whose very halls he was now leading S- & his father twd. The boy was summarily charged w/ theft of a stolen vehicle, tho, since the carriage hadn't actually gone anywhere, the sentence was flea bargained down to probation.

As the three approached the sanctuary/station, S- recognized the towering clock, its mangled hands & dangling Roman numerals faintly illuminated against the nite sky. He recalled his earlier visit, accompanied by Mr Smolet who dubbed the jigsawed complex "Government Row," rhyming 'row' w/ cow. "The town's municipal heartbeat," the banker had asserted as he doled out cigar-halves to passing executives.

Orson led the way to the drab bldg said to house some of the city's most notorious criminals—as well as many an inmate. ABANDON HOPE Y'AWL WHO ENTER was carved in stark hieroglyphics above two solid oak doors set in a frame artistically rendered to resemble gaping jowls. Metal teeth, doubling as hinges, dared anyone entering to prepare to be swallowed, chewed up & regurgitated. Stubbs squeezed S-'s arm & turned as if to slink away. Undeterred— perhaps oblivious to the danger—S- trudged up the gray stone steps, Orson & the reluctant Stubbs trailing behind.

As the three breached the threshold, colored strobe lights & a screeching siren announced their arrival. Several officers ordered the trio to raise their arms before herding them thru a mental detector, strapping each to a Fibber Rater. Separated thus, they were then interrogated—hounded, actually—until each confessed his view as to whether the chicken preceded the egg, the egg the chicken, or—as the GOOD BOOK documents—both magically appeared on the sixth day after PUP had cut some kind of cheese.

In adjoining cubicles, males & she-males in ill-fitting uniforms pounded noisily on typewriters, polished badges, oiled handcuffs, or tested billy clubs on anyone out of uniform. At the front counter, sergeants & lieutenants waved subpoenas, removing bits of habeas corpus from btwn their teeth as they stamped half-a-davids, which secretaries & office clerks then signed off on before converting into confetti.

After S-, Stubbs & Orson were pronounced unfit for general consumption, the trio was herded on, no one quite sure where 'on' was. They were steered in conflicting directions, waylaid for half an hour in the LADIES ROOM before an officer on a cross-dressing break led them to an official looking doorway. POLICE CHIEF W. W. WILLOUGHBY was stenciled on its glass window, the bold block letters X'd thru & 'Callow Gutwright' scribbled below it.

S- entered first, greeted by an unshaven officer clad in flannel pj's. Leaning back in a swivel chair, interim Police Chief Gutwright cocked a curious eyebrow as he scrutinized his three visitors. S- stood flanked on one side by Stubbs, on the other by Orson.

"Soooo," the Police Chief crooned, blowing out his finger after pretend-shooting S- btwn the eyes, "i kneeeew you would make your way here sooooner or lateeer. I hope you've brought your suicide note."

"We've come to see my brothers," Orson blurted, dashing behind S- when the Police Chief re-cocked his finger.

"Yooou've had @ least thirteen years to see your broothers, young man. I assuuuure you, they look quite the same...tho perhaps a tidbit saddier, i'm afraid. I'll have you know we took the crutches from the younger one lest he attempt escaping by hobbling off disguised as a cripple—you handicapped are sooooo clever." The interim Police Chief raised an admonishing eyebrow. "The older one...we're still interrogating him. Our orders are to find out how he gets his pizza dough so crisp, yet fluffy.

"Truth is, you've couldn't have come @ a worsier time," the chief added w/ a sigh. Having only that nite been called down from the Dept of Incompetence, the new Chief of Police proceeded to complain about conditions in the men's bathroom, its maintenance under the joint jurisdiction of his own dept & the Ministry of Oxy Morons.

As Gutwright railed about unflushed toilets, overflowing latrines & no place to set his shaving kit w/out other officers absconding w/ his razors, S-'s eyes were drawn to various charts plastered along the office walls. PUBLIC ENMITIES was printed in bold black letters atop each chart, each then subheaded: B-election, C-election, D-election & so on. S- scanned the unfamiliar names: hogbobins, flatlampets, unicorns, pagens, wickets, coyøtès, mahogans, commie bastards, centaurs, doodoo birds, clovis, et als, etceteras. Scrutinizing the K-, L- & M-election charts, he noted the name 'Nibian' in btwn Tinkerbell & fairy godmothers. Thereafter, on subsequent lists, the name rose higher in prominence. Soon 'Canaan' began to appear, along w/ several chess clubs & countless barbershop quartets—four-part harmony apparently having gone out of favor. The final chart, subheaded S-election, was only half-filled & contained a good deal of white space. On one line, 'Lugwort' was preceded by a question mark; on another, Dregs, written in pencil, had '?misc' scribbled after it in parentheses.

His eyes glued to this last chart, S- failed to hear Stubbs stutter or Orson translate his father's demand to know the charges brought against Weed & jj. Fumbling thru the clutter atop his desk, the interim Police Chief fished out an official-looking clipboard. He flipped repeatedly thru the same several pages, finally alighting on a pink onionskin document stamped: OFFICIAL.

"Looks like two counts of impiersonating a Brittlebaum," he pronounced, glancing @ them sideways before puckering his lips. "Robbery & attemptied rape."

"Rape?" the janitor mumbled.

Tossing the clipboard aside, the substitute C of P leaned back in his chair, propping his feet on the desk corner. "Seems your boys done stole a fat wad of One, then went to a Grad-fest impiersonating rich persons. Now had they won, don't tell me after the wedding ceremonkey, they wouldn't have forced themseeeelves upon that pooor, unwilling Brittle girl." The Chief of Police paused, his lips puckered as he counted his fingers. Momentarily distracted, he had to begin again. And again. Frustrated, staring @ his digits as if admonishing them for failure to cooperate, he finally used a few to aim a pretend gun twd S-'s head, S-'s eyes still lasered in on the final chart.

"Wondering what theeeese are, are you?" the C of P asked, glancing @ the chart S- was scrutinizing. "Found 'em in the attic-basement. These eighteen charts here span the entire hisssstory of human e-vil-ution." The officer stepped proudly to the final chart.

"This heeeere is a list of this year's potential turkeys. As you can see, Dimlets are the favoorite, followed closely by your Dibildogs. Next we have those darn Scuttlecocks, who, as you can see, have edged out the once-popular Nibian. Sadly, our Nibian population has been a-dwindling in recient years. We're attemptying to remeeeedy that situation. That effort, however, has been held up for i don't know how many years by our Committee on Slooooow & Painstakingly Teeedious Deliberaaaation."

Rummaging thru the pile on his desk, the interim Police Chief located a magic marker, promptly adding another name to the list. "This here, Harold Johnstone…" he pointed to the name he had just written, "…my grade schoooool nemesis. Told him i'd get him back someday, tee hee. And i think it's finally time we add those nasty Nabors next doooor." He scribbled the additional name, misspelling it, crossing over it & attempting a new misspelling. He was on his third attempt when a loud commotion diverted his attention. Dropping the marker, the C of P smoothed his pajamas & picked @ some lint before dashing from the room. S-, Stubbs & Orson quickly followed.

Shouts & counter shouting emanated from the hallway, interrupted occasionally by unabashed cursing as a ragtag flock of bug-eyed, severely bruised citizens were corralled into a processing pen. A motley assemblage of pear-shaped people w/ cantaloupe complexions (Dimlets, S- was to learn) were being pushed & shoved,

318

whipped & kicked into the enclosed structure. Mixed in among the Dimlets were several residents of Crooked Town, their heads awry, their smiles bent out of shape, their hearts apparently broken beyond repair. S- recognized several Dixsticks as well, their limp rods dangling & despondent. A man in a blood-splattered butcher's apron looked familiar, tho S- could not recall from where. The butcher seemed overly protective of an elderly woman who clutched her purse & continually asked if anyone knew the way to San Jose. S- spotted Erle Greaves, struggling to stay on his feet. Tho Erle's scars were nearly healed, new bruises of a greenish-purple tint had taken root.

"MORE CANDIDATES FOR THE TURKEY SHOOT!" someone shouted, the interim Police Chief ordering his officers to handle the merchandise gently.

"Gutwright! Callow Gutwright!"

The Police Chief looked in several directions. "Over here," the voice called again before Gutwright zeroed in on the prisoner in the bloodied apron.

"It's me. Clyde," the butcher shouted. "Our kids used to play Lynch the Riffraff together, remember? You & me graduated near the bottom of the same class. Mediocre High. Remember the wedgie I once gave you? Sorry about that. Listen, there's been a mistake. I'm no Dimlet. I hate Dimlets. I was even fined once for selling a few as chopped liver. Check your records."

The Police Chief shrugged. "Sorry, Clyde. Noooo can do. You're a conflict of my lack of interest. But it's real good to see you!"

A female officer tapped Gutwright on the shoulder. "Chief, we can't seem to locate the proper paperwork. All we found is this here sign-up for the police potluck."

Removing more lint from his pj's, the C of P sighed & issued a reluctant okay; each prisoner was subsequently identified, fingerprinted & assigned a dish to bring before being whisked away.

"Such a nice young man," the elderly woman said of each officer shoving her farther down the hall.

Retreating to his office, followed by S-, Orson & Stubbs, the interim Police Chief again fished for his clipboard, reviewing the pink onionskin report on Weed & jj. "It seeeems, you have one of twooo options," he announced, eyeballing Stubbs from the corner of his eye. "One, you can trade in thisssss one," he pointed his gun finger @ S-, "in exchange for your two sons. You knoooow how many bonus points he's worth." Again he pointed @ S-, this time cocking his thumb before pretend-pulling the trigger. Receiving no response, the interim C of P shrugged. "Oooor, you can get whatever Brittle girl they attempted to raaaaavage to confess she would

319

have actually reliiished their unwarranted advances...tho i highly doubt that. Still, you neeeever know what perverse thrills some Brits too big for their britches get out of circumventing their rule books. Do that & get the peeeerson they stole from to drop the charges...& all that would be left is impiersonating a Brittletibaum, which we cooouuld reeduce to impiersonating an affluent Woodbee. For that...your sons might get off w/ a year or twooo of probation."

Stubbs mumbled incoherently, waving both arms like a traffic cop intent on misdirecting traffic.

"He wants to know the girl's name," Orson translated.

The C of P checked the clipboard. "Looks like they intended to bid on a Mzzzz Peneloooopy Smooolet. I suppoooose, since your friend here currently oooowns Mz Smolet, pending litigation, we could reduuuce that charge to attemptied adultery per husband's consent."

Stubbs again mumbled, re-misdirecting traffic.

"What about the robbery?" Orson translated. "Who did they steal from?"

"Some store owner, i think." The officer flipped thru additional documents. "Yes, here it is...a fishing-gear merchant...owner of a switch, bait, tackle then snap a photo shop. Someone by the name of...here it is…someone named Perman: Perman Radcliffe."

* * * * *

UNDER COVER OF the same darkness S-, Stubbs & Orson had strolled thru on their way to the Police Sanctuary, Neimann Gorge found himself climbing thru the boarded windows of the literary infirmary. Flashlight in hand, the emboldened libarian began reviewing statutes, dusting off dossiers & brushing up on all the laws he hoped the City & Counting Government might @ least feel compelled to pretend to adhere to—knowing full well there was no guarantee. By morning, as on an other side of town Sur Harry's wife began to crow, Neimann felt sufficiently armed, his papers & documents arranged in reversed alphabetical order & properly footnoted as he marched defiantly to the Counting Commissioner's office.

There he was instantly collared by a muscular, purple-eyed receptionist who set aside her nose tweezers to insist they arm wrestle before allowing him an audience w/ the ultra-busy Commissioner. As he was rolling up a sleeve, Neimann glimpsed a piebald head pass outside below the windowsill. He dashed to the window, spotting the Commissioner tiptoeing down the alley, then dashing @ full speed upon reaching the street. The libarian gave chase, following the trail of watermelon seeds until he mounted the front steps of the counting official's supurban residential suite.

Gathering his breath, Neimann knocked violently & rammed the doorbell w/ an impatient thumb. He pounded on the door until a piebald woman wielding a flyswatter appeared. Before Neimann could speak, the woman attacked, the swatter stinging his face & thwacking his chest & raised elbows. But Neimann refused to leave until the Commissioner agreed @ least to hear what he had to say. Only after the flyswatter broke, dangling precariously by its bent handle, did the ranting woman concede, stepping aside. She gave Neimann one last swat on the rump as the libarian squeezed by. Neimann followed the remaining trail of watermelon seeds into the family feeding-room, where a slipper-clad Commissioner was tossing slabs of marinated bambino into a grumbling feeding duct.

Planting his feet firmly, Neimann stated his purpose in carefully practiced monosyllables—all the better, he had reasoned, to be understood by even the least educated, linguistically challenged public official. Quickly reverting to his old habits, however, he was soon over-stuffing his prepositional phrases w/ cumbersome qualifiers while dangling more modifiers than he knew to be socially acceptable. He chronicled every legal argument every legal practitioner had used since Cain had clobbered Abel, then hired an attorney to plea bargain the sentence down to eternal damnation. Finally, he resorted to words no one save he ever used or understood—convinced these would be impossible for the Commissioner to refute.

The Counting Commissioner never batted an eye. Consulting his watch every few minutes, Donald Dicker reached for his standard dictionary (the pasteurized edition), each time proving conclusively Neimann didn't know what the Samuel T Hill he was talking about.

As Neimann persisted, the Commissioner wondered out loud what an unemployed libarian might taste like to a grumbling feeding duct, especially if said libarian was diced into digestible pieces & marinated in a tasty cream sauce. The Commissioner rubbed his abdominous belly, calling his wife to inquire where she or he might have left the pickaxe.

Neimann held his ground, talking louder when the Commissioner stepped momentarily into an adjoining room. Only when the Commissioner returned, pickaxe in tow, did Neimann abandon all argument to beat a hasty retreat, Mrs Commissioner brandishing a fresh flyswatter as the libarian tumbled down the porch steps, landing prone on the unforgiving sidewalk.

Wandering aimlessly, Neimann finally steered his feet twd the jigsaw puzzle known as GOVERNMENT ROW. Marching first to the Dept of Offensive Odors, he was informed in colorfully foul language that, no matter how convoluted & well-researched his legal arguments, his reasoning basically stunk.

Tail btwn his legs, the libarian then spent hours banging his head against the door of the Dept of Brick Walls until a sympathetic clerk directed him to the Bureau of Double Standards, housed in the same duplex as the Division of Unity. Unable there to get his grievances adequately redressed, Neimann was sent to the Dept of Disappointed Hopes & Dreams, where he was instucted to take a number. As it was standing room only, the former libarian stood in a crowded corner, chewing on his pride until closing, upon which he was told he could either go home or face a hefty fine.

The soles of his shoes suffering no less than the souls of his feet, his knees about to buckle under, the libarian nevertheless remained determined to give his cause one last try. He trudged resolutely up the porch steps of the Smolet Manor, ringing its doorbell thrice, inbtwn rings practicing protruding his chest up & out. He knocked, then pounded on a window, sighing w/ renewed hope when he saw the shadow of a beach ball approaching. The town's most powerful banker waddled into view, struggling to open each door in turn. A short lifetime later the two men stood face-to-face.

Chewing ferociously as he eyeballed the unexpected visitor, the banker listened impatiently as Neimann prattled on about something upon which the entire fate of civilization apparently depended.

"You know what a tie clasp looks like?" the banker finally asked. When Neimann nodded in the affirmative, the banker waved him inside.

Leading Neimann to the family den, Smolet fell to his knees, instructing the libarian to start @ the other end. Tho Neimann had renounced the One, & all who groveled before it, he assumed the One to be the end-all & be-all of the banker's intellectual capacity. While feeling behind the bureau, Neimann decided to go for the banker's jugular. Couching his argument such that the entire fate of civilizing civilization rested on the reopening of his literary infirmary, Neimann made sure to conjugate his adjectives to his nouns such that the word 'one' appeared as often as possible.

In his introductory statement, Neimann capitalized the O, advancing to a capital N, then a capital E. Within his supporting arguments, while he ransacked the bureau drawers, he capitalized the O & the N together, advancing to the O & the E together, & finally, the N & the E. By the time he was rummaging under the sofa cushions, all three letters were couched in uppercase, several times followed by exclamation marks. Against his own better judgment, the libarian sprinkled in phrases like "PUP be praised" & "Where there's the ONE, there's a way."

Still on his knees, the banker paused, staring @ Neimann in wide-eyed disbelief. "Are you soliciting the One?" he finally asked.

Neimann stammered, his forced smile beginning to melt. "Does the GOOD BOOK not state that 'He who genuflects can count on the ONE's generous reflex'?

"Just a small One," Neimann petitioned. "In hard cold cash...if that's possible. Just enuff to open the libary so our economic scholars can formulate how to retail whatever fruits they harvest from the tree of knowledge onto the open market—@ a substantial profit, of course."

Grunting, swearing & dusting his hands, Smolet struggled to his feet, his face beet red, his jowls jiggling as if barely able to contain their outrage. "I thought you bookworms were smarter than that. You above all people, Mr Gorge. As much as i sympathize w/ your cause—as important as thwarting the forces of ignorance, bigotry & low test scores may be—the One, sir, is on vacation; relaxing on a sunny beach in some place called the Caribbean. Surely you recognize the One is not invincible. Right now, it's resting; gathering its strength for what is sure to be a very taxing bulloting process."

As he spoke, the banker gently tho firmly guided Neimann by the elbow back onto the front porch, adding parenthetically that as soon as the S-electoral dust had settled & the One assumed its rightful place @ the right hand of the ONE, he, Charles Dinero Smolet, would most certainly bring the libarian's concerns to the One's attention. He would even go so far as to consult PUP personally on the libarian's behalf.

The jettisoned Neimann stood on the front porch, hearing the door close firmly behind him; the deadbolt clicked even more firmly. Realizing the banker hadn't offered him a cigar—not even half of one—Neimann understood he had been summarily rebuffed. Soundly, in fact. The libarian stared @ the walls of the Smolet Manor, its windows, its panels, its pillars—for all their splendor, all indifferent to his desperate plight.

As he wobbled twd home, Neimann's imagination began to conjure images he wished for all the world not to face. In vivid detail he saw the disapproving glower of his Aunty McAsser, her hard-hearted stare now a permanent fixture in his tense household. He envisioned the dark stains & wet puddles that now w/ increasing frequency appeared on his bookcases. Tho his Aunt blamed Pythagoras, Neimann had other suspicions.

These images too unbearable, he pivoted in mid-stride, whirling in a new direction as he conjured up scented candles & the aromatic potpourri that always permeated Mz Pritt's cozy studio apartment. He basked in the image of her sympathetic smile, could feel the enticing, sensuous walk of her fingertips up & down his bare chest. The farther he walked, however, the shorter each stride. He pictured himself standing in her doorway, defeat etched on his long face, Kate gently probing, her questions forcing him to confess his complete, abject failure. He imagined his Kate graciously suppressing her disappointment, secretly wondering if this was the man she wanted to be saddled w/ the rest of her life—tho not saying anything, of course.

Again he pivoted, dreading yet preferring the disparaging glares of his aunt & Bratwurst to the disappointed smile of the woman he longed above all else to believe him faultless.

Rounding a block of rowhouses, Neimann nearly tripped over an abandoned shoe. Inside the Hush Puppy he found a foot, one whose odor he swiftly recognized. Picking the shoe up, he walked on, stumbling upon an ankle attached to a shin, one he also recognized. He quickly found a calf, topped by a recognizable knee. Adept @ deductive reasoning (& a lifelong fan of the legendary Sheerluck Ohms), the highly resourceful Neimann soon made his way down a back alley & up a rickety fire escape. Pressing an ear to the door, he heard a commingling of familiar voices. Ignoring the social etiquette known as knocking, he burst thru the door, his gleeful smile met by the angry stabs of five startled faces. Several of his bookworms jumped to their feet, scurrying like cockroaches as they dashed to obstruct his view of something gurgling lethargically atop a waterlogged table.

"What's going on here?" he demanded, tossing Sedgewick the misc body parts. "What are you all up to?"

As Ruth readied her whip, Edmund & Hector gripped their root bottles by the necks. Heidi stared @ her mismatched shoes as Sedgewick fumbled to pull himself together.

"You're making explosives, aren't you?" Neimann pushed past Edmund to examine the glass rollercoaster tepidly emitting puffs of anemic steam. "But it isn't working, is it?"

Heidi & Sedgewick stared @ the floor as Edmund defiantly puffed out his chest. Hector gripped his root all the tighter while Ruth steadied her whip.

"That's because you haven't been listening to a word i've said," Neimann scolded. "Whether we're talking chemistry, cosmology, thermodynamics, nuclear physics—the guiding principles are always the same. So too in politics, war, religion, social upheaval, marriage, you name it—you want to shake things up, you need massive quantities of Either/Or."

Several bookworms cocked their young eyebrows as Neimann tsk, tsk'd them, shaking his head. "Either/Or. You know: Positive vs Negative, Us vs Them, Matter vs Anti-matter, North vs South, East vs West, My Way or the Highway. Nothing creates an explosion like rubbing two implacable forces together. The more vigorously you rub, the greater the kaboom. What exactly are you planning to blow up, anyway?"

As no one answered, Neimann called on Heidi.

"A vault," the girl confessed.

"A what?"

"A vault."

"A vault?" Neimann repeated.

As Heidi & Sedgewick nodded, Edmund & Hector again gripped their bottles, Ruth's cat-o'-nines also on standby.

Neimann looked in turn @ each of his protégés. Spotting the soiled copy of **Cooking Up Mischief**, he demanded Edmund hand him the manual.

Flipping thru the pages, the librarian found the appropriate footnote & the corresponding recipe for concocting Either/Or from scratch. Skimming the instructions, he expounded on how in Nature, as in life, there was Harmony & Chaos. "Harmony exists when various forces work together for a common purpose," he explained. "Chaos arises when Force 'A' decides it's either *Them*...or *Me*; either *This*...or *That*; *My Way* or the *Bye, Bye Way*. But Force 'B' responds w/ a No Way, Jose; we'd rather you die first...

"Here we go." The librarian readjusted the flame, re-proportioning the sodium bicarbonate before systematically adding additional droplets of cow manure concentrate & dashes of paprika. "This should do the trick." Soon the mixture began to fizz, gradually bubbling w/ increased agitation. When the chemical compound threatened to boil over, the librarian held back on paprika & recommended the Either/Or be allowed to simmer. "Repeat three times," he instructed, "& you'll have an explosive so compacted, you can fit it in a baby's pacifier."

Grabbing a nearby rag to wipe his hands, Neimann looked @ his humbled scholars. "So why do you need to blow up a vault?"

As the other bookworms exchanged furtive glances, Edmund's left jaw espoused its unwavering commitment twd the advancement of the causes of freedom & the ending of all tyranny. His right jaw inserted its equally unwavering commitment to redistributing the world's overabundance of One, said redistribution crucial to the advancement of universal, far-reaching humanitarian & altruistic aims.

"In other words, you're planning to steal from the rich to give to your friends," Neimann interpolated.

Heidi stepped fwd, nervously smoothing her bangs. "Actually, sir...the plan is to mainly keep the One out of the hands of the Powers that do DO...@ least till S-election is over."

Hector cracked his best smile. "We also figure, after we spring for a couple cases of root, we'd hand some over to you, Mr Gorge...so you can reopen the libary."

Neimann's eyes lit up, his smile just as quickly fading as he observed Hector systematically crack every available knuckle. Edmund too was smiling as if advertising a new & improved revolutionary toothpaste. Just how naïve his bookworms believed him to be, the libarian wasn't sure. He turned & added a few more drops of manure to the chemicals simmering contently on the lopsided table.

He hummed as he adjusted the flame, confident that as in chemistry, so too in life. Tho one could never account for exactly how a cookie would crumble, he understood how, w/ the right ratio of Either/Or, one could @ least be sure that cookie would indeed crumble. Commissioner Dicker, Sur Harry D'leBaum & that fat hypocrite of a Smolet were all about to have their cookies crumbled. If he couldn't triumph, neither would they.

Neimann reached again for **Cooking Up Mischief**, noting in the appendix the section *To Fuse or Not to Fuse*. After scanning the instructions he called for assistance: "Heidi, Sedgewick, give a hand here, will you?"

* * * * *

Commonly known as the wild turkey, the MELEAGRIS GALLOPOVO became extinct a millennium ago. Fortunately for our micropolis, our earliest forbears meticulously documented their first encounters w/ these peculiar creatures. One scholar affectionately described the MELEAGRIS as a cross btwn a chicken & a circuit court judge. Unfortunately for the obnoxious critters, the vocal sound they emitted was strikingly similar to a common Brittlebaum expression disparaging one's mother's sexual proclivities. Thus our distant ancestors passed laws forbidding such fowl language. But, as these laws were blatantly ignored by the miscreant featherbrains, our forbears had few alternatives but to shoot the gobble-gobblers wherever one appeared. Thus began our tradition of the annual Turkey Shoot. And when there ceased to be any more GALLOPOVO, in order

326

to preserve the honored tradition, our industrious City Council saw
fit to designate new, 'honorary' turkeys among the general (which is
to say, the generally disliked) population.

Upon concluding her report, the voluptuously plump Rosie Guile collected her papers. Standing beside her, Professor Major-Lieutenant General Armstrong Cody rubbed his bullet as he balanced precariously on his tiptoes. Surrounding the pair were the twenty-one aspiring candidates competing for the seven seats on our City Council.

Ollie Garky, Jr XIV, stood most prominent among them, due partly to his glowing galaxy of acne, partly to his commanding girth, but mainly because of the three boxes of donuts he generously shared w/ the others competing on the Brittlebaum ticket. The Hon. Clarence Sayles cordially grabbed two of the powdered variety while Adm Warron Peece opted for one dipped in chocolate caramel, lightly coated w/ chopped nuts.

Alongside his fellow candidates, Bill (aka Buck) Smolet stood unsmiling, coins falling from his pockets each time he sat, rose, turned, or bent nervously to re-tie a combat boot. Thus the man-child was surrounded by many a Woodbee & Dreg candidate vying for the quarters, dimes & nickels landing amongst them. Standing nearest the Professor-General was Filkin Grimspoon, his pockets stuffed w/ greenbacks, protruding like so much lettuce on an open-face BLT sandwich.

Dressed in military fatigues, brandishing a riding whip, Professor Cody thanked Mz Guile for her stimulating presentation, patting her on the buttocks & rubbing his bullet as he watched her sashay away. Commanding the others to follow, he led the entourage down the Tower of Power & into the stadium, stopping @ its perimeter. He about-faced btwn two of the twenty-one bullot boxes lining the arena.

"Ĕach of you will bĕ stationĕd in onĕ of thĕsĕ," he explained, pointing w/ his whip. After citing the booth's dimensions & its distance from the farthest point w/ in shooting range, he cautioned the candidates on the illegality of killing a fellow citizen for no good reason—even a Canaan, Dimlet or one of those dang Diphthongs.

"Fortunatĕly," he added, "our laws havĕ providĕd scorĕs of pĕrfĕctly good rĕasons for killing thosĕ most of us wouldn't mind doing w/out. Somĕ rĕasons arĕ, of coursĕ, sanctionĕd by our City Chartĕr; somĕ ĕtchĕd in ĕrasablĕ ink in thĕ margins of thĕ GOOD BOOK; othĕrs mĕrĕly in currĕnt fashion—to fall out of favor should somĕ plĕading hĕart libĕrulĕ start bĕllyaching so as to gain a fĕw points w/ thĕ lĕast-likĕly-to-votĕ populacĕ among us."

327

His cold eye cocked in Filkin Grimspoon's direction, the Professor smacked his whip against a booth. Momentarily distracted, the politician failed to feel the General pluck a few bills from the lawyer's back pocket.

"Ĕach of you shall bê allottêd three stonê-throwêrs or stonêrs," the Professor-General continued, lifting a sample stone from one of several buckets & rubbing it to demonstrate its smoothness. "Ĕach stonêr shall bê providêd an êndlêss supply of thêsê to toss @ your chosên turkêys, so as to flush thêm out of hiding. As you can sêê," the General pointed to the arena, "to makê things morê challênging, wê'vê addêd numêrous barriêrs for your turkêys to hidê bêhind. In addition to thê swings, slidês & monkêy bars our cadêts usê during rêcêss, thê stadium has bêên strêwn w/ trêê stumps, cardboard bouldêrs, usêd baby carriagês, womên's sêê-thru lingêriê, markêd-down furniturê, prê-fabricatêd gravêstonês & a fêw sênilê rêsidênts from a nêarby nursing homê, thêsê voluntêêring to sêrvê as dêcoys.

"Your stonêrs sêrvê two purposês," the Professor explained further. "First, to gêt your turkêys to comê out from hiding...that way you can gêt a clêarêr shot. Morê importantly, to gêt your turkêy to cursê—cursê you, cursê PUP, cursê this micropolis, it doêsn't mattêr—any cursê a pêrfêctly justifiablê rêason to blow thêir gonads off. Any quêstions?"

After fielding several questions, most involving directions to the restrooms, the Professor-General led the candidates to a shooting rink. Along a waist-high parapet were numerous cap guns, carbines & high caliber rifles, an economy-size Gatling gun, an AK-747, an automatic M-19, several hand-grenade launchers, a sawed-off double-barrel bazooka & a handheld nuclear device w/ optional circus cannon attachment.

"As in any truly dêmicratic sociêty," the Professor stated, "hê or shê w/ thê greatêst Onê gêts first dibs in choosing a wêapon. Bê surê to bring plênty of cash. Promissory notês, as I am surê you arê all awarê, won't cut it. Yês, Mr Grimspoon."

"I was wondering, Professor. Do you by chance have any literature, something w/ pictures, perhaps, indicating the best place to shoot a turkey so as not to kill but to merely maim severely?"

"Ĕxcêllent quêstion," the Professor conceded, one hand patting the lawyer's shoulder, the other relieving the politician of more lettuce. "Bêar in mind, maiming êarns thê lêast amount of points. A clêan kill êarns you half a point; blowing a turkêy to smithêrêêns is a full point. You maim a turkêy & an opponênt finishês him off, you forfêit that quarter point. Most importantly, you losê a point if your targêt is not hêard to clêarly cursê. Of coursê, êvên if thêy only yêll 'Ouch!' that counts as an êxplêtivê.

"Thêse rulês may sêêm arbitrary, gêntlêmên, but thêy arê basêd on a thoro knowlêdgê of social history. History has provên ovêr & ovêr that thê morê rêprêssêd, abusêd & humiliatêd a pêoplê...thê morê frustratêd, hopêlêss & hatê-fillêd thêy bêcomê...thus thê morê likêly thêy rêsort to violêncê, crimê & othêr passivê-aggrêssivê antisocial bêhaviors...giving us êvên morê justification to shoot thêm down likê turkêys."

The Professor-General stared directly @ Grimspoon, then @ Buck. "Rêmêmbêr, killing is not a right; it's a privilêgê."

Confident he had made his point, Professor Cody encouraged the candidates to sample each weapon. The practice rink was soon swarming w/ squirrels, marmots & groundhogs who had 'volunteered' to strap on roller skates & serve humanity by becoming rapid-moving, ricocheting targets. When the last marmot lay gasping for breath, condemned to die of slow radiation poisoning, Professor Cody led the candidates down a corridor into a standard-issue military classroom.

As the candidates either sat @ a desk or clustered around a table piled high w/ finger food, the Professor-General yanked down an overhead screen. While the Brittle candidates snacked & the Woodbees & Dregs competed for the coins tumbling from Buck's pockets, Buck & Grimspoon stared @ the CONFIDENTIAL, TOP SECRET chart, crisscrossed by colorful arrows, fancy decals & corporate logos. Below the words CONFIDENTIAL, TOP SECRET was the subheading:

PUBLIC ENMITIES*
(*Subject to change)

Pointing his whip, the Professor read off the list of names, beginning w/ Dimlets & Dibildogs, passing thru Harold Johnstone & the nasty Nibblers next door, onto the Suite Idlelynes, Mel Lodee & the Harmonic Diversions, all the way to the bottom, rolling his r's & enunciating each enmity w/ meticulous care. As he rubbed his bullet & rustled his medals, he reminded those present that one as-yet-to-be determined enmity would be designated ENMITY OF THE YEAR, thus earning the lucky annihilator DOUBLE DAILY BONUS POINTS.

"Now this is whêrê things gêt intêrêsting," the Professor continued, smacking the chart w/ his whip before pulling down a second chart.

From the corner of his eye, the General noted Buck suddenly sit up straight, the man-child's rigid body leaning fwd as the riveted blue eyes studied the screen. The chart was a kaleidoscope of photographs displaying a spiraling circle of odd-looking characters, each of whom shared a severe lack of fashion sense along w/ thick tufts of disheveled hair. The captions identified each as: B-, C-, D- & so on, all the way to R-. Each headshot revealed a thin if not scraggly beard, a gaunt chin & eyes so deep & dark as to suggest a flaw in the photo or perhaps holes in the screen.

"Of coursê, wê don't havê any of thêsê participating in this yêar's shoot," the Professor sighed, his eyes lasered in on Buck. "Not yêt, anyway. But should thêrê bê onê—a latê êntry pêrhaps—not only do you gêt tên points for lêvêling onê, but êvêry succêssful kill thêrêaftêr bêcomês worth twicê as much. Daily Doublê Bonus Points quadruplê. Clêarly, your bêst stratêgy is to shoot onê of thêsê first thing." The Professor concluded by striking the chart w/ his whip.

Raising both screens, the Professor-General bade the candidates enjoy the fresh fingers, shipped all the way in from a local nursery. He further offered anyone interested additional practice in the rink; several, including Grimspoon, accepted the offer. "I suggêst you build your strêngth, as wêll as cultivatê a hêalthy thirst for bloodcurdling cussing," he encouraged. "Gêt plênty of rêst; clêan thosê gunsights & nurturê thê itchinêss in thosê triggêr fingêrs.

"At êasê, gêntlêmên. Class dismissêd."

Chapter 28

The evolution of our venerated demicratic society had taken a winding, rather circuitous route before arriving in its perfected form on the shores of this, our fair province. During its prenatal & Paleolithic periods (what historians/anthro-apologists call the 'middle human epoch'), demicratic societies would gather only their wisest—these to choose among themselves who was most wisest & therefore best fit to rule over its ever-expanding flock of complacent dummies. These rulers, brimming w/ boundless wisdom, even devised means by which dumber animals would be ritually sacrificed so as to perpetuate their (i.e. the wisemen's) prevailing wisdom. Till one wise guy, a philosopher @ that, noted how the older/wiser he became, the more he recognized how little he truly understood. Other wise guys of the period noted this same phenomenon & soon it was postulated that he among them who knew the least must surely be wisest of all.

From there evolved the Neolithic or 'late-middle human epoch' where the least knowing of citizens gathered to select who among them knew the absolute least—that person being therefore most fit to rule over those who knew considerably more. Like their predecessors, these rulers also sanctified the sacrificing of dumb animals (tossing in a few wisemen for good measure). Thus were these fwd thinking leaders able to perpetuate their all-pervasive learnéd ignorance onto succeeding generations.

In time, other demicracies were forged, these able to entice their elected leaders w/ shiny coins & rare rocks found in the ground, on the grounds such rocks, being hard to come by, must by definition be 'precious.' As these least knowledgeable of rulers increasingly fell under the spell of coveting precious metals, said rulers increasingly became selected according to their ability to hoard/attract andor confiscate these precious coins & stones—usually by inducing others thru an act called 'enslavement' into the back-breaking privilege of digging up said stones & handing them over under pain of a private conversation w/ a cat having nine tails.

Of course, we speak here of our more primitive demicracies from that late-late-middle epoch of human history, which, according to most scholars, ended circa a few months ago. From the ashes of these floundering forefathers, we in our time have perfected the science of social debate & compromise, combining the best aspects of all the above into a system the envy of the uncivilized world.

Crouched Canaan-style on the floor @ the foot of his bed, Buck Smolet reviewed the above information in his Civic History textbook, reading it thrice to be sure he understood its full implications. Bemused @ best, he read further:

Continuing the tradition of sacrificing our wisest while heeding the advice of those who know least, our founders decided its governing council should consist of seven chairs, each to be purchased by anyone hoarding a majority of precious coins & stones—seven chairs, incidentally, because the good PUP had seen fit to give each person two hands on which were five fingers: two plus five equaling seven.[2]

The First Chair (as decreed by the Ecclesiastical First Council of the Second Church for the Trinity of the Four-Sighted PUP) was to be made of only the highest quality oak, w/ a high ornate backboard, hand-carved, its headrest a symbolic crown of blue velvet w/ highlights of inlaid gold & rubies. The two chairs seated to its immediate left & right were to be of similar design tho the fiber could be of reconstituted plywood, the crown painted w/ a high gloss latex, gold glitter optional. The next two chairs were to be variations on the La-Z-Boy, these so the elected officials could nap during any lengthy discussions yet sit upright when it was time to be instructed how to vote. The final two chairs were to be of the metallic folding kind, able to be stacked in an adjoining storage room should the other five members not care what these two remaining council members had to say. Who sits in which chair is always to be determined by a Turkey Shoot, s/he w/ the sharpest eye surely possessing the more farsighted of visions.

Setting the textbook aside, Buck rose from the floor, his course of action clearly obvious. He recognized the paramount importance in securing First Seat on the council. Clearly, no other chair mattered. To ensure his rightful place @ the head

---

[2] To seal beyond debate that this was indeed the will of the ONE, said founders further documented how the good PUP saw fit to provide those very same persons w/ two feet attached onto which were usually five toes – also totaling seven, thus staunching further debate.

of all things Brittlebaum, he needed the highest number of points & for that only the latest in state-of-the-art mutilation technology would do: the biggest rocket launcher, the deadliest ammunition, the most accurate gun sight. Once in charge, he could lay down his own rules, rearranging everything the way he thought it should be run...not as his overbearing Uncle Harry would have things, or even his servile excuse of a Pupa. Plus, once S-elected, he'd also be in prime position to give that medal-chested Professor-General a piece of his mind.

Shedding his fatigues, the man-child crawled confidently into bed. Visions of Lieutenant-General Cody rubbing his bullet, his great-uncle pointing out the best turkeys & his Pupa stuffing his pockets w/ an endless supply of One circled Buck's imagination as he drifted snugly into slumberland.

* * * * *

THE FOLLOWING MORNING, as the yellow-eyed mistress in the sky stretched her long, sultry legs, yawned & slipped on a sheer azure dressing gown, Pearl climbed eagerly thru S-'s trap door. The bright-eyed pre-adolescent was surprised to see her father's corpulent figure centered on the loveseat, his jowls jiggling, his eyes shifting nervously. After pulling herself thru the entrance, she stared @ its narrow passageway, perplexed as to how her father could have made his way thru.

A half hour earlier, S- had been equally surprised. He too had stared in disbelief as his landlord/employer/former partner squeezed his way in, waddled to the loveseat & plunked himself down as if he owned the place. For several moments S- watched the banker chew in silence, the banker's shadow rising—first to inspect what S- had done to the apartment, then to search for something it never managed to find.

"There has been a bit of a, uh, misunderstanding," the banker began, looking everywhere & anywhere except @ his tenant. "This whole affair has been uh, blown out of uh, all proportion." Raising his arm, Smolet rubbed the perspiration from his brow.

"This uh, thing w/ my uh, daughter—i mean, of course, you've the right to uh, you know...impregnate her—w/ her uh, consent, of course. After all, you won her fair & uh...."

Abandoning its search, Smolet's shadow raced to the banker's side, helping the financial officer sit up straight, patting his quivering hand, leaning in to offer words of reassurance.

"In fact," Smolet continued, regaining a bit of his composure, "i'd uh, be honored to have you as my, uh, whatdoyoucallit?...my son-in-law. Yes, my son-in-law." The banker reached to adjust his glasses, astonished to discover he had forgotten them. When he went to stroke his beard, that too was missing.

"This uh, trial really wasn't my idea," he went on, his shadow continuing to whisper in his ear. "My uncle—my uncle-*in-law*—was the one who... Still, i guess it, uh, is *somewhat* my fault. But i promise you, after tomorrow when Buck, i mean Bill...when Bill sits in the First Chair, i'll uh, speak to my uncle personally & get this uh, whole mess straightened out."

The banker's shadow backed away, testing the financial officer's ability to remain upright on his own. Pleased & relieved, the shadow again leaned in, whispering in Smolet's ear.

"There is uh, just one thing." Looking directly @ S-, the banker extended his arms, displaying the cufflinks @ the end of either sleeve. "I still haven't found the tie clasp & could uh, really really use your help. It's a matter of life & uh...death, actually. If we don't find it soon, i can't uh, guarantee what will happen—to me, to you, to your impending marriage. We uh, only have till this evening before the bank closes."

The banker turned, falling silent @ seeing Pearl's head pop thru the trapdoor. His face flushed as his daughter approached. Pearl scanned the room before staring @ him as if seeing a perfect stranger.

"Shouldn't you be in school?" he reproached.

"Pupa!" Pearl countered, hands on her hips. "It's Pre-S-election Day!"

"Oh, yes. That's right. I...i forgot." The banker wiped his brow & rose slowly, his shadow dashing over, ready to assist him. "Think it over," he urged S-.

Without hesitating, S- assured his landlord there was no need to think it over. Explaining he had another matter to attend to first, S- stated he would happily resume his search as soon as he reported to the bank. Tentatively addressing his future father-in-law as partner, S- extended his hand. An awkward moment ensued, Smolet's shadow accepting S-'s hand immediately, the banker slowly following suit, supplementing the handshake w/ an embarrassed smile.

As the hands released, Pearl sprang @ her father, the startled banker nearly toppling backward as the pair collided. Clasping her father around his formidable hips, Pearl powdered his protruding abdomen w/ kisses. The banker's shadow dashed to Smolet's rescue, bolstering him upright as the girl showered him w/ declarations of undying love, promising to do so forever & ever. Smiling awkwardly, Smolet patted his daughter btwn her pigtails, gently prying her from his hip. As the banker

334

slipped down the trapdoor, Pearl marveled @ how his belly never once touched the opening's rim.

"Where are we going?" she asked moments later as she watched S- put on his shoes. Glancing up @ the youngster, S- explained he had important business to attend to. "Grown-up business," he added, suggesting tagging along might not be appropriate. Pearl pshaw'd & stomped her foot, her shadow covering its ears & making faces. While S- expertly tied his shoes, the girl recited the opening verses of the 'Spoiled Brat Credo' which in essence granted her the PUP-sanctioned right not to obey any rule she didn't feel like adhering to. His shadow more on the girl's side than his own, S- finally acquiesced, sighing as the two shadows high-fived, Pearl jumping up & down in gleeful triumph.

Descending from the attic & about to step outside, Pearl suddenly pulled away. "I almost forgot," she declared, trotting back up the stairs. Dashing into her room, she rummaged among her dolls, finally yanking something off one's ripped nose. Again descending the stairs, she detoured, barging into her father's cocoon.

"Pupa?" she called. "Pupa?"

No one answering, the portraits on the walls staring down in eerie silence, she ran to the sports jacket hanging on the back of her father's chair. Slipping something in its pocket, she exited, returning to S- & taking his hand, explaining there was something she kept forgetting to give her Pupa. "He'll find it," she concluded, closing the last of the front doors as she & S- negotiated the moat & headed downtown.

* * * * *

Upon learning where they were headed, Pearl leapfrogged over a legless panhandler. Tho she had never been to Perman's Bait, Switch & Tackle Shop, she knew it was far enuff away for them to play several rounds of her favorite game—a game no one played better than S-. She dashed ahead, her delighted eyes on the lookout for a clever place to hide.

Initially the game had perplexed S-. The two had played it first in the libary. That time Pearl had eluded him for nearly half an hour before he caught on. Since then, having observed her shadow, he had come to understand the way she thought— not thought exactly. He couldn't quite explain it but the girl was prone to follow certain sporadic impulses—the same impulses his own shadow liked to detour down. As he had come to trust these impulses—despite simultaneously doubting them—he inevitably found himself in proximity to wherever Pearl had hid. There

335

he might glimpse her shoe or the hem of her dress, sometimes hear the faint hint of suppressed giggling. It was his shadow who suggested they pretend to be baffled. They'd scratch his head & look about in all directions while maneuvering to stand just w/in Pearl's reach. No longer able to contain herself, the girl would inevitably jump out, shouting "Boo!" Her laughter proved contagious, sending ripples thru his body as well as hers. The longest of walks seemed to fly by when she was w/ him. Thus it was but a short time later the pair arrived @ Perman's Bait, Switch, Tackle Then Snap a Photo Shop.

No sooner had they entered when Mr Radcliffe poked his bald crown around a corner. The shop owner wore a broad grin, his eyes twinkling as he welcomed S-, wrapping both palms around the hand S- extended. He patted Pearl on the cheek, ever so pleased, he said, to make her acquaintance. Scratching his sideburns, the shopkeeper quickly turned to the subject of his upcoming photo exhibit.

"The gallery is rented & the opening gala will be here before you know it. Let me get you an application. You can fill it out here—or take it home."

As Perman scooted away, the door again opened. Mrs Farrago entered, young Eve tugging on her mother's hesitant sleeve. S- introduced the pair to Pearl, then to the returning shopkeeper, informing Perman Mrs Farrago had an important favor to ask of him.

"I'm not exactly good @ talking in public," Mrs Farrago apologized, her face flushed, her hands conducting a spastic symphony to a no doubt bewildered orchestra. "Not having one ounce of Brittle blood, i wouldn't deign to consider myself capable of holding a public conversation—even in private—but you see my husband, bless his mop, had to work today &..."

Mrs Farrago prattled on, Eve underscoring her mother's more important pronouncements. Looking from Eve to S- to the flustered Mrs Farrago, the store merchant nodded graciously, rubbing his chin & suggesting they step into the backroom, where perhaps Mrs Farrago might feel more @ ease.

"Jasmine," he called, leading the others past the counter. "Would you mind minding the store a few minutes?" Appearing promptly, his wide-eyed daughter readily complied, smiling @ the passing entourage, encouraging them to take their time.

Cluttered beyond capacity w/ defective fishing gear, leaking boxes of photo supplies & other haphazardly stacked merchandise, the backroom nevertheless provided a comfortable corner for the fivesome to congregate in. Perman offered cold drinks to anyone interested. He then listened attentively as Mrs Farrago conducted a train wreck of a narrative, frequently jumping track, winding thru perilous switchbacks, boring deep into dark tunnels only to derail before reaching any semblance of light @ the end of said tunnels. Her voice frequently cracking, the matron revisited territory already covered & just as frequently wandered into cul-de-sacs she had difficulty turning her thoughts around in. Perman nevertheless smiled patiently, amused & grateful every time Eve would parenthetically insert an important clarification. S- also came to the tortuous narrative's aid. With the duo's help, the shopkeeper finally grasped the gist of what was being requested.

"I understand," he injected during one of the rare moments Mrs Farrago paused to take a breath, "but your boys did steal what was not theirs. What is more, they violated my son's trust. My son has a very trusting nature, Mrs Farrago. Whether Wignut, Nibian, Wetdweller or Cur—it doesn't matter. My son believes in doing unto others & this is how that trust gets repaid?"

"I'm not one to contradict one such as yourself," Mrs Farrago stumbled on. "I mean, what gives me the right, being raised on humble pie & taught to always assume the position, to presume that one such as yourself..." Mrs Farrago continued, Eve parenthetically pointing out the stolen money had been recovered & Weed & jj were repentant & sufficiently punished.

Mrs Farrago further noted in her circuitously roundabout way how, this being S-election season, every mother would rather see her sons in General Admission seating rather than in the arena dodging stones & being shot @ for using foul language—which she assured the shopkeeper her sons would never use, excepting, being in jail, who's to say what kinds of words they might pick up & fall into the habit of repeating when stones & bullots were flying all around them.

As the conversation stumbled on, a restless Pearl wandered back into the fishing/photo shop. Pretending to inspect the fishing hooks & angleworms, she hid from view, spying on the scantily clad woman-child rearranging merchandise behind the counter. She listened as the girl-not-quite-an-adult sometimes hummed & sometimes sang.

Most of her acne having cleared up, Jasmine's large round face radiated something Pearl found intriguing. Pearl found herself envying the snug-fitting brassiere w/ its flowery, almost see-thru pattern. She liked especially how the matching panties hugged the girl's tight narrow buttocks. The calves shapely, the thighs firm & muscular, Pearl found herself admiring every graceful curve & contour of this specimen of feminine confidence. She stepped boldly from her hiding place & approached the counter. "You're the girl in the photos," she declared.

337

Jasmine turned, her curious gray eyes scanning the pigtailed pre-adolescent. "What photos?"

"The photos my brother took."

Jasmine pursed her lips. "Who's your brother?"

"Buck. Buck Smolet. Tho now we're supposed to call him Bill."

As she stared into Pearl's hazel eyes, Jasmine's brows furrowed. "Why would Buck be taking pictures of me? I thought he hated my naked guts."

Pearl shrugged. "All i know is you're the only thing he takes pictures of—used to take pictures of. Now he's too busy running for City Council."

Jasmine looked up, Pearl also turning as Mr Radcliffe poked his head thru the backroom curtain. "Jas, honey, would you mind calling your brother? Tell him it's important—some people need to speak to him."

As the woman-child headed twd the far stairwell, Pearl watched w/ admiration. She noted the bare feet confidently plodding the wooden floor. She wondered if she too might someday walk w/ such grace, if she too might fit as snuggly into flowery undergarments. Even Jasmine's voice as the girl called up the stairs won Pearl's approval.

The woman-child repeated her call until a disheveled Edmund came bounding down the steps.

Upon learning his father's request, her irritated, rusty-head of a brother grimaced, complaining of never being able to get anything done w/ people always pestering him all the time.

"Did you know Buck Smolet had been photographing me?" Jasmine inquired as Edmund stomped past. "I thought you said he hated me & everything i stood for." Ignoring his sister, Edmund nearly plowed into Pearl, sidestepping the girl @ the last second. He passed by, lifting the curtain & disappearing into the backroom.

Edmund's thin, freckled face quickly registered something close to fear as his eyes narrowed in on S-. He clutched the back of the nearest chair, bracing himself as both sides of his cheeks erupted into spasms. Barely listening as his father made introductions, he conjured up images of the store surrounded by pudgy policemen, no doubt hoping his father might extract a full confession before they burst in to drag him away. He pictured the other Lugworts still upstairs...perhaps already being herded into a paddy wagon parked in the back alley. He shifted on his feet, certain the Powers that DO would not even give him the benefit of a mock trial before dragging him handcuffed to the turkey pens. He glared hatefully @ S-, wishing his eyes might turn into knives if not double-barreled, grenade-launching six-shooters.

338

"Son, how would you feel if we dropped the charges against that jj fellow & his brother Weed?"

Edmund glanced over @ his father in disbelief. His jaw ceased twitching as he surveyed each face staring curiously into his.

"Their mother here—their entire family in fact—seem to feel the boys are genuinely sorry. And you & i know that being the day before S-election... Well, you've often said you oppose the death penalty—except, of course, in cases where people deserve it. What do you say, son?"

A relieved smile curled both sides of Edmund's cheeks. A similar smile erupted on the shopkeeper's face as he & his magnanimous son agreed to forgive & forget. Growing quickly impatient w/ his father's paternal hugs & pats on the back, Edmund slithered back to his room. A proud & glowing Perman gathered his hat, happy to accompany Mrs Farrago & Eve to the municipal jailhouse.

S-, along w/ Pearl, declined to join them, indicating they were past due @ the First Smolet Pedestal & Pizzeria.

The mild mid-morning had just finished a quick shower, the sky's moist blue skin gleaming as S- & Pearl waved goodbye to Perman, Mrs Farrago & Eve. Pearl dodged the sparse raindrops, dashing from storefront to dogwood to box elder to prickly ash. S- followed @ a more leisurely pace, winking @ the trees tilting slightly or shifting their branches to accommodate Pearl as she frog-leaped from canopy to green canopy. By the time the two approached the stone lions guarding the First Smolet Pedestal steps, the silver droplets had all but dissipated save for a few pearl-shaped hitchhikers sparkling in the plaits of Pearl's pigtails.

The youngster skipped down the freshly mopped halls, sliding as she nearly passed her father's office. Finding the door ajar, she barged in, dashing over to her startled father. The banker's cheeks were as ashen as his hair. He stared @ his daughter as if looking thru her. Pearl nonetheless threw her arms around his neck. With machine gun rapidity she fired a volley of kisses on his cold cheeks.

"S- told me everything," she blurted.

As S- stepped thru the doorway, Pearl whirled around, noticing the sour expressions on three visitors gathered in her father's office.

"Oh, hi, Uncle Harry," she called, running to her great uncle. "Guess what?"

Sur Harry shrugged his sloped shoulders. Pearl announced S- & Penny were to finally be married. She added Bill would no longer need to kill S- & once Penny moved into the attic, she would get her big sister's room...including all her sister's hula hoops!

Her great uncle glowered as her father affected a nervous chuckle, making light of "kids w/ their youthful imaginations." The banker bade Pearl bid hello to Commissioner Dicker & Professor Cody, the latter w/ a fedora in his lap, one hand rubbing his skull. Pearl dutifully curtsied to each, the banker then suggesting she run along, smiling weakly @ his three unamused visitors before fumbling thru a desk drawer. Finding some keys, he gestured for S- to take them.

S- stepped cautiously past the three sullen-faced men. Accepting the keys, he turned, acknowledging the uniformed officer playing a mournful melody on his medals, the Commissioner nursing a rumbling belly & Sur Harry burping an impatient derby. As S- exited, the banker called him back.

"Perhaps you should begin in the basement," the banker suggested, removing the chain around his neck.

Rising & handing the key to S-, Smolet ushered both S- & Pearl from the room. Closing the door, he waddled back to his chair, searching first for his glasses, then for the false beard. With his eyes magnified, his sagging chins well obscured, he turned back to his solemn guests. "Now, gentlemen, where were we?"

Leaving her father's office, Pearl dashed to the basement, coming first to the boiler room. With the aid of a stepladder, she climbed over & behind the furnace.

Moments later, S- appeared. He carefully inspected every surface, checked each corner, reached under, around & behind every pipe, pump & meter. He inched gradually twd the furnace. Methodically he circled the multi-armed, fire-breathing heating unit. Pearl adjusted her position accordingly. When satisfied no tie clasp was to be found, he rubbed his chin & scratched his head.

Wonder where she could be hiding? his shadow whispered.

No sooner did S- repeat the question than Pearl pounced monkey-like onto his back, her human paws covering his eyes. "Guess who?" she beseeched, hardly able to contain her giggles.

"Hmm," S- speculated, pretending to rub a goatee. "Are you that rhinoceros w/ an incurable sweet tooth?"

"Nooo," Pearl responded.

"Are you that purple elephant dreaming of becoming a ballerina?"

"Nooo!"

"Then you must be that alien, the one from the planet Borthrax...come to earth to turn our bullets into bubble bath."

340

"No, no, no," Pearl insisted, leaping from his back to dash into the next room. There too she hid, this time crouching behind several storage boxes.

Overhead shouts & foot stomping permeated thru the ceiling. Pearl scrunched lower when she heard what sounded like gunshots.

Directly overhead, her Uncle Harry was whacking his cane on the sides of her father's desk. For dramatic effect, the aristocrat would grab the nearest porcelain lamp or ceramic vase & smash it in a corner of his trembling nephew's office.

"Calm down, Harry. Calm down," a cooler, more collected Commissioner urged, all the while handing the aristocrat the next breakable item to toss.

An equally composed Professor-General played a dissonant refrain on his medals as he reminded the banker of the severity of the moment. "You know how this works, Charliê. Wê can't win w/out thê Onê. Thê S-êlêction Commission closês in fivê hours. Wê can't afford to wait anothêr minutê."

"Bbear in mind, Charlie," the Commissioner added, "your own son's ffuture is riding on what happens ttomorrow."

"We've been telLING you this for weeks," Sur Harry chimed in, smacking his cane before picking up a bronze bust & tossing it thru a window, glass shattering as the banker cowered.

Grappling w/ his false beard, Charles D Smolet pleaded for patience. In choppy, incomplete sentences, punctuated by intermittent gulps & incoherent stammering, he apprised his guests of how the First Smolet vault operated on a timer—this not just for security reasons but because said timers happened to be on sale @ the time of their purchase—a sale no one in his right wallet would have passed up. Smolet assured them how only that very morning he had checked the vault, how the One lay perfectly intact & was in fact antsy to be of service to their cause.

"However," he said after another bust went careening thru another window, "once the combination is reset, the timing system automatically kicks in. It is not due to release," Smolet looked @ his wrist as if the watch he had neglected to wear was nevertheless there, "till 4:30, a good half hour before we close."

Dodging an airborne vase, the banker dropped to his knees, hiding below his desk.

"You need tto understand, CD," he heard the Commissioner explain, "tthat gives us less than an hour to ttrek over to Government Row. That's bbarely enuff time to get our candidates registered."

"Thên wê nêêd to gêt to thê Acadêmy to purchasê thê biggêr wêapons & stockpilê thê ammo bêforê thosê Woodpêckêrs can buy any."

Smolet rose to his feet, his jowls jiggling as he chewed on his options. He wormed his way twd the door, careful not to turn his back to his visitors. "Maybe i could get one of the pizza boys to hurry the timer along," he suggested, smiling weakly. "After all, the same timers we use on the vault are used on our ovens."

Opening the door, the banker slid thru, delicately closing it behind him. Leaning against the doorframe, he glanced repeatedly @ his invisible watch, intermittently looking both ways as well as @ the ceiling as if assessing which direction might offer the most secure escape route. As he again looked @ his missing watch, he wondered how S- might be faring.

Oblivious to the noise above him, S- had exhausted nearly every room in the basement. About finished in the storage space, he had but one room left. Pearl meanwhile stood outside the door of that very room, reading its warning:

PRIVATE
FOR NO ONE ONLY
KEEP OUT
THIS MEANS YOU!

She jiggled the doorknob, but the handle refused to budge. She frowned in disappointment, that disappointment lasting but half a moment. She flashed on a new idea, her eyes sparkling like fireflies @ the thought.

He'll never find you there, her shadow concurred.

The girl cheerfully skipped past Stubbs, @ that moment mopping the steps. She gingerly traipsed up the stairs he had just swiped. The janitor chewed tobacco & mumbled something about some people's kids. When she reached the landing, Pearl indulged in a pretend game of hopscotch. As she hopped down the corridor, she chanted a short refrain: R24, L73, R45.

Stubbs cursed under his breath, then saw S- approaching. Unaware his sons were in the process of being released, the janitor stared @ S- w/ his usual deadpan expression. Tho there was something he felt he needed to say to S-, what that something might be he couldn't quite wrap his pride around. He returned to mopping, pondering if it might be better not to say anything @ all. To his relief, S- stopped in front of the door marked PRIVATE.

There S- fumbled w/ the keys the banker had given him. He tried several, his shadow insisting he try the lone key usually worn around the banker's neck. When S- obliged, the key slipped easily into the lock, the deadbolt clicking w/ confident finality. He was turning the knob when his entire body was abruptly jerked backwards.

An octopus of rough dry hands grappled w/ his arms & neck. Two hands tried to choke him while several others attempted to hold him down. He struggled against three assailants, all in dark blue uniforms, their yellow badges perpetually falling off, each occasionally pausing in his/her assault to pin or tape the loosened badge back on. Nearby a fourth officer, half her hair in curlers, hunched over an instruction manual.

"Uppercut to the lower chin," she read, after which a fist rammed into the underside of S-'s jaw.

"Swift kick to groin w/ favorite knee," the woman called, S- suddenly hunching over in excruciating pain.

"Right hook to the chin."

He felt a sharp blow to his leg.

"His *chin*, stupid, not his shin!"

As S-'s knees found the floor, he saw other officers in blue giving Stubbs the same treatment, one punching & pummeling, two deciphering the instructions from a manual, a fourth pulling away to tie an errant shoelace.

S- watched droplets of his own blood spot the floor Stubbs had just mopped when someone grabbed him by his hair, yanking his head back. Bringing her hooked nose inches from his face, the officer paused as if confused. Referring again to the manual, she returned her face, this time giving S- her ugliest sneer. "Ready for a little turkey shoot?" she smirked, flashing a devious grin before emitting her best bloodcurdling cackle.

One story above, CD Smolet was also suffering severe stomach cramps. His roiling tummy refused to settle down, his swirling brain painfully aware that nothing short of crawling under his desk could save him...& actually, not even that. Sur Harry & Commissioner Dicker were converging on either side of him.

Ever the cool diplomat, Professor Cody reached in his vest, extracting a pocket-sized handbook. Said to offer time-honored techniques for soliciting cooperation even from deaf & dumb mutes, the manual suggested beginning w/ the systematic breaking of a reluctant's fingers.

The banker cringed in terror, plunging his frankfurters into his coat pockets. Just as quickly, his right hand popped back out, a glittering gold tie clasp wedged btwn his plump, startled fingers. R45, the tie clasp announced.

Just as suddenly a loud boom shook the entire bldg. All four men were thrown to the floor. Pictures tumbled from the walls; file cabinets rattled violently open as books dive-bombed from their shelves. Cracks slithered up the drywall while everything made of glass dove to its death. Had the three men in Smolet's office possessed the ability to see thru floorboards, they would have seen a small enclave of very petty officers abruptly drop two bloodied bank employees to scamper up the nearest staircase, barely holding up their ill-fitting pants & running back for their badges as they stumbled over one another. Could they see thru walls, they would have seen several stealthy, rather youthful figures—one apparently having left his brain @ home—slither like guilty cockroaches thru an emergency exit. As it was, they saw nothing save the banker quickly jump to his feet & move faster than any of them believed humanly possible.

No sooner had Smolet been thrown to the floor when his shadow was up, rushing from the room, dragging the stumbling banker along w/ it. Smolet's arms & legs moved more on instinct than from anything resembling his own free will. Gripped by an unsettling fear, nothing around him registered: not the paintings tumbled from the walls, the broken flowerpots spilling their dark guts, the papers strewn like giant confetti floating gently to the floor. Employees were splayed around the main floor; doughboys flat on their backs, some still in their chairs, were a blur to the panicked banker. There was only the pull of his frantic shadow & the bass-drum pounding of his erratic heart.

Rounding a corner, still stuck to his shadow, the banker slammed into the rancid smell of burning sulfur as he battered @ the thick dust, choking on smoke & dust particles searing his throat. The double-thick walls that held the door leading to the vault now displayed a huge gash, the door nowhere in sight. The gaping hole was wide enuff for two Brittlebaums abreast to pass thru. The steel vault, touted for its impenetrability, stood twisted, the thick bars that held it in place melted, welded together into a bizarre abstract sculpture.

Fearing the others were close behind, the banker frantically weighed his options. Surely they'd discover the vault blatantly empty, had in fact been empty for years. Lacking sufficient time to transfer the One from the basement room marked PRIVATE, he decided a diversion was needed, something to block or @ least impede

344

their entering the vault. His brain a swarm of uncooperative bees, the banker failed to feel his shadow again pull away.

When the shadow let out a sudden gasp, the gasp registered as a lump in Smolet's throat. A new terror seized the banker as he stepped into the vault. First he saw a familiar dress, noted the buckled shoes & knee-high socks, then the mangled crisscrossed legs. The lump in his throat plummeted to his chest, his knees buckling as he crawled more than walked to the limp figure slumped in the far corner like a discarded carcass. His body seized by spasms, Smolet fumbled w/ the lolling head, the listless arms, he & his terror-stricken shadow hoping against hope the hazel eyes might yet open, the face crack its playful smile, the smirking lips suddenly shout, "Boo! Ha, ha, ha. Fooled ya!"

Collecting their composure, Sur Harry, Commissioner Dicker & Professor Cody followed the banker @ a less hurried pace, arriving shortly to the area clouded w/ plumes of smoke & scattered debris. Coughing & choking, they covered their mouths, waving their arms to assist their eyes. They came finally to the bank's vault, its hefty steel door dangling by one severely mangled hinge. Inside they found nothing save the banker bowed on one knee, hunched over what appeared to be a rag doll the size of a small human, its bloodied limbs twisted & lifeless. The vault shelves, neatly aligned & perfectly undamaged, stood empty.

The three community leaders moved aside as S- arrived panting, his body nearly as bloodied as whatever was dangling over the banker's quivering knee. They scoured the outside perimeter, hoping the thieves might have dropped a few bills or a couple of coins, if only by accident. The three pillars of the community grew increasingly despondent, further annoyed by the wailing banker whose shoulders heaved uncontrollably as Smolet threw his head back & bawled @ the top of his lungs.

"Thêy'vê clêanêd us plumb out," the Professor whispered, moving out of range of the blubbering banker. "Wê'll bê lucky if wê can afford pêashootêrs aftêr this."

Sur Harry smacked his cane against the wall, dislodging a few crumbling bricks. "Any chance we can postPONE S-elecTION, DonNIE?"

The Commissioner shook his head as he cupped both arms around an upset belly.

"Ddon't think so, Harry. I'll do my bbest, but i don't tthink so."

Chapter 29

TRY AS THE THREE PILLARS of our community might, S-election Day would not be postponed. Tho an emergency meeting was called, most Brittlebaums, resenting the interruption during their dinner hour, failed to respond in any significant number. Commissioner Dicker did manage to draft an order postponing the festivity, further managing to rouse a rather putrid-smelling Ollie Garky from his deathbed to sign the hastily drafted order. However, by the time the edict had passed thru a few chinks in the Dept of Walls...which forwarded the document onto the Dept of Why Not?...which provided a thick dossier of perfectly sound reasons why S-election should *not* be postponed (these promptly rescinded by the Dept of Because-I-Said-So), the postponement order had found its way to the Ministry of Oxy Morons, whose night crew accidently placed it on a desk piled high w/ lemon- & cherry-filled donuts. The sticky—tho admittedly tasty—filling oozed onto the official document, rendering it too gooey to pass thru the copy machine. Thus the final order fluttered its way into a nearby wastebasket, where it was promptly buried under the mounting pile of empty donut boxes.

To buy more time, Commissioner Dicker further ordered the clock above Government Row rewound & consequently turned back, said task also assigned to the aforementioned Ministry of Oxy Morons. To the Commissioner's dismay, the mangled hands, already under the strain of having dragged their feet for decades, snapped off completely, suggesting to those prone to genuflect upon said clock, that our micropolis had entered THE END OF TIME, which further confirmed their nagging suspicion that all action was futile anyway.

Meanwhile, those few Brittlebaums Sur Harry managed to wave a threatening stick @ were urged to raid their piggy-banks, to sell off any unwanted children & sue any & all neighborhood panhandlers for the return of any cash any Brit, during a lapse in good judgment, might have deposited in said hobos' cups. Thus, by robbing Peter & not paying Paul, the Brittlebaum Party was able to @ least register their seven candidates.

Pacing his Tower of diminishing Power, Professor-General Cody, after rubbing both bullets profusely, hit upon the idea of raising the fee on all weapons to be leased to the one-&-twenty candidates. Gaining the approval of council members Ollie Garky, Clarence Sayles & Warron Peece, the price on the AK-747, the automatic M-19, the hand-grenade launchers, the Gatling gun & the handheld nuclear device were placed significantly beyond the price range of all but two of the competing candidates—these being Filkin Grimspoon & William Dinero Smolet.

The following morning proved hot & balmy. The golden-haired mistress smiling from her throne slid into a hot pink dress, doing everything in her sultry power to dissuade our excited citizenry from leaving their air-conditioned cocoons. She trickled sweat down necks, soaked the backs of shirts & blouses, beaded foreheads. She blew gusts of hot arid air, sent summer hats scurrying, rendered thick wigs unbearable & unwashed armpits doubly so.

As each competing candidate paraded by, trailed by supporters & well-wishers, mobs of spectators gathered to cheer & jeer. The casually dressed Dreg candidates waved their cap guns, pistols & Lugers; one toted a chipped, mother-of-pearl handled derringer, another a refurbished, sawed-off shotgun, only one barrel still functioning.

The Woodbee candidates carried rifles—the better dressed the Woodbee, the higher caliber the ammo, the more ornate the gun sight. A roar rippled thru the crowd as Filkin Grimspoon strutted by, a portable Gatling gun strapped on his back, belts of ammunition crisscrossing his casually formal, modestly sockless attire.

When the immaculately dressed Brittle candidates arrived, a hush followed by low murmuring ran thru the crowd. The chunky Ollie Garky, Jr XIV, the bejeweled Clarence Sayles & the medal-chested Adm Peece each carried the latest in slingshot technology. Their fellow candidates had had to settle for slingshots of an earlier design. Conspicuously absent from the parade was Buck Smolet. Heads turned, mouths whispered & ears perked up @ the onslaught of rumors, most suggesting the Brittle's best marksman would not be participating due to a death in the family.

"I could unDERstand if it was his own death," Sur Harry grumbled, kicking the bullot box especially rigged for his great-nephew. "That i might EXcuse! Hail, famiLY memBERS die all the time! He should have antiCIPated all continGENcies & planned accorDINGly! Isn't that right, ProfesSOR?"

"Thê lad may show up yêt," Professor Cody kept insisting, wearing a bulky trench coat despite the blistering temperature. The Professor-General entered the empty booth, immediately shedding numerous pounds in the form of a used, somewhat rusty rocket launcher.

Keeping guard as the Professor shed still more pounds in the form of ammo stuffed in his jockstrap, Sur Harry launched into a relentless attack on anything vaguely resembling a fly. The swinging & thrusting dissuaded any & all officials from coming near enuff to discover the secret of the Professor's miracle weight-loss program. Sur Harry was still thrusting & parrying when the first warning bell sounded & those buying popcorn, soft drinks & souvenirs hurriedly waddled back to their seats. When a second bell clanged, the roar of the crowd, the stomping of feet, the munching of caramel pupcorn proved deafening.

The frantic scurrying of the honorary turkeys drew cheers & thunderous applause. The live targets were chased out of their pens, each desperately seeking safety behind the fabricated tree trunks, cardboard boulders & discounted, fire-resistant used furniture. Shouts rang out louder as stoners wearing special fluorescent vests hurled rocks to flush out the cowering chickens, who cursed & brandished middle fingers as they dashed for new cover. With each "dam you" or "you son-of-a-brit," shots kapowed out of the bullot boxes, bullets ricocheting, turkeys screeching, the crowd cheering louder every time a turkey spun, pirouetted, then slammed face down onto the freshly mown grass.

Filkin Grimspoon wielded his cumbersome Gatling gun, firing hesitantly, careful not to waste a single bullet. The lighted scoreboard tallying the minute-by-minute results showed him swiftly falling behind. Even his Brittle opponents edged past him as their slingshots fired poison darts. When one particularly defiant Dixstick pulled something from his pants & waved it threatening, Grimspoon found the boy in his crosshairs & pulled the trigger w/ determination.

A rush of adrenalin coursed thru the lawyer's veins as bullets rained down around the lad, finally slamming him to the ground. A smile curled up the sides of the politician's cheeks. He found another turkey in his sights, waited for the offending

"Ow" & pulled the trigger w/ similar determination, netting similar results. The tally on the scoreboard quickly shifted in his favor as he amassed multiple points, his bullets soon achieving the force of exploding rockets, each kill sending spasms of approval thru the cheering crowd.

"I was just having fun," he later confided to adoring school children. "The secret to doing anything well is to enjoy doing it," he encouraged them, recounting the overwhelming victory he enjoyed that blistering sunny afternoon. Only much later, in his memoirs, did the celebrated politician reveal just how his Gatling gun came to miraculously fire exploding rockets. "A voice kept whispering in my ear," he would relate, his autobiography commissioned by the Dept From Historical Fact, cowritten by his one-time mistress Rosie B Guile.

When he dared turn around, Rosie wrote in her flowery cursive, *he found himself flanked by three wisemen. One liked to draw PUP tents over the letter e, another sought the wisdom of the ONE by thumping on ripe watermelons, while the third kept muttering, "FolLOW me, folLOW me & i will grant you my virgin niece."*

Before the astonished Grimspoon could blink an eye, his Gatling gun transformed into a rocket launcher, albeit a rusty one—one that nevertheless allowed him to take out half a dozen cursing turkeys in a single shot, thus amassing many more times the points of his closest rival.

On the heels of such a miracle, Grimspoon easily secured first chair on the City Council, ushering in a new era in Brittlebaum-Woodbee relations. Supported by fellow Woodbees on the council & ignoring the Dregs still looking for their folding chairs, his first decree was to strip those turkeys not too badly mutilated of all clothing. Said clothing was then presoaked, washed, bleached & re-stitched so as to fulfill his commitment to help clothe the clothesless.

In a further act of mercy, he ordered the release of all surviving turkeys. Thus the two remaining targets—an elderly woman trying to find her way to San Jose & Erle Greaves, who had refused to curse his stoners or the candidates or the cheering crowd—were set free.

During the weeks that followed, order was swiftly restored to our fair micropolis. Those of us @ headquarters—including card-carrying members of the Union of Spies, Double Agents & Turncoats—were granted our jobs back. New myth-o-lizers, ones made of durable flexi-glass & less prone to clogging, were passed around like crandy, allowing those of us in the Dept From Historical Fact to complete this report as well as the other eyewitness accounts commissioned by our Joint Committees on Conjecture, Fabrication & Ad Hoc Wishful Thinking. Barbershop quartets were once again raised to their previous high esteem & those nasty Nabors next door were allowed to relocate to a more exclusive neighborhood—so long as they agreed to remain downwind.

But the crown jewel of the Grimspoon Administration was the coveted motion to end all war. Heavily favored in those initial weeks, the legislation was soon opposed—mainly by a vehement Filkin Grimspoon himself. While philosophically embracing the ending of all war "once & for all, for all time, into perpetuity," as he @ one time asserted in speech after stirring speech, the esteemed head councilman nevertheless insisted that the council should keep all options open. He pushed for language calling for the abolition of war 'except in times of peace' andor 'during periods of hostility—said hostility being real or imagined.' Over time, all bills pushing for the end of all war were killed—murdered in fact, stabbed in the back during several intense backroom negotiations, Councilman Grimspoon washing his hands of the whole matter.

During subsequent months, extending into the subsequent millennium, our City Council, our citizenry, our Brittlebaums, Woodbees, Dregs, our Wetlanders, Butterbutts, Dibildogs, Nibians, et al, continued to bicker, their politicians to dicker, our pundits to engage in the fine art of splitting hairs—usually w/ the blunt end of a sharp axe. At the behest of the now 6.75-star Professor Major-Lieutenant Colonel-General Armstrong Cody, new, nastier names were added to our collective lexicon, while new dictionaries permitted the GOOD BOOK to be reinterpreted so as to remain consistent w/ whatever people happened to be feeling @ any given moment. New rule books were mass-produced accordingly. Thus the continued evolution of our demicratic system had been assured—@ least until the now highly anticipated, forthcoming T-election.

* * * * *

As those of us in positions of authority well knew, that T-election might not be for a century or two. And who could predict when the advent of Z- would happen?...that epoch whereupon we would come to the *TRUE* END OF HISTORY, human beans thereafter to live in perpetual perfection...@ least for the few weeks before someone again pissed PUP off.

Thus, after a few weeks of ruffling feathers, we—our new City Council as well as our townspeople—slipped back into our normal routines. As is their wont, citizens continued to nervously break down, some losing an arm, a leg, a liver, a conscience; some losing their head, a few forfeiting a heart; some going out of their minds, others merely out of their senses. Many found strength in speaking from both sides of their mouths or by refusing to see what was clearly in front of them. Still others scrounged about for things they never found or, in sheer frustration, lashed back @ things they couldn't see, much less affect.

Yet for one household the old routines were destined never to resurface. For months the sugarcoated exterior of the Smolet Manor remained bitterly sour. The shutters brooded, drainpipes wept & gutters gushed, glum & heartbroken. A wistful wind circled the silent chimney, clouds tiptoeing by as if passing a funeral procession. Even the mulberry, neighboring junipers & daffodil beds ceased their once-irrepressible whistling, singing softly in the wind no longer an option. The surrounding hedges hunkered down as if anticipating an early autumn followed by the long, bitter chill of winter.

So too w/in the manor's stark interior. Its owner, the once irrepressible Charles Deniro Smolet, increasingly had trouble constructing complete thoughts. His heavy head, often resting in his splayed palms, was home to a fractured brain, one swirling w/ random, often contradictory, images: Pearl in pigtails, clutching his thick leg...the smacking of Sur Harry's cane...the One piled high in the room marked PRIVATE, waiting to be secretly slipped into the vault...the dissonant melody of Professor Cody's medals. As the banker's eyes roamed the confines of whatever room he found himself mulling in, his mind traveled back to memories of Pearl—Pearl @ two years old, newly discovering how to hurl oatmeal...& as a toddler, giggling each time his pudgy fingers did the spider tango around her belly button.

In another part of the same manor, Mrs Smolet dressed for the role of a zombie. Wrapped in mourning gauze, she roamed her domain like a lost soul looking for a coffin to climb into. Her neglected houseplants watched in somber silence, drawing what little nourishment they could from the thin slivers of sunlight passing thru curtains now rarely opened. The lady of the house wore down every slipper she donned, refusing to pick up her feet as she dragged herself half-heartedly to every empty destination. Her only solace lay in creeping into the bedrooms of the sleeping Buck & Penny, staring @ the rise & fall of their shallow breathing, panicking if either held a breath too long. When she finally crawled into her own bed, she would press her back against that of her husband, who silently pressed back. Once or twice the couple speculated tentatively on perhaps creating a Jewel or maybe an Opal, tho, when it came to any follow-thru, neither possessed the energy, much less the passion.

Meanwhile, no longer welcome @ Gladiator U, where quitters never win, the heir to the Smolet misfortune had taken to the climbing of maples & the straddling of elms. Slipping out each morning, Buck sought the tallest, most knot-riddled tree in any given park or nature observatory. He observed w/ mounting curiosity how each elephantine bough contained its own muscular contours yet seemed willing to conform to his own provided he met it half way. Secure in a powerful oak's sinewy branches, he gazed out as far as his watering blue eyes could manage. Seated above the rest of the town, he pondered complex conundrums such as how all horizons managed to elude one no matter how fast one ran to try to overtake them.

His back pressed against one of his solidly rooted friends, Buck spent each day daydreaming, sometimes for hours @ a stretch. Some of his thoughts proved painful; others shimmered like fluttering mirrors. Pearl would appear often, he bouncing her off a bed or sofa, she giddy & undaunted, jumping to her feet & tackling him around the knees. S- also paid frequent visits to his brooding imagination. Buck pondered the many times he'd observed S- staring off into space, or @ some flower or annoying bumblebee...almost as if the bee or bud were speaking some secret language. When Buck tried it, staring @ a leaf, for instance, he could only peer @ its green waxy sheen for so long. He might note the lighter shade on its underside. One side might be smooth & slippery while the other bristled w/ tiny near-invisible hairs. But after observing the stem branching thru the leaf's underside like prolonged skinny fingers, what else was there to learn? Always w/out thinking, he'd snap the leaf in half, wondering immediately why he had done that. The leaf was now ruined. Clasping his hands behind his head, Buck wondered if S-, despite his peculiar habits, knew something the rest of them might still be trying to figure out.

While Buck ruminated to the sound of rustling leaves, S- ruminated in his bare feet, walking the length of his now silent attic floor. Even when he sat, his mind paced. When he slept, his fingers remained awake, drumming on the side of the bedframe until his body awoke to rejoin it. There was a roiling in the pit of his stomach, a vague sense that everything was somehow his fault. Had this then been his destiny? Had the man in the libary...the darkroom equipment...the mysterious notes w/ their fancy handwriting—had they all been leading him to this? He thought back to the trial, recalling the pensive smile of the girl named Belinda. Had she known? Or suspected? If she did, why had she opted to say nothing? Why had she handed him no note, no instruction on how to proceed? No warning to turn back as

Erle Greaves had done. She merely shook his hand, sending that familiar ripple up his arm & down his spine.

Clicking on a light he had just clicked off, S- recalled the secret passageway Pearl had shown him.

Penny's smile flashed in his mind. The appeal of Penny's presence suddenly seized hold of his imagination. Feeling about his attic wall, he located the panel behind which lay the hidden door. As the narrow, winding staircase offered no light, he had to feel his way along, finally stumbling into some boxes where the stairs eventually ended. He rapped softly on the surrounding walls, hearing finally a rustling accompanied by the soft plod of footsteps. Light swiftly stabbed his eyes as a door opened.

Stepping back, Penny smiled sadly, allowing him entry. Returning to her bed, she plopped down among piles of scattered photographs. S- entered & found a chair, watching as Penny sifted thru the various photos until selecting one to place inside a photo album. Turning to a new page, she rummaged for another photo, hooking a lock of hair behind one ear & brushing her dark bangs to one side.

S- sat transfixed as he watched her movements. He felt content. A sense of peace welled up inside him as he sat there in silence. Soon a longing seized him. He thought to reach for her, to take her hand or run the back of his own hand along her smooth cheek. Yet he hesitated. He feared how she might react. He sensed a chasm btwn them, a gulf he dare not cross. Tho the lawsuit against their marriage had been dropped, neither he or his bride-to-be had ever mentioned what should come next.

"She loved you, you know." Penny peered into his confused eyes, her own eyes nearly identical to those of her deceased baby sister. All of the glossy photos in the album were of Pearl.

"She probably never told you that," Penny continued, "but when you're that young, you don't need to." Smiling wanly, Penny's eyes remained locked onto his. "You just know it.

"I keep thinking how excited she was about getting my room once you & i..." Penny looked around the room. "Funny...i've always hated this room, but it was all she could talk about. I guess we're just built that way." She shrugged & went back to her task.

"After the wedding..." S- stopped, noting the panged expression on Penny's face.

"You know we can't. Not now. And i think you know why."

S- nodded tho, in truth, he didn't know.

"Pearl was our soul," Penny continued, her lips quivering. "She was the heart beating thru this family. I didn't understand that until she was gone. She had something me & Buck, Mummy & Pupa had lost...something we had all given up a long time ago, thinking we were somehow better off w/out it. Yet there were times she could still pull it out of us. She pulled it out of you." Wiping her eyes, Penny stared @ the photos spread out in front of her. "I'm not sure i'm making any sense, but somehow i've got to be what Pearl once was. For this family's sake. For Pupa, Mummy—especially Buck. We all need it. I don't even know if i'm capable, i just..." Again Penny looked away.

Sifting thru the remaining photos, she selected a final picture, slipping it into the final sleeve of the album. She closed the album & handed it to S-. "Here. I've put this together for you."

S- accepted the hefty book, running his palm across the cover's coarse texture. He placed the album in his lap & opened to the first page. Pearl, in a seven-by-nine glossy headshot, smiled up @ him, her eyes bold & brash. "Bet you can't find me," she challenged.

S- flipped the page, barely catching a glimpse of the girl fleeing as she slipped behind a large wooden barrel, the hem of her bright orange dress still visible. She popped her head out. "That's cheating. You turned the page too fast. Close your eyes this time...& count to three thousand."

S- closed his eyes, counting only till he could contain himself no longer. He opened his eyes & turned the page. There the wizen-faced oak smiled back @ him. Flanking his old friend was a grove of sycamores & alders, their palms waving in greeting. S- scoured the foreground, then the background for even a hint of an orange dress. The oak rolled its eyes, whistling w/ impatience, discreetly pointing its chin, deliberately steering S- away from where Pearl lay hidden. Finally, w/in a flowerbed of azaleas & tiger lilies, S- detected a pair of hazel eyes.

"Boo!" Pearl popped her head out & smiled. "Okay, this time you gotta give me a big head start. Keep counting till you run out of numbers." In a flash, the girl was gone.

S- closed the album. Slowly rising, he moved twd Penny, bending to kiss her proffered forehead. As his lips pressed gently, as he tasted her skin & whiffed her scent, he heard a sudden pop—as if something had snapped. Returning to his attic, he resumed the game of hide & seek w/ the elusive Pearl.

You know what that snap was, don't you? he asked himself.

"Yeah," he sighed back. "I know."

```
⌐────────────────────────────────────────┐
│                                         │
│        W E L C O M E                    │
│                                         │
└────────────────────────────────────────┘
```

a bold banner broadcasted above the entrance of a warehouse turned temporarily into an art gallery. Townspeople had come in droves to support their burgeoning local talent. Many in fact had heard rumors of a new talent (a genius, some had suggested), who @ the tender age of however old he was, was already producing masterpieces. S- was grateful his half a dozen photographs were also attracting sizeable attention. He attributed this mainly to his many friends showing up to display their support.

All dolled up, the Farrago females arrived soon after the doors opened. Mrs Farrago, in particular, couldn't praise S-'s efforts enuff, encouraging everyone w/ in earshot to come gawk @ his work. "Not that i'm an expert or contain even a molecule of Brittle blood," she qualifed her enthusiasm, "but i know what i like...& these i really like."

While the matron rubbed elbows w/ women in spaghetti-strap evening gowns, their hair done up like meatballs, their husbands usually sauced, Eve wrangled her younger siblings. Tasha & Josh wore one of Mrs Farrago's multi-armed creations such that should either wander off, they wandered together. Thus the ever-vigilant Eve could quickly spot the multicolored suit & lasso the pair back to her side.

A slender & neatly groomed Margaret entered, cradling a newborn. At her side was a girl S- first mistook for Eve, tho this girl was taller & rounder about the face & arms. Margaret beamed when she saw S-, gently jostling the baby, who stirred, balled its tiny fists & smiled up @ his mother. "S-, i'd like you to meet my sister, Martha," she said. "Can you believe it? It's a miracle. She came home just in time to help little Tyler be born. Plus, now i have someone to watch him while i look for a part-time job. Isn't that great?"

Eve's older twin extended both hands, wrapping them warmly around S-'s hand, rising on her tiptoes to peck his cheek. "Everyone's told me so much about you," she added, gently squeezing his hand before letting go.

Shortly thereafter, Weed, Joseph, Orson & jj entered, Joseph having returned home early from running away so as not to miss the opening. jj hobbled in on a single crutch, using it more to point out favorite photos than to lean on. After embracing S-, Weed blushed @ seeing his own image on the gallery wall. He was in two photos. In one he was mixing paints, a blank canvas staring back @ him like a child waiting to have its face painted. In the other he was lost in his task, portions of ocean, cloud & trees just beginning to emerge as if they had been there all along, merely waiting for someone to unveil them.

While Weed stood staring, his father arrived, beaming w/ pride @ seeing his son's image. The janitor refused to move aside as others vied for a more unobstructed view of the two much-pointed-@ photos. Stubbs turned eventually to S-, recalling what it was he had wanted to say that day in the bank. S-, however, waved the comment off, the two men settling for an affectionate bear hug. They pried themselves apart only to better listen in on a conversation percolating nearby.

Drs Buncle & Oswald were standing before the two photos of Weed, magnifying glasses in hand, tobacco pipes clasped btwn their lips as they examined the photos w/ surgical interest.

"The painting in the photo is almost as exquisite as the photo itself," one postulated.

"More exquisite," the other insisted. "And it raises the question: 'which is the greater work of art? The art created? Or the artist who creates it?'"

The men called over Neimann Gorge, who stood nearby, the statuesque Mz Pritt hanging onto the libarian's arm, more fascinated w/ Neimann's left earlobe than by anything on the walls. Neimann pondered the doctors' questions, emitting a formidable volley of four & five syllable adjectives, finally concluding neither question could be adequately answered, as one question presupposed the cognoscibility of the other. "Or vice versa. You, gentlemen, have stumbled upon one of art's great paradoxes," the learned libarian concluded w/ a graceful upswing of his pointed nose.

"I'd like to find who the artist in the photo is, tho," he continued. "I think such plein-air neo-classical primitivism, w/ its hint of the pittura metafisica, would go splendidly in the new basilica. I did tell you, didn't i? We'll be breaking ground the first of the new year."

As the three men speculated further, S- watched Penny & Buck, who had just entered the hall. Initially wandering aimlessly, Penny managed to meander to the refreshment table, encountering Jasmine by the punch bowl. The two girls embraced, Jasmine clad in an apricot nightie w/ white frilly lace lining the hem, collar & sleeves.

Penny turned to introduce Buck, who stood bare-chested & in boxers, his feet bare, his hair uncombed. Jasmine kissed his humbled dimple, immediately introducing the girl standing to her left. S- squinted, doing a double-take as he recognized the clean-shaven face & small, timid head. Her hair bubbling w/ curls, Heidi Kilborn reached to shake Penny's hand. She nodded to Buck, then looked about the crowd, her probing glance unduly interested in the back of Weed's head.

When a finger tapped his shoulder, S- turned, his delighted eyes alighting on a perfectly aligned, clear-eyed Erle Greaves. The two men hugged passionately, Erle then shaking S-'s hand profusely. S- was struck both by the faint aura around Erle's head & the small entourage of followers trailing his friend. Several sucked on double-barreled saxophones, jotting notes & conferring over everything their leader said. Launching into a diatribe on how there was nothing like being slapped in jail to set a man free, Erle invited S- to a campfire sermon, one of a series he was giving to his ever-expanding fan base.

As Erle was providing directions, encouraging S- to bring his own marshmallows, a commotion rang out near the gallery entrance. Applause & whistling erupted as Councilman Grimspoon entered, his entourage—including bodyguards—three times the size of Erle's modest following. Perman, Jasmine & many of those in attendance dashed over to shake the Councilman's hand, some dropping on one knee to kiss the politician's jewel-studded brass-knuckles. Mr Radcliffe called for everyone's attention, warmly introducing the Councilman as 'the new OnE,' placing a fatherly hand on a three-piece- suited, cherub-cheeked Edmund, who stood to the Councilman's right. Edmund smiled from both sides of his well-fed cheeks, his eyes darting like pinballs as he looked around the gallery. Spotting S-, the freckled redhead frowned, one side of his face sneering, the other curling in a broad, unabashed grin.

"Where'd you get your eye?" S- heard someone asked. He whirled around to gaze into the smiling face of Belinda Grimspoon. His mind swimming thru a swamp of conflicted emotions, his tongue did several back flips as he stared into the twinkling green eyes. Adding to his confusion was his vague recollection of the Councilman's niece towering over all others. Yet here she stood, she & he of equal height.

The willowy woman-child probed him w/ questions as she scrutinized his photos, moving onto the photographs on the adjacent walls. S- followed as if pulled by invisible string, a churning in his stomach, a dizziness in his brain somehow different from what he associated w/ the stranger he had been seeking, whom he hadn't thought about for weeks. He contemplated her every question, grappling to frame clever or @ least intelligent responses. Painfully aware of his own inadequacy, he was nevertheless surprised, relieved, really, when the elegant enchantress didn't seem to notice or care how stupid he sounded.

Finally she turned to face him, looking deeply into his eyes. "So what's your name?" she asked.

S- fumbled, heat rushing to his face as he clutched a nearby beam for balance. The voices around him melded into a cacophony of chaos as he waited for the room to cease spinning. *Would you excuse me a minute?* he managed to blurt.

"Of course. I'll be right here."

S- staggered away, his feet having a mind of their own, his head daring him to look back. When he did, the girl was studying another photo. As if sensing his gaze, she glanced over her shoulder. "I'm not going anywhere," her smile reassured him.

Gaining his footing, S- made his way to the restrooms, tumbling into the one designated MEN'S ONLY. His eyes stabbed by the sheen bouncing off the walls & floor tiles, he leaned over the sink. He ran the faucet, splashing cold water onto his face. He dried his cheeks & chin with a paper towel while taking deep breaths. Grabbing another towel to dry his hands, he caught his reflection in the mirror. No towel in its hand, the mirrored image crossed its arms, smiling @ him as if waiting to be acknowledged.

"So," the reflection chuckled, extending its hand, "we meet @ last."

About the Author

(photo by Kit Hedman)

BEST KNOWN AS performance poet SETH, Gregory Seth Harris lives in Denver, CO. He is author of the poetic memoir A Black Odyssey, a collected works using Homer's epic to chronicle his own journey as a Black poet in contemporary America. A published short fiction writer, in a previous life, Harris wrote and performed radio theater comedy.